Born in Hampshire, Sam Baker studied politics at Birmingham University before going into journalism. After successfully re-launching teenage magazine *Just Seventeen* as *J-17*, she spent five years as editor of *Company*. She was also editor of *Cosmopolitan* in the UK and is now editor-in-chief of *Red*. She has one grown-up stepson, and lives between Winchester and central London with her husband, the novelist Jon Courtenay Grimwood.

THE STEPMOTHERS' SUPPORT GROUP

Eve, a journalist in her thirties, never imagined being a stepmother. But when she falls in love with Ian, he comes with a ready-made family of three children. Seeking moral support, she meets up with friends in similar circumstances. Firstly, there's best friend Clare, a teacher and single mother. But it's Clare's sister Lily who provides the truly sympathetic ear. Then there's Mel, starting a new relationship — and a new business. And homebody Mandy just wants a happy family life for herself, her kids and her new step-kids. Cups of coffee become bottles of wine, and the get-togethers become a regular fixture. But the friendship is tested when the five women are forced to confront new futures as well as unwelcome figures from the past . . .

SAM BAKER

THE STEPMOTHERS' SUPPORT GROUP

Complete and Unabridged

CHARNWOOD
Leicester

First published in Great Britain in 2009 by
HarperCollins*Publishers*
London

First Charnwood Edition
published 2010
by arrangement with
HarperCollins*Publishers*
London

British Library CIP Data

Baker, Sam, *1966* –
   The stepmothers' support group.
   1. Stepmothers- -Fiction.
   2. Female friendship- -Fiction.
   3. Large type books.
   I. Title
   823.9′2–dc22

   ISBN 978–1–44480–190–3

Published by
F. A. Thorpe (Publishing)
Anstey, Leicestershire

Set by Words & Graphics Ltd.
Anstey, Leicestershire
Printed and bound in Great Britain by
T. J. International Ltd., Padstow, Cornwall

For my favourite boys, Jon and Jamie.
Thank you for letting me be part of your
little family.

A stepmother is not a mother. She can help you with your homework and make dinner, but she should not be able to decide when you should go to bed.

Delia Ephron

1

'Look,' he said. 'Stop worrying. This is going to be fine.'

'Ian . . . '

'I mean it. I've told the kids to behave. We're going to Hamley's afterwards. All you guys have to do is say hello to one another.' A muffled noise came from the other end. 'OK?' Ian said, his tone changing. 'See you soon . . . It's Eve,' she heard him say to someone. 'We'll do that later. I've already told you.'

'Oh God, *Dad* . . . '

And then the line went dead.

The girl's voice was the last thing she heard. It was young, very English; much more confident than she had been at that age. Hannah? Eve wondered. It sounded too grown-up to be Sophie. She was still wondering when something else hit her.

I've told the kids to behave.

Why did they need telling? Ian was always saying how sweet and polite they were, all things considered. Maybe the devil was in that last detail.

This was like taking her driving test, plus getting her A-level results and having a root canal all rolled into one. Maybe throw in a job interview, for good measure. Actually, it felt worse than all of that. Much worse.

Her stomach was empty, hollowed out and

1

queasy. If she'd eaten anything worth throwing up, she would have done so, right there on Charing Cross Road. An anxiety headache pushed at the edge of her vision; and the first decent spring day of the year would have hurt her eyes, if only it could have found its way past her enormous sunglasses. When she'd tried them on they had given her an air of nonchalance, or so she'd supposed. But now she was horribly afraid they made her look like a bug-eyed, frizzy-haired insect. A *Dr Who* monster to send small children screaming behind the sofa.

Come on, Eve, she told herself. *You're thirty-two, a grown woman, with your own flat, a good job . . . And they're not even four feet tall.*

On the other hand, those knee-highs held her future in their tiny chocolate-smeared hands. It was an unnerving thought. One that had kept her awake most of the night.

Thirty minutes later, from where she stood on the pavement, gazing across Old Compton Street, three small heads could be seen in the first-floor window of Patisserie Valerie. Ian's three children were blonde; of course they were. She'd known that. It wasn't as if she hadn't seen enough pictures. Anyway, what else would they be? He was fair, his hair cropped close to his scalp. And Caroline had been blonde, famously so.

Not that Eve had ever met Caroline, but her cheek-bones, knowing smile and flicked-back hair had been famous. They sat above her by-line in *The Times*, and even those who had never

2

read her column knew her face from *The Culture Show* and *Arena*, not to mention that episode of Jonathan Ross's Friday night chat show that came up whenever Caroline Newsome's name was mentioned.

More gallingly, the same smile could still be found on Ian's mobile, in various endearing family combos. Caro's hair could just as easily have come out of a bottle, Eve thought uncharitably, but with genes like theirs, what were the chances of Ian and Caroline Newsome producing anything but Pampers-ad worthy cherubs?

Get a grip, Eve told herself.

As she loitered, the sun cleared the skyline behind her and hit Patisserie Valerie's upstairs window, lighting the angelic host above. If she stood there much longer she was going to be late; which she had categorically, hand-on-heart, promised would not happen. And if Eve was late Ian's anxiety would only increase and, God knew, his stress levels were through the roof already.

('This is a big deal,' he'd told her on the phone the night before. As if she didn't know it. 'I've never . . . ' he'd paused. 'They've never . . . met one of my *friends* before.'

Eve had never heard him so tense. His obvious worry only served to increase hers.

'And please don't be late,' he'd added. 'You know what it's like with children. You have to do *what* you say you'll do, *when* you say you'll do it.'

Eve didn't know *what it's like with children*.

3

That was precisely the point. She didn't have any.)

If Ian was strung out, then the only one on Team Eve would be Eve. And with those odds she'd be lost. As if to rub it in, she caught sight of herself in a window below the awning. An average-looking brunette, with a mane of curly hair — a bit frizzy, a bit freckly — grimaced back at her.

Her trench was flung over a blue and white matelot top and jeans. Battered Converse completed the look. Kid-friendly, but not scruffy, was the look she'd been going for. Low-maintenance yummy mummy. Elle Macpherson, the high street version. Not afraid of a little dirt, more than able to handle the mothers' race. (*Do stepmums do sports day?* She pushed the thought from her mind. One thing at a time.)

Rummaging in her leather tote, Eve pulled out a blue carrier bag. Sliding the children's books out (bribes, peace offerings, late birthday presents, Easter egg surrogates that wouldn't rot tiny teeth . . .) She tucked them under her arm, scrunched the plastic under the other crap at the bottom of her bag and took a deep breath. Marching purposefully through the crowds clustered around the café's door, she pushed it open and headed for the stairs at the back.

★ ★ ★

Even in a café full of brunch-seeking tourists, there was no missing them. The round table by the window looked like an accident in a cake

4

factory. Eve took in the mix of Power Rangers, Spider Man and My Little Ponies using an assortment of cream slices, éclairs and croissants as barricades, jumps and stable walls, and grinned.

'Eve!' Ian shouted the second he saw her. His voice was loud, too loud. His nerves radiated around the room like static, drawing the attention of a couple on the next table. One of them started whispering.

Pushing back his chair, he knocked a plastic figure from the table. Three pairs of long-lashed blue eyes swivelled in Eve's direction.

'You made it!'

'I'm not late, am I?' Eve said, although she knew she wasn't. She'd set two alarm clocks and left her flat in Kentish Town half an hour early to make sure she arrived on time.

Ian glanced at his watch, shook his head. 'Bang on time.'

'Hannah, Sophie, Alfie, this is Eve Owen, the friend I've told you about.'

Eve smiled.

'Eve, this is my eldest, Hannah, she's twelve, Sophie is eight. And Alfie, he's five.'

'And two months,' Alfie said firmly. The matter corrected, he returned to twisting Spiderman's leg to see how far it would turn before dislocating at the hip.

Smiling inanely, Eve felt like a children's TV presenter.

'Hello,' she said.

Three faces stared at her.

'I'm Eve,' she added unnecessarily, putting out

5

a hand to the girl sitting nearest. Hannah might be twelve, but she looked older. Already teenage inside her head. And way taller than four feet. She exuded confidence. 'Hannah, really nice to meet you.'

'Hi.' Hannah raised one hand, in token greeting, then used it to flick long, shiny golden hair over her shoulder, before reaching pointedly for her cappuccino.

'And you must be Sophie.'

The child in the middle was a smaller, slightly prettier and much girlier version of her sister. Except for Levi jeans, there was nothing she wore, from Converse boots to Barbie hair slides that wasn't pink.

'How do you do?' Sophie said carefully. She shook Eve's hand, before glancing at her father for approval. He nodded.

'I'm Alfie,' the boy said.

'Hello Alfie.'

'Do you like Spiderman or Power Rangers? I like Power Rangers, but Spiderman is all right. You can be Venom.' Recovering a plastic figure from the floor, he shoved it into Eve's outstretched hand.

'That's kind,' she said, feeling stupidly grateful.

'Don't be so sure,' said Ian, tousling the boy's hair until the tufts stuck up even more. 'All that means is your figure gets bashed.'

'Venom's the baddie,' said Alfie, as if it was the most obvious thing in the world. 'He has to lose, it's the law. Can we eat our cakes now, Dad?'

Without waiting for permission, he grabbed

the nearest éclair, one twice as big as his hand, and thrust it mouth-wards, decorating his face, Joker-style, with chocolate and cream.

'Sit, sit, sit,' Ian said, pulling out the empty chair between his own and Hannah's. 'I'll get you a coffee. Black, isn't it?'

You know it's black, she wanted to say. When has it ever been anything else?

She didn't say it, though. And she resisted the urge to touch his hand to tell him everything would be all right. Hand squeezing was out of bounds. As was reassuring arm touching and even the most formal of pecks on the cheek. They'd been lovers for nine months, but this was something new and Eve was still learning the rules.

This was more than girl meets boy, girl fancies boy, girl goes out with boy, falls in love, etc . . . This was girl meets boy, girl fancies boy, girl goes out with boy, girl discovers boy has already gone out with another girl, girl meets boy's children.

In other words, this was serious.

★ ★ ★

Eve never expected to fall for a married man. Well, widowed, to be more accurate. But married, widowed, divorced . . . It just hadn't occurred to her this was something she'd do. In fact, like boob jobs, Botox and babies, it was one of those things she'd always have said, *No way*.

But then she'd stepped off an escalator, into Starbucks, on the second floor of Borders on

Oxford Street over a year earlier. It had been Ian's choice, not her idea of a good venue for an interview; too noisy, too public, too easy to be overheard. She'd stepped off the escalator, seen him at a table reading *Atonement*, her favourite book at the time, and felt a lurch in her stomach that said she was about to commit a cardinal sin.

He was tall and slim, with a largish nose, made more obvious by his recently cropped hair. But it was the brooding intensity with which he read his book that attracted her. Before he'd even looked up, she'd fallen for her interview subject.

She never expected to fall for a married man.

Eve ran that back. Actually, she'd worked hard not to fall for anyone. She could count on one hand the number of lovers she'd had in the last ten years. And she didn't need any hands at all to count the number whose leaving had given her so much as a sleepless night.

She had her job, features director on a major magazine at thirty-two, and, apart from one serious relationship in her first year at university, she'd never let anyone get in the way of what she wanted to do. And, if she was honest, she hadn't let that get in the way, had she?

So, falling for Ian Newsome was more than a surprise. It was a shock.

Life didn't get messy immediately.

Caroline had been dead for nine months when Eve interviewed Ian; and it was another six months before they ended up in bed. All right, five months, two weeks and three days. But from the minute he stood up, in his jeans and suit jacket, to pull back her chair, Eve was hooked.

And during that first meeting he wasn't even the most accommodating of interview subjects.

He hadn't wanted to do the interview at all. He was there, surrounded by tourists, two floors above Oxford Street, under duress. Caroline's publishers had insisted. *Precious Moments*, a collection of her columns documenting a three-year battle with breast cancer was due for publication on the first anniversary of her death. And Ian was morally, not to mention contractually, obliged to promote it.

Since a large percentage of the money was going to the Macmillan Trust, which had provided the cancer nurses who had seen Caroline through her last days, how could he refuse?

It was a given that *The Times*, Caroline's old paper, would extract it; so he agreed to an interview with their Saturday magazine to launch the extract, plus one further interview. Of all the countless requests, he had chosen *Beau*, the women's glossy where Eve was features director.

The first thing he'd said was, 'Can I get you a coffee?' (Eve recognized it for the power play it was, but let him anyway.) The second was, 'I won't allow the kids to be photographed.' He fixed Eve with a chilly blue gaze as she took a tentative sip of her scalding Americano and felt the roof of her mouth blister.

Great start.

'I'm sorry,' Eve said, hearing her voice slide into 'case study' mode. 'But we'll need something.' She tried not to run her tongue over the blister. 'I did make that clear to your publicist right from the start.'

Ian's mouth set into a tight line. So tight, his lips almost disappeared. 'And *I* made it clear,' he said. 'No photography would be allowed. That was my condition. After all they've been through, losing their mother and . . . And everything. Well, protecting them, giving them some . . . normality. That's the most important thing. I'm sure you understand.'

'Of course, I do.'

Eve forced a smile, racking her brains for a way to salvage the interview. She did understand, but she also understood that Miriam, her editor, would kill her if she came back empty-handed. There were pictures of Caroline they could buy from *The Times*, obviously enough. Also pap shots, taken when she was leaving hospital. Only Miriam would want something new. Something personal.

Something that would strike a chord with *Beau's* readers, many of whom were in their thirties. The point at which Caroline had discovered, while feeding Alfie, that she had a lump in her breast. A lump that turned out to be what everyone thought was a not-especially life-threatening form of cancer.

Eve thought fast. She only had an hour with the guy. The last thing she needed was to spend half of it squabbling over pictures. Then it dawned on her. 'You're a photographer? I bet your family album is stunning. How about a snap of Caroline with the kids, when they were much younger, before she was ill? The children would scarcely be recognizable. Your youngest,

Alfie, would still be a baby. Surely that wouldn't infringe their privacy?'

'I'll consider it,' Ian said grudgingly. His scowl said the subject was now closed.

★ ★ ★

The feature was a success. After that early hiccup, Ian had talked candidly about Caro's life and very public death, even giving Eve some lovely quotes on the children he clearly adored. The following day, he'd e-mailed her three 'collects' — snapshots from his family album of Caro and the children when they were small. The pictures had never been seen before or since. It was only later, after the interview was published, that Eve looked at the spread and realized there was only one of Ian, standing in the background, behind Caroline and her triumvirate of beatific angels.

'Well, he *is* a photographer,' the editorial assistant said. 'He was behind the camera.'

All the same, something about the shot troubled her.

Eve couldn't have been more surprised when, a week after the issue containing Ian's story went off-sale, her mobile rang and it was him.

'I hope you don't mind me calling.'

'No, not at all.' Eve tensed. She'd been expecting him to ball her out the week it was published; to say he hadn't said this or didn't mean that, but his tone wasn't what she'd come to expect from enraged or regretful case studies. And it wasn't as if they could have lost his

11

pictures because they were digital. So what did he want?

'It's just . . . I was wondering if you'd like a coffee sometime?'

Even then Eve hadn't been entirely sure he was asking her out on a date. And to begin with it wasn't a date; it was a coffee. And then another. And another. Between then and now, Ian Newsome had bought her an awful lot of caffeine.

★   ★   ★

'I bought you all something,' Eve said now, as she took off her trench and slung it over the back of her chair. She tried not to notice Hannah eye her stripy T-shirt. Whether the girl's expression was disapproval or amusement was hard to tell, but it certainly wasn't covetousness. Maybe she'd tried too hard, Eve thought. Maybe the girl could smell that, like dogs smell fear and cats make a beeline for the one person in the room who's allergic.

'Here,' she said, offering a copy of Philip Pullman's *Northern Lights* to Hannah. 'I loved this. I hope you haven't read it.'

Hannah smiled politely but didn't put out her hand. 'I have, actually. When I was younger . . . '

'But thank you,' she added, when Sophie nudged her. 'I loved it.'

The book hung in midair, hovering above mugs of cooling hot chocolate. Eve felt her face flame, as she willed Hannah to take the book anyway. The girl studiously ignored it.

12

Eve could have kicked herself.

This was tough enough as it was. Why had she taken a risk like that? It would have been so much easier just to ask Ian what books they had. Only she'd wanted to do it on her own. She'd wanted to prove she could get it right.

'Oh well,' Eve said, admitting defeat. 'I'm sorry. I'll exchange it for something else.'

'Thanks. But there's no need.' Hannah held up a dog-eared magazine, open at a spread about *Gossip Girl*. 'I prefer magazines anyway.'

'What about me?' demanded Alfie. 'What did you buy me?'

'It's not your turn,' Sophie said, punching Alfie's arm. 'It's mine.'

'Ow-uh!' Alfie's face fell. But when he saw Eve watching, he grinned. His heart wasn't in being upset.

Regaining her confidence, she gave Sophie a brightly-coloured hardback. 'It's the new Jacqueline Wilson; I hope *you* haven't read it too.'

Sophie's squeal reached Ian as he returned, holding a large cup and saucer that he'd been waiting at the counter to collect. 'What's the matter?' he said. He shot Eve an, I've-only-been-gone-two-minutes-is-everything-OK? Glance.

'Look,' Sophie said, waving the book. 'Look what Eve got me!'

'Aren't you lucky?' Ian looked pleased.

'What's Eve got me?' Alfie asked again.

'For God's sake Alfie,' Hannah said. 'Don't be so rude.' She was grown up enough to sound like her mother. Well, what Eve remembered Caro sounding like from hearing her on television.

13

'That's enough,' Ian said, rolling his eyes. 'Chill, both of you. And Hannah, you know I don't like you saying for God's sake.'

Hannah scowled.

Nervously, Eve offered Alfie a copy of *Charlie and the Chocolate Factory*. With Roald Dahl's words and Quentin Blake's illustrations, it was a book she loved. She still had a copy somewhere, probably in her parents' attic.

'Hey Dad, look,' Alfie said, snatching it. Immediately whatever chocolate wasn't smeared on his face was transferred to the book's cover. 'Spiderman's got a new hovercraft.' He sat one of his plastic figures on the book, before turning to Eve.

'You be Venom.'

'Later,' Ian said. 'Let Eve eat her cake first.' He smiled at her, then glanced at the table, a frown creasing his face. 'Alfie,' he said. 'Where *is* Eve's éclair?'

2

'They're . . . Well, cute, I guess.'

'Cute?' Clare Adams said.

'Yes, cute. Small, blonde, cute.'

The woman leaning on the work surface turned to look at her. 'They're children and there are three of them. There has to be more to say about them than, *they're cute.*'

Eve was in the kitchen of her friend's flat in East Finchley. It was a small flat, with an even smaller kitchen. As it was, there was barely room for the two of them. When Clare's daughter, Louisa, got home it would be full to capacity.

Rubbing her hands over her face, Eve felt the skin drag. The magazine's beauty director was always telling her not to do that. But Eve did it anyway, pushing her face into her hands hard enough to see stars. How could one hour with three children be so draining?

'OK, let's be honest about this. Cute, well brought-up . . . And lethal. Like a miniature firing squad. Only some of them wanted to shoot me more than others.'

'Now we're getting somewhere,' said Clare, flicking off the kettle just as it was coming to the boil. 'You know, I don't think a cup of tea is going to cut it.'

Heading for the fridge, she peered inside at the chaos of Louisa's half-eaten sandwiches and jars that had long since lost contact with their

15

lids. Emerging with half-empty bottles in either hand, Clare said, 'Already opened bottle of Tesco's cheapest plonk or own brand vodka and flat tonic?'

'I'm sorry, I didn't think to bring wine,' Eve said. 'I just . . . fled, I s'pose.'

After leaving Patisserie Valerie, Eve had made the journey on the Northern Line from Soho to East Finchley on autopilot, not even calling ahead to make sure Clare was at home. Although Clare was almost always home at weekends. A single mum, with a teenage daughter on a secondary school teacher's salary, she rarely had the spare cash for a bit of light Saturday afternoon shopping.

And when she did, it was Louisa who got the goodies.

'You want me to pop to Tesco Express on the High Road?' Eve asked, reaching for her bag.

'No need.' Using her arm, Clare swept aside exercise books to make space on the table for a bottle of Sicilian white and two large wine-glasses. 'All I'm saying is, it's not Chablis!'

★ ★ ★

When Ian first announced he'd like her to meet his children, Eve had thought they'd make a day of it: shops, a pizza, perhaps the zoo. An idea Ian rapidly squashed.

At the time she'd been hurt, maybe even a bit offended.

But now . . .

Now she was grateful he'd insisted they keep

16

their first meeting brief. 'So as not to wear them out,' he'd explained. Eve couldn't help thinking that she was the one in need of recuperation.

After Patisserie Valerie came Hamley's for Alfie and Sophie, and Topshop for Hannah. Ian had grimaced when he told Eve. And Eve had wanted to hug him. Ian hated shopping. For him, Topshop on a Saturday afternoon was like visiting the nine gates of hell, all at once.

'You are good,' she whispered, when the children were packing their possessions into rucksacks, carrier bags and pockets. Or, in Alfie's case, all three at once.

'It's in the job description.' Ian kept his voice light, but his meaning was clear. He was their dad, and not just any old dad, not an every-other-weekend one, or a Saturday one. He was full-time, 24/7, widowed.

He was the there-is-no-one-to-do-it-if-I-don't model.

★ ★ ★

As Eve recounted her meeting with Ian's kids, badly chosen books and all, Clare sipped at her wine. It was more acidic than when she'd opened it the night before, allowing herself just the one, after Louisa went to bed. Well, Lou claimed she'd gone to bed. Clare knew better. Her daughter had probably spent a good hour on YouTube; only turning off her light when she heard footsteps on the stairs.

Clare had learnt the hard way to choose her battles, because, as a single mum, there was no one to back her up. If Louisa and she argued, it seemed much more serious. Besides, if they weren't there for each other, who was?

Clare had saved hard to buy a laptop for Lou's thirteenth birthday; taken in extra exam marking to pay the monthly broadband bill. *It will help with your homework*, she told Louisa at the time. If Clare was honest, it was about more than that. She wanted Lou to fit in and have the stuff that her friends had, not always to be the one who went without. Not that the reconditioned Toshiba from a computer repair shop on Finchley Road was the latest thing, but it could pass for new, and it worked, and Louisa had been ecstatic. The expression on Lou's elfin face when she first turned it on made all the long nights at the kitchen table marking exam papers worthwhile.

Occasionally, Clare felt her life was one long night at a kitchen table. After Louisa was first born, it had been a pine table in Clare's mother's kitchen in Hendon; revising for the A-levels she'd missed, what with being eight months pregnant. At Manchester University, it had been an Ikea flat-pack in a grotty student house she'd shared with three others. One of whom was Eve. It was Eve who lasted. The others came and went, endlessly replaced by yet more students who freaked out at the idea of having a toddler around to cramp their style.

Now it was a pine table again. And, even now, Clare couldn't work until Lou was asleep, the flat was still, her light came from an Anglepoise lamp that lived in the corner during the day, and

18

the low mutter of the BBC's *World Service* kept her company.

Not normal, she knew.

Clare had been sixteen when she met Will. She'd been smitten the first time he walked into her AS level English lit class, his dark floppy hair falling over his eyes. By the end of the second week they'd been an item, a fixture.

He was her first boyfriend, her first true love and, so far as she knew, she was his. At least, he'd told her she was. They'd done everything together. First kiss, first love, first fumble, first sex. Life had been a voyage of mutual discovery. And then, halfway through the next year, she'd become pregnant and everything — *everything* — had come crashing down.

Her mum and dad only got married because her mum was pregnant, with Clare. Her nan had married at seventeen; giving up her factory job to have five children and a husband who spent most of his life in the pub. It was the one thing Clare had promised herself would never happen to her.

A mistake like that, it could ruin your life.

Will had laughed when she'd said that. Said people didn't think like that any more. He'd been trying to get her into bed at the time. Well, he'd been trying to get his hand inside her knickers on his parents' settee while they were next door having drinks. Like a fool, she'd believed him.

Clare wasn't sure what happened exactly. They'd always been careful. Originally, she only went on the pill because she didn't think condoms were enough. After Will stopped using condoms, Clare never, ever missed a pill. But a vomiting bug went around college, and that was enough, apparently.

Everyone, from her mum to Will and Will's parents told her to do the sensible thing, and 'get rid of it'. Even her dad would have had an opinion, Clare was sure of it; if he'd ever bothered to show an interest in what she did, or even sent a birthday card in the five years since he'd left.

'What do you mean? You want to have it?' Will said, sitting in the recreation ground not far from her home. Clare watched the ducks try to navigate a Tesco shopping trolley masquerading as an island in the middle of their lake.

'I want *us* to have it,' she said. 'Us. It's *our* baby.'

Out of the corner of one eye she was aware of Will staring at his knees. Once, his curtain of hair would have hidden his eyes, but he'd had it cut shorter and removed his earring for a round of medical school interviews.

'*Our baby*,' she said, turning to stare at him. 'We would have had one eventually, wouldn't we?'

Will refused to catch her eye.

'Wouldn't we?'

It was only later she realized he'd never answered the question.

'If it's *our* baby, then it's our decision,' he said, trying to harden his voice. But Clare could hear it tremble as he spoke. 'And I don't want a baby. I'm too young, Clare. *We're* too young. What about university? What about those novels you're going to write? And me? Seven years of medical studies. How can I do that with a baby?'

'We can manage,' Clare promised. 'Both of us, together.'

She was fighting a losing battle. She knew it, and Will knew she knew it. 'No,' he said finally. 'We can't manage. And *I* won't do it.'

★ ★ ★

Hurtling into the kitchen, Louisa threw her skinny arms around Eve. 'Hello Auntie Eve,' she said. 'Mum didn't say you'd be here.'

'That's because *Mum* didn't know,' Clare said.

Louisa raised her eyebrows.

Eve had known Lou since she was a baby, and been an honorary aunt — the kind whose job it was to provide presents, play-dates and an impartial ear — almost as long. But it always amazed her how unlike her mother Lou looked. Where Clare was stocky, Louisa was wraith-like. Taller, lankier, olive skinned, with eyes so dark they were almost black, and a curtain of shiny black hair that kept falling into her eyes. A black T-shirt carrying the logo of a band Eve didn't recognize, black jacket, skinny jeans and a pair of sneakers that were almost Converse. The girl had emo written all over her.

'Mum,' said Louisa, heading to the fridge. 'What's for lunch?'

'Lunch was two hours ago and if you think I'm cooking again you've got another think coming.

21

If you're hungry, you can have what's left of last night's risotto or make a sandwich.'

Her daughter's nose wrinkled in disgust. 'A sandwich?' she said, sounding like Edith Evans playing Lady Bracknell in *The Importance of Being Earnest*, her last school play. 'I'm going to look like a sandwich if I eat any more. Anyway, there's nothing to put in one.'

'I'll do a shop tomorrow. For now, there's cheese, peanut butter, marmite, jam . . . ' Clare recited a list of jars in the fridge and hoped the cheese hadn't yet developed a crust.

'They're all empty. And you know I don't eat cheese,' Louisa said, spotting the bottle. 'Can I have a glass of wine?'

'You know you can't,' Clare sighed. 'Have orange juice.'

Louisa opened her mouth to object.

'Don't even start. Auntie Eve and I are trying to have a conversation. A *private* conversation,' Clare added pointedly.

It was no use.

As the mother-daughter combat bounced back and forth, Eve listened as Clare negotiated her daughter down to marmite on toast now, plus a glass of orange juice, with the promise of a takeout pizza later as a Saturday night treat. Apparently, Louisa didn't regard mozzarella as cheese. Eve couldn't imagine ever having a conversation like this with Hannah.

'Kids,' Clare said, as Louisa bounced out, orange juice sloshing as she went. 'That's all they are you know. A mess of emotion done up to look scary.'

It was Clare the schoolteacher speaking.

'I know . . . I know.' Draining her glass, Eve reached for the bottle and topped herself up to the halfway mark, before emptying the rest into Clare's. 'And I can't begin to imagine what Ian's have been through. But the eldest, Hannah, I don't think she has any intention of giving me the slightest chance. It's like she's already decided to hate me.'

'How old is she again?'

'Twelve, going on twenty.'

Clare shot her a warning glance. 'A year younger than Louisa,' she pointed out. 'Can you imagine how Lou would react to a new man in my life? Not that that's going to happen any time soon. She'd hate it.'

'You think?'

'I *know*,' Clare said firmly. 'Hannah doesn't hate you. She hates the *idea* of you. She'd hate any woman who threatened to come between her and her dad.'

Looked at objectively, Eve could see Clare was right.

'But right now,' Eve protested. 'I'm just a friend of her dad's.'

'Yeah, right.' Clare rolled her eyes. 'Of course she knows. How many of their dad's *friends* have those children met since their mum died? I mean, think about it. How many times have they traipsed into London to meet someone and then been taken to Hamley's or Topshop as a reward for good behaviour?' She looked at Eve questioningly.

'Zero, nada, zilch. Am I right?'

'Oh bollocks,' Eve said. 'D'you think so?'

'I know so. They might be children, but they're not stupid. Certainly not Hannah. The little ones might take you at face value, for now, but Hannah? Twelve going on twenty, as you put it? No way.'

Eve took a gulp of her wine. How could she have been so naive?

'To be honest,' Clare said. 'I'm surprised Ian was dumb enough to think she'd fall for it. Lou wouldn't, and nor would any of her friends.'

Eve could have kicked herself. It had seemed such a good plan, but with the benefit of hindsight, its flaws were glaring.

'Still, at least he tried. I've told you about Lily's boyfriend, Liam?'

Lily was Clare's sister. Nine years younger and a lot closer to Louisa in looks than she was to Clare. Eve hadn't seen her for years.

'The divorced one? Sports reporter?'

'Not-quite divorced. But yes, that one. He just threw Lily in at the deep end. Her and the kid, *and* his ex. I don't know who was more traumatized. If that wasn't bad enough, a couple of months later, she has to field his kid for an entire afternoon by herself.'

'God,' said Eve. 'Why?'

'His shift changed and he *had* to cover the FA Cup.' Clare mimed inverted commas around the 'had'. 'He didn't even ring his ex to explain. She only found out he wasn't going to be there when she delivered Rosie, and Lily opened the door. I had Lily on the phone almost hysterical. Didn't have the first clue what to do. Didn't know what to feed her, anything . . . I mean,' Clare asked, 'would you?' Her voice rose.

Clare had never been much of a drinker, but when she got drunk, she got drunk. Eve was familiar with the signs.

'I should probably go,' she said.

'Not yet.'

Eve waited.

'I've had a brainwave! You could meet up with Lily. Compare notes.'

'Clare . . . '

'I'm serious.' Standing up from the table Clare found the cups and put the kettle back on. 'Have to be instant,' she said. 'And I think I'm out of digestives.'

'I know. You haven't done a shop.'

Eve hated Nescafé, but wouldn't dream of saying so. Fresh coffee was a luxury Clare only allowed herself once a month, on payday. And when the packet was empty, it was back to instant again. Occasionally, Eve would bring coffee herself, only she'd been too strung out by meeting Ian's kids to bring anything, apart from her problems.

If she was honest, that was something of a pattern. Eve arrived with something for Louisa, a bottle of wine for Clare, and her problems. In return, Clare listened, although rarely without comment. That was the price of access to Clare's shoulder.

'It's a good idea,' Clare insisted. 'You know it is. If you're going to do this . . . ' She looked at her friend. 'And I assume you haven't fallen at the first hurdle?'

25

Eve shook her head. Of course she hadn't. How pathetic did Clare think she was?

'Then you're going to need all the moral support you can get. And who's going to understand better than Lily, who's in the same predicament?'

3

If Clare hadn't been coming along *to say hello* . . .

Check they both showed up more like, Eve thought wryly. She'd already had a text and a call on her mobile to make sure there was no last-minute work crisis. If not for Clare coming, Eve would have cancelled.

But even the most mundane night out was a big deal for Clare. She didn't do it often — couldn't afford the time, energy or money that four hours away from Louisa invariably cost, both in bribery and babysitters — and every occasion was a military operation of childminders, Tube trains and precision timing.

In the two weeks since Clare suggested a three-way get together, Eve had seen Ian only a couple of times. Both snatched drinks on his way home from work. They'd spoken on the phone another half a dozen times, and texted and e-mailed often, but she hadn't once mentioned Clare's plan.

What was the big deal anyway?

And mentioning it would involve being honest about how hard she'd found meeting his kids, how upset she'd been about Hannah's rejection of her present. Easier by far to continue with their mutual pretence that it had gone well.

Closing the feature she'd been editing for what felt like days, Eve shut down her computer. The

27

piece was a profile of Kate Winslet by an award-winning interviewer. Eve pulled her make-up bag from a desk drawer and began retouching her face. Award-winning interviewer maybe, but she was a famously bad writer, well-known for delivering what were, basically, six-thousand-word transcripts for a two-thousand-word interview.

But features editors continued to commission her because her name opened doors. Hollywood publicists loved her and always approved her, so she always got used. Eve wondered if the old soak ever read the interviews printed under her name; and whether she really believed the award-winning writing was hers.

A stiff drink was deserved, for cutting the feature by half and turning what remained into half-decent prose, but she wasn't going to get one. Clare had suggested Starbucks on Carnaby Street and Eve had agreed. Central enough to be convenient for none of them, it was busy enough for them to have a coffee each and call it quits if the whole thing was as big a disaster as Eve expected.

An hour, she decided. An hour and a half, max.

Then she was out of there.

⋆ ⋆ ⋆

'I'll be an hour, tops,' Lily Adams told the stage manager at the Comedy Club, as she grabbed her purse and kicked her backpack under the desk of the ticket office. 'I've got to do this to humour my sister. I'll relieve you at eight, promise. Eight-thirty, absolute latest.'

'Eight it is,' he said, waving her away.

There was no irritation in Brendan's voice.

Stand-up had always been Lily's great love. Right up to the point she got hammered at Soho House with a couple of the comics who'd just done a one-off charity special, got talking to, and laughing with, some journalist they knew called Liam Donnelly, and woke up in his bed. Somehow one night had turned into weeks, and then weeks had turned into months; now Liam was Lily's great love. Or so she was telling everyone.

Helping out in the ticket office, and being general dogsbody at the Comedy Club in Piccadilly was as close as Lily got to the career she'd temporarily put on ice. For now, it was close enough. She had other things on her mind. Although what Clare thought 'discussing her problems' with some old friend that Lily hadn't seen for years would achieve, Lily didn't have the faintest idea. Not that she could avoid it.

'I've booked a babysitter,' Clare said. Pulling her old, 'don't let me down after I've gone to so much trouble' guilt trip again. It worked, of course. It always did.

Privately, Lily thought that if her sister's life was tough, Clare had only herself to blame. She hadn't had to have the baby after all. Although Lily would never dream of saying such a thing, and felt bad for even thinking it. She adored Louisa and couldn't imagine life without her pint-sized partner in crime. But honestly, nobody *forced* Clare to become a single mum at eighteen. More importantly, nobody forced her to still be a single mum nearly fourteen years later.

That particular call was down to Clare.

Lily had been nine when Clare announced she was pregnant, and was having it no matter what anyone else said. She could still remember the rows that rocked their Hendon terrace. As days dragged into weeks, Lily began to feel ever more invisible. She went to school and came home again. Went to Brownies and netball practice. Went next door to play with Bernice. Inside the house the argument raged. Lily might as well not have been there.

Lily had lost count of the nights she lay awake, plotting her escape. She wanted to run away and find Dad, then they'd be sorry; if they even noticed. But she never did run away. And Dad had been gone five years, anyway. Six, almost.

When the baby was born, Lily went from see-through to utterly invisible. The day Clare took baby Lou away to university in her push-chair, Mum had shut herself in her bedroom and sobbed and sobbed.

At the time Lily didn't care. She had her mum back.

At the bottom of Carnaby Street, Lily stopped to check her reflection in a shop window. Not exactly smart — jeans, T-shirt, Paul Smith jacket lifted from Liam's wardrobe — but these were her theatre clothes and she was on her break. What else could Clare expect? Her fine dark hair was newly washed and tied back in a knot, her make-up minimal, but there if you looked close enough. That would do. It would have to.

★ ★ ★

Clare was already sitting at a low-level table pretending to reread *Jane Eyre* in sympathy with her GCSE students when Eve arrived. Of course she was, Eve thought fondly. The one with the most on her plate and the furthest to travel still managed to get there early and keep a bunch of German students out of the three most comfortable leather armchairs in the whole place. She'd even got the coffees in.

'Let me,' said Eve, reaching for her purse. She knew the evening would have cost her friend at least twenty quid before she even stepped out of her front door.

'No need,' Clare said. 'Anyway, it's easier saving the chairs if there's a cup in front of each. You can get the next round.'

Eve didn't say she was hoping there wouldn't be a next round.

'There's Lily!' Clare exclaimed.

As Eve turned, Clare began waving at a tom-boyish figure peering through the window. The girl raised her hand so briefly it was more twitch than acknowledgement, and began weaving between tables to reach the door.

'*That's* Lily?' Eve asked.

'Uh-huh. Hasn't changed a bit, has she?'

As Eve watched the girl working her boyfriend's clothes in a way that was only possible with the confidence and body of

31

someone under twenty-five, she wondered if Clare realized how long it was since they'd last seen each other. Lily had been at school. And now she was here. Cool, effortlessly stylish, with that no-age aura that made her appear both older and younger than her twenty-three years. Eve felt strangely intimidated.

'Hey,' said Lily to no one in particular. She swung skinny denim-clad legs over one arm of the chair and lounged against the other. 'Very long time no see.' She turned to her sister. 'So, where's the fire?'

'Good to see you too,' Clare said.

Rolling her eyes, Lily slouched even further, causing two of the German boys to look over. And keep looking.

Eve, whose newly-hip Jaeger dress and skyscraper heels had seemed so right at the office, felt instantly overdressed.

'So,' Clare said, calling her meeting to order. 'The reason we're all here . . . '

Lily sighed. 'There's three of us,' she said faux patiently. 'Perhaps you'd like me to take minutes?' Some things hadn't changed, she still had her annoying little-sister routine down pat.

'The reason we're here,' Clare repeated, 'is because we're stepmums. Well, you two are, sort of . . . And since I have to suffer you both moaning, I thought it might be better if you moaned at each other.'

Eve couldn't help laughing. 'I'm sorry,' she said. 'I didn't realize I was that bad!'

'Oh, Lily's worse. Liam this, Liam that

. . . The problem is, I'm not sure I'm on either of your sides.'

'You're not?'

'No,' said Clare. 'I'm not.'

'Then whose side are you on?' Eve demanded.

'The children's.'

Eve was shocked. She'd only come because she didn't want to let her friend down. Now Clare was stitching her up. Out of the corner of her eye, she saw Lily had frozen, her latte halfway to her lips.

'Don't look so surprised.' Clare seemed almost pleased by their reaction. 'When you've had one like ours, you're hardly going to side instinctively with the stepmother.'

'Oh for crying out loud,' Lily said, banging her cup down hard enough to slop coffee over the edge. 'If you're going to start whingeing on about Annabel again, I'm leaving.'

'I'm not. I'm just saying, remember what it's like from the kids' perspective. They don't ask for a stepmother.'

'But we barely even saw her,' Lily said crossly.

'Yes, we did.'

'*No, we didn't.*'

Eve started to rummage in her bag, looking for her mobile, a lipstick, anything to remove her mentally, if not physically, from this conversation.

'We did. What about that trip to the cinema and . . . '

'Yes. I know!' Lily almost shouted. 'The pizza from hell.'

'Maybe I should go?' Eve started to get up.

'No!' Both sisters rounded on her so swiftly the students crowded around the next table turned and stared.

'Dad left us for the stepmonster,' Clare resumed her story as soon as Eve had returned to her seat.

Eve knew what was coming; she'd heard it all before.

Drunken midnight rants at their student house, with one ear on a baby monitor, segueing into hissed updates every time a birthday or Christmas was missed. When her father began missing Louisa's birthdays too, Clare was livid. The fact he didn't even know his granddaughter existed was deemed irrelevant.

Clare's hatred was impressive in its consistency. Annabel was a blonde-bobbed, designer-clad bitch who stole her father from under his children's very noses. Her father wasn't exactly an innocent party in this particular fairy tale, but Clare never seemed to mention that.

Stealing him, however, wasn't Annabel's number one crime.

Her number one crime, the sin that led to rows, recriminations, and ultimately an estrangement lasting nineteen years and counting, was that Annabel had tried to usurp their mother. When, as Clare never failed to point out, they had a perfectly good one, already.

The scene of Annabel's crime was an Italian restaurant in north-west London. And the way Clare told it, it began with Annabel sending Clare and Lily to the toilets to wash their hands before eating, and went downhill from there.

Couldn't they sit up straight? Why weren't they using napkins? Hadn't their mother told them how to hold a knife properly?

The list grew longer with each telling.

Finish their mouthfuls before starting another. Surely their mother didn't allow them to leave their crusts at home? (The answer was no. But what self-respecting thirteen-year-old would admit that?)

When the woman asked Clare if she'd ever heard of the words *please* and *thank you*, lunch turned ugly. Who could blame her, Clare said, if she accidentally knocked an almost-full glass of Coca-Cola over her father's girlfriend's smart cream trousers? (She was thirteen, for crying out loud. Thirteen and trapped. Who wouldn't do the same?)

Lily sighed loudly.

But as Eve pictured a teenage Clare nudging her elbow towards that glass, it wasn't her friend she saw. The skinny face that stared defiantly as sticky brown liquid splashed across the table was Hannah's. And suddenly the story didn't seem as clear-cut.

'Liam's got a little girl, hasn't he?' Eve asked Lily. Her attempt to move the subject on could hardly be less subtle. 'How old is she?'

'Rosie,' Lily said. She'd obviously planned to say as little as possible, and leave as quickly as she could, but even she looked grateful that Eve had stopped Clare in her tracks. 'She's three. Adorable, in a girly way. Yours?'

'Not really mine.'

'They never are,' Lily said, sounding far older

35

than her years. 'That's the whole point, isn't it? So, how old are they?'

'Hannah's twelve, going on fifteen. Sophie's nine and Alfie's five and two months. And don't you dare forget the two months!' Eve smiled. 'I've only met them once. And that was terrifying enough.'

'Three of them! I can barely cope with Rosie.'

'I know the feeling,' Eve said. 'I had no idea it would be so hard. They're just kids, after all.'

'*Just kids?*' Clare said. 'You're kidding, right?'

'Of course,' Eve smiled weakly. 'I wanted them to like me so much. That's why I bought them the books,' she explained to Lily. 'That was my big mistake, right there. I shouldn't have bothered. Especially without running it by Ian first. I opened myself right up and now I'm afraid I've blown it.'

'What does Ian say?' Lily asked.

Eve stared at her hands. 'I haven't told him,' she admitted. 'We haven't really seen each other properly since. And I don't want to worry him.'

Don't want him to think there might be a problem, more like, she thought.

'Is that usual?' Lily asked.

'What?'

'Going a fortnight without seeing him properly?'

'Not really, but it's not unusual. It depends on both our work, his childcare arrangements — he has an au pair, but he tries to be home as much as possible to cover homework — that kind of thing.'

'We talk about it all the time,' Eve continued.

36

'How to spend more time together, I mean. But Ian wants to take it slowly — for the sake of the kids. It's a difficult balancing act. I'm trying to understand, but it's not easy.'

'So much of our relationship has been like this,' she continued. 'Cups of coffee, quick drinks on his way home, dinner and the odd evening at my place. We've managed a night away a couple of times, but overnighters are rare . . . Understandably enough,' she added, for fear of sounding bitter. 'They're going to their grandparents' in a couple of weeks, so he'll stay with me then.'

She felt like a teenager, aware her face lit up at the mere thought of a whole twenty-four hours together.

Said out loud it sounded paltry, embarrassing. A grown woman excited by a Saturday night sleepover. 'It's the kids,' she repeated. 'He wants to ease them in gently.'

It was a well-worn line. One she trotted out every time anyone asked after her love life.

'You can hardly blame him,' Clare put in, plonking three full mugs on the table in front of them. 'They've lost their mum, after all. The last thing they need is to feel they've lost their dad too.'

Eve and Lily had been so engrossed they hadn't noticed Clare was gone until she'd returned with the second round of coffees.

Lily nodded thoughtfully. 'So, he's a proper dad,' she said. 'Unlike Liam.' She smiled indulgently. 'He's an every third weekender. And then only when he remembers.'

'Liam forgets?'

'Oh yeah,' Clare said. 'He'd forget his head if it wasn't screwed on.'

'My turn,' Eve said, reaching for her purse.

'OK,' said Lily. 'But I'll get the next round.'

Clare raised her eyebrows.

'If there is one, obviously,' Lily added hastily.

'It wasn't that much,' Clare said, looking at the ten pound note Eve was holding out to her. When Eve rolled her eyes, Clare took it anyway. It would pay her Tube fare home.

'Back to Liam,' she said. 'And his convenient bouts of amnesia.'

'Don't start,' said Lily, but her tone was light and the smile reached her eyes as she pulled a picture from her wallet. It showed a slightly thickset man, with dark curly hair and crinkly brown eyes. He was good-looking, if you liked the type, and he knew it.

'Looks like Jimmy Nesbitt with longer hair,' Eve said.

'God, don't tell him that,' said Lily. 'He's vain enough as he is.'

'I'm not sure Eve meant that as a compliment.'

Lily caught Eve's eye and both women grinned. 'Thing is,' she said, 'I know Clare doesn't appreciate his finer qualities . . . '

She ignored her sister choking pointedly on her coffee.

'But I love him. I've never met anyone like him. He's funny and clever and . . . '

'The sex is great,' said Clare.

'Clare!'

38

'You're telling me it isn't?'

'OK, the sex is great,' Lily grinned. 'You're just jealous.'

'Seriously, though,' she returned her attention to Eve. 'If you'd told me a year ago I'd be taking on a guy twelve years older than me with a three-year-old kid I'd have told you to dream on, so I guess that makes it a bit more than great sex.'

Lily smiled again. 'But, yes, he forgets, a lot . . . '

'And you can't do that with a kid,' Clare completed for her.

'Never make a promise you can't keep.' Eve put in. She had heard it from Ian, about a zillion times. Never fight a battle you can't win. Let the small stuff go. Concentrate on the things that matter.

'Well,' Lily said. 'Let's just say, reliability isn't Liam's strongest point. Not even where Rosie's concerned.'

'Understatement,' Clare snorted. 'Tell her about the FA Cup quarter-final.'

'Not his finest moment. Rosie comes every third weekend. Liam picks her up Saturday, takes her back Sunday. He fixes his shifts around it. We both do, if we can.'

'Which paper's he on?'

Lily named a tabloid.

'Anyway, that's how our free Saturdays are spent, babysitting.' She glanced at her sister, and Eve was impressed to see Clare remain silent.

All of Clare's were spent babysitting.

'So, he got a call late Friday night saying they

needed him to cover the quarter-final. To be fair, he did try to get out of it. I heard him. But his editor wasn't having it. And, ultimately, work's work. The paper comes first, everything else is second. That's what he's like. What he's always been like.'

Now *that* Eve understood.

Taking a gulp of coffee, Lily said, 'He couldn't face calling Siobhan — his ex — at midnight. I didn't blame him. It's not exactly amicable at the best of times and this was going to cause a huge row.'

Clare nodded. She'd obviously heard it before. 'When he left next morning, I just assumed he'd call her on his way to work. I was on the verge of phoning the Comedy Club to see if they needed any shifts covering, when his doorbell rings. So I picked up the videophone assuming it's the post or something. There's Siobhan, with Rosie, Angelina Ballerina rucksack and all.'

'God!' said Eve, horrified. 'What did you do?'

'What could I do?' Lily shrugged. 'I let her in. Siobhan was furious. Man, did she give me a piece of her mind. It's funny how she's changed the goalposts to suit her. She refused to let me anywhere near Rosie in the beginning. But then Liam told her that if she wanted every third weekend off, Rosie would be spending it with us or she'd be making other arrangements. So she backed off.'

'New boyfriend,' Clare said. 'Wants some time for herself.'

For a split-second Eve's eyes met Lily's.

'So there I was — and there Liam wasn't,' Lily

continued. 'I was at least as furious with Liam as Siobhan was. Being lumbered with his kid without anyone even having the decency to ask, but there was no way I was going to let Siobhan see that.'

'What about Rosie?' Eve asked. 'Did her mum take her away again?'

'Fat chance!' Lily was emphatic. 'She dumped her on the settee, turned on CBeebies and shut the flat door so she could spit venom in the privacy of a communal stairwell. She said I could tell Liam she expected him to deliver Rosie back at the usual time and she'd be having words with him. Then she buggered off. Can't say I blame her. But talk about kicking the cat.'

Eve was blown away by the young woman's calmness. She wasn't sure she would know how to cope with this now, let alone when she'd been Lily's age.

Maybe she could learn something after all . . .

4

His dark head was burrowed into the pillow, and his flat silent but for the sound of his breathing when Lily finally pushed open the door to the bedroom she shared with Liam. As she stood in a strip of light from the hall, she couldn't help feeling a pang. A bit of her wanted to reach out and stroke his hair. Another bit wanted a quiet life and some sleep. She couldn't risk waking him, and didn't want another scrap, because scrap was all they had done since Rosie's last visit.

If they were speaking at all.

Surely this wasn't how it was meant to be? Surely this wasn't what having kids did to you? Even kids who weren't your own.

Reaching back to click off the hall light, Lily heard a floorboard creak, making Liam grumble in his sleep and burrow further under the duvet. She waited for him to settle, before shutting the door and shucking off her clothes, her eyes adjusting to the quasi-darkness of south London, visible through a gap in his curtains.

God knows she loved him. She just hadn't bargained for this. She was twenty-three, twelve years younger than he was. And suddenly she was being referred to as Mum by Polish waitresses in Pizza Hut.

When I was your age I was married with a three-year-old.

Her mother's voice echoed through her head.

Yes, Lily thought, as she always did. *And so was Clare*. Well, not the married bit. That was precisely why Lily was determined to do things differently.

What had she been thinking, getting involved with a not-quite-single dad? It wasn't as if she hadn't been out with boys with baggage before. In fact, the bigger the baggage the better she liked it. If Lily had a type it was tall, skinny and arty . . . All cheekbones, hipbones, angst and assorted undesirable habits.

So what was she doing with a slightly stocky sports reporter who came with a child attached? It didn't bear thinking about.

Except, of course, thought hadn't come into it. Their second bottle of Pinot Grigio — or was it the third, who knew? — had seen to that. And the sex was amazing, even drunk. Or should that be especially drunk? But when her wine goggles came off, Lily hadn't moved on in her usual easy-come, easy-go way. Moving on hadn't even entered her head.

Somehow, Lily Adams, who never let a man get under her skin, let alone in the way of her ambition to make it on the comedy circuit, had found herself organising her weekends around a three-year-old. That was something they didn't mention in all those magazine features about the Dos and Don'ts of twenty-first-century relation-ships. Where were the features on falling in love with a man with baggage? The ones about how to handle his ex, know Peppa Pig from Iggle Piggle, or planning your Saturday around trips to the playground.

Making a mental note to suggest those to Eve next time they met, Lily slid into bed beside Liam.

To Lily's surprise, her brief coffee with Clare and Eve had turned into a long yack; only ending when a Portuguese barista, with *trainee* written across his back, started mopping up around them. Lily had serious grovelling to do when she got back to the Comedy Club, gone nine, to find the show almost at the first interval and Brendan cashing up the till himself.

'Sorry,' she said. 'Really sorry. It won't happen again.'

'Whatever.' Brendan's shrug suggested it couldn't matter less. 'But, next time you want an evening off, just book it like everyone else.'

So when the show finished, and the stragglers and autograph hunters had gone, she insisted he head to the pub with the crew for a pint before closing time. She stayed behind to lock up. It meant braving the night bus with its drunks and letches, but in the circumstances it was the least she could do.

'Lil, that you?'

The sleepiness was obvious in Liam's voice, as he rolled over and draped his arm heavily across her hip. 'S'late . . . You OK?'

Her body instinctively curled into his. 'Work,' she whispered. 'It was my turn to lock up.'

'Look, I'm sorry about the Rosie thing,' Liam said, his sleep-fogged breath hot against her ear. 'My fault entirely. Should have called on my way to the match. And then it was too late and . . . '

I know, Lily thought, you gutless sod, you chickened out.

'Sorry you got landed with my shit.' He nuzzled the back of her neck, and she could feel him hardening against the base of her spine. Despite herself, she pushed against him. 'It won't happen again,' he promised, sliding one hand up to her breast, the tips of his fingers grazing her nipple. 'I'll straighten it out, I promise. You do believe me, don't you?'

Her brain didn't, not really.

But for that moment at least, her body did.

★　★　★

Two hours later Lily was lying, eyes wide open, staring at streetlamp shadows and passing headlights on the ceiling. It wasn't the itchy-eyed insomnia she'd suffered since childhood, the kind that guaranteed her migraines by the following lunchtime.

She was warm and her body relaxed; she'd even been dozing since they'd finished making love and Liam had sunk back into his usual impenetrable slumber. No, she'd been woken by a thought. And now that thought was bugging her.

Liam and she had barely gone forty-eight hours without sex since they met, let alone two weeks. And it hadn't escaped her notice that he'd made peace in the nick of time for Rosie's next visit. Now that thought was playing on her mind. Was he really sorry? Had he missed her as much as she'd missed him? Had he been as unhappy

45

about the quarrelling as she was? Or was he just worried he might have to field his daughter on his own for twenty-four hours?

No, she wiped the thought from her mind. Liam was many things, but calculating was not one of them.

★ ★ ★

'Any luck with that case study?'

Eve was on the phone to Nancy Morris, a regular contributor to *Beau*. What should have been a straight-forward 'four women who . . . ' feature had turned into a nightmare when the fourth case study had pulled out that morning. The shoot was in two hours. Somewhere in London there had to be a woman aged twenty-eight to forty-five, who had turned emotional trauma into business success and could get to a photographic studio in Chalk Farm by two o'clock at the latest.

'I've got two possibilities,' said Nancy. 'If Miriam hates them we're up shit creek without a paddle; not to put too fine a point on it.'

Eve laughed. *Beau*'s editor was notoriously choosy. Did they have the right age range, geographical spread and racial mix? And that was even before she'd approved photos of them. 'Tell me what you've got.'

'I'm e-mailing you the pics now. They can both do a shoot this afternoon, but the first is best, by a mile. Her name's Melanie Cheung. She's thirty-five, and she sold her home and ploughed all her savings into an internet fashion business after her marriage fell apart. You've probably heard of it, *personalshopper.com*?'

Eve had. It was one of those genius, 'why didn't I think of that?' ideas, mixing the high-end edited choice straight-to-your-desk ease of NET-A-PORTER, with a personal shopping service. When you signed up, you just put in your sizes, budget, colouring and examples of items and labels you already owned to give an idea of your personal style. And every week your *personalshopper* e-mailed you a tailor-made list from their new stock. Click on the items you liked, and they'd be delivered by six p.m., provided you ordered before one p.m. (And lived in London, of course. Everyone else had to wait twenty-four hours.) Not that Eve had bought anything. Most of the items had 'investment' sized price tags.

'So there's a good entrepreneur-rises-from-ashes-of-failed-marriage story,' Nancy was saying. 'And I think, if we dig around, there might be an I-wanted-kids/he-didn't angle. If that's not mud-dying the waters too much. I'll play that by ear, if that's OK?'

'Sure,' Eve said.

'She lives in London, of course. Which means we have three London-based case studies. But realistically, at this short notice, anyone who can make a shoot this afternoon is going to be here already. Plus, she's Chinese, so not blonde.'

'Thank God,' Eve said. 'We've got three blondes already. You sure she can make it?'

'Surer than sure. To be honest, I've already teed her up. I had to.'

47

Eve sighed. 'Is it worth me even looking at the other?'

'Probably not,' Nancy said, as she gave Eve the top line on the alternate case study. She was right. Although the woman had set up a business, she was selling scented candles from her Notting Hill living room, there was nowhere near enough human interest to garner readers' sympathy. Also, she was blonde.

'We'll go for Melanie,' Eve said, forwarding the photo to her editor, having added the relevant details. 'I know Miriam usually demands a choice, but there's no time to mess around. I'll square it with her.'

★ ★ ★

'Tell me again why there's only one option?'

'Because the other is blonde and we've got three of those already. Plus, her marriage hasn't fallen apart and she didn't launch one of the most successful start-ups of the year from the ashes of her relationship.'

'And why do we have three London-based case studies?'

'Because we're paying David a thousand quid to do the shoot and she has to be at the studio in under two hours.'

Miriam wasn't thrilled. But Eve also knew her boss could spot the difference between a rock and a hard place, as surely as she knew when she was wedged between them.

With her editor squared, Eve headed down the office to the picture desk. Thank God Melanie

Cheung was size 10. That way, they'd be able to scrounge some samples from the fashion department, before they were returned to the designers.

One of the designers, Caitlin, was regaling the picture editor with a weekly update of the dating woes of a thirtysomething singleton.

'You could hardly move for groovy dads,' Caitlin was saying. 'You know, sexy, slouchy thirtyish, maybe forty-something, cute little kids in matching jeans and kiddie Converse. All carrying eco-shoppers stuffed with locally grown asparagus. Although, I mean, how local can it be if you buy it in Queens Park?'

'So what's your problem?' Jo, the picture editor, asked. 'I thought hunting down a groovy dad was your preferred weekend pastime.'

'Me and the rest of the single female population of north London,' Caitlin sighed. 'Anyway, the problem with the Queens Park farmers' market crowd is they usually come with a groovy mum attached!'

The art department rang with laughter. 'You don't live anywhere near Queens Park,' Jo said. 'What were you doing there anyway?'

'Hunting. I had a tip-off,' Caitlin said, lowering her tone and pushing subtly highlighted hair out of her blue eyes. 'Anyway, I have a plan.'

Jo waited.

'Even groovy mums and dads split up,' Caitlin said. 'So somewhere in there has to be a groovy separated every-other-weekend dad. That means changing my MO. From next weekend, I'm going to take my sister's kids as bait and disguise

49

myself as a groovy estranged mum. That gives me five days to train my nieces to answer to Phoebe and Scarlett. If you see me hanging by the organic cheese stall with two adorable little girls, do me a favour — don't blow my cover.'

Jo grinned. Looking up from her screen, she spotted Eve. 'Got one?'

'Yup,' said Eve. 'And she's perfect. She's sample size and can be there by two.' She gave a bow to accept the applause that wasn't forthcoming.

'What d'you think of Caitlin's idea?' Jo asked. 'I mean, you're the expert. Does it sound like a plan?'

'Sorry, groovy dads, not my specialist subject.'

Jo and Caitlin snorted in unison. 'Hello!' said Caitlin. 'Earth to Eve Owen. Ian Newsome is the patron saint of them all. Added to which, he's famous. Famous and a widower, which makes him the Holy Grail too. All the sympathy, none of the nightmare ex-wife. Come off it. All you need now is the rock and you're home dry.'

Caitlin paused, waiting for Eve to reply.

When Eve didn't, Caitlin tilted her head to one side, a look of expectation lighting her face. 'You haven't split up, have you?' Far from sounding sympathetic, her voice revealed thinly veiled excitement. Eve realized her colleague was a split-second away from asking if she was ready to on-gift Ian's phone number.

'In your dreams,' Eve said.

Was Ian a groovy dad? It had honestly never occurred to her.

Maybe he was.

In fact, Ian and Caroline Newsome had been the full groovy mum and dad package.

'Come on Eve,' Caitlin's words echoed up the office in Eve's wake. 'Tell us how you pulled it off.'

Eve shrugged and kept walking.

She shrugged because, in all honesty, she didn't know how someone like her — just pretty-enough, just bright-enough and just successful-enough — had bagged a catch like Ian Newsome. And having met his children, she didn't know how on earth she was going to keep him, either.

5

'I'm sorry it's been so long.' Ian rolled over and planted a lingering kiss on her forehead. 'I couldn't get any decent overnight cover. Also, to be honest, their suspicions have been on high alert since they met you. Especially Hannah's. They're not stupid, after all.'

Eve wriggled up the mattress, so his lips trailed down her face until their lips met. His blue eyes were open, staring into hers as he began to do previously unimaginable things with his fingers. They didn't say anything else for a long time.

★ ★ ★

'I know it's not ideal and I promise it won't be for ever. Now they've met you, that's the first hurdle over with. We just need to take it slowly, give them a chance to get used to the idea of there being someone else in our lives,' he paused. 'Someone important.'

Same subject, different setting.

They had dragged themselves out of bed and were now camped on Eve's living room floor sharing an impromptu picnic.

Joy surged through her. She felt irrationally, stupidly happy. As if she were fifteen again. Not that she'd ever felt like this when she was fifteen.

Smiling, Eve reached over the tea towel that doubled as a tablecloth, laden with pitta bread, hummus, carrot sticks and tubs of salads, to squeeze his hand. 'I understand,' she said. 'The kids come first. You don't need to explain.'

'I do, though,' he said. But his smile was grateful as he leant forward to kiss her again. As he did, the front of his shirt fell open, and Eve couldn't help but stare at the trail of fair hair that led down his lean body into the waistband of his jeans.

When they were together, she felt sick with longing.

She loved him so much she felt physically ill with wanting. And when they were apart too, most of the time. It was just that, sometimes, at night or on a Sunday, when Ian had spent the weekend with the kids, and she'd exhausted Sky Plus and was on her fifth DVD of the day, she couldn't help wondering if they really stood a chance.

There was no way he would have allowed her within a mile of his children if he wasn't deadly serious. But this wasn't a regular, every other weekend stepmum arrangement. There would be no collecting the children on Saturday morning, dropping them back on Sunday evening, and having the following weekend to recover. This was full-time, 24/7.

She didn't know if she could handle that. More importantly, she didn't know if the children would let her try. But she did know she wanted to.

The bottle of Sauvignon Blanc shook in her hand as she refilled his glass and then her own. When she looked up Ian was staring at her. 'You all right?' he asked.

'Of course.' She smiled before taking a sip. A gulp would have given her away.

'Can I talk to you?'

Eve laughed. 'Funny how you don't ask if you can fuck me. And now you ask if we can talk!'

'Eve, be serious.'

'I was, sort of . . . Of course you can. Either or both,' she couldn't help adding.

The tension left his face and he slid a hand down the front of her dressing gown to cup her breast.

'Talk first,' he said, crawling around to her side of the picnic, and lying beside her, his head on his elbow, his face serious.

'I need to tell you something,' he said.

'So, tell me.'

'I'm so grateful, Eve . . . for everything, but above all for your patience. Believe me, I do know I'm asking a lot.' She waved his apology away. 'But there are other things about Caro and me. Things that might help you understand . . . About Hannah.'

'What's she said?' Eve asked, before she could stop herself.

'Nothing.' Ian held up a hand. 'Chill, OK. It's going to be harder for her than for the others because she's the eldest. When Caro became ill Hannah was seven. So she remembers . . . ' He hesitated. 'What it was like before, I guess. She remembers things the others don't. Especially not Alfie. He never really knew his mother. Not properly.'

Caro and me. The words tasted sour in Eve's

mouth. And she hadn't been the one to speak them. When she looked up, Ian was watching her, obviously wondering whether to continue.

'What does Hannah remember?' Eve asked gently.

Ian rubbed his eyes. His skin had greyed, and in the fading light he looked older. For the first time, tiredness showed in the lines of his face.

'Caro was ill for three years. Think about that. Hannah was ten when she died. A third of her life,' he sighed. 'The third she was old enough to remember properly.'

Eve felt her insides knot. She'd wanted to hear this. She needed to know how it had been. Not the public-friendly version Ian gave in interviews. Had given *her* in an interview. But how it really was. Now it was coming, she was afraid of what he might be about to tell her.

'Go on,' she forced herself to say.

'When Caro found the lump we didn't tell Hannah or Sophie there was anything wrong. Even the hospital visits were fairly easy to hide. Alfie was tiny, the others were used to her being away. But then Caro needed a mastectomy.'

Wrapping her robe more tightly around her, Eve waited.

'She didn't want to have to hide away every time the girls came into the bathroom or our bedroom. And, of course, she couldn't breast-feed Alfie any more. So, we told them.'

'What?' Eve asked.

'Mummy needed an operation to make her better.'

Eve nodded.

55

'Then, for a long time, Caro was in remission. And then, suddenly, she wasn't. And the rest, as you know, is terrifyingly well-documented. But it's not so much the illness that I need to explain to you. It's my relationship with Caro.'

She felt sick. Eve wasn't sure she did want this conversation after all. 'Your relationship?' she managed.

'Yes, I'm horribly afraid Hannah has worked it out. The others haven't. Unless she's told them.' Ian stopped, as the full implications of that hit him. 'She wouldn't,' he said. 'I'm sure she wouldn't.'

Somehow both their glasses were empty again. Eve refilled Ian's, but when she shifted to fetch another bottle, he reached out to stop her. His grip on her wrist was gentle but solid.

'Please,' he said. 'If I stop now, I'm never going to start again. And I need to tell you. I need you to know everything. If we're going to . . . if we're going to make this work.' He stared at her. 'We are, aren't we?'

She sat down. Her heart was pounding. 'Yes,' she whispered.

'Look,' he said. 'The night Caroline died I wasn't there. All right? I wasn't there. Oh, I'd been there up to then. I'd been at the hospice for weeks. Originally she came home when we realized radio and chemo were only making things worse. But eventually she had to go into a hospice. For the kids' sake. For mine, for her own, I don't know . . . But we said it was for the kids.'

Ian took a gulp of wine, then another.

'I took them to see Caro most days, after school. Or her mother did, when I was working. Although, by the end I'd stopped accepting commissions. We didn't want the kids to live their day-to-day lives in a house where their mother was dying. Of course, they knew she was ill, very ill. But going to visit, even someone who's unrecognizably ill, is different from sitting in the same room as them day after day. If you're six, I mean, or ten.'

'Or even thirty-eight,' he added, almost to himself.

'I'm talking about Sophie and Hannah, because Alfie was only three. I'm not sure what he knows, even now. He's like 'Is Mummy in heaven, Daddy? That's good. You be Venom, I'll be Spiderman'.'

Eve smiled, she couldn't help it. It was so *Alfie*.

Ian nodded.

'Anyway,' he said. 'The night Caro died I took the children home, gave them a bath and put them to bed. Hannah wasn't asleep. I knew that, because I could see light under her bedroom door. Although I pretended I couldn't. It was our ritual. Still is. After I tucked her in, we had a long conversation about Mummy and angels. I wasn't expecting her to get much sleep that night.'

He looked so haggard by the memory Eve wanted to comfort him, but didn't know how, so she remained silent and hoped that was right.

'Gone eleven,' Ian said. 'My mobile rang. I knew it was the hospice before I even looked at the screen. They'd agreed to call my mobile instead of the house to avoid disturbing the kids. Caro had lapsed into unconsciousness. They thought it would be soon. Her mother was there already. Her father was on his way. Could I come back?'

This is it, Eve thought. *Whatever he's been wanting to say.*

'Eve, I didn't even stop to think. There was nothing to think about. I just said no. Someone had to look after the kids. Someone had to get them up, washed, make their breakfast. Someone had to carry on, and that someone was me. That was the way life was. The way I knew life was going to be from that moment on. That's what I told the nurse, and it's what I told Caroline's mother when she called two hours later to tell me her only daughter had gone. She was kind enough to pretend she believed me. But the truth is, I didn't want to be there. I was done.'

Ian took a deep breath, and Eve watched him wonder if he was really going to say what he was about to say.

'The truth is,' he said. 'We'd been done for years. Caro and I were only together because of the kids and the cancer; not necessarily in that order. Caro knew that, although we rarely spoke about it. And I assume her parents knew; but they were kind, they never judged me. They still don't. The thing . . . the thing that worries me . . .'

He shrugged and eyed his now empty glass.

'I'm fairly sure Hannah knows too.'

Dusk had fallen while they were talking, and

58

the room was dark but for an orange glow from a street light through still-open curtains, and the tiny screen of the CD player, which had long since fallen silent. For once, the Kentish Town streets around Eve's one-bedroom flat were quiet, without even the wail of a distant siren.

With Eve, the room held its breath.

It felt to Eve that whole minutes passed before he spoke again. As if they'd slipped into a slower time zone and if they went outside they'd discover time had passed everywhere but there.

'I had an affair,' he said. 'So did she. One. More than one. I don't know. It didn't mean anything. It was symptomatic, I guess. Before Alfie was born. He was — what do you call them? — an Elastoplast baby, meant to stick us back together again. Poor little sod. Of course, he couldn't. How could he? I wasn't in love with Caroline, hadn't been for years. She wasn't in love with me, not any longer. We stayed together for the children, then I stayed for the cancer, then she started that damn newspaper column and our life — our family — became public property. With no way out, except the inevitable.'

6

Eve had just discovered the real meaning of walking on air. Ian had stayed Friday night and Saturday night too, leaving on Sunday only to collect his children from Caro's mother to take them to his own parents in West Sussex where they were all staying for the rest of half-term.

Another first in a weekend of relationship firsts.

A full, blissful, domestic forty-eight hours together, and Eve knew she was in deeper than ever. And Ian was too, she was sure of it. He'd never have told her about Caro, about his infidelity, about hers, if he wasn't. Far from being thrown by it, she felt her confidence surge.

If she ran into Caitlin now, she could say, hand on heart, big smug grin on her face, 'Yup, you're right. I've bagged the cream of groovy dads. So hands off!'

Print-outs of the pictures from last week's feature shoot were already on Eve's desk, with a Post-it note from Jo, the picture editor.

'Nice work,' said Jo's hastily scrawled note. 'They're all fab, but Melanie Cheung is STUNNING.'

No kidding, Eve thought, flicking through the printouts. The line-up of case studies was on top. No prizes for guessing which one was Melanie, even if she hadn't been the only non-blonde. Her solo portrait was even better.

Eve was about to pick up her desk phone when her mobile rang. *Ian mobile* flashed up on its screen.

'Hey, you're up early.'

He laughed. 'You've got a lot to learn, Alfie's been up so long he's had second breakfast.'

'Second breakfast?'

'I blame *Lord of the Rings*. All those hungry hobbits. Can you talk?'

Eve glanced around. The office was empty. 'Nobody in yet but me. What's up?'

'Nothing. I've just been thinking, wondering really, if you'd like to come around to the house at the weekend? Saturday lunch, maybe? See the kids in their natural habitat. If you're free, that is?'

If she was free? Eve couldn't help grinning. Of course she was free.

'Sure,' she said casually. 'I'll just check my diary.'

'If you're not, it's . . . '

'Ian!' She laughed. 'I was kidding! Of course I'm free. What time do you want me?'

★   ★   ★

Sliding her mobile back into her bag, Eve collected her thoughts and picked up her desk phone, punching in Nancy Morris's number from memory.

'What a result,' she said when Nancy answered. 'Melanie Cheung looks fabulous — if her story is even half as good we've had a lucky break.'

61

'Good?' said Nancy. 'Her story's brilliant. She's Chinese/American, from Boston, but don't let that put Miriam off,' she added hastily, knowing how the editor could be about non-Brit case studies. 'She meets this British guy in New York, they have a whirlwind romance, he proposes and she moves to London to be with him. She was a lawyer there, pretty high-flying by the sound of it, and she chucked it all in for him. From what she says the whole episode sounds out of character, but hey, we've all been there.'

Speak for yourself, Eve thought. Never one for grand romantic gestures, it wouldn't have occurred to her to let anything so insignificant as love get in the way of life. Well, not until Ian. Now she wouldn't rule out anything.

'Like I thought,' Nancy said. 'It was a classic she-wants-kids/he-doesn't scenario. She was in her early thirties, clock ticking, and he wouldn't even discuss it, said kids weren't consistent with his lifestyle, apparently. He ended it, although she won't talk about that on the record. If you ask me, she was gutted. You don't look the way she does unless you've spent a considerable amount of time on the heartbreak diet.'

'Uh-huh,' Eve murmured by way of encouragement. Heartbreak had never had that effect on her. Maybe her heart had never been sufficiently broken.

'Her parents are crazy for a grandchild,' Nancy continued. 'Last of their line and all that, and blame her for the breakdown of the marriage. Her mother, old-school Chinese, accuses her of putting her career before doing her duty and having a family, which, according to Melanie, couldn't be further from the truth. Anyway, the whole thing makes her re-evaluate her life. So she sells the duplex in Holland Park that was her divorce settlement and ploughs every last penny into her internet start-up. Which, as we now know, is reckoned to be the new NET-A-PORTER.'

'Fantastic,' Eve said, typing her password as Nancy spoke. A hundred and eighty e-mails awaited her. At least ninety per cent of those would head straight for the trash. 'I'm almost glad the first case study pulled out.'

'It gets better,' Nancy said, the grin obvious in her voice.

'Not possible.'

'The ex? He's Simeon Jones.'

Eve racked her brain, but the name didn't ring any immediate bells.

'Call yourself a journalist. He's that hedge fund guy. And not just any old hedge fund guy, either. He's the king of them, been all over the society pages since he married Poppy King-Jones, the model. You know the one. Working-class girl from Rotherham made good.'

OK, now there was a bell ringing.

'C'mon,' Nancy was getting frustrated. 'Less than two years after he dumped Melanie 'cause he didn't want to start a family, the guy is married to a supermodel and the father of a one-year-old. Although not necessarily in that order! Tell me that's not a good story?'

Eve was impressed, but not *that* impressed. 'So we throw a society ex into the mix,' she said.

'Is that going to add to the story? I think it'll just turn readers off.'

She'd have had more time for Melanie Cheung if she hadn't turned out to be one of those women who'd go to the opening of an envelope. Because that was the only place you met men like Simeon Jones.

'God,' Nancy said. 'There's no pleasing some people. No wonder Miriam rates you . . . Melanie Cheung crawls from the ashes of her divorce to launch the most successful start-up of the year, recently valued on paper at least at — ' She named an eye-watering figure. 'And her 'celebrity ex' throws it all back in her face by rushing off to procreate with one of this country's biggest models.

'So, not only does Melanie have to handle being dumped for one of the world's most beautiful women, she can't even open a magazine without seeing her ex with his picture-perfect new family. The family he refused to have with her.

'And on top of that, she's recently started seeing a new guy, Vince something or other, I forget what. She met him through the business. It's early days, by the sound of it, and he's just dropped a ten-year-old daughter from his first marriage on her from a great height. Now he wants Melanie to meet her, the daughter, not the ex . . . Surrounded by kids, and not one of them hers. Tough, huh?'

'Fascinating,' Eve said. 'But I think we need to stick to our angle: how divorce spurred her into launching a business.'

'Well, you'd better not be so snotty when she calls you.' Nancy sounded put out.

'*Calls me?* Why would she call me?' Eve felt herself tense. 'Tell me you didn't promise her copy approval?'

'*God no.* What do you take me for?'

'So, why is Melanie Cheung going to call me?'

'That's what I've been trying to say. I told her about your club.'

'My . . . *What club?*'

'Oh you know, the stepmother thing. That get together you have for women landed with other people's kid-shaped baggage.'

Eve wanted to smack her head on the desk.

'Nancy! That was a coffee. *One* coffee. With one other woman, plus her sister. It was just for moral support.'

'Well, whatever. Club, support group, coffee morning. I mentioned it to Melanie and she asked if you'd mind if she came along. So I said, contact you.'

'Thanks,' said Eve.

'That's OK,' Nancy replied, the sarcasm going right over her head. Or maybe not. 'Melanie says she needs all the moral support she can get. So I gave her your work number and e-mail address. She's going to call to find out when the next meeting is. If you don't want her to come, all you need to do is tell her.'

Next meeting.

What next meeting?

Her good mood evaporated, Eve stabbed irritably at her keyboard, deleting e-mails. She could kill Nancy, really she could. Mind you, she could kill herself more for mentioning it in the first place. *You're a journalist for crying out loud. The first rule is you never tell anyone — especially not another journalist — anything that you don't want to see in print.*

As she dumped updates from *dailycandy, mediaguardian, style.com, mediabistro* and the *Washington Post* without bothering to open them, her eyes alighted on a name she'd been entirely unfamiliar with until a few days earlier. But it wasn't just Melanie Cheung's e-mail address that made Eve's heart sink. It was what Melanie had written in the subject box:

Stepmothers' Support Group.

★ ★ ★

'Melanie? You in there? There's a call for you . . .'

Clambering to her feet, Melanie Cheung peered around one of the dozens of plastic-shrouded fashion rails that lined her stockroom. If *personalshopper.com* carried on growing at this rate they were going to have to out-source fulfilment, and do it soon. The warehouse off the Caledonian Road had seemed perfect eighteen months ago when she was setting up, not least because Melanie could live above the shop. Now she could barely move for cardboard boxes. Her company was growing too big and too fast. Melanie knew that was better than the alternative. In the current climate, the entire shopping population of London didn't have enough fingers to count the number of start-ups

66

that had gone under in the last year. And now the recession was squeezing more. So the scale and speed of the company's success terrified Melanie.

Terrified and thrilled her.

This monster was hers. The first thing she had done for herself — done at all, in fact, beyond shopping and smiling and making small talk — since she moved to London as Mrs Simeon Jones, and the mere thought made her heart pound with excitement.

'Tell them I'll call back,' she said. 'I'm kinda busy right now.'

'Already did,' said Grace, Melanie's office manager, right-hand woman and what passed for friend. Scratch that, *only* friend. 'But she's pretty persistent. It's from that magazine you did an interview for last week. She says you're expecting her call. Eve someone. Sorry, I didn't catch the surname.'

Melanie swallowed hard. Now she'd really done it. 'OK . . . ' she said. 'Tell her I'll be right there.'

'Melanie Cheung speaking.'

Two years after the split, eighteen months after the decree absolute, it still surprised her how easily she had become Melanie Cheung again. Melanie Jones had vanished as quickly as she'd appeared. Sometimes it seemed to Melanie as if the other her had only ever been a ghost. The real her had always been there, lurking just beneath the surface, biding her time, waiting to make her move.

'Hi, this is Eve Owen,' said a voice on the

other end of the phone. 'From *Beau*.'

The woman sounded cool; official, if not exactly unfriendly. 'I got your e-mail. And, to be honest, I think Nancy might have given you the wrong impression.'

'In — in what way?' Melanie's heart was pounding.

This probably wasn't what she'd thought it was. Probably the woman was just calling to check some facts, but still Melanie had to resist the urge to check her reflection in the small mirror that hung on the back of her office door.

'Well, we're not really a group, to be honest. Or a club, or anything like that. We're just friends, well, two of us are. And we've only had one meeting, so far. And that wasn't so much a meeting as a couple of cups of coffee. And one of us isn't even a stepmum.'

'Oh.' Melanie didn't know what she'd been expecting, but it certainly wasn't this. 'It's just that Nancy — your reporter — well, she said . . . '

'So I gather. Anyway, to get to the point, I've spoken to the others.'

'The other members?'

'Like I said, it's not a club, so there are no members. But I've spoken to my friend Clare, and she's spoken to Lily, who's her sister, and we've decided . . . '

Melanie sighed. To say this woman sounded reluctant was the understatement of the year. But if she'd learnt anything from her ill-advised marriage to Simeon Jones it was that there was no such thing as a free handbag. If something

68

sounded too good to be true, in Melanie's experience, it usually was.

She was about to put the woman out of her misery, tell her not to worry, it was all a misunderstanding, when Eve spoke again. 'We're meeting Tuesday week at seven. Starbucks on Carnaby Street. Come along if you're free. You can meet the others and we'll, you know, see how it goes . . .'

For several seconds the words didn't sink in.

'Unless you don't want to?' Eve said, slightly too quickly. Her tone was part-relief, part-irritation.

'No, no. I do,' said Melanie. 'That's . . . perfect. Just perfect. I'll see you then.'

7

'You remember Eve?'

The small blonde girl sitting cross-legged on an old rug peered shyly through her fringe. 'Hello,' she said. 'I finished my book. It was good.'

'Hello Sophie,' Eve said. 'I'm glad you liked it.'

'Alfie hasn't read his,' the girl said, 'He says it's Venom's vehicle.'

Eve smiled inside. Were small girls in some way programmed to tell tales? 'That's fine,' she said. 'It can be whatever Alfie wants it to be. Where *is* he anyway?'

A thundering on the hall stairs, in no way proportionate to the size of the shoes using it, answered her question. 'Eeeeve,' he shouted, launching himself into the room. 'Have you bought me a present?'

'Alfie!' Ian said.

Eve just laughed, there was no way she'd get caught out like that again. Alfie was easy enough to buy presents for, but then she'd have to buy presents for the other two and that meant finding something Hannah wouldn't reject.

'No presents this time,' she said. 'It's not a special occasion.'

Alfie cocked his head to one side as he processed the information. 'Oh,' he said. 'When *is* a special occasion?'

'Christmas,' Eve said, thinking on her feet.

'Easter, your birthday, that sort of thing.'

His face crumpled in confusion. 'But you gave me *Charlie and the Chocolate Factory* and it wasn't my . . . '

Eve looked at Ian in panic.

'It's OK,' Ian said, rumpling Alfie's hair. 'That was different. That was a late present because Eve missed Easter.'

'Oh,' Alfie seemed satisfied. 'What's for lunch?'

'What would you like?' From the way Ian asked, Eve gathered he already knew the answer.

'Pizza!' Alfie yelled and galloped from the room, leading his imaginary army in search of a takeaway menu, which, apparently, was in his bedroom.

'Red wine? White wine? Beer? Tea?' Ian asked, as he led Eve back into the hallway. At some point its original black and white Victorian floor tiles had been lovingly restored. Eve tried not to wonder by whom.

'White please, if you've got one open.'

'What do you think?' he asked, pushing open the door to the kitchen. Sun poured through a large bay, bouncing off the white walls and giving the scrubbed pine table and cupboards a golden glow. 'Like it?'

'What's not to like?' she gasped. Eve couldn't imagine owning a place like this. You could fit her flat twice into the kitchen alone. 'It's beautiful.'

Throwing a glance over his shoulder before he pushed the door to, Ian slid his arms around her. 'So are you,' he said and kissed her.

'Daddeee!' a wail came from halfway up the stairs and Ian rolled his eyes. 'Talk about timing. Take a seat,' he nodded at the old pews that lined either side of the table. 'While I go and sort that out.'

★ ★ ★

'Ian? Where's Hannah?' Eve asked when Ian reappeared. It was less than a minute later but enough time for Eve to analyse every inch of the room's polished terracotta floor, clean white walls and minimalist white china. If it hadn't been for Sophie's drawings stuck to the fridge and a muddy lattice of paw prints on the kitchen window the room would have been just a little too immaculate.

'Oh, around somewhere. In her room probably.' Ian shrugged and stuck his head in the fridge. 'Pinot Grigio all right?' But his body language was nowhere near as casual as his words, and Eve felt her confidence dim a little.

★ ★ ★

An hour sped past. Eve and Ian laid the table, washed salad leaves and mixed olive oil and vinegar to make dressing, while Alfie and Sophie skittered in and out. From Sophie, Eve learnt the paw prints outside the window belonged to next door's cat. From Alfie, she learnt that Spiderman beat Venom every time.

As Ian chatted, about photographing some up-and-coming artist, about Alfie's school, about

72

his occasional problems with Inge, the new au pair, Eve dared to let herself hope there might be other Saturday lunchtimes like this.

Sunday lunchtimes as well. Maybe a Saturday night in the middle, too.

'So, what d'you fancy?' Ian asked, shoving Alfie's tattered takeaway menu into her hand and interrupting a reverie that had included Ian, shirt undone, jeans, bare feet, making fresh coffee and toast some Sunday morning.

'Oh,' Eve jumped, feeling caught out. 'Anything. Really. Just get what you usually would.'

'Now that's reckless.' He grinned. 'In this house that could mean tuna with bacon bits and pineapple ... I'd better go see what Hannah wants. It changes from week to week.'

Letting her hand drop, he pulled open the kitchen door. 'Oh!' he said, but recovered quickly. 'Hannah. How long have you ... I mean, I didn't realize you were there.'

When Hannah stepped into the room Eve resisted the urge to shiver; she could have sworn the sunshine dimmed and the temperature dropped a degree or two. The girl's long fair hair hung loose and the white shirt she wore over her jeans looked vintage, but more granny's attic — or even grandpa's — than charity shop.

'Not long,' Hannah said, glancing at Eve. Eve saw the girl give her outfit a cursory one-two. 'I was coming to say hello but I wasn't sure if it was OK to interrupt.'

'There's nothing to interrupt,' Ian said levelly. 'You remember Eve, of course.'

'Hi Hannah,' Eve said. 'I love your shirt.'

'This?' Hannah shrugged. 'It was grandpa's.'

'It's lovely,' Eve said, meaning it, but the girl had already turned away.

'I hope you haven't phoned yet,' she said to her father. 'I want to change my usual order.'

*　*　*

The pizzas were from Domino's, the ice cream was Ben & Jerry's, the washing up was virtually zero and, somehow, the kitchen still looked as if a hurricane had hit it. Hurricane Alfie. The polar opposite of Hannah, who perched at the far end of the table, in the opposite pew, speaking only when spoken to; she was like a cold front that hadn't quite decided whether or not it was going to blow in.

And even though she had changed her pizza order three times — the last after Ian had placed the order — Eve couldn't help but notice Hannah ate almost nothing.

None of your business, Eve told herself. And since no one else seemed to notice, let alone comment, she helped herself to another slice of vegetarian supreme with jalapeños, sipped her Pinot Grigio and watched Ian juggle Sophie and Alfie's constant demands. She'd never seen this side of him before — this side of any man, come to that, since in her thirty-two years she'd never before dated a man with children, and the only other man in her life, her father, just wasn't that kind of dad.

'Alfie, drink your juice. No, no cola, you know

74

you're not allowed cola.'

'Makes him even more hyper than usual.' This as an aside to Eve.

'Sophie, wipe the tomato sauce off your hands before taking pudding. Chocolate or vanilla ice cream? No, we don't have strawberry . . . Because you said chocolate when I did the order.'

It was an endless litany and Eve was surprised to find she loved it. And if she looked up occasionally to see Hannah watching her from under her hair, well, that was only to be expected, wasn't it?

★　★　★

'Well, I think we can call that a success, don't you?' Ian said, when the pizza boxes were in the recycling bin, the plates were in the dishwasher, Alfie and Sophie were in front of a DVD, and Hannah was wherever Hannah went doing whatever Hannah did. He emptied the remnants of the bottle into Eve's glass.

'Really?'

Ian slid onto the pew beside her, wrapping an arm around her shoulder and leaning back against the wall. He looked as exhausted as she felt. 'You don't think so?'

Eve wasn't sure how truthful she could be. 'We-ell,' she said. 'I was glad just to survive, to be honest.'

'You did more than survive,' Ian said pulling her towards him. 'You were brilliant. They really like you.'

75

Eve leant into him and closed her eyes. He was right, of course. It had gone much better than she'd feared; give or take Hannah's silence, although even that could have been worse. But still Eve was knackered. She'd only been there three hours and didn't think she'd ever been so emotionally drained. How anyone did it full-time — even with 'help' — she couldn't begin to imagine. Maybe it was different if the children were your own; maybe some switch in the brain was automatically flicked. That was what Clare always said. But Eve wasn't convinced.

When she opened her eyes Ian was gazing right at her, as if trying to decipher her thoughts. . He looked almost shy.

'Do you think you could *survive* longer?' he asked.

Instinctively, Eve glanced at her watch. 'Why not? I haven't got anywhere else to go.'

'I didn't mean that.' He paused, his nerves getting the better of him. 'I meant, could you survive longer than a Saturday afternoon . . . a week, maybe? Or just a few days if a week's too long? It's just we're going to my parents' place in Cornwall for a couple of weeks in August, and I thought it would be a good opportunity for you to spend more time with the kids. And me, of course.'

He smiled.

'And, erm . . . if you'd like to, at the same time, I mean . . . I'd like you to meet my parents.'

★ ★ ★

76

Melanie Cheung hadn't been this nervous since her first date with Simeon, maybe even before then. Shaking the thought from her mind, she tried on and promptly discarded another outfit, before reverting to wide-leg jeans, smock top and flats. Exactly what she'd have put on if she hadn't been thinking about it at all.

And certainly no date with Vince had ever engendered this sense of excitement or dread. Theirs wasn't that kind of relationship. This was no bad thing; she didn't want it to be that kind of relationship. Stomach-churning excitement was not part of her plan right now. Easy and comfortable was what Melanie needed. Someone to chat about the day's work and watch DVDs with — and it was what she'd had, until Vince had dropped his ten-year-old daughter on her.

You look just fine, Melanie told herself as she knotted her shiny black hair at the back of her head, slicked on lip balm and grabbed her jacket. *Better than fine.*

If she messed around any longer she'd be late. And she didn't want to give the other women — the group, the club, whatever they were — any excuses to reject her. They had enough already, given that she hadn't yet met the child she was going there to talk about.

C'mon, Melanie, she thought as she ran down the stairs, pulled the door to behind her, and stuck her arm out at a black cab, which sped straight past. *Chase down your inner lawyer.*

She had managed it the day she did her presentation to the private equity firm who agreed to help finance *personalshopper.com*.

That had taken reserves of guts she'd forgotten she had since moving to London. As had pressing send on her e-mail to Eve Owen, *Beau's* features director, inviting herself to the next Stepmothers' Support Group meeting. She could manage it now.

Another cab passed without a light on, and then another.

Shit, now she really was going to be late. If she walked really fast she could be there — covered in sweat, but there — in about twenty minutes, maybe thirty. The Tube, on the other hand, would take a fraction of that; signal failure, overcrowding and bodies on the line permitting. Melanie hated the Tube, just as she'd hated the Subway in Manhattan. It was hot, stuffy, dirty and crowded, especially at this time of the day; the tail end of rush hour. But Kings Cross to Oxford Circus was ten minutes on the Victoria line, and since ten minutes was as long as she had, she headed underground anyway.

The truth was, Melanie was lonely. Her yearning for someone to talk to, someone who didn't work for her, someone who might just 'get her', was more powerful than any fear of rejection. Her sense of isolation had been growing ever since she'd left her home, her friends and her hard-won career in Manhattan to follow Simeon to London. Infatuation made you do stupid things; but as stupid went, falling for Simeon's lines and finding herself divorced and alone in London took some beating.

It wasn't that Melanie didn't know anyone here. But the people she knew were hedge fund wives, the women on the charity circuit. Other women with nothing to do but spend what was left of their husbands' money on personal trainers, high-maintenance and time-consuming beauty regimes, and expensive meals they never ate. That wasn't Melanie's scene, much as she'd tried to make it so to keep Simeon happy.

More than anything, she missed her friends. The women she'd had to resist the overwhelming urge to go fleeing back to the second Simeon told her he'd instructed his lawyers to make her a *reasonable* settlement, and suggested she instruct her own lawyers to accept it.

But it wasn't their reaction that had stopped her . . . The inevitable, *we told you so* her mind's eye could see on their faces. No, what stopped her was her family; her mother in particular, who had also *told her so*. Far more explicitly.

It had been bad enough making the call home to tell them her marriage was over. She wasn't about to go creeping home with her tail between her legs, too.

* * *

Was it mean to ask Clare to arrive at six-thirty, instead of seven, so they could talk before the others arrived? It wasn't exactly true to the spirit of a support group. Even Eve wasn't a hundred per cent convinced by her own excuse that she and Clare were friends and this was something just for her friend's ears. Already, after only one meeting it felt unfair to exclude Lily. The adult Lily had been a revelation to Eve — smart,

79

ballsy, irreverent and full of common sense. Like her sister, in fact, but without the enormous chip weighing her shoulder down.

Clare, as usual, wasn't prepared to humour Eve.

'You invited Melanie,' she said matter-of-factly. 'Your choice. Either this is a support group or it's not.'

Eve shrugged. 'She might not show anyway. I wouldn't, if I were her.'

The fact that Eve could hear the petulance in her own voice annoyed her, because she hadn't said what she wanted to say at that point. Which was, '*Whose choice?*'

The group had been Clare's idea, and she'd pretty much bulldozed Eve and Lily into it.

'We're going on holiday,' Eve said instead. Trying the words for size. As if speaking them aloud might break the spell and it would cease to be true.

'You're what?' Clare yelped. 'When did this happen? Why didn't you tell me?'

Eve grinned. 'I haven't seen you. And I'm telling you now.'

'There's such a thing as the phone! Anyway, you did phone me. Why didn't you tell me then?'

'Only just happened,' Eve said. 'Anyway, I wanted to tell you in person. You know I went around for pizza on Saturday?'

'Mmm-hmm.'

Eve could see what Clare was thinking: *Yes, and I knew it had gone well because I didn't hear from you.* God, had her friend always been this transparent? For that matter, had she?

Still, Eve was grateful when the flicker of resentment that crossed Clare's face didn't translate into words. Instead, Clare said, 'What is it with pizza?'

'Kid-friendly, I suppose,' Eve said. 'If the world wasn't full of every-other-weekend dads I swear Pizza Express and Domino's would go out of business.'

Clare snorted.

'Anyway, it was good. Well, as good as can be expected. Hannah wasn't exactly friendly, but she wasn't *unfriendly*.'

No head-to-toe soakings in cola, thought Eve, though she didn't say it.

'And the other two were great. Sophie spent most of lunch relating the entire plot of that book I bought her. And Alfie's adorable, it's like he's adopted me. Ian says not to take it seriously. It's my novelty factor, plus the fact my Spiderman tolerance threshold is unfeasibly high. We managed a full three hours. Impressed, huh?'

Clare nodded. 'So,' she said. 'About this holiday?'

'We-ell, holiday might be a slight exaggeration,' Eve said, trying unsuccessfully to conceal her excitement. 'When school breaks for summer they're going to Cornwall for a couple of weeks — Ian's parents have a place there — and Ian suggested I join them. Not for the whole time, just for a week at the end, so it's not too much for the kids.' *Or me*, she added in her head.

'What holiday?'

Neither of them had seen Lily arrive. 'Don't

tell me you and Ian are getting away from it all. Just the two of you?'

'Can tell you don't have any kids!' Clare snorted.

Lily ignored her. 'Not you and Ian?' she asked Eve.

Eve grinned, aware the euphoria she'd barely been able to contain since Ian made the suggestion was now flooding her face. 'Me, Ian, Alfie, Sophie and Hannah . . . ' For now, it didn't seem necessary to mention that, for some of that time at least, Ian's parents would be there too. Clare would have plenty of theories on that, Eve knew. She also knew that right now she didn't want to hear them. She was more than capable of adding two and two and getting an accurate total without Clare's help.

'No way!' Lily surprised Eve by flinging her arms around her. And Eve was instantly reminded of Louisa. 'That's great. Real progress. How did it happen?'

Eve was opening her mouth to begin the story again, when a slight draught made them turn towards the door. 'Not now,' Clare hissed. 'No time.'

Even though the others had no idea what Melanie Cheung looked like, beyond the vague description Eve had given Clare over the phone, there was no doubt in their minds that Melanie was now standing in the doorway, peering across packed tables towards the corner where they sat. She was clutching what looked like a waiting-list-worthy Hermès Kelly bag to her chest as if it was body armour.

'Oh God Eve,' Clare murmured. 'Tall, slim, gorgeous. Your basic self-esteem crusher.'

'Shut up.'

Raising a hand to wave Melanie Cheung over, Eve had to share Clare's misgivings. What could this woman — all expensive handbag, effortless style and shampoo-ad hair — possibly want with them?

'Thank you, so much, for letting me come along. I really appreciate it,' Melanie Cheung said, when she'd settled into the seat they'd saved for her and Lily had returned with two skinny lattes and a bottle of water. 'Are the others on their way?'

'Others?' Eve looked at her, confused. 'What others?'

'Well . . . I thought . . . I mean, I know you said it wasn't so much a group . . . ' Melanie looked flustered, as if she wanted the ground to swallow her up.

'There are no others,' Clare said with a smile, taking control of the situation. 'Just us. It doesn't matter, does it?'

Melanie shook her head, but it looked as if it did matter. A lot.

'Eve, you already know, sort of. She's a new stepmum . . . '

'Not exactly,' Eve protested.

'As good as,' Clare continued. 'To three children — her partner, Ian, is a widower. Lily's my sister and has a three-year-old stepdaughter.' Lily didn't bother to correct her. 'And I'm not a stepmother at all,' Clare said. 'But I had one, so that gives me a different perspective on things when it's needed.'

'And when it's not!' Lily said, but she was smiling.

'What about you, Melanie?' Eve said, conscious of the other woman's discomfort. 'What's your story?'

Gingerly, Melanie placed the bag she was still hugging — either as protection or in case she'd need to make a quick getaway — on the seat beside her.

'I'm divorced,' she said, raising her voice slightly to be heard over the low-level chatter around them. 'My ex recently remarried and had a child — not in that order. A little boy with his new . . . wife. But that's not strictly relevant. I mean, it's not as if Barty's my stepson. He's nothing to me. And that's kind of odd in itself, don't you think?' She paused, obviously embarrassed at how much she'd revealed so quickly. The others looked everywhere but at her, while Melanie sipped her latte and tried to regain her composure.

'Anyway . . . I've been seeing this guy for a couple of months now, I met him through work. His name's Vince, his company set up *personalshopper*'s computer systems. It was all going really well, no pressure, just an easy-going thing. No strings — well, not many. Exactly what I needed after . . . well, after . . . you know . . . '

They did. Even if Eve hadn't already filled them in, Melanie's divorce was well enough documented for anyone who ever read the gossip columns.

84

'And then I found out he's been married before. Vince, that is. He just tossed it into the conversation, like it was nothing; just one of those things everybody did in their twenties.'

'Not me,' Clare said.

'Me neither,' Eve agreed.

'That's what I mean,' Melanie continued. 'And on top of the unmentioned marriage, it turns out he has a daughter who's ten. She lives with her mother but he sees her every other weekend, and a week or so in each of the school holidays.'

'How d'you mean, you 'found out'?' Lily asked, sketching inverted commas in the air. 'You mean he kept it secret?'

'No, not exactly,' said Melanie. 'He just hadn't thought to mention it and I didn't think to ask. Well, you wouldn't, would you? But I know what you must be thinking. I mean, how do you date someone for two, nearly three, months and not tell them something that significant? And, to be honest, I feel like an idiot. How can you not know your boyfriend has a kid?'

'*I* wasn't thinking that,' Lily said, with a shrug.

'Really?' said Clare turning to her. 'I was.'

Melanie gave a nervous laugh. 'But it's not just that. It's like one minute it's all easy-come, easy-go, the next he's got a ten-year-old daughter and therefore, by extension, so do I.'

She paused, clearly panic-stricken. 'It's not that I don't want to meet her. I do. It's just . . . I'm terrified. I don't have the first clue how to handle it. What to say, what to do.' Taking a deep breath, Melanie looked around at the other

85

women. 'I'm pathetic, aren't I? I'm scared of a tweenager I haven't even met.'

'And, not unreasonably, a bit pissed off with Vince for putting you in this position without warning,' Lily added. 'I don't call that pathetic.'

'Not at all,' Eve added. 'If we're anything to go by, out-and-out terror is entirely normal.' She was gratified to see that Melanie, who'd looked on the verge of tears, smiled.

'When did you find out your guy was a dad?' Melanie asked Eve. 'If you don't mind me asking.'

'It was a bit different,' Eve said. 'I knew long before I met him.' And she ran Melanie through a potted history of her and Ian.

'What about you?' Melanie asked Lily, when Eve had finished.

'Pretty much straightaway,' she said. 'A week in, maybe two at most. But that's Liam for you. He wouldn't see what the big deal was. It was, 'Can't see you Saturday babes, it's my turn to have the kid. Don't suppose you fancy coming round too, do you?''

'Really?' Eve said, eyebrows raised. 'You're kidding? Liam let you meet Rosie that soon? How did he know it was going to last? You and him, I mean.'

'What? You don't believe in love at first sight?' Lily grinned to show she wasn't serious. 'And I didn't meet Rosie that soon. But only because I refused. Liam would have wheeled me along on our second date, no doubt about it. To him, it's not that big a deal. He thinks we think too much. And, sometimes, listening to us beat ourselves up, I wonder if he doesn't have a point.'

'Anyway,' said Lily. 'Where was I? Oh, yes. I didn't meet Rosie that first time. It would have been too soon for Rosie, and frankly it was too soon for me. I mean, you meet this guy, you basically laugh each other into bed, then you wake up next morning and he's like, 'Oh by the way babe, how d'you feel about brat sitting at the weekend'. Call me old-fashioned, but I say that's a bit too soon!'

The group burst out laughing and Eve took the opportunity to start a coffee run. As Melanie reached for her purse Eve waved her away. 'You get them in next time.'

'Not for me, thanks,' Lily said, reaching for her jacket and backpack. 'I've got to be back at work five minutes ago. Lovely to meet you, Melanie. Sorry to run out on you. See you soon.'

★ ★ ★

Melanie watched Eve and Lily hug each other and then head in different directions, Lily to the door, Eve to the counter, as Clare called her daughter to check she was where she said she'd be, doing what she said she'd be doing. At home doing homework.

Did they realize what they'd just said? Melanie wondered. *Next time.* For the first time since landing in London, Melanie felt on the verge of something, some people, who might truly, in time, become her own friends.

★ ★ ★

'That whole Lily/Liam thing kind of puts things in perspective,' Melanie said when Eve had returned with two more coffees and a herbal tea for Melanie. 'I mean, this might sound odd to you . . . but, Vince and I, it's just not that kind of relationship. If he'd gone straight from first date to 'meet my kid' I would have run a mile. I've so had it with big romantic gestures . . . ' She paused. 'Vince is nothing like my ex. Thank God. We just like each other's company. So I guess I can understand.'

'That's all very well,' Clare said and Eve winced, knowing her friend was about to punch right to the heart of the matter. 'But didn't he have any photos of her? Of his daughter?'

'Um,' Melanie looked uncomfortable. 'He might do. I mean, yes . . . yes, I'm sure he does but usually we hang out at mine. It's not much, just a couple of rooms. But it's above work, so it's easy. I've only been to his place once and it was, late. You know . . . ' Her voice trailed off.

The others smiled to show they knew. Well, Eve did. She'd only set foot in Ian's house once so far. But it was a long time since Clare had been anywhere else with anyone else. Late, or otherwise.

* * *

The Tube to Finchley took even longer than usual. The Northern Line was sweltering, not just from that day's heat but from decades of muggy, smoggy summers, the memory of which seemed to have lingered in the tunnels, just

88

waiting to burst out at the slightest rise in temperature above ground. Why was it, Clare wondered, leaning her head against the murky glass, that seventy degrees above ground translated into ninety degrees below?

'Ladies and gentlemen, I apologize for the delay,' came the driver's voice over a tannoy. 'We are being held in the tunnel and hope to be on the move again shortly.'

Clare sighed as her watch reached and then passed nine.

Damn it, there went another seven pounds.

She'd been hoping to make it back in time to sneak under the wire of three hours. But 9.05 might as well be 9.55 where babysitters were concerned. Even the, supposedly cheaper, teenage variety. Like traffic wardens, they showed no mercy. A minute was as good as an hour.

Perhaps Lou was right, Clare thought, totting up the cost of that evening's meeting and feeling nausea rise as the sums approached forty pounds. Forty? How could four hours out of the house and a couple of cups of coffee set her back forty quid? Maybe Lou had a point. Perhaps she *was* old enough to stay home alone. Her daughter was now fourteen after all, and if the girl was to be believed, all her friends were allowed to stay home without a sitter.

Mind you, if Lou was to be believed, her friends were allowed to do a lot of things she wasn't. Staying home alone was just the tip of the iceberg.

The train lurched, then lurched again. As it

gained momentum a through-breeze temporarily relieved the cloying heat.

It was tempting, Clare had to admit. Lou got the appearance of freedom and Clare would be twenty, even thirty, pounds richer; and maybe the concession would buy Clare a reprieve. Not to mention a little more time to decide what to do about the many other things that Lou's friends had that she didn't. Those grenades Lou lobbed willy-nilly at Clare when they had one of their few, but increasingly ferocious, rows.

Well, ferocious on Lou's part, at least.

Recent grenades included, in no particular order: a dad (always a direct hit, that one), a family (obviously Clare didn't qualify), grandparents (not granny, *proper* ones, two sets, they came in pairs, apparently), an iPod, a TV in her room, cousins, free run of Topshop, a Saturday job, a holiday . . .

The orange glow of streetlights made Clare blink as the Tube train clattered out of the tunnel on its approach to East Finchley station.

Nearly home.

Clare knew the storm was coming. She'd felt the clouds on the horizon as Lou banged around their tiny kitchen picking holes in everything her mother suggested she eat for supper. Pasta was *boring*. Fish fingers and chips were *for kids*. Jacket potato was *too slow because we don't even have a microwave*. And no, she wasn't interested in the remains of a moussaka Clare had soothed herself cooking for last night's supper.

Nothing was right.

Nothing was good enough.

Everything was crap.

'Don't say crap,' Clare said instinctively, earning herself a scowl from her daughter. The signs were familiar. Blissfully rare, at least to date, but Clare had seen enough to know they heralded a fight. What she couldn't work out was what this one was going to be about.

'Why not?' Lou shouted, giving the fridge door a slam. 'It *is* crap. My. Life. Is. Total. Crap.'

Clare opened her mouth to rebuke Louisa, and shut it again. The storm was coming, she might as well get it over with.

'Everybody else goes on holiday,' Lou had yelled. 'You don't have to listen to them talking at school. Bridget's going to Ibiza. *Her* mum and dad have rented a villa for a month. *A WHOLE MONTH*. Madeleine's mum and dad are taking her to Crete. And they're letting her take Callie with her. And Charlie's going to Turks and Caicos.'

Clare was pretty sure Lou didn't even know where Turks and Caicos was, but that didn't lessen her daughter's frustration.

'Amy's going to her mum and dad's cottage in Norfolk for the whole summer . . . ' she continued. 'The whole summer, Mum! All my friends are going somewhere. And I'm stuck here!'

Groaning audibly, Clare wondered if she'd be able to get away without telling Lou that Auntie Eve was going to Cornwall with her boyfriend and his children, to stay in their grandparents' holiday house. Lou would find so many faults with that sentence Clare could hardly bear to think about it.

The words echoed inside Clare's head as the Tube doors finally opened and she stepped off the train into a balmy north London night. The venom with which Lou had spat her resentment at the comforts she didn't have that her friends did . . . And unspoken, the words that had sent Clare fleeing from their flat for fear of hearing them, knowing she couldn't bear it if she did. Knowing that if she let Lou say those words, the words she knew her daughter was thinking, things would change for ever between them. 'And I'm stuck here,' Lou had screamed before her bedroom door slammed shut behind her.

With you.

8

'This it, love?'

Eve peered from the taxi's window across a gravel drive littered with dusty four by fours and expensive but low-key cars to a solid farmhouse built from weather-beaten Cornish granite. Above the screech of seagulls she could hear the squeals of small children.

'Sounds like it,' she said, pushing a ten pound note and some loose change into the driver's hand as she took the case he hauled from the boot.

It looked like it too. Eve wheeled her case between a Subaru and a Lexus, and narrowly avoided squashing a Power Ranger standing guard on a manhole cover. She bent to collect it, then stopped. *Alfie was here*, it said. He might not thank her for moving it.

The front door was on the latch for late arrivals and opened at first push. Dragging her case across a flagstoned hall, she lent it against a wall and slipped Hannah's birthday card and present (Topshop vouchers — no chances this time) from her handbag, then folded her jacket — creased from the heat, the journey and being clutched too tightly — and dumped it on top of the case beside her handbag. There was no doubt the house itself was empty; but the shrieks of children and low-level murmur of adult conversation was louder now. Eve took a deep breath.

She was in no doubt what a big deal this was, not just for Ian and his children, but for his entire family. For more than two years since Caroline's death, there had been nothing and no one in his life but the children, and getting them from one day to the next. And now, here was Eve . . .

Although, somehow, meeting his parents had turned into something even bigger. What Ian hadn't made clear — at least not until there was no turning back — was that she'd be meeting the extended Newsome clan at the same time.

'It'll be great,' Ian had promised when he'd called from Cornwall earlier in the week to check her train times. 'The weather's amazing and it's meant to hold. So Ma thought it might be fun to have a barbecue in the garden, Saturday lunchtime. It's Hannah's birthday, so it's her party really. My parents will be there, obviously. My brother, his wife and kids are coming over from their place in Devon. There's a cousin or two, nothing too terrifying. Oh, and a couple of neighbours.'

Safety in numbers, that was what he'd said. Hiding in plain sight. There'd be so much going on it would take the focus off her, off them. Far from being the main event, she'd be just another guest on a lazy summer's afternoon. And that had made sense to Eve. At the time. But that was before engineering works on the line from Paddington had added ninety minutes to her journey and she'd felt obliged to call Ian with an offer of making her own way from the station. How hard could it be, after all?

94

Smoothing down her top, she followed the noise.

An open door to her right led into a large sitting room that stretched from front to back. Its parquet floors were barely visible beneath a chaos of threadbare Persian rugs, and mismatched chairs and sofas covered with cushions and throws. The effect should have been a fight in a jumble sale, instead it was relaxed and cosy.

At the far end, French doors spilled out onto a terrace and lawns that led across to the fields beyond the garden's limits. This was some holiday home, bigger by far than her own parents' only home. A fold-out table inside the doors was laden with presents, some opened, some still neatly wrapped, and in the middle, in pride of place, stood a large birthday cake iced in pink with a large, garish number thirteen, marked in candles. To Eve's eye, the pastel icing bore Sophie's unmistakable hallmark.

Propping her card against a pile of unopened presents, Eve moved to the French doors. The lawn was packed. *A few friends?* She'd hate to be around when Ian's parents organized a large party. Where the terrace met the grass she could see Ian, standing by the large brick barbecue, talking to a stockier man wearing a navy and white striped apron. At first glance he looked nothing like Ian, but on closer inspection his nose gave the relationship away. Eve guessed she was looking at Ian's younger brother, Rob. The 'boys' were obviously on barbecue duty. Ian's eyes found her and his face broke into a grin.

'Eve!' he called. 'You made it! Over here!'

A dozen heads swivelled, Meerkat-like, faces full of ill-suppressed curiosity. Smiling nervously, Eve looked for the quickest route from where she stood to Ian's side. Not that she expected this to afford her much protection. As she did so a small whirlwind swirled through the tanned legs and deck shoes of a group that stood drinking Pimm's on the terrace.

'Eeeve!' shouted Alfie, hurling himself at her, another small boy in tow. 'Did you bring me a present?' Although they had now spent several Saturday lunchtimes together with no further gifts forthcoming, this was still his preferred opening gambit.

Resisting the urge to hug him, Eve bent down to ruffle his hair instead.

'Hello Alfie, what you up to?'

'Winning!' He grinned and turned to smack a black Power Ranger against the other boy's toy. Eve wondered if anyone had ever explained the concept of playing nicely to Alfie.

Someone else obviously felt the same way.

'Alfie, behave. Now go and tell Daddy we need him over here.'

The woman who spoke was tall, slim and elegant in a beige cotton skirt and white short-sleeved blouse and cream sandals. Around seventy, she had the stature and aura of someone much younger, someone used to people noticing her. Someone like Caroline, had Caroline lived to see her eighth decade.

'But Graneee . . . '

'Alfie,' the woman's voice was gentle but firm,

96

'go and fetch Daddy for me, there's a good boy. And take Danny with you.'

'How do you do?' The woman held out her hand with a smile. 'I'm Elaine, Ian's mother.'

'I'm Eve,' said Eve, unnecessarily. 'It's nice to meet you. I'm so sorry I'm late. The train . . . '

The woman waved her apology away.

As she did so, Eve couldn't help noticing that Ian's mother took in every particular of Eve's appearance.

'I'm delighted to meet you, dear. You're something of a hit with my grandson, I gather. And my son, of course, but I imagine that goes without saying.'

No, thought Eve. She would never tire of hearing it. Instead she smiled with relief. 'I'm very glad to hear it,' she said. 'They're something of a hit with me too.'

'Eve . . . you've obviously met my mother.' Eve felt a warm arm slide around her waist and resisted the temptation to sink gratefully into Ian.

'Come on,' he said. 'You look like you need a drink. Ma, another Pimm's?'

Ian's mother waved her half-full glass and shook her head. 'Not for me dear. I'd better go and see what your brother is burning on the barbecue.'

'How was that?' asked Ian, leading her by the hand to a white-clothed table that had been set up at the side the terrace with metal buckets full of iced beer and bowls of punch. 'Survive the first encounter?'

Eve took an indecently large gulp of Pimm's

and nodded. 'So far so good,' she said, hoping she sounded more confident than she felt. She glanced behind her. 'One down . . . Ooh, about twenty total strangers to go.'

'You don't have anything to worry about,' he said. 'Everyone here wants me to be happy. And you make me happy.'

A wave of pleasure flooded through her.

He leant forward and, for a split second, she thought he was going to kiss her full on the lips in front of his entire family, but his mouth slid sideways and he nuzzled her cheek before pulling back, just as Sophie appeared at his side and wrapped her arms around his middle. 'Daddy,' she said.

'Have you said hello to Eve yet?'

Sophie shook her head and her pink braided topknot bobbed. 'Hello Eve,' she said. 'Did you see the cake I made for Hannah?'

Ian laughed. 'I think Granny might have helped.'

'Excellent icing,' Eve said.

Sophie glowed. 'That bit was mine.'

'Definitely the best bit,' Eve agreed. 'Much too good eat.'

Ian choked on his beer and whispered, 'Nice try, but you don't get out of it that easily.'

★ ★ ★

Half an hour later Eve had completed a circuit of the entire garden, been appraised and assessed by twenty pairs of eyes and shaken as many hands. Other than Ian's immediate family — his

98

brother Rob, Jill, his wife, and their children Danny and Ella — she remembered not a single name.

Rob had given Eve a hug, kissed her on the cheek and said he was glad — really glad — to meet her finally. (He was so obviously genuine that Eve was embarrassed to find herself almost reduced to tears.) Jill, on the other hand, eyed Eve with unbridled curiosity. Not unfriendly, but not friendly either. If looks could talk, hers would say: *Rebound!* After all, how could Eve — all wild hair and flushed face, freckles leaping out at the first hint of sun — compete with the cool elegance of Caroline?

But there *was* no competition. Already Eve could see that to compete with Caroline was to lose before she began. What Ian liked, Eve was beginning to understand now she'd met his family, was that she bore no resemblance to Caro, or to any of the other women in his life, whatsoever. A tall, blonde mother, a tall blonde sister-in-law, and the ghost of his tall blonde late wife. Whereas she . . .

Give yourself a break, Eve thought.

And give them a break too, while you're at it. They have a vested interest. Who wouldn't, after all this time?

'You OK if I give Rob a hand?' Ian asked, when they'd done the rounds. He looked as relieved as she felt.

'Sure. Is there anything I can do to make myself useful?'

'Well, we'll need tomato sauce, mayonnaise and mustard from the kitchen. Shall I show you

99

where it is?' His over-the-shoulder glance to where Rob stood brandishing a lethal-looking metal fork didn't pass Eve by.

'That would defeat the object,' she said. 'There are only so many places it can be.'

Skirting the crowd in an attempt to steer clear of any more and-what-do-you-do? small talk from guests whose names she'd already forgotten, she passed Hannah, sitting on a wooden bench in the corner of the garden, iPod firmly plugged into her ears in a not remotely subtle attempt to ignore her relatives, neighbours and knee-high cousins. Until now, Eve hadn't noticed that Hannah was by far the oldest of all the children. No wonder the girl was hiding. One of those family celebrations that's for the family, not the birthday girl.

'Hi,' Eve said, waving her fingers so Hannah knew Eve was talking to her. 'Didn't see you earlier. Happy Birthday.'

Hannah reluctantly pulled one bead out of her ear, 'Oh, hi.' She was wearing skinny jeans, Havaianas flip-flops and a black waistcoat over a T-shirt. She shrugged. 'Thanks.'

That's it? Eve thought. *Oh hi, thanks.*

'Cool iPod,' she said, it was small and silver, the latest design, and definitely not the one Hannah had been carrying the first time they met. 'Present?'

'Uh-huh, Dad got it for me.'

Eve tried to conceal her disquiet. Shouldn't Ian have told her that? There was so much she didn't know about Ian's life with his kids. It was like standing at the top of a cliff, with the thinnest of ropes, waiting to jump off. Unless it was like standing at the bottom without any ropes at all — no equipment, just her bare hands — and being expected to climb to the top.

'Um, well, it's lovely,' Eve said, certain she looked as pathetic as she sounded. 'I'm, uh, I'm looking for the kitchen. Can you point me in the right direction?'

'In there.' Hannah jerked her head towards the nearest window. Her grandmother was clearly visible through the glass. Eve was glad she'd at least tried to make an effort with Hannah. Still, she was none the wiser about how to reach the kitchen.

'Um, thanks,' Eve said. 'I'll let you get back to it.'

Head down, Eve walked away, and feet first into one of Alfie's battles.

'Who's winning?' she asked, scoobying down.

'Me,' Alfie said, oblivious to the fact he was the only one playing. *Doh* he might as well have added.

'Where's Danny?' Eve asked.

'His mummy.' This was clearly explanation enough.

In that second Eve made her decision. 'I need to find something,' she said. 'Can you help me?'

He peered up through tufts of hair. 'Like hide-and-seek?'

'Sort of. I have to get Daddy some ketchup. I thought you might be able to show me where it lives.'

'Tomato sauce?'

Eve nodded.

101

'All right.' Alfie scrambled to his feet and wiped his fingers on his already grubby shorts. 'This is easy,' he said and marched off towards the house, ploughing through adults as if they were invisible. 'It's in the kitchen. I'll show you where. But we have to put it back in the right cupboard, with the lid on properly, or Granny gets cross.'

Eve didn't know where the kitchen was. But thanks to Hannah she knew one of its windows looked out on the back garden. So when Alfie entered the house through a different door, crossed the hall and made for the stairs, she was sure that wherever he was headed, it wasn't the kitchen.

'Hey, Alfie,' she said. 'Ketchup? Kitchen?'

'I want to show you something,' he said, already halfway up. 'Come and see my room.'

The house was silent, and even with Alfie as her guide, Eve couldn't shake the feeling she was trespassing. 'Alfie,' she repeated, 'Daddy asked me to get the ketchup.'

'In a minute. Come on!' the look Alfie gave her was withering: *Don't be such a girl*.

At the landing, the small boy vanished through the first door he came to. His room was tiny, but then so was Alfie. It was also crammed with furniture. Two single beds, two white bedside tables, a not-quite-matching chest of drawers and one of those flat-packed wardrobes with a flowered curtain where a door should be. There was scarcely any floor to see; but what there was, was littered with shoes, discarded clothes and toys. The diamond-paned window above the

102

beds was open; the smell of cooking, and the clink of glasses and chatter and laughter seeped in from below.

'This is my bed,' Alfie said, flinging himself onto the nearest and disturbing an elderly labrador that was clearly trying to get some peace. 'And this is Ben, Grandpa's dog. He's old,' Alfie said, shoving his face against Ben's, so they were nose to nose. The dog didn't look wildly impressed.

'You can sit on Daddy's bed.'

Eve's smile froze on her face.

Daddy's.

Of course it was.

Ian hadn't mentioned the sleeping arrangements. But since, as far as the children were concerned, Ian and Eve were 'just good friends' and had done little more than hug in their presence, there was no question of sharing a room, let alone a bed. That was for mummies and daddies. Not daddies and daddies' friends.

And what about Tom and Elaine? Ian's parents knew, didn't they? That she and Ian . . . that they were . . . ?

Of course they did. They weren't born yesterday.

A mess of emotion swept through Eve. This was like being a teenager again. Worse, in fact. At least when you were a teenager you knew the rules and did everything in your power to break them. Now everything was flipped on its head. It gave her a headache just to think about it.

But Eve was impressed, too. It was so very Ian.

One of the many reasons she'd been so blown

away by him. Right from the start, right from their first conversation, he'd made it completely clear the children came first. No matter what. No exceptions. Not for him. Not for anyone. Not even, Eve saw now, for her. This was going to take some getting her head around. And the sooner she managed it, the better.

'It's a good room, isn't it?' said Alfie. He was bouncing up and down on springs that sounded as if they'd last been oiled in 1935. 'I like sharing with Dad. He won't let me at home. Says I'm big enough to sleep on my own.'

'It's a very good room,' Eve agreed. The dog, now irredeemably disturbed, jumped off, yawned and pushed his way through the slightly open door, in search of a new place to sleep, or food, or both.

Now she'd had a chance to look around Eve could see all the signs of Ian's occupation. The coat draped over the top of the wardrobe was big boy's not small boy's. The shoes kicked into one corner were a mishmash of Ian's huge feet and Alfie's tiny ones. And the books on the bedside table, Roald Dahl and James Lee Burke . . . Although, thinking about it, both of those could have belonged to Ian. The plastic figures on the floor, though, were most definitely Alfie's.

'Smile.' Ian's voice from the doorway took her by surprise. Her expression as he clicked the shutter was one of confusion, rather than the pleasure she felt when she realized he'd taken a picture of Alfie and her together.

'Two of my favourite people,' he said, clicking again. 'But I hate to tell you . . . unless Alfie has

104

a secret stash — and anything's possible — you're not going to find the tomato sauce in here!'

Eve flushed. Embarrassed.

'I'm showing Evie our room,' Alfie said, saving Eve from having to choose between confessing to being a snoop or grassing up a five-year-old.

Ian's eyes met hers. 'You're sleeping in Sophie's room,' he said. 'She's moved in with Hannah for the night. I hope that's OK?'

'Of course it is,' Eve said with feeling. 'I was expecting the sofa.'

★　★　★

It was gone eight before the stragglers left and Ian disappeared to coerce an exhausted and over-excited Alfie and Sophie into a bath and their beds. Hannah used his vanishing as an opportunity to commandeer the sitting room, and turn on whatever reality show was flavour of this month.

Feeling like a spare part, Eve went to see if she was needed in the kitchen.

'Ghastly,' said Ian's father, as he staggered in with a plastic sack full of rubbish. 'Not all it's cracked up to be, entertaining.' Tying a knot in the top of the sack, he said, 'People descend like locusts, eat the place bare, then leave their rubbish all over the lawn and push off, leaving me to clear up. Remind me why we do it?'

Elaine patted his arm as he passed. 'The pleasure of seeing the people you love enjoy themselves, perchance,' she said, smiling. 'Your eldest granddaughter's birthday, maybe?'

He pulled a face and went to get another bag.

'Can I persuade you to dry?' Elaine asked Eve, who was loitering awkwardly by the doorway.

'Of course. I was just about to offer.' Eve was conscious how pathetic that sounded. As soon as Elaine shut the door, then headed not for the sink but the fridge, where she liberated a half-full bottle of Chablis and two glasses, Eve realized she'd been had. It was a trap.

Should she start washing up anyway?

The elderly woman read her mind. 'Sit down, my dear,' she said. 'Keep me company while I put my feet up and have a drink I actually taste.'

Eve knew the feeling. She felt much the same about food. She hadn't tasted a thing all day, even though she'd eaten like it was going out of fashion.

Taking a chair, Eve perched on its edge and hoped she didn't look as nervous as she felt.

Elaine filled two glasses and pushed one towards Eve. And then, having raised her glass in silent salute, she said, 'I hope you don't mind, but there are a couple of things I'd like to say.'

It wasn't a question, so Eve picked up her glass too; more for something to do with her hands than anything else, and made herself sit back in the chair.

Ian's mother took another sip, longer and slower, and closed her eyes. When she opened them, they were steely, almost as if someone else was suddenly in residence.

'I hope you understand what you're taking on,' she said. 'Ian's not just their father, he's both

106

parents in one. I don't know what sort of deal you and he have, but you need to understand that those children must be part of it. Will always be part of it. He wouldn't let it be any other way. And nor, I assure you, would I.'

Eve held Ian's mother's gaze for a few seconds, then looked down at her own glass. Condensation was dripping onto her fingers.

'Those children have been through a lot. And Hannah more so than the others.'

Although Elaine held up a hand to stop Eve speaking, Eve had no intention of uttering a word. 'I'm sure she's not easy. Any fool can see that. But what I am saying is it's up to you to make it work. You're the adult in this equation. Hannah's the child, whatever she likes to pretend otherwise. And she misses her mother terribly.'

Eve nodded, slowly. She was listening with every nerve in her body, but she hadn't a clue what Elaine expected her to say.

'However scared you are, her fear is far greater. Remember that.'

'I will,' Eve managed.

'I watched my son go through a lot,' Elaine said. 'Far more than any mother wants to see her child suffer. Caroline's death was awful, just awful. And why she had to write that damn column I don't know. Ian hated it, we all did. But then I suppose he's told you that. All we can do is hope they never make the film.'

Eve felt her eyes bulge in horror, and buried her face in her glass before Elaine could see her shock.

What bloody film?

107

She forced herself to push the question to the back of her mind. *Save it,* she urged herself. *Don't let her see you don't know.*

She would ask Ian later — if she ever got him on his own.

'Caro was no saint, you know,' Elaine was saying. 'I'm sure he's told you that, too. If he hasn't — out of respect for her memory, or some such — I'm telling you now. No matter what you've read in the papers, she wasn't some heroine. Oh she was brave, braver in public than in private, is my understanding, but who isn't? But ill or not, courageous or not, Caro wasn't perfect. Mind you, I don't doubt that Ian is less than perfect when you're not his mother.'

Elaine smiled, her eyes were softer now. 'Now,' she said. 'I want my son to be happy. And if you make him happy — and you must, or he wouldn't have invited you here — that's good enough for his father and me. But I'm telling you it won't be easy. In fact, prepare yourself for it being very, very hard. But you will have me on your side, that I promise you. While you are on Ian's side, Tom and I will always be firmly on yours.'

She reached across the table, and placed a thin hand over Eve's own. Despite its papery skin, her grip was strong.

'You are the first, you realize that?'

Eve nodded. She hadn't been sure before this weekend, but now it was obvious. Oh, she was certain there had been women before her; one-nighters, maybe two, but they hadn't mattered enough for Ian to let them into his and his children's life. Or, for that matter, his parents'.

'Good. That's clear then.' The old woman was reaching the end of her speech. 'But if you hurt him or my grandchildren . . . I assure you, my dear, I may be old, but I'm tougher than I look. You won't know what hit you.'

'I won't,' Eve said, finding her voice in the face of the older woman's resolve. 'Hurt them, I mean. I love Ian, Mrs Newsome . . . '

'Eve?' The kitchen door opened and Ian's head appeared around it. He took in the table, the wine, the two glasses and the ghost of a hastily withdrawn hand. 'Mum? What's going on?'

Pushing back her chair, Elaine climbed to her feet. 'Nothing dear. Eve and I were just having a little chat.'

'Eve?'

Eve drained her glass in one. She felt as if a tsunami had washed over her and she had come out the other side. Alive, just barely, and clinging to a tree.

'Uh-huh. Like your mother said. Just a little chat.'

9

'Wake up, wake up, wake up!'

Hammering, loud, long and very, very hard. Eve wasn't sure if it was inside her head or outside, but she knew it hurt. A lot. Surely she hadn't drunk that much? Mentally she tried to tot up the Pimm's, the glasses of rosé, then there was a bottle of beer and that final glass of Chablis . . .

'Wake UP!'

No, definitely outside her head, but now inside the room. Inside the room, on her bed and, if she didn't open her eyes in the next few seconds, she imagined it would be on her head.

'Alfie, stop!' came Ian's voice. 'What bit of 'Let's take Eve a cup of tea and wake her up gently' didn't you understand?'

Eve opened one eye and found herself nose to nose with a small blond boy, his hair standing on end at the back of his head, where he'd slept on it and so far evaded all threat of a brush.

'Hello,' she said, hauling herself onto one elbow and risking a small hug. He hugged her back and she was surprised to feel a surge of something more than pleasure.

'Would you like a Jammy Dodger?'

'Alfie . . . ' Eve could hear a warning note in Ian's voice, but it was too early in the day for her family code-breaker to be functioning.

'Erm, no thanks. It's a bit early for me.'

'See, I told you she . . .'

'*Pleeeese* Eve, you gotta have a Jammy Dodger.' It was one of those wails that could go in either direction.

'OK, OK . . . I'll have a Jammy Dodger.' If it mattered that much, the least she could do was have a biscuit with her tea.

'See Dad!' The little boy jumped off her bed and raced for the door, his Spiderman pyjamas a whirr of blue and red. A second later, she could hear his feet as he pounded down the stairs.

'What a pushover,' Ian said. 'Budge up.' She moved her legs to one side and he perched beside them, squeezing her knee through the floral duvet. 'You're just too easy.'

Eve grinned. 'Speak for yourself.' But before either one could find out just who was easy around here, she spotted a flash of pink bobble lurking beyond the door.

Just as well, as the door crashed open again, and Alfie appeared carrying a plate with four Jammy Dodgers skidding around precariously. By the time the plate reached Eve, two had vanished.

'We're not allowed biscuits before breakfast,' said a voice from the landing. Sophie sounded put out.

'Granny said OK.' Crumbs sprayed from Alfie's mouth as he spoke. 'I can have a biscuit if Eve does.'

Eve heard a bedroom door slam.

'A biscuit. So, where's the other one?' Ian asked. But it was too late, the second Jammy Dodger had gone from Alfie's dressing-gown pocket to his mouth in a flash.

'Alfie!'

'*Can't didn't won't!*'

'Alfie, what have I told you . . . ?'

But boy and biscuit were long gone. Eve realized she had, indeed, been had. Used up and tossed away by a five year-old mercenary who knew a fast track to a snack when he saw one and wasn't above using it.

'*Can't didn't won't?*' she asked

'All-purpose denial.' Ian couldn't help grinning. 'Can't do it, didn't do it, won't do it. One size fits all.'

Eve was impressed. Maybe it would work on Miriam? 'I didn't even know they made Jammy Dodgers any more.'

'I know, disgusting things. They're all E-numbers. Reckon they must be in the granny handbook. Those, and those horrible sports biscuits with icing on one side and pictures of stick men playing tennis and cricket on the other. She has a limitless supply of the damn things. Dread to think what their sell-by date was. Begins with nineteen probably. Used to drive Ca — ' he stopped, aware of what he'd almost said.

Caro mad, Eve wanted to finish for him. Of course it had, of course Caroline would have been the queen of organic. No E-numbers in the Newsome household then, that was for sure.

They were saved by a second flash of pink in the gap where door met hinges. 'Would you like a Jammy Dodger?' Eve said, looking past Ian, to where she knew Sophie lurked on the landing outside.

Silence.

'Sophie? Would you like a biscuit?'

A be-bobbled head peered around the door into Eve's room. 'Am I allowed one, Daddy?'

'I don't see why not,' Ian said. 'Just this once.'

The girl ventured in, coming just close enough to the bed to take the remaining biscuit before backing away again. She was already dressed in denim jeans with pink embroidery on the pockets and pink everything else.

'Thank you for lending me your room,' Eve said. 'It was kind of you. Your bed's very comfortable.'

The girl smiled, pleased, but didn't speak.

'What d'you say Sophie?' Ian coaxed.

'It's OK, but my sleeping bag's really prickly.'

Eve burst out laughing.

'Sophie!' Ian rolled his eyes.

'Well,' she said, bottom lip wobbling. 'It is.'

'I'll swap you for your duvet if you want,' Eve offered.

'No,' Ian said. 'You won't. Anyway, Granny and Grandpa are going today so there'll be enough duvets for everyone tonight.'

* * *

Breakfast at the cottage was chaotic, all dogs, children, Rice Krispies and spilt milk, but that was as nothing compared to the fight for the children's bathroom. Were mornings always like this? Eve wondered. Getting to the office on time was about the full extent of her usual morning achievements. How Ian got three kids washed,

113

dressed and to school with all the necessary equipment and all before nine, she had no idea. And as for doing it without them looking as if they'd been dragged through a hedge backwards . . . it was beyond her. OK, so he usually had Inge, the au pair, who had returned home for a holiday . . . but, even so, Eve was impressed. And slightly appalled. Although there was no way she'd let Ian's mother get a whiff of that.

'Can I give you a hand?' she asked Ian's father, as he staggered downstairs, carrying a large suitcase. He stopped, taking advantage of the opportunity to rest the case on the bottom step and catch his breath. 'If you can lift this you're tougher than you look,' he said. 'But I'm not about to find out. Ian would kill me if you did yourself a damage.'

His eyes were Ian's, but twinklier. Ian's without three years living in the shadow of his late daughter-in-law's cancer, and two years of child bereavement counselling. Although who knew what the old man's eyes had seen over the years?

Tom handed Eve the car keys. 'How about you open the boot for me?'

So Eve unlocked the Volvo estate and then watched, feeling useless, as the old man lugged the leather case across the gravel, pausing halfway to catch his breath before bundling it into the boot.

'Are you sure I can't help?'

'You are helping,' he said, fixing those eyes on her. Not so twinkly now.

Another Newsome family trap, Eve realized, only this one she'd helped spring herself.

'More than you know.'

Eve blushed.

The old man squeezed her arm. 'You survived Elaine's interrogation for a start!' His twinkle was back.

'It wasn't . . . '

'Don't deny it, my dear. Braver men than you — no offence intended — have fallen at that hurdle. Take it from me. I've been married to Elaine for forty-five years, I've seen her disapproval. It can be ugly.'

'Thanks, Mr Newsome.'

'It's Tom. I've told you, call me Tom.'

Ian's father leant forward and grasped Eve's shoulders — part affection, part, she suspected, simply holding himself up — and kissed her firmly on both cheeks. 'Well done, my dear. And welcome.'

'Come on, you old fool, we're going to spend the rest of the day on the A303 if we don't start soon.' Ian's mother was on the doorstep, Alfie loitering around her legs. Her expression told Eve nothing other than the fact that they were likely to be late.

'Where's Hannah?' Tom said, to no one and everyone.

'Coming,' said Ian appearing around the side of the house, Ben panting and tail-wagging at his side. 'I sent Sophie to tell her you're off, so she's to get up pronto.'

The girl's grandmother glanced at her watch, her face registering the time. 'Channelling her

115

inner teenager,' Eve said.

Ian shook his head. 'Outer teenager. She's thirteen now. We'd better get used to it.'

Eve wasn't sure what 'it' was. But she had a horrible feeling they were going to find out.

10

The envelope sat on the kitchen table where it had rested for the past two hours. Not for the first time that morning, Clare thanked all manner of Gods she didn't believe in that it was the summer holidays and, in true teenager style, Louisa was still asleep gone eleven a.m.

And if Lou wasn't asleep, she was at least lazing in bed and leaving Clare in peace, to get on with 'whatever schoolteachers do in the school holidays', as Lily used to say.

This had to be the first summer her younger sister hadn't made some scathing remark about teachers getting a nice long break. Clare had always ignored her, anyway. She'd developed a talent for that over the years, ignoring the things people said that hurt or wounded her. Even her mother and sister had no idea how much of her holidays Clare spent working. Some was to earn extra money, like marking exam papers. The rest, preparing lessons for the coming term, rereading set texts (although if she had to read *Jane Eyre* one more time, she would scream) was just the kind of stuff that, as a teacher, she was expected to do but never got any thanks for. At least she could do it at home. Not that Lou really needed her there any more. Now the need was all on Clare's side.

If it hadn't been the holidays Clare wouldn't even have known the letter was there until she got back from school; which was rarely before five-thirty, and almost never before Louisa.

That thought brought bile to Clare's throat.

What if Lou had found the letter first?

What if, curiosity stirred by the unfamiliar handwriting, she'd opened it? Lou wasn't allowed to open her mother's mail, obviously. But it wouldn't be the first time. Last time, Clare had bollocked her to within an inch of her life, but last time it had just been an overdue bill, with *Open Now* in red on the flap.

Just a bill . . . There was no such thing as *just a bill* in Clare's house. But it was an official letter, not a personal one. Albeit one that told Lou facts her mother would have preferred her not to know about the state of their finances.

Turning the envelope over in her hand, Clare swallowed hard. Funny how she'd recognized the handwriting the second she saw the letter on her mat, even though it was fourteen years since the last letter. That one's contents had been altogether neater, more studied, more thoughtful, bearing all the signs of having been written, torn up and rewritten a dozen times. Not that there was anything about this letter that hadn't been thought through: every word had been planned, analysed and assessed for potential misinterpretation. But the writing still bore all the hallmarks of every doctor's hand Clare had ever seen. One part legibility, to two parts haste. Perhaps they taught it at medical school. If Clare hadn't known better she might have thought it was from her own GP.

No such luck.

Sun streamed into her kitchen, throwing the outline of her sash window onto the pine table. That window was one of the things that had sold the flat to her. (Well, that and the price, obviously. She knew she'd been lucky to afford a one-and-a-half-bedroom flat in a decent part of north London, even on the grottiest of grotty edges.) The window, and the way the sun poured into the kitchen in the morning, and her living room in the evening. When they'd first moved in, Clare had nurtured dreams of stripping the boards back to a sweet soft golden pine and buying antique rugs. It had taken her years to get around to sanding the floors, and antique rugs were still way beyond her budget, even from eBay and of questionable age.

Still, she had the sun. Her grandmother always said the sun shone mostly on the righteous. Personally, Clare would have preferred something a little more concrete. But she'd had her chance.

* * *

The sun had streamed through the blinds of the maternity ward fourteen years earlier. On the morning of June fourteenth, when a nurse had wheeled Clare back to her ward with the tiny puce-faced, freakily hairy baby that was Louisa Lilian Adams in her arms. It had to be Will's, the hairiness, because Clare was as mousy as anyone could be.

Beautiful and vulnerable, the baby was a part of her now. And although little Louisa

119

represented the end of so many of Clare's hopes and ambitions, Clare loved her instantly, feeling her heart expand with more emotion than she'd imagined possible. Beside this, what she'd felt for Will paled into insignificance. Beside this, he was nothing.

★ ★ ★

And sun had streamed through the windows of an examination hall thirty-five miles away, as Will sat the last paper of his biology A level. Whether he knew the baby was due that day — was, in fact, three days late — Clare had no clue. But Will was meant to be the one with the maths brain, the one who wanted to be a doctor, so presumably he knew that forty weeks translated into nine months, which translated into three trimesters; of which, she'd just reached the end of the third.

She also had no clue that — unwilling to depend on Will's mental arithmetic — her mother had contacted his parents, until the letter arrived, a week after Clare got home from hospital.

The handwriting was his; the cheque most definitely not.

'Ten thousand pounds,' said Clare's mother, her voice full of awe. It was partly how impressed her mother sounded at their generosity that made Clare fling the cheque and the brief letter accompanying it across the kitchen table in disgust.

'How fucking dare he?'

'Clare, please . . . ' Her mother's attempt to calm Clare only enraged her further.

It didn't help that she hadn't slept for two days, her nipples were sore and she couldn't pee without being reduced to tears.

'Think what you can do with ten thousand pounds. Just *think* for a minute. Please.'

Clare didn't need to think. She wasn't stupid, she knew. She could start again. She could pay her way through university without having to work evenings and weekends and every second of every holiday. She could buy a proper cot, more baby clothes, a buggy . . . She could give some to her mother to thank her for her support, despite her initial, highly vocal, reservations. She could put it into a savings account for Louisa's future.

She also knew she wouldn't.

He didn't want their baby. She didn't want his money. He couldn't pay off his conscience that easily, she refused to let him.

She took back the cheque before her mother had a chance to realize what she intended to do, and began to tear it, obsessively, into tiny, tiny pieces. Pieces so small no one could put them back together again. Scattering the fragments onto the floor like confetti, Clare said, 'He doesn't want Louisa, fine, that's his choice, but I won't be bought.'

She had never regretted Louisa, not for a second. But there had been many times since, when Clare considered what she could have done with ten thousand pounds and regretted not taking the money.

★ ★ ★

Clare didn't need to reread Will's letter. She'd read it twenty times already, since lifting it from the mat with a pile of bills, mailers and the local paper. There wasn't even that much to read.

> *Dear Clare*
> *I realize this will come as a surprise to you, after all this time.*

Surprise? Shock. Bombshell. Fucking nightmare. All or any of the above. But surprise? That had to be the understatement of the year. Words had never been his strong point. Nor had imagination. Will had always been more of a facts and figures boy.

> *I've been out of our daughter's life for far too long but I'm now in a position to make amends to her. If you — and she, of course — agree, I'd very much like to get to know her. Please call me [he gave a mobile number] and perhaps we could meet to discuss putting matters on a more formal footing.*
> *Kind regards*
> *Will*

That was it. Nothing more, nothing less. No, *I'm sorry.* No, *Forgive me.* No, *I made a terrible mess of things, please give me another chance.* Not that she would, but hey, it wouldn't hurt to have him ask.

122

Who would have known a note so potentially earth-shattering could also be so cold, so formal, so . . . emotionally constipated.

It was the *Kind regards* that killed her.

No *Best wishes*, no *Love*, just regards. And how kind could his regards be if he could do this to her after so many years? Cluster bomb her carefully constructed world with a sky full of toxic memories. Just because he could.

Fourteen years of silence. No birthday cards. No letters. No, 'I saw Will's mother in Marks & Spencer and she asked after you and her *granddaughter*'. (That was the other thing Clare sometimes wondered, in her too frequent three a.m. moments when she couldn't sleep. All right, so Will had hardened his heart; but didn't his *parents* care? Didn't Will's mother ever see a little girl in the street and wonder about her own granddaughter? Didn't she wonder if Lou was taller, shorter, prettier, cleverer or sportier? Weren't Will's parents even the tiniest bit interested in the lanky, lovely, too-smart-for-her-own-good girl their son — however reluctantly — had fathered?) And now this. I want to come back into our daughter's life.

Our daughter.

Clare's laugh cut harshly through the silence of her kitchen.

But his words weren't the only thing that made her frown into the dregs of her fourth cup of coffee that morning. It was the fact he'd sent a letter at all. How had he known where to find her? How did he know she hadn't married? That Lou didn't have another father now? A different surname?

But then, she hadn't exactly hidden herself and Lou away. They had, she supposed now, hidden in plain view. The facts of her life common knowledge to anyone interested enough to ask. All the same, she didn't live what you might call a public life. She wasn't Eve, with her face and her e-mail address in a magazine. Or even Lily with her dreams of being a stand-up comic. Anonymous was what Clare had set out to be and she had unquestionably achieved it. An ordinary woman, with an ordinary job and an ordinary life, in an ordinary London suburb. With nothing to mark her out but her love of cooking, and an ability, born of necessity, to conjure a healthy supper containing all five main food groups out of leftovers for her beautiful, brilliant daughter.

And still he'd found her.

And if he knew where she and Lou lived, how long before he turned up in person?

At the far end of the narrow hall that ran the length of the flat, the muffled sound of cupboards and drawers opening and shutting told Clare that Lou was stirring. And as Lou's bedroom door creaked open, and Clare's daughter shuffled from bedroom to bathroom, grumbling a cursory greeting before slamming and locking the bathroom door, and all the possible consequences played out in her mind, Clare knew that she could not, would not, allow this to happen.

Clare's daughter.

Not Clare and Will's daughter.

Clare's.

Louisa Adams not Louisa Drew.

It was not Clare who had deprived Louisa of her father's surname. He had not wanted Clare and he had not wanted his daughter, and so his name had not gone on her birth certificate. If he hadn't wanted her fourteen years ago, Clare was determined he could not have her now.

Picking up the letter, she began to tear it, obsessively, into tiny pieces.

★ ★ ★

Eve and Ian were sitting in the garden of the Fort Inn, looking at the harbour. They'd been there most of the afternoon. Slowly sinking a bottle of iced rosé between them and chatting as they watched Alfie work off a chocolate-ice-cream-induced carbohydrate high by lobbing his toys off a table onto the grass, running around hyperactively collecting them, only to toss them again, higher and further. Sophie was sitting on the swings with a cluster of other small girls who also displayed a bias for all things pastel. Hannah — all cut-off denims and string bikini top — had vanished to the surf shops in search of surfers hours ago. Eve could only assume that Ian knew her rough location thanks to some mystic parental osmosis.

Would she ever get used to this 'eyes in the back of your head' business; or was that one of those things you instinctively developed when you had a child of your own? If so, Eve was horribly afraid she would never acquire it.

'You OK if Hannah doesn't come back to the

house with us tonight?'

'Of course.' Eve smiled at Ian, hoping her relief didn't show. 'What's she doing?'

'Staying over at Leonora's. Cassia and Simon say no problem, we can pick her up on our way back to London tomorrow morning.'

OK? thought Eve. *Bloody delighted more like.*

Hannah's presence — a glowering cloud — had been the only dampener on an otherwise idyllic week. She was constantly plugged into the parallel universe of her iPod, and refused to eat anything anyone else did, only to empty the fridge in the middle of the night when she thought everyone else was asleep.

It wasn't Hannah using food to control everyone else that bothered Eve. God knows she'd done enough of that herself when she was thirteen — and beyond — and she was sure Alfie and Sophie barely noticed.

No, it was because Eve felt that Hannah only did it because she knew it got to Eve. And nothing, but nothing, Eve did or said made any difference. She'd tried keeping out of the way and she'd tried being friendly; she'd tried mate, surrogate mum, cleaner, cook and bottle-washer. All to no avail.

'Ian . . . ' she began.

Now, relaxed by alcohol, sunshine and sheer distance from London and real life, seemed like a good time to voice her worries. Ian seemed to be some kind of alchemist where kids were concerned. Clearly he knew a magic formula, perhaps he could be persuaded to share it. 'Ian, I . . .'

126

Her sentence was interrupted by a familiar wail.

'Back in a sec.' Ian was on his feet and over the small wall that separated the pub's garden from the beach before Eve knew it. Seconds later, the wailing stopped.

'Let me guess,' she said when he returned. '*Can't didn't won't?*'

'Pretty much. Alfie pushed Harry or Harry pushed Alfie, who knows? Both probably. Either way, both are completely innocent and prepared to swear it was Venom wot done it.'

They both laughed.

'Who's Harry?'

'Random small boy. But from the way the woman over there leapt to her feet then sat back down when the yelling stopped, I'd hazard a guess that's his mum.' He nodded to a slim, tanned woman in shorts and vest top, her highlighted hair tied in a chic knot at the nape of her neck.

The woman nodded back and Eve felt a twinge of jealousy. The sea air, so kind to the sun-bleached, bronzed surf bunnies, had turned her own curls to frizz and her pale skin pink with freckled splotches. She glanced down at her legs hoping they might have tanned slightly since the last time she looked. When she glanced up, Ian was looking at them too, a smile she hadn't seen on his face all week. To judge by the rest of the holiday, she could tell him right now he was on a hiding to nothing. Mind you, if Hannah was away tonight, maybe . . .

'Ian . . . '

'I . . . '

They started talking simultaneously and stuttered to a halt. 'You go,' Eve said, already reconsidering the wisdom of sharing her worries about Hannah when he clearly had other, altogether more fun, things on his mind.

'I just wanted to say, thanks.' Under cover of the table, he rested his hand on her leg and stroked her bare thigh. Eve's insides turned molten. The week had been wonderful, just not on that score. It was like being under permanent guard, with Hannah their self-appointed chaperone, staying up late into the night, patrolling the corridors to ensure there was no sneaking between rooms, and only finally allowing herself to sleep as dawn approached.

Right about the time Alfie was guaranteed to wake up and take over his shift.

It was worse than being a teenager. Apart from the quickest of quickies in the downstairs loo when Alfie and Sophie had been glued to the TV and Hannah had still been asleep, they hadn't managed so much as a snog in the kitchen under the guise of washing up without various pairs of small feet thundering towards them from all corners of the house. Eve was beginning to feel she might explode. And if Ian carried on doing that with his hand, she would. Right there in the pub garden.

'Eve,' Ian said. 'I've had the most wonderful time. The best time since . . . since . . . Well, I've had the best time ever.'

'You don't have to say that.'

'I mean it. I don't think I've ever been so happy.'

'Not . . . ?'

He put up a hand to silence her. 'Shhh.'

Good grief, did she have a death wish? Embarrassed at her own stupidity, Eve glanced around to make sure no beady eyes were watching or small ears flapping. Although, of course, it went without saying that Ian would already have made sure of that.

'Me either,' Eve said. 'Thank you for letting me be here with you. For letting me be part of your family.' That, she knew, was the biggest of deals for him. How big had become obvious the moment she met his parents.

Suddenly, both his hands were holding hers across the table. Eve stroked his tanned forearm with her free hand, smoothing sun-bleached hairs. The past week had taught her to be permanently on alert for knee-high intervention. But none came.

'Look,' he said. 'This feels right. I want us to be like this all the time.'

'Me too.'

'Then marry me,' he said.

Eve stared at him. Her brain not computing.

'Marry me,' he repeated. 'Please.'

Yes, yes, yes, screamed her heart. But her mouth wasn't cooperating any more than her brain.

'Are you sure? I mean . . . It's a bit unexpected.'

Shut up! screamed her heart.

'Eve,' he said, 'I know it's a bit out of the blue, but I love you, the kids love you.'

The euphoria drained away as quickly as it had come.

'I'm sorry,' Eve said, fixing her eyes on the weather-battered wood of the table between them. 'But they don't.'

She was praying he could see it all over her face how much she loved him back. How much she wanted to say yes. There were just other things she had to say first.

'At least I don't think so. Not yet.'

'I do, Alfie does, Sophie's fond of you, so that's only a matter of time.'

'But Hannah doesn't.'

He stopped. His face clouded. He couldn't lie, wouldn't lie. She knew that. 'That's true,' he said slowly.

Ian couldn't have said anything else and still been the man she loved; but even so, Eve wanted to weep. Hannah didn't. There it was, the elephant in the room dragged kicking and screaming into the open. And if she didn't, how could Eve and Ian be together, let alone marry?

'Hannah wouldn't like anyone who might take her mother's place,' Ian said, finally. 'And you would be. I mean, not literally, but in my life at least. It's not personal. It's nothing you're doing or not doing. It's the mere fact you exist. Give her enough time and she'll come around.'

'I . . . ' Eve was thinking of all the reasons why not. And the one very good reason why. She loved him.

'We can take it slowly,' he was gabbling now, tripping over his own words. 'You could move in. Get the kids used to . . . to us . . . to being a family . . . and then, next year, even the year after if you want, we could make it, you know, permanent.'

Before she knew it, Ian was out of his seat. She hadn't heard the telltale wail. Had Ian seen something she hadn't? Was Alfie all right?

When she looked back, he was half-kneeling beside her. 'I love you,' he said. 'I've never felt like this before. Never. Marry me. Please.'

Eve was conscious she was grinning like an idiot now. Oblivious to the couple on the nearest table staring openly, oblivious to the lanky blonde teenager in cut-off denims and sequinned bikini top watching from the entrance to the pub garden, headphones plugged firmly in her ears, Eve threw her arms around Ian.

'Yes,' she whispered. 'Yes, please.'

11

'Let's see it then.'

'What?'

'The rock, of course.'

'No rock. Not yet. He hasn't got me a ring yet. Didn't want to presume to choose one for me.'

If she was honest, Eve knew it was also partly because his proposal had been utterly out of character; a spur of the moment decision, borne on the wave of their successful holiday, but she wasn't about to let a small detail like that get in the way of her happiness. For what felt like the nine hundredth time since she'd returned from Cornwall, Eve prepared her punchline: 'There's a diamond ring that belonged to his great-grandmother. If I like it, he's going to get it resized to fit.'

'Not . . . ?' Lily was temporarily aghast.

Eve knew what she was thinking. She'd thought it too for a split second when Ian first mentioned the family heirloom. 'No!' she said. 'No way. Caroline never had it.' And the unspoken implication, that Caroline hadn't been as important, as significant . . . that Eve was special, made her grin all the broader.

'Oh my god,' Melanie gasped. 'Is this man perfect or what?'

★ ★ ★

'What? What's going on?' Clare watched the other three look up guiltily, and wondered what she'd missed. Eve, in particular, she thought, looked as though she'd been caught rifling through someone's handbag.

Clare's train had been stuck in a tunnel on the Northern Line for the past twenty minutes. She was hot, she was sweaty and the bad mood that had settled over her since Will's letter arrived was congealing into a malignant shroud.

She hated being late and she was in no mood for the girly hysteria emanating from their corner of Starbucks.

She also, for some reason she couldn't pin down, felt excluded.

This wasn't how it was meant to be, this group had been her idea. Clare had been so pleased with herself, so happy when Eve and Lily hit it off and wanted to meet again. She'd even persuaded Eve to let Melanie in, but now the evenings were gaining a life of their own. That was what Clare had wanted. Only now it was happening, she wasn't sure she liked it.

'I got you a skinny latte,' said Melanie, a little nervously. As if she'd been caught stealing Clare's seat. 'I hope that's right. If not I can go get you something else?'

'That's perfect, thanks.' Clare forced a smile. Just because her life was shit right now — right now, that was a laugh — it didn't give her the right to piss on everyone else's party. And clearly there *was* a party going on here.

Dropping her bag on the floor, she kicked it under the table, where it landed next to the

Mulberry tote she knew had been handed down to Eve by her boss. M&S's finest p-leather might cut it in the staff room, but it didn't stand scrutiny here.

'What's going on?'

Lily beamed at her.

Clare looked at Eve. Yes, she definitely looked awkward. Embarrassed, even.

'If you don't tell her,' said Lily, giving Eve a meaningful stare, 'I'm going to.'

Eve smiled. Now she looked at her, Clare realized there was something different. Had she cut her hair? Dyed it? Been for some sort of miracle facial?

'Ian proposed.'

'You what?' Clare caught herself. 'I mean, Wow, congratulations. When did *that* happen?'

'Recently.' Eve had obviously read her mind, or at least part of it, and leant forward, putting her hand on her friend's. 'I called you from Cornwall, several times. Your answering machine's broken. There's something up with your mobile too. Where've you been? I've been desperate to talk to you.'

Clare didn't have the heart to tell Eve's lit up face that her answering machine wasn't broken, it was turned off. It had been turned off since Will's letter arrived. Now she was terrified he'd call, or even worse, simply turn up on the doorstep. As for her mobile, that was just old. Old and crap. The kind of phone that made teenagers smirk when she took it out on the bus.

'So, it was obviously a good holiday,' she said tightly, a prickling in her nose threatening

134

emotion at being the last to hear her old friend's news.

'The best.' Eve was glowing; it wasn't a dye job, or a trip to the hygienist, she really was radiating happiness. Clare felt a pang of jealousy. It was a long, long time since she'd felt like that. Not since . . . Well, not for a long time. She listened as Eve told them all how it had happened, trying to relax and shake off her black mood. Eve was her best friend, why couldn't she just be happy for her?

'So, when's the big day?' she asked. 'Or haven't you thought about that yet?'

'Oh God, not for ages. Next year. Year after. If it was down to me I wouldn't bother at all, but it's important to Ian. He wants the kids to understand it's permanent. But we're going to take things slowly, get them used to the idea first.'

Clare noticed that Eve carefully avoided making eye contact. *Not kids*, she thought. *Hannah*.

'So I'm going to move in,' Eve continued. 'As soon as I can find a tenant for my flat. And we'll take it from there.'

Out of the corner of her eye, Clare saw her sister mime sticking fingers down her throat. Eve had seen her too. So had Melanie, who looked appalled.

'It's all right,' Eve said, laughing. 'I'm making myself want to vomit too! This is not like me at all, is it Clare?'

'Never met a woman less interested in marriage or babies . . . ' Clare shrugged.

That was true. When they were at university Clare would have sworn Eve would do anything — *anything* — to avoid what she'd once been heard to call, with an entirely straight face, *the subjugation of marriage*. There had been boyfriends, but none had been around for long. And that was always down to Eve. *Low jerk threshold*, she said. She'd rather hang out with the girls. She had better things to do than chase after jocks, stoners and pretty boys. Clare always assumed this would change when Eve met *The One*. Although why she, of all people, should believe that . . .

Clare had met *The One*, and look where that had got her.

★ ★ ★

'That was me, too,' Melanie ventured. She'd been sitting quietly, sipping chai latte (not that she'd have admitted it to Clare) and taking in the conversation, watching Eve grow more radiant with each telling, and feeling pangs of envy tinge her pleasure for her new friend.

That was what love did to you, she guessed, wondering if this was how she'd looked when Simeon proposed; if her girlfriends had sat in the Gramercy Tavern and watched her radiate love, goodwill and happy-ever-after, like some sort of Jimmy Choo-shod fairy tale princess.

Not all men were like Simeon, she reminded herself. The way Eve told it, Ian certainly sounded like a decent guy, possibly even the real thing, assuming there was such a thing.

When the others turned to look at her, Melanie wondered why she'd spoken up.

'I just mean, I was Ms No-marriage, No-kids, No-way,' she ventured, meeting their gaze. 'Always had been. Ever since high school. My parents were gutted. Oh, they said they were proud when I got my place at Brown, graduated *cum laude* and was fast-tracked at Singer, Bartlett & Nash, the corporate law firm I joined, but my mom would be the first to tell you that she'd rather I'd just married a nice guy from Boston — a nice Chinese/American guy, obviously — kept house and had kids . . . And then I met Simeon and boom. Six months later I'm on a plane here. Honestly, in my high school yearbook, I was girl most likely to succeed — aka girl *least* likely to chuck it all in and follow some guy halfway around the world. My friends nearly died of shock when I told them I'd given up my job and the lease on my rent-controlled apartment to marry some Brit. They thought I was crazy. I guess they still do . . .'

And they wouldn't be wrong, Melanie thought. In fact, they'd be so far from wrong they were right. How had she made such a mess of her life?

The mere thought of the tight-knit group who'd seen Melanie through her Manhattan years, gave her an almost physical pang. How were they? Where were they? Far more than her ex, and definitely more than her family, she missed her New York girlfriends so much it hurt.

'And I did all that, only to get publicly

137

dumped by one of the world's richest men,' Melanie finished lamely.

'It's not your fault the guy's an arse,' Lily said gamely. 'I mean look at you — gorgeous, brainy and a successful businesswoman. Simeon's loss is Vince's gain. How *is* Vince anyway?'

'Oh, he's fine.' Melanie didn't feel like talking about Vince either. She was beginning to feel a fraud, she was here as a stepmother, but had still to meet the stepchild in question — and she was in no hurry to do so. In fact, the thought made her stomach lurch.

'How's Louisa?' she asked Clare, hoping the others would let her get away with the feeble attempt to deflect attention.

'As fine as can be expected when everyone's been on holiday except her. Everyone's got an iPod except her. Everyone's allowed to stay home alone except her . . . ' Clare shrugged. 'You get the picture.'

The truth was they'd had another row before Clare had left the flat. The Northern Line had not been entirely to blame for Clare's tardiness. It had merely compounded things. Having promised Lou that she would be allowed to stay home alone next time Clare spent an evening with the Stepmothers' Support Group, Will's letter had forced a panicked rethink and she'd reneged on the deal. Something she hated to do where Louisa was concerned and promised herself she never would.

Clare felt another rush of fury. *Thanks a lot, Will*, she thought. *As if you haven't fucked up my life enough already.*

'Her father's been in touch.' The words took Clare as much by surprise as the others; she hadn't been planning to say them. Not being a stepmother-type problem, this wasn't one for the SSG.

'You're kidding?' Eve leant forward, her face full of shock. She clasped Clare's hand. 'Will? *Your* Will?'

'Not *my* Will,' Clare said, freeing her fingers. 'Very definitely not *my* Will.'

'Oh my God. Are you OK? What did he say?'

Sensing that this was not a conversation for mere acquaintances, Melanie headed for the ladies and another round of coffees, leaving Clare to fill Eve and her sister in on the letter.

'How did he find you?' Lily asked.

'I've been wondering about that,' Clare said, her chin in her hand. 'You don't think Mum . . . ?'

'Mum? No! No way.' Lily was emphatic. 'So far as I know, Mum hasn't so much as bumped into Will's mother in the street for over a decade. And, if she did, she'd hardly just hand over your address. Apart from anything else, she knows you'd murder her.'

'How then?'

'I hate to say it,' said Eve. 'But it's not that hard. You haven't changed your name, and you live in roughly the same area, give or take a few postcodes. Even without Facebook, Friends Reunited or any of that stuff, there are probably people from home who know you're still in the vicinity, know you became a teacher. And you're on the electoral register, aren't you? You vote.

You pay council tax. I bet you're not even ex-directory?'

Clare scowled. Why would she be ex-directory?

'Well then, the most basic search would probably throw up half a dozen Clare Adams in their early thirties with your postcode.'

'Is it that easy?' Clare knew she sounded appalled. It had simply never occurred to her that anyone would want to find her.

'Pretty much,' Eve said. 'Any vaguely competent journalist could find you in under an hour with the most basic of information. If Will was really determined to make contact and hired a private detective — '

She held up her hand at Clare's protest. 'Calm down hon. I'm not saying he did. I'm just saying *if*. It's not hard to find someone if you know how to look. You don't even really need to know where.'

It was Lily's turn for a question: 'What did you do with the letter?' she asked.

'Tore it up. What d'you think I did with it? Left it on the side for Louisa to read? Put it in a red velvet box with all his other treasured love notes?'

Even Melanie, who'd just deposited four full mugs on the table, winced.

Lily just stared.

'Sorry,' said Clare. 'Sorry, sorry, sorry. I didn't mean to have a go.' She was staring down at a steaming latte, hoping the tears that brimmed in her eyes wouldn't spill over. 'It's just . . . how *dare* he?'

'God, what a nightmare,' said Lily. 'What right

140

does he have to come barging back into your life like this?'

It wasn't a question. Clare shrugged, her eyes fixed firmly on her coffee, wishing she hadn't got into this. She wasn't ready. She didn't have the faintest clue where to go from here, other than outside for a cigarette she didn't even smoke.

'What are you going to do?' Eve asked gently. 'Have you told your mum?'

'No, and I don't know,' Clare said sadly. 'All I know is he gets to see Lou over my dead body.'

Lily and Eve exchanged glances, silently negotiating whose turn it was to get shot. Somehow Eve lost. 'Clare . . . ' she paused, hoping for divine intervention. None came. 'I know you don't want to hear this.'

Clare glared at her. 'Don't say it then.'

Eve ploughed on. 'My love, I'm sorry, but it's not that straightforward. And you'd know that too if you were thinking straight. I mean, private detectives or not, Will's obviously determined. He's made the effort to find you and Lou. I could be wrong, but I don't think he's going to go away just because you don't respond to one letter. He's going to get in touch again. And next time, or the time after, it may not be by letter.'

'At some point he's going to phone.'

Clare looked up from where her finger traced circles in the cooling froth. 'I know.'

She wasn't stupid. Why else had she turned off her answering machine? Not that the others knew that. 'And I'll ignore him,' she said firmly. 'Again and again. Until he goes back under whatever rock he crawled out from . . . '

141

There was a long, hideous silence. The kind 'cut with a knife' was invented for. It was enough to make Lily wish Melanie hadn't bought that last round of coffees. Still, someone had to say something. And it looked like it was her.

'Oh,' Lily said, her faux brightness fooling no one. 'On an entirely different subject, there was one thing I wanted to mention.'

'Don't tell me Liam's done it again!' Eve said.

'No — well, yes, of course he has. He's Liam, isn't he? But that's not it. I wanted to ask if I can bring a new member to the next meeting.'

Eve didn't look opposed to the idea. So Lily glanced at Clare to see how she'd reacted, but her sister was still engrossed in her froth peaks.

'I mean, Melanie came,' Lily said. 'And I don't know about you two, but I think that's been a good thing. It's like we're more of a group now.' She smiled shyly at Melanie, who smiled gratefully back.

'And personally,' said Lily. 'I've found it helpful. I mean, I know Liam has his faults, but he has good points too. And no,' she stuck her elbow in her sister's ribs to get her attention, 'they don't all involve sex.'

Clare managed a weak grin.

'Anyway,' Lily continued. 'I was talking to one of his neighbours, Mandy. I've seen her around, in the Indian newsagent on the corner, buying milk and such like, and we always chat. Then the other day she invited me in for a coffee. Anyway, she's like, you know, a *proper* stepmother.'

Lily grinned at Eve and Melanie. 'No offence, but we're just stepmothers in waiting. Me and you more than Eve now. But Mandy's got a tough gig, she has three kids of her own, all boys between twelve and sixteen, and the guy she lives with has a girl and a boy, fifteen and twelve. His kids don't live with them, but they're there most weekends . . . '

'*Five kids?*' Eve said.

'Yeah, and none of them get on. Plus Mandy's ex is a stingy bastard . . . Excuse my French,' Lily glanced apologetically at Melanie, who shrugged. She'd obviously heard worse in behind-closed-doors negotiations. 'Since John — that's her new bloke — moved in, Mandy's ex has started refusing to pay maintenance. I mean, what a shit. They're still his kids, and John is still paying his ex for his kids, of course. So, on top of everything, they're really skint.'

'Sounds grim,' Eve said.

'Look,' Lily said. 'I know Liam's not going to win any awards for dad of the year, but he'd never do a thing like that. Frankly, after spending half an hour with Mandy, I was counting my blessings. That's how I came to tell her about us. Although, to be honest, I was a bit embarrassed because I have such an easy ride of it compared with her. Anyway, Mandy seemed interested so I said I'd ask you if she could come along.'

Lily had prepared a speech, only that hadn't been it. Ad-libbing was one of the things she loved about stand-up. It was all in the timing, and she was good at finding the right words on the fly. The flip side was she couldn't stick to a worked-out speech if her life depended on it. That was probably why she'd never been able to

143

pass a language oral exam either.

'Any objections?' Lily looked at Eve, Clare and Melanie in turn. Each woman nodded agreement. *Why not?* their expressions seemed to say. *In for a penny.*

Smiling her annoying kid sister smile she'd perfected twenty years earlier, Lily beamed at Clare, who until that moment had been self-appointed chairperson. The boss of them, just as she'd been the boss of Lily for as long as Lily could remember.

Slapping her hand flat on the table, Lily said, 'Motion carried.'

12

Number withheld.

The phone was ringing. It had been ringing every half-hour for most of the day. This had been going on for three days now, and Clare knew she couldn't let it carry on. Apart from anything else, Lou was pissed off at not being allowed to answer the phone. Pissed off and downright suspicious.

Eve had been right. Lily too.

Clare had known that the minute Eve opened her mouth. Before that, really. Will was back in her life after fourteen and a half years. And he wasn't going to go away any time soon. Maybe if she hadn't said anything to the group it wouldn't have happened. Maybe if she hadn't told them it would all have gone away.

Don't be so stupid, she told herself.

If she wasn't going to answer it, the only thing to do was to put her answering machine back on. It might not be Will at all. It could be someone trying to flog her home insurance. How dumb could she get? Sitting here in fear of the phone when it was probably just some poor sod in a call centre in Mumbai.

So Clare plugged the machine back in and sat on her sofa, watching it, waiting.

Twenty minutes later she was still sitting there and the machine was still silent. Coffee, she decided. Although she might as well take it intravenously she'd drunk so much lately. The kettle was boiling when she heard the first ring, a click, and her machine burst into life.

Clare and Lou Adams aren't available to take your call right now. Leave your name and number and we might call you back. Then again, maybe not.

The voice and words were Lou's. Clare had meant to make her change them, but had never got around to it. Now she couldn't help feeling the message was meant for today.

Clare . . . ?

That voice. One word, one syllable, and she knew it was him. The boy on the bench staring at his knees instead of looking her in the eye. The boy on the bench saying he didn't want a baby with her. Not now, meaning not ever. As ducks circled the sunken Tesco shopping trolley and Clare felt — and would swear this on her own life — a kick inside.

She stood in the doorway hovering between kitchen and living room, staring as the green light flashed, bringing his voice back into her life.

Um, I'm guessing I've got the right Clare? I'm looking for Clare Adams who grew up in Hendon and went to King Henry in the early nineties. This is Will, er, William Drew. If it's you, Clare, you know why I'm calling and obviously I won't go into it here . . .

Almost fourteen and a half years of suppressed fury propelled her across the living room and her hand was lifting the receiver before she could stop herself.

'How fucking dare you?' she exploded. 'How

146

dare you call my home and threaten me?'

'Clare? Clare, is that you?' Same voice, but now it was in her ear she could hear it was older, had matured. As, of course, had its owner.

It was a voice that said doctor. *Now Mrs Adams, what seems to be the problem?*

You! You're the problem!

'Yes, it's me,' she said, feeling the fight drain from her body as quickly as it had flooded in. 'Who were you expecting?'

'Louisa sounds . . . She sounds *feisty*,' he said. 'On the answer phone, I mean. Like her mother.'

It wasn't true and Clare knew it. Maybe she had been like that once, back then. But not for years. Fourteen years of single-motherhood had ground the feistiness out of her. The most you could say for Clare Adams now was that she was dogged.

'What do you want?'

'I want — I mean, I would like — to see my daughter.'

'Well, you can't.'

'Please, at least consider it.'

'Why? Why should I?'

'Why not? No, don't answer that. It was a long time ago, Clare, things change. I've changed.'

What did that mean? Clare wondered. What was he trying to say? Had he changed towards her? Did he have . . . regrets?

'I think we should meet,' Will was saying. 'At least talk about it. Please?'

Clare didn't trust herself to speak. Now her fury had lessened she could feel herself softening towards him and she couldn't let that happen. She couldn't let Will back in. She felt the silence of her indecision lengthen between them.

'Clare,' he repeated. 'Like it or not, Louisa *is* my daughter. And I want to see her, get to know her . . . Provide for her.'

'A bit late for that.'

'You know that's not entirely fair . . . '

Yes it is, Clare wanted to scream. *Go back where you came from.*

But she could hear a key in the lock at street level, a door slam and oversized teenaged feet stamping up the lower flight of stairs.

Clare wanted to hang up, but she knew Will would only call back. Now, or later. And when he did, she might not be the one to answer the phone.

Lou might.

'OK,' she said. 'I'll meet you. But not here. You're not coming here.'

The footsteps were louder now, dragging on the final flight of stairs, complaint implicit in each worn-to-death Dr Marten-clad footstep. Clare wondered what she'd done — or not done — for Louisa this time.

'Tell me where,' she said, her voice low. 'Somewhere away from here, somewhere in the centre . . . '

Somewhere there was no chance of Lou seeing them. Putting two and two together and coming up with fourteen.

★ ★ ★

'Erin! Erin! Over here!'

The statuesque model turned, all raven hair

148

and crimson lips, and smiled, setting off an explosion of flashlights.

The red carpet outside the Victoria & Albert Museum was thick with models, designers and fashion industry celebrities. For the first time since arriving in London as Simeon's accessory of the season (aka his latest wife), Melanie slipped past the paparazzi unpapped. Only one of them even so much as threw her a glance. Something about her expensive hair, designer gown and almond eyes obviously rang a bell. Then he clocked Vince beside her. No, said the photographer's expression, just another fashion nobody.

Not an unwelcome experience for Melanie, but new all the same. In the weeks after Simeon left her, Melanie had been unable to step outside without one of the paparazzi who camped there taking her picture. But they weren't looking for glitz and glamour, then. They'd been after something different. Melanie as heartbroken stick with which to beat Simeon Jones, billionaire shagger about town. Although to be fair to Poppy, which Melanie was disinclined to be, it was she who had taken most of the flak. Poppy King was the other woman, the home wrecker, Melanie the victim; Simeon was just a bit player in the media's girl-on-girl blame game.

'You OK?' asked Vince, squeezing her hand.

'Uh-huh.' Melanie forced a smile to her lips. Try as she might, she couldn't make it reach her eyes. *C'mon Melanie*, she thought, pushing through the revolving doors into the entrance hall. *You can do this. It's not like you haven't done it a thousand times before.*

She hadn't wanted to come to the Fashion Awards at all. In the three years she'd been with Simeon, Melanie had been to the opening of more envelopes than most people manage in a lifetime. Simeon had insisted on it. His job depended on his profile, and, as far as he was concerned, his profile — their profile — was her job. Private views at galleries in Mayfair, designer store openings on Sloane Street, black-tie charity fund-raisers, and luncheons for ladies who lunched.

But being nominated for a British Fashion Award was a huge deal for *personalshopper*. The column inches and resulting hits on her website, an astonishing seventy per cent of which led directly to sales (according to Vince), could be bigger still.

'It's recognition enough to be nominated,' she told Grace when the invitation arrived. 'We won't win, so there's no need for me to go. It's a waste of my time and *personalshopper*'s money . . . Both valuable resources,' she added pointedly, pushing from her mind the much-needed publicity; the opportunity to network; the fact that not bothering to show was just plain rude, not to mention selfish.

And Melanie Cheung had been brought up to be neither rude nor selfish. The fact was, life was beginning to feel good away from the limelight. Slowly but surely, thanks to *personalshopper* and Vince and even the SSG, Melanie was beginning to feel like herself again. Melanie Cheung, straight-A student, fast-track lawyer, a success on

150

her own terms and no one else's. She'd always been a back-room girl at heart. She minded her own business and let other people mind theirs. Vince was the same, which was one of the things they had in common.

Grace had just rolled her eyes and shrugged. 'Have it your way,' she said, turning on her heel and heading out of the office, muttering not quite under her breath, '*chicken*.'

That was all it had taken.

And so here Melanie was, wearing a liquid jersey vintage Halston gown in metallic grey borrowed for the night, Vince by her side — looking, if she did say so herself, pretty hot in an Armani tux, omnipresent stubble shaved off in honour of the occasion. Tending towards the craggy, his looks had slid into place as he progressed through his thirties. He had probably always looked forty — and always would. And every second woman — those who didn't stop her to tell her how much they loved *personalshopper*, how, in fact, *personalshopper* had changed their lives — glanced her way anyway, Melanie was pretty sure, to eye Vince.

'Who knew,' Vince whispered, 'that internet shopping could change the world? If only someone had told Angelina Jolie, she could have saved herself the inconvenience of adopting all those orphans.'

Melanie snorted champagne bubbles up her nose.

Even Vince had begun to relax. In the Mercedes on the way from Kings Cross, Melanie had wondered if she was doing the right thing bringing him as her plus one. After his ninth attempt to knot his bow tie, the tension in the back had been so obvious she'd been tempted to lean over him, open his door and push him out.

In the end she'd settled for scolding him.

'For crying out loud, Vince,' she said. 'You're meant to be here as my moral support, not the other way around. If you didn't want to come, all you had to do was say.'

He'd looked at her, sheepish. His brown eyes sad, his bow tie still undone, the unruly salt and pepper hair he'd spent the best part of ten minutes trying to comb down before they left, springing back up. 'Sorry, Melanie,' he said. 'I just . . . Well, I'm out of my league here.'

'Don't be crazy, you look gorgeous. I would!' she winked.

'I don't, but thanks,' he squeezed her knee through the fabric of her dress. 'But that's not what I'm talking about.'

Melanie waited.

'I don't even know what I'm supposed to say to these . . . fashion people. They're going to ask what I do, I'll tell them *systems* and that'll be that. B-o-ring!'

'*Personalshopper* would be nothing without your software. They'll all be trying to poach you.'

Vince rolled his eyes; a faux yawn turning into a real one.

'Anyway. You don't have to say anything if you don't want to. Just stick to *Hello* and *What do you do?* In fact, scratch that, or you'll be asking Alexander McQueen what he does, and that would not be good. Anyway, you're not coming to talk to them, you're coming to talk to me.'

Then she'd set about knotting his tie once and for all.

★ ★ ★

'Is it my imagination,' Vince asked, after Melanie had spent five minutes making small talk to an up-and-coming designer. 'Or am I the only straight man here?'

'Not quite,' Melanie said. 'Why? Fancy your chances?'

'As if.' Vince leant in and kissed her neck. 'I'm just thinking, with all these women around, I should have brought my mates!'

'That's it! That's my next business idea,' Melanie said, laughing. 'An on-line dating agency putting women in fashion together with men in systems. Seriously, though, they're not all gay. Most men in retail aren't . . . '

Only Vince wasn't listening, not really.

'Melanie,' he said. 'I was thinking . . . ' Putting out his hand, he dumped his empty champagne flute on a passing tray and took up a new one.

'How about Saturday to meet Ellie?'

Melanie took a gulp from her own glass to hide her shock. She shouldn't be taken aback, not really. She'd been expecting this for weeks. Secretly thankful with each weekend that passed without it. 'Well,' she said, playing for time. 'You certainly pick your moments.'

'Not really,' said Vince. 'Look, forget I mentioned it.'

'I just wasn't expecting it right now,' Melanie

153

said hurriedly. 'Of course, yes. I'd love to meet Ellie.'

'Really? You will?' Vince slid an arm around her waist and squeezed her. 'Thanks. I've told her so much about you. You'll love each other. I know you will.'

Melanie wasn't so sure — Eve's unhappy experiences with Hannah and Lily's, admittedly funny, retelling of her elder sister's behaviour when she met their father's new wife at thirteen were enough to give anyone the jitters. She was almost glad when the call for dinner echoed around the foyer, ending their conversation.

Since their skinny, blonde minder was nowhere to be seen, Melanie and Vince joined the crowd shuffling up the marble steps and along a maze of corridors that led to the gallery where the dinner tables were laid.

'Wow,' Vince muttered, more than once. Melanie wasn't sure whether at the Victorian nudes or the dress Kate Moss was just about wearing.

Their minder, Charlotte, caught up with them just as they descended the grand stone staircase into the gallery. 'Ms Cheung, Ms Cheung,' she called, pointing to a table near the centre of the long thin room, just in front of the stage. 'Your seats are right over here.'

It was a good table, one of the best.

Wondering if that was significant, Melanie decided it wasn't and reached back to clutch Vince's hand. Only to discover he wasn't there. As the staircase had split in two halfway down he'd become separated in the crush and taken the other direction. Casting around Melanie saw him standing forlornly at the foot of the other staircase. He looked about twelve.

'You sit down,' Charlotte said. 'I'll get him.' She muttered darkly into her headset and disappeared between tables.

Conscious the hem of her borrowed gown was dangerously close to everyone else's five-inch heels, Melanie hitched up her skirts and began weaving through the crowd towards her table, nodding to those who nodded to her as she pushed past. Whether they knew her as Mel Jones or Melanie Cheung, she had no idea.

There was now only one table between Melanie and her seat, but every inch of the space surrounding it seemed full of photographers, even though an unmissably huge sign at the top of the staircase announced 'No Photography'.

The only way forward was through them, so she put her head down and ploughed on.

She was nearly there, home dry, when one of the photographers called: 'Poppy! Over here Poppy!'

Melanie froze. She could have misheard. And there might be a dozen Poppies who warranted a paparazzi frenzy . . . but somehow Melanie knew she hadn't, and there weren't. This was the British fashion industry event of the year. If Poppy King-Jones was in the country, of course she'd be here. Why the hell hadn't anyone thought to warn Melanie? If only to give her time to prepare herself.

Melanie knew why.

Because if they had warned her she'd have pulled out.

Frantically, Melanie looked for a way to avoid the inevitable. The thing she'd successfully avoided for two years. Until now.

The crowd behind was pushing her, sweeping Melanie inexorably forward. To her left stood an almost full, white-clothed table laden with silver and glass, arranged around the most implausible floral centrepiece she'd ever seen. To her right was the table around which the photographers swarmed. Her own was beyond that.

'Poppy! How did you lose the baby weight so quickly?'

'Let's have a shot with Simeon!'

At what point the scrum put two and two together and got a scoop, Melanie didn't know. But one of them did, and it was probably the man with the beard and glasses who had clocked her an hour earlier. Melanie only knew she'd been recognized because his camera was suddenly in her face.

'Mel, Mel Jones, isn't it?'

'It's Cheung. Melanie Cheung.'

'Mel, give us a smile.'

'Simeon Jones's ex?' The whisper went around. 'What's she doing here? Where?'

Melanie saw the exact moment Simeon turned in her direction, his eyes scanning the crowd for her, his expression pitched between annoyance and horror. Bespoke Savile Row dinner jacket, silk shirt, immaculately-knotted bow tie. Simeon couldn't see her; that much was obvious. But she could see him.

Them.

This was clearly not part of his plan. And

156

Melanie knew, to her cost, that Simeon hated things not going to plan. In Simeon's world, there was zero tolerance for surprises.

At least, she thought bleakly, he'd been as much in the dark about her attendance as she'd been about his. A small mercy, but better than nothing.

Somewhere an organizer was experiencing the excitement that came with knowing they had — unwittingly, or not — unleashed a PR maelstrom to dominate the next morning's papers and guarantee the Fashion Awards blanket coverage. The poor winners would barely get a look-in.

'Mel. Over here.'

'It's Melanie, actually,' Melanie said, her voice quiet but firm, scarcely audible above the shots. 'Melanie Cheung. And I mean it, no pictures, thank you.'

But no one was listening. Or if they were they chose not to hear — and a phalanx of photographers turned their cameras on her. Melanie forced a smile. Knowing the drill, knowing she had no choice. She gave the photographers three pictures and then turned her back, hoping tears hadn't reached her eyes before the final shutter clicked.

'What was that about?' Vince demanded when she reached their table.

Melanie couldn't look at him.

'I said,' he whispered, a shade louder than strictly necessary. 'What was that about?' He didn't bother to fix the smile to his face that she had glued to her own for the benefit of the rest of the table.

'Simeon,' she hissed through gritted teeth.

'What about him?'

'Simeon,' she repeated. 'Simeon and Poppy.'

'What about it?' Vince said. 'What's he got to do with you now?'

Before she could stop herself, Melanie turned on him, 'For Christ's sake, just leave it alone, will you?'

★ ★ ★

What followed were the longest three hours of Melanie's life. Three gruelling courses of food she didn't want or taste, peppered with small talk and blatant staring, during which Vince spoke only to ask if she needed water, and downed glass after glass of his own. Something cold, dry and white, and definitely not mineral water. When *personalshopper* didn't even get a special mention for Highly Commended, it was a relief.

★ ★ ★

'What the fuck was that?'

Their chauffeur had barely shut the car door before Vince started in.

He was pissed. Pissed and pissed off, and Melanie didn't blame him. Trouble was, she was still so shell-shocked she couldn't bring herself to much care either.

'Don't,' she said. 'Vince, just don't, not now. OK?'

'Don't 'Vince, just don't' me,' Vince almost spat. 'It's not OK.'

Melanie had never seen him like this, never had cause to, and she knew it wasn't good. How could it be? It wasn't the side you saw of someone in the early days of a relationship. At least not if that relationship was going anywhere.

'You drag me to . . . that room full of arseholes and twiglets, then you ignore me for the entire evening because . . . because your fucking ex and his new girlfriend are there?'

'She's his wife,' Melanie said. 'The mother of his child.'

'Whatever. I don't give a fuck who she is. I care about the fact my so-called girlfriend has just treated me like shit in front of . . . in front of everyone. You drag me into your world and then do that to me.'

'It's not my world.'

'Well, it's fucking not mine!'

Melanie didn't understand why Vince didn't understand.

How would he feel if he was confronted with his ex and her new husband for the first time in front of five hundred strangers and every paparazzo in London? How would he like being splashed on tomorrow's papers, next week's gossip mags and all over the internet, indefinitely?

Outside the limousine's windows, Hyde Park loomed in the darkness as the car passed the Albert Memorial and curved up towards Park Lane. Vince was still muttering, but Melanie wasn't listening. Staring blindly at the back of their driver's head, she wondered if he was

159

listening to Vince's rant. Or whether it was all in a day's work to him. She knew chauffeurs were paid not to listen, but that didn't mean they couldn't hear.

As the car approached Marble Arch, Vince leant forward. 'Hey,' he said rudely, tapping the driver on the shoulder. 'Let me out here, will you?'

'Right here?' the driver asked. He didn't need to point out that right here was in the middle of the three lanes of traffic circling the Marble Arch roundabout. It might have been midnight, but central London was still in gridlock.

'That's what I said. Right here.'

'You're the boss.'

'Vince, don't be stupid.' It was the first thing Melanie had said for several minutes. Her voice sounded hollow even to her. 'How will you get home?'

'I'll get a cab or a night bus, like the rest of London.' Vince paused. 'Public transport,' he said, 'it's what real people use.'

If she hadn't been so anaesthetized by shock, confusion and alcohol, his words might have stung. Instead she just stared at him. Seeing how fury hardened his face and narrowed his eyes. For a moment she wasn't even sure she recognized him.

'I love you,' he said, hand resting on the door handle, 'but I'm buggered if I'm going to be with someone who's in love with someone else.'

The car door swung open, narrowly missing a motorbike filtering between the two lanes.

'I am not in love with Simeon,' Melanie said

160

irritably. *Men. Why did it always have to be about other men?*

'So you say.' Vince was looking at her. As if waiting for her to do something, say something. Quite what, she didn't know.

'You aren't over him, that's for sure.'

13

'Matt! How much longer are you planning to be in there?' Mandy shouted through the locked bathroom door, not for the first time in the last hour.

On the other side, water thundered down, and downstairs Mandy's ancient boiler wheezed on.

'Matt!' Mandy yelled again, this time banging the heel of her hand against the wood.

The water slowed to a drip and plastic rings clattered as the old shower curtain was yanked back.

'What?' came her eldest son's voice.

'I said,' Mandy tried to suppress her exasperation, 'how much longer?'

'Not long. Going out soon.'

And the water started up again.

Glancing at her watch, Mandy sighed, seven-thirty p.m. Where had the afternoon gone? Wandering into her room — her and John's room, Mandy corrected herself — she tossed a box of Schwarzkopf root retoucher onto the bed. It bounced, and landed on the floor.

Oh well, her roots would have to do. It was the thought that counted, after all.

Mandy had been debating getting her roots done at the salon on Clapham High Road ever since Lily invited her to the SSG, only she hadn't got around to it. Just as she'd debated doing a home dye job. Debated it, bought the kit, just

162

hadn't moved fast enough to grab the mid-terrace's only bathroom when John left to take Jack and Izzy back to their mother's.

At the far end of the landing, the shower stopped and, in the kitchen below, the boiler stuttered gratefully to a halt. Mandy could hear her eldest son bang shut the medicine cabinet door. Through force of habit, Mandy snatched up the hair dye from where it still lay and headed for the bedroom door. With three teenage-ish boys in permanent residence and another two teenagers in and out, you had to move fast in this house.

Minutes crawled past as Mandy kept one ear on the bathroom and the other on the street outside for the sound of John's Peugeot. Finally, the bolt slid back and Matt shuffled past to his room. Waiting just long enough for him to get inside, she slipped around the door, almost sprinted along the landing and pushed open the bathroom door. A cloud of hot steam and Lynx assailed her, sodden towels were strewn over the flooded floor, condensation misted the mirror and every tile. No wonder mould was forming in the ceiling corners.

'Ma — ,' Mandy started. And stopped. It would be quicker just to clear his mess up herself.

When the bathroom was tidied, clean towels found, dirty ones bundled into the laundry basket, and she could see her hand in front of her face and her face in the mirror, Mandy pulled the dripping shower curtain from the bath, turned the hot tap on full and returned her attention to the box of dye.

Idly she dangled her hand under the tap to check the temperature, and snatched it away. Cold. Not just cold, the water was freezing. Mandy turned the tap off and then on again, just to check she hadn't been running cold by mistake. No, still cold. The immersion tank was empty.

'Bloody kids,' Mandy muttered, twisting the tap irritably and pulling the plug. Matt had used all the water. Looked like her roots would have to go *au naturel* after all.

Defeated, Mandy headed downstairs to iron the boys' school shirts. Now there was an exercise in futility. But still she did it every Sunday night without fail, because there was no way Mandy McMasters's boys were going to school looking like tramps. If they came home looking like tramps . . . well, that was another thing entirely.

Sometimes it amazed Mandy how long she spent doing things that looked as if they hadn't been done fifteen minutes later. Ironing, washing, cooking, cleaning. All things that were satisfying for, ooh, five minutes. And then all signs of her hard work were obliterated by the appetites, scuffling and clomping size ten feet of five teenagers.

★ ★ ★

The obviously uneasy woman who hesitated in the doorway of Starbucks looked as if she was about to turn around and walk straight out

164

again. West Soho they called this area now, according to a sign outside. But whatever they called it, the street, the café, the area, they weren't her kind of thing.

She was turning to go when someone called her name.

'Mandy!'

She'd left it too long to make her decision. Story of her life really. So she sat at the chair they'd saved for her, nodded hello as Lily introduced them all, although she didn't really take in their names, and thanked Lily for the coffee, when it arrived. But what she really wanted to say was, 'Why the hell did you invite me here?'

Mandy imagined herself as the others must see her; smart but cheap knee-length skirt (navy), knee-length, re-heeled boots (black); round-necked jumper (pink). Her work clothes were the only ones she had that were remotely smart enough.

Of course, there was that purple Monsoon wrap dress from a few years back; bought shortly before Dave moved out. She could still remember twirling in it for him to admire, while he hissed in irritation and tried to see the football scores around her.

How much? he'd demanded, when *Final Score* was finally over. *A bloody fortune.* Immediately trampling on all the joy she'd drawn from choosing the dress, trying it on and buying it in a sale.

That thought, the memory of Dave, nearly finished her off. What little self-confidence she'd brought to the table shrivelled and died.

What on earth was she thinking?

Risking a glance up from her extortionately-priced mug of coffee, her eyes met those of the woman with the mass of dark bouncy curls. Mandy forced a smile, and looked away before she could see if it was returned.

I don't belong here, she thought. *I should never have come.*

What was it her mother always said? *Don't get ideas above your station. Don't give yourself airs.* There were plenty more where those came from.

Mandy sighed.

The coffee wasn't even that good, she thought, sipping its dregs to avoid making any more accidental eye contact. Not that much nicer than instant; certainly not enough to warrant the price at any rate. It was watery, and too milky for her taste.

It was only when Lily asked for an extra shot, and the glamorous-looking Chinese woman demanded skimmed milk on the side that Mandy realized she could have done the same.

It hadn't occurred to her.

You ordered a coffee, it came, you drank it. She didn't spend much time in coffee shops. Who had the time? Come to that, who had the money? Not her, that was for sure.

The glamorous-looking one, the one with the long, shiny hair and beautiful almond eyes, whose clothes even Mandy could tell must have cost Mandy's entire monthly maintenance (when Dave bothered to pay at all), was telling a

166

complicated story involving an award ceremony, an ex husband, a new boyfriend and a big row. It seemed to Mandy that she was more upset about her ex and his new wife than the row with her new man. But Mandy didn't say so, obviously. She was the new girl.

'Grim,' Lily said.

'Has it occurred to you,' said Lily's sister. 'That you're more upset about seeing Simeon with Poppy than you are about the row with Vince?'

Mandy nodded agreement, as a chorus of disapproval ricocheted around their table from the others.

'Clare!' the curly-haired one cried. 'You just can't help yourself can you?'

'Jeezus,' Lily added. 'Call a spade a bloody shovel, why don't you?'

'It's just an observation,' Lily's sister said. 'And since when did we introduce censorship? Melanie asked what we thought. That's what I think. Vince is right. Melanie's not over Simeon, if you ask me. And she did, didn't you Melanie? Ask, I mean.'

Melanie nodded bleakly, clearly wishing she hadn't asked.

Mandy was warming to Lily's sister, a few years older and obviously sensible, not that Mandy could see a family likeness. And not that warming was the right word. Clare was too prickly for that, wearing her opinions like armour. But still, Mandy liked her for having the courage to say what Mandy had been thinking. Mandy was drawn to people who said what they thought. More than that, she admired them, precisely because she never did.

'You're wrong,' Melanie said. 'I don't want Simeon back. I wouldn't have him back if he came crawling on bended knee.'

'That's not the same thing at all,' Clare pointed out. 'There's a big difference between wanting him back and being over him.'

'Takes one to know one,' muttered Lily.

Clare scowled at her.

'Enough about me,' Melanie said brightly, fooling no one. 'Tell us about you Mandy. Lily's told us a bit already, but I'd like to know more.'

The other four women turned, and Mandy felt blinded, like someone had undipped their headlights and shone them in her face. She hated being the centre of attention. Even on her wedding day, if she could have avoided being in the photographs she would have done.

'Um, not much to tell really,' she said, tugging at her Next skirt (fifty per cent off, last season's sale) and wishing she'd worn jeans instead. Not that her jeans looked anything like the ones Lily and Melanie wore. Hers were strictly weekend jeans, more suited to gardening and housework than coffee up West.

'Of course there is,' Lily said reassuringly. 'Go on.'

'Honestly,' Mandy said, seeing there was no way out of this. 'It's all pretty ordinary really. I'm divorced, obviously. We were together twenty years, married seventeen. I've got three boys, teenagers, near enough. Matt, the eldest, he's sixteen. He's like me — quiet, bit of a plodder, just keeps his head down and gets on with it, with luck that will be enough to get him through his GCSEs next summer. Jason's the youngest, he's twelve. Nothing bothers him apart from his stomach and football. And then there's Nathan,' she took a breath and looked at the women watching her. Where to start with her middle son? 'He . . . gets more like his father with every passing day. Not just physically, although there's no denying the likeness, it's more his personality. Human bulldozer. Just like Dave.'

Mandy gave a shudder and hoped no one else noticed. Please God, she thought, mentally lighting a candle, don't let Nathan turn out to be too much his father's son.

Realizing the others were waiting, she picked up where she'd left off. 'Dave's my ex, he walked out three and a half years ago now. I'm not sure which of us was more relieved in the end. Doesn't see much of his kids, only pays up when the CSA makes him. And doesn't see why he should pay at all now John's moved in. John's my, erm, boyfriend,' she explained unnecessarily.

It was a strange word, *boyfriend*. Mandy still couldn't get used to it, and it sounded even more wrong when applied to a forty-three-year-old. But what else was there? Partner was too women's magazine. Lover was too Jackie Collins. Other half sounded like a sitcom.

'Dave says he won't pay to have some other bloke live in his house. Which is complete b — rubbish. For a start, it's not his, it's mine and his kids' now. And he's not paying for *some bloke*, he's paying for his children's food, school

169

uniforms, that kind of thing. Not that what he pays even begins to cover it. Anyway, John has two kids of his own to pay for.'

'How did you and John meet?' Lily asked.

Mandy looked embarrassed. 'Through work. I work at that solicitors above the butcher's. You know the one?'

Lily didn't, but she nodded anyway.

'Worked there since the boys started school. Part-time, just to make a bit of extra cash. They let me go full-time after Dave left. John works in the council offices just down the road. Funny how we never came across each other before. He came in when his wife said she wanted a divorce. When he came to pay his final bill, we got talking. He asked me for a drink and we went from there.'

Thank God, she thought, but didn't say.

At the point he'd asked, it had just begun to dawn on Mandy that she had to 'get back out there'. It was either face the horrors of dating again or spend the rest of her life on the shelf. Dating? On the shelf? Where did those words come from? Sometimes she felt as if she'd gone to bed one night and woken up in the 1950s.

'And what about John's children?' Eve was asking. 'How do you get on with them?'

Eve looked genuinely interested. So interested, in fact, that Mandy half expected her to whip out a notepad.

'They're good kids,' Mandy said, finding her voice. 'They come to us every other weekend. Well, Jack does. He's thirteen, the same age as Nathan, and he gets on OK with my boys. But

Izzy's fifteen. It's not that we don't get on. We do. And I'm fond of her, actually. She's a good kid. But, you know, she's *fifteen*.'

Mandy gave the others a meaningful look.

'Fifteen's bad?' Eve asked. She looked worried. 'I'm having enough trouble with thirteen.'

'Try fourteen,' said Clare. 'That's worse.'

'I just wasn't expecting having a stepdaughter to be so complicated,' Mandy said apologetically. 'Like I said, mine are boys, so I'm used to the noise and the mess. Their teenage stuff starts a bit later. And even when they're properly moody it's different. Matt either locks himself in the bathroom and fumigates the house with Lynx, or shuts himself in his room and plays rap so loud the entire terrace shakes.'

She glanced at Lily, who laughed and nodded, 'It's true. You can hear it out on the street. Still,' she grinned to show Mandy she wasn't complaining, 'we've all been there.'

'Izzy's fine,' Mandy said. 'She just doesn't want to spend her weekends hanging out in a house full of teenage boys, and I don't blame her. She wants to see her dad, but she'd rather see him on his own. And she's not interested in me. She's got a mum after all, and the only boys she's interested in are older than Matt and hate rap.'

'The indie crowd,' Lily said, nodding.

'It's called emo now,' Clare told her.

Lily rolled her eyes.

'I had this idea we'd be one big happy family,' Mandy said. 'But it's not happening. Izzy stayed over once, but there's not really room for her. My boys have their own rooms and Jack normally sleeps on Jason's floor, but Izzy had to sleep on the settee. Between you and me, I think the lack of space is just an excuse. She comes for Sunday lunch sometimes — not that she eats it — and that's about it. John seems happy enough with it, but it's not how I imagined it would be.'

Mandy caught Eve and Clare exchanging a glance. She didn't know what their glance meant but it made her nervous. She stopped.

'Weekends must be a barrel of laughs,' Lily said.

Mandy shrugged, too intimidated to continue.

'Sounds hard,' Eve said. 'I thought I had it bad, but I've only got three to deal with and none of them are mine. At least Ian and I aren't having to try to glue two sets of reluctant kids together.'

'Blending, they call it,' Clare said, in teacher mode.

'Feels more like liquidizing most of the time,' Mandy laughed.

'Well, it makes me feel like a fraud,' said Melanie.

Mandy was taken by surprise. 'Really?'

'Absolutely. Mind you I feel like I'm here on false pretences every time we meet. Here I am angsting about a child I haven't even met yet and you're juggling five. I can't even cope with the idea of one.'

'I'm sure that's not true,' Mandy said.

'It is,' Clare and Melanie said in unison.

'We-ell,' said Mandy. 'It wasn't exactly part of the plan. But it's what there is and I have to make the best of it.'

★ ★ ★

Her plan, if she'd been the kind of woman to have one, would have included roses around the door and adorable children playing in the garden and a happy marriage — for life — to a man who came home from work every day at six, maybe seven. They'd sit down for the supper she'd cooked, while the children, all clean and neat in their pyjamas, watched television and went to bed when they were told. And that was how it had been, for a time. Give or take the roses, and the clean, well-behaved children.

She hadn't ever wanted much, Mandy thought.

For a girl like her, nice but ordinary, bright but not academic, attractive enough, but not stunning, meeting a man who earned enough to pay for a nice house and was happy for her to stay home and bring up their children was as much as she could hope for. It was certainly all she'd wanted.

And for a while, she'd had it.

Or it had looked that way from outside. A four-bedroom terrace at the wrong end of Clapham, three well brought-up boys, a husband who ran his own building company; not swimming in money, but enough for essentials and, occasionally, treats. The kids and Mandy had never really gone without. Materially.

Divorce. Single motherhood.

Living with a man who had kids with another woman, while your teenage sweetheart, the boy you thought you'd spend the rest of your life with, the groom you promised to love and honour moved in with his secretary. Now *that* had never been part of her plan.

But was it worse, really, than being married to someone who used you as a cleaner and a childminder and only came home when he wanted his clothes washed? Because that was what her life with Dave had become by the end. And for most of the middle too. Dave had been having an affair. Maybe affairs, Mandy didn't know which. Even now, he denied it. Furiously, aggressively, terrifyingly. Although he'd moved in with Angela from work quickly enough, and as far as Mandy was concerned that was all the proof she needed.

★ ★ ★

'Grim,' Lily repeated, when Mandy reached the end. *Grim* seemed to be a Lily word.

'Yes,' Mandy agreed. 'Grim is right.'

'D'you think anyone's life works out?' Melanie asked. 'Like the plan, I mean? If they do, I've yet to meet them. Mine didn't. If you'd told me when I was in my twenties, a fast-track corporate lawyer, that I'd end up the dumped trophy wife of a billionaire ego maniac and publicly humiliated by a bimbo in Versace I'd probably have slapped you!'

174

'Millionaire,' Lily said.

Melanie looked at her.

'Not billionaire. The recession must have hit him like everyone else.'

'Here's hoping,' said Melanie, draining the dregs of her latte.

'I know exactly what you mean about plans,' Lily said. 'I was in an accessories shop the other day — buying pink glittery things, as you do — and it hit me. How did this happen? What happened to the comedy circuit, performing at the Edinburgh Fringe, becoming the first woman to win a Perrier Award?'

'Not the first,' Clare said. 'That's been done.'

'Well, two years running, then. And then, wham, bam . . . I meet this gorgeous, interesting, sexy — drunk — Irishman,' she laughed. 'And suddenly, I'm twenty-three years old and spending my Saturdays choosing between pink sparkly and purple sparkly with a three-year-old. Like, hello?!'

'Hang on,' Clare said. 'If we're going to talk about plans being wrecked, how about me? I was going to be the twenty-first-century Jane Austen, remember?'

The look Clare gave Lily was sad. 'You don't remember, do you?'

Lily shook her head. 'I was too young for that version of you.'

'Instead you got the single mum at nineteen who spent the rest of her life teaching the works of bloody Charlotte Brontë to classes full of fifteen-year-olds who'd rather be reading celebrity magazines.'

175

'Who wouldn't?' Lily said, and Mandy burst out laughing.

'What about you?' she asked Eve. 'What was your master plan?'

Eve shrugged. She wasn't sure she liked this game. She'd been planning to tell them about moving to Chiswick, about her growing relationship with Alfie, about how Hannah was still so furious with her dad for moving Eve into their family that she was barely speaking to either of them. But now didn't seem to be the time.

'Me?' she said casually. 'Oh, I was never much of a one for plans.'

Clare snorted, sloshing coffee onto the table.

'Give me a break,' she said. 'You've had a five-year plan ever since I first met you. Get your degree. Get a job on a magazine. Get that promotion. Then get the next one. The only part of your life there's never been a plan for — to my knowledge — is the love bit. Ironic really, when you look at how things have turned out.'

* * *

Laughing she turned to Eve. But Eve wasn't laughing, she wasn't even looking at Clare, she was staring hard at the table.

What? Clare wanted to ask. *What did I say?* But there was no chance of making eye contact, Eve was making sure of that.

Thinking back to college there had been the one guy, Clare remembered. But, so far as she knew, Eve — as ever — had done the dumping.

It had been in the second year, and this one,

176

Steve, she thought his name was. Yes, Steve, that was it. He was tall, lanky, thin-faced with floppy hair and small wire-rimmed glasses, when vanity allowed him to wear them. Studied English and played bass in an Irish folk-rock band. Not that he was Irish.

Now Clare thought about it, most of Eve's five-minute men had looked like Steve. Even Ian probably, back in the day, before time took its toll and he shaved his hair off altogether rather than watch it recede.

This Steve guy had hung around their student house for half the second year, waiting for Eve to throw him a bone, poor bastard. At least that was how it had looked to the other girls in the house. They'd almost felt sorry for him, when they weren't ripping the piss out of him behind his back for being so pathetic. He was an OK bloke. And he hadn't even been *too* freaked out by Louisa toddling in and out, although that was relative.

But when the summer term started, Steve was gone and Eve was non-committal as to why. When Clare finally cornered her to ask what had happened, Eve just shrugged. She had exams to pass and Steve was getting in the way; he was getting too heavy; and besides, they didn't really have anything in common (delete as applicable). Why she'd let Eve get away with stonewalling her, Clare would never know.

And to judge by the look on Eve's face, that was not about to change now.

★ ★ ★

If only she knew, thought Eve. And, not for the first time, was beyond grateful that Clare didn't.

'OK, OK,' Eve said. 'I admit it. Not so much plans as mantras. No men messing up my life. No marriage getting in the way of my career. And definitely — *definitely* — no kids . . . ' she hesitated. 'Mine, or anyone else's.'

14

Ian's house was quiet. Well, as quiet as any house could be that contained a five-and-a-half-year-old boy glued to back-to-back episodes of Power Rangers turned up so loud the sash windows shook. Ian had taken Sophie to ballet classes and Hannah riding. Then he was going to Waitrose to get some last-minute bits for lunch.

Eve was glad of the peace. A squabble, a couple of near misses and a full-on argument about gumboots. It wasn't really how she'd expected living together to be.

To judge by the deathly silence coming from the stairs to the loft conversion, Inge was spending her day off asleep in her room at the top of the house. Eve didn't blame her.

Alfie had begged to be allowed to stay behind with Eve. He didn't want to go to the *boring* shops to buy *boring* food. So Eve, still surfacing from sleep that had only come as daylight and the dawn chorus arrived, promised to keep an ear on him. One ear was right. She was sure he'd already consumed his entire weekend's allowance of TV-viewing. The television was turned up so loud she could hear every zap and kapow through the black-stained floorboards of Ian's bedroom.

Her and Ian's bedroom, Eve corrected herself. *Our* bedroom.

It certainly didn't feel that way. At best, Eve

179

felt like a guest; at worst, an interloper. Either way, she didn't feel like the house — or even this room — was remotely hers. It still came as a surprise when she opened the wardrobe door and found her clothes inside.

Flinging on yesterday's jeans and a clean T-shirt, she wandered barefoot onto the landing. The door to Hannah's bedroom was firmly shut. But with Hannah safely out of the house it took all Eve's willpower not to try the handle. The urge to take just one tiny peek inside Hannah's world was almost overwhelming, but Eve resisted.

She'd been granted entry to Sophie's room several times in the past couple of weeks. It was common-or-garden tweenager, floor-to-ceiling High School Musical, Hannah Montana, you name it . . . And she was scarcely out of Alfie's room. ('Come and look at this, Evie. Come and play battles. You haven't said night night. Evie, where are my jammies?' As if she had the faintest idea where his jammies were. That was Ian's domain, and Inge's.) 'Don't worry about the mum-stuff,' Ian had said. 'Just get your head around being here first. You can worry about the rest later.' *Good job, too*, Eve thought. Just living here, under this roof, was so much harder than she'd ever imagined.

★　★　★

The thought of Alfie's tufty head sticking out from under his Spider Man duvet, his sleepy blue eyes struggling to stay open as he claimed not to be even the littlest bit tired, and could she

180

read him just one more story made her heart swell in a way that surprised her.

Eve adored Alfie.

The feeling grew with every passing day. And she knew, instinctively, that he loved her back, in the unquestioning way only small children can. It wasn't that he thought of her as his mummy. He didn't, not for a moment. Alfie would no more call her mummy than he would eat carrots (unless they were pureed and hidden in a bolognese sauce).

She was Evie, and Alfie adored Evie. It was that straightforward.

Even Sophie, Eve dared to hope, was coming round. Ian's younger daughter had even scooched up next to Eve on the sofa the night before, for the latest screening of *HSM3*.

But Hannah . . .

Where to start with Hannah? Eve didn't have the faintest clue.

Hannah was furious.

It wasn't that she didn't feel for the girl. She did. Eve's parents were still together after almost forty years of marriage, come hell or high water (and both had come at various points, and then receded). The most she'd had to contend with as a child was hissed disputes behind a firmly closed kitchen door; and two, maybe three, window-rattling rows. So Eve couldn't begin to imagine how it felt to lose your mother at such a young age and then to be landed with someone else in her place. But, as far as Eve could see, Hannah had decided to hate her almost before she'd met her. And nothing Eve could say or do (short of leaving, she suspected), seemed to make any difference.

She'd tried being friendly, she'd tried generous, she'd tried big sister and kindly aunt. She'd tried inclusive and she'd tried keeping right out of the girl's face. Only the latter had cut any ice at all. And then only because it meant Hannah could carry on as usual, by ignoring her. Without saying a word (beyond 'No' and 'Meh', always accompanied by an exaggerated roll of the eyes), Hannah had made it clear that she, and her room, were firmly out of bounds. The varnished wooden door, with its childish *Hannah's room* plaque, was inoffensive enough, but such was Hannah's hostility that it might as well have had a bio-hazard sign on the door screaming. *No Eves Allowed!*

Sighing, Eve crept downstairs. *Crept.* That just about summed up everything she'd done since she'd moved in three weeks ago.

She picked her way past a pile of plastic men, abandoned mid-battle halfway down the lower stairs, a pink hoodie belonging to Sophie, and a pair of trainers that had not yet made it up, grateful for the obstacles. Navigating them gave her something to do other than examine the classically — framed black-and-white photographs that lined the staircase.

Caroline and the children; Caroline alone; the children in a group; the children individually and in various combinations. Hannah through the ages, growing more like her mother with every birthday. Sophie, a mini Hannah, only developing her father's watchful look in the last few

182

years. And Alfie . . .

Alfie as a baby in Caroline's arms. Alfie as a toddler at his mother's feet. Alfie, this summer, firmly and resolutely himself, his face a picture of concentration. What he was concentrating on no one would ever know, but Eve suspected several plastic men lost their lives as a result.

And, at the bottom, a beautiful triptych of Caroline, probably in her mid-twenties, slim and striking and happy. The kind of woman who turned heads, not because of her beauty, but because of her presence. The portraits could only have been taken by someone who loved her. As Ian obviously had.

Don't, Eve told herself. *That was then. He loves you now.*

Except for the framed photograph on Sophie and Alfie's bedside tables (and, Eve had no doubt, Hannah's too) those were the only pictures in the house of Caroline on her own. *Hannah's favourites*, Ian had said, catching Eve's glance and feeling the need to explain their presence.

Hannah's favourites. A phrase Eve was beginning to recognize as shorthand for something that cannot be moved or changed. *The children like them. It makes them feel secure.* Phrases that signalled both the beginning and end of any conversation about interior decor.

To be fair to Ian, which Eve was trying very hard to be, there were no heart-warming photos of the entire family to make her feel even more excluded. Ian had stayed firmly behind his camera. Or, if he hadn't, he'd been considerate enough to remove the evidence before Eve moved in. Although Eve suspected he'd never been there in the first place, since no other evidence of Caroline had been removed from the house in deference to Eve's sensibilities.

Other than the bedroom — *their* bedroom, she corrected herself — which Ian had refurnished and redecorated after Caroline's death; the house was more or less as she'd left it. Give or take a lick of paint and a few photos.

'It's not Caroline's house, it's mine and theirs,' Ian had said gently when they lay in bed on the night she moved in, after making awkward love. Try as she might, and she had tried, Eve was unable to let go. She didn't know what was wrong with her. Not easily spooked, she just couldn't relax. And it wasn't only the three pairs of small ears on the other side of the bedroom door.

She wasn't sleeping in a dead woman's bed, Ian had promised her that. Not that either of them had used those words. But she was in a dead woman's house and she felt . . . Eve knew it sounded stupid, but she felt somehow watched.

'It's the children's home,' Ian had protested. 'They've lived here their whole lives. I can't just redecorate, not yet. They've got enough to take on board right now. Give it time, Eve. Let them get used to you being here first.' He rolled over and pulled her towards him. 'Now let's see what we can do about your stress levels.'

★ ★ ★

Despite the letting agents' dire warnings that the market was flooded with Buy To Lets, it had taken no time at all for Eve to rent out her flat in Kentish Town.

Disconcertingly quickly, the agent had found a tenant who wanted to move in at the end of the month and was happy to hand over three months' deposit and sign a year's lease on the spot. Before she knew it, Eve was clearing her 'personal effects' and apologizing to her beloved chesterfield sofa (her first big purchase as a home owner) for the inevitable cigarette burns to come.

Her clothes and shoes hadn't presented a problem, although Ian didn't pass up the opportunity to roll his eyes and wonder aloud where his own clothes were meant to go when hers took over an entire wardrobe. Cushions, some pictures, a couple of throws and box after box of books were loaded without comment into the back of the Volvo estate he'd borrowed from his parents.

It was the crockery that started it.

'Why do we need these?' he asked, as she opened a kitchen cupboard and began to load plates and glasses into a cardboard box. Some of it was just old white stuff, the few remaining bits from the set her mum had bought when Eve left home for university. It had no value but sentimental. But the rest was her beloved mismatched china and glass painstakingly found on long Saturday afternoons spent trawling flea markets and junk shops.

Eve stopped packing. 'What d'you mean what

do we need these for? You Newsomes do eat, don't you?' She turned to him grinning, about to move in to kiss him, but the look on his face stopped her. Tired, drawn, irritated, definitely. But love's dream about to move in together? No.

'Eve,' Ian said, tension entering his voice. 'We've got cups and plates and glasses and bowls. You name it, we've got it coming out of our ears.'

'You can always use more,' she said lightly. 'Especially when there are tiny terrors around to smash them.' Ian pulled a face. That was unarguable. The last time she'd been around, Alfie had put paid to a mug. It wouldn't be the last.

'I rest my case,' Eve said, and returned to her packing with an uneasy sense that the subject was not closed.

In the end they'd compromised on two large boxes of china, which Eve had filled to overflowing with as many second-hand cups, saucers, plates and glasses as she could squeeze in. The Mexican jug wouldn't fit, so she stuffed it in a holdall under her sweaters. But that was before Rug-gate.

'Eve, the car's full,' Ian said, looking pained as she rolled up the Afghan that covered the boards of her living room. 'And we don't need any more rugs. We've got rugs coming out of our ears too.'

'It's just one,' she replied. 'I know it's not antique, like yours, but I like it.'

'There's nowhere to put it. And anyway,' Ian said reasonably, 'won't your tenants need it?'

'They're bringing their own,' Eve lied easily.

186

She had no idea what her tenants planned to bring and didn't really care. This was the rug she'd bought when she'd got the job at *Beau*. 'We can take up one of the others, can't we?'

Ian opened his mouth to speak and shut it again, seemingly admitting defeat.

So she brought the rug anyway. And now it sat, still rolled up and tied with string, in the attic space, behind a small door in Inge's room. Eve couldn't help feeling she was the one who'd been defeated.

* * *

And then there were the wellies. Not Eve's. Eve didn't own gumboots. Hadn't since she was about ten years old. And since she didn't possess a pair of her own, it was hard to complain about the others.

Initially, she hadn't even noticed them. Not the first week anyway, but in her second week in the house, Alfie announced he wanted to play in the garden; and since it had done nothing but rain for the previous twenty-four hours and the garden was a sea of mud, Ian announced wellies were in order.

'Where are they?' Eve asked.

'By the back door. Can't miss them.'

He was certainly right about that, Eve thought, as she stood in the matchbox-sized room that separated the back door from the utility room. Lined up against the wall was a neat row of wellies. A row that started with teeny red ones for Alfie and ended with Ian's enormous green Hunters, with two pink pairs in rising sizes, followed by a smaller pair of Hunters in between.

Anxiously, Eve eyed the anoraks hung on hooks above. It wasn't rocket science to guess there would be five in ascending order. It was like something out of Goldilocks and the three bears. Who's been sleeping in my bed? Well, they all knew the answer to that one.

'What's keeping you?' Ian said. 'Don't tell me you can't . . . ' His voice stopped as abruptly as he did in the doorway. 'What?' he said, seeing her face. 'What's the pr — ' His eyes followed hers and he stopped mid-sentence.

'Erm, Ian . . . ' Eve couldn't quite believe what she was seeing. 'Are these . . . are these Caroline's wellies?'

'Of course,' he tried to laugh it off, but his discomfort was obvious. 'Whose did you think they'd be? The first Mrs Rochester? My mad wife locked in the attic?'

But Eve wasn't laughing. 'Is this really necessary?' she whispered.

'Necessary?'

Eve's whisper turned to a hiss. 'Yes, *necessary*. I mean, I know she's their mother, but it's a long time ago now. Do you really need to keep Caroline's bloody wellies?'

In the kitchen, Alfie and Sophie's chatter died. Only *The Archers* carried on talking, oblivious to the tension.

'Shhh,' he whispered. 'Don't swear. The children will hear you.'

'What do you expect?' she snapped.

188

His shoulders slumped and when his eyes met hers they were beseeching. She knew what Ian was going to say, but she was determined to make him say it anyway.

'Just leave it, will you? Please. For the children.'

15

Thick, black coffee bubbled to the top of the cafetiere and threatened to overflow. Eve inhaled deeply and felt a little of her tension slip away. She was tempted to fetch her favourite vintage cup and saucer from the utility room where Ian had stashed her boxes of china, *Just for now*. But she didn't. It might make her feel more at home, but if Ian and the girls came back he might take it personally, and she didn't want that, not today of all days. Instead, she pulled out a chunky off-white mug from an eye-level cupboard above the kettle where she now knew the mugs were kept, and sloshed coffee into that, then filled a glass with orange juice and shouldered open the door to the sitting room.

'OJ, Alfie,' she said, holding out the glass.

'Evie!' he cried, not taking his eyes from the screen.

'Here.' She pushed the glass into his hand. 'Drink.' She had learnt quickly that where Alfie was concerned, single-syllable instructions were most effective.

Bottom lip protruding comically, Alfie shook his head. 'Had some,' he promised. Eve knew that wasn't true. Not because his expression gave him away, he was far too skilled a fibber for that, but because the carton of orange juice had been in the fridge door and there were no sticky orange stains on the kitchen table. If Alfie had

190

already drunk juice, there would have been stains. Wherever Alfie had been, whatever he'd just eaten, there was always a trail of evidence.

'Who's winning?' she asked, trying a different tack.

'The goodies,' he said, his eyes still glued to the TV.

Thirty seconds later he took a guzzle of juice. And thirty seconds after that the glass was empty.

Attention span of a gnat, Eve thought, tucking her feet under her and trying, for all of ten seconds, to follow the plot, such as it was.

There were things she could be doing, like tidying up this bomb-site for a start. But sitting on the sofa with Alfie at her feet, and Ian's house quiet but for the battle noises bursting from the TV, she felt comfortable for the first time in weeks. Just as long as she didn't look beyond Alfie and the television. If she did, she'd remember that virtually nothing in this room belonged to her, except for the cushions against which she leant and some books on the bottom shelf nearest the door. A shelf that Ian had cleared to make way for her. It was a start, she told herself. Take it slowly. Inevitably, and sooner rather than later, she was sure of it, they would buy some things together, things that would be theirs — Eve and Ian's — not Ian and Caroline's.

Ian was right, she knew he was. One thing at a time.

As the credits rolled Eve seized her chance. 'We need to clear up, Alfie,' she said. 'You know what's happening today?'

Alfie frowned at her. 'Swimming?'

'No, Alfie! You know! What's happening today?'

'Zoo?'

'Alfie! Eve's friends are coming,' she reminded him. 'Clare and Louisa. Remember?'

He frowned, as if processing the information. 'Why do I have to tidy up?'

'Because Eve's friends are coming and it mustn't be messy.' Eve wasn't sure why she kept referring to herself in the third person when she talked to Ian's children. It was as if by doing so, she could pretend she wasn't really there.

'*My* friends,' she corrected. 'You'll like them. Clare — she's a teacher . . . '

Alfie made a face and Eve forced herself not to laugh. 'And her daughter, Lou,' she continued. 'They're coming for lunch.'

'Can we have pizza?'

'Yes, pizza and pasta. But first we need to clear up.'

Eve left Alfie in charge of putting his plastic men into their box, without much hope of it actually happening, and returned to the kitchen to remove all evidence of Alfie's breakfast before she started making lasagne, pretty much the only thing she could cook.

★　★　★

'Wow!' Lou said as they turned the corner into Ian's street. 'Nice work, Auntie Eve.'

Wow, indeed, Clare thought, lightly punching

192

Lou's arm. 'Behave,' she said. And Lou grinned. Clare wasn't sure whether that meant she would or she wouldn't. She hoped, for Eve's sake, Lou would.

Ian's house was halfway along a poplar-lined street. An imposing double-fronted Victorian house in a perfect state of repair, right down to the original black-and-white tiled front path. Original features. That was the understatement of the year. This place was Clare's fantasy house. Her dream home. She'd never wanted Mandy's roses around the door. A solid period house with a bit of character in a good part of London would do her.

In another life, she thought, pushing open the wrought-iron gate.

Even the gate was newly painted, Clare noticed. A tasteful, glossy black, as if Ian had been scrubbing, polishing and painting in preparation for Eve's arrival. And the leaves that had fallen from the trees had been swept away. Clare wondered if Eve had even noticed the gesture. She suspected not. Eve had been in near hysterics the last time they spoke. Something to do with gumboots.

Before Clare had a chance to ring the bell, the front door swung open revealing a small blond boy who just about came up to handle height. He looked suspiciously as if he'd been standing sentry at the letter box, waiting for them to arrive.

'How do you do?' he said, and put out his hand politely. 'My name's Alfie.'

'Hello Alfie,' said Clare, trying not to grin. She

took his hand and returned his firm, cartoon-like shake. 'My name is Clare, and this is my daughter, Louisa.'

'Lou,' said Lou. 'I keep telling you, Mum. Nobody calls me Louisa, any more.'

'You're a teacher,' Alfie said solemnly. 'Eve said so. I have to let you in.'

Clare smiled encouragingly. 'That would be nice,' she said, when he didn't move.

'Well, let them in, then,' said a voice behind the little boy.

Clare had seen a picture of Ian in *Beau*, and several more relaxed shots on Eve's mobile, but she had never met him in the flesh. It pissed her off, if she was honest, that her best friend would move in with someone — not just move in, but agree to marry him — without even letting Clare give him the once-over. After all, what were best friends for, if not to vet your boyfriends?

Not that she'd seen much of Eve since Ian had proposed, anyway. And Clare missed her. Missed the gossipy e-mails, late-night texts, and phone calls that had been a mainstay of their friendship for over ten years. But she pushed that from her mind. Her friend was happy and in love, that was enough for Clare.

Ian wasn't really Clare's type. Mind you, it had been so long that Clare wasn't sure what her type was any more. Male, two legs, two arms, one head, minimal emotional baggage, no mental health issues, in gainful employment, would have been a start. But she could see instantly why Eve had fallen for Ian. Tall and lanky with a strong nose and cheekbones like wing mirrors. He had Eve stamped all over him. She'd never known anyone to be as consistent as Eve in her tastes. Not that Eve would ever admit that.

'You must be Clare,' Ian said, shaking her hand and ushering them past Alfie. 'And you must be Lou.' He smiled, more at Lou than Clare. To Clare's untutored eye, he looked knackered, but the smile reached his clear blue eyes and softened his angular face.

Tall, slim and good-looking if you liked the type, amazing house, good with other people's children . . . Small matter of coming with three kids bolted on, but hey, you can't have everything. *Yes, Clare thought, Ian is quite hot. Nice work, Eve.*

When Clare ruffled her daughter's hair, Lou threw her a curious look and batted her hand away.

'It's great to finally meet you both,' Ian was saying. 'I've heard so much about you from Eve. I'm sorry we didn't meet before. You must think I'm so rude.'

'Not at all,' Clare lied as Ian closed the door behind them. 'I'm sure you had enough to worry about. It's nice to meet you now, though. Thank you for inviting us. I've never been to this part of Chiswick before. It's beautiful. Lovely street . . .'

Shut up, Clare, she thought. Stop gabbling. You're thirty-three and you're behaving like a star-struck thirteen-year-old. In fact, the fourteen-year-old standing next to you is far cooler. But Clare didn't.

'Beautiful house,' she continued, as Ian led

them through the hall. It *was* beautiful, and enormous, but there was something slightly off about the atmosphere. It felt wrong, tense, almost. Yes, that was it . . . It was almost as if the house was tensed, waiting for something to go off bang.

Don't be daft, Clare told herself. *You're transferring. You feel tense, Ian clearly feels tense, no doubt Eve does, wherever she is.* Come to that, where was Eve? Clare glanced up as she passed the stairs, and did a double-take. Weren't there an awful lot of photographs of the dead wife?

'Have you lived here long?'

She could have kicked herself. She didn't need to, Lou did it for her.

'Mum!' Lou hissed.

Ian smiled, looking wan. 'Quite a while. We, er, I bought it a long time ago, when the area was still cheap. It was cheap and quiet and near good schools, the perfect location if you're starting a —'

He flapped his arms helplessly, and Clare wanted the ground to swallow her. *Great start*, she thought.

★   ★   ★

'Clare!' Eve yelped. She tossed her oven gloves aside and shot across the room, flinging her arms around her friend. 'You made it!'

'We've come from north London not the North Pole.' Clare grinned, and Eve hugged her again, harder.

196

'I've missed you,' she muttered at the side of Clare's face. 'I'm so glad to see you.'

'Chablis?' Eve said, glancing at the bottle in Clare's hand. 'Don't be silly, you can't afford that. Any old cheap plonk would have done.'

It was a relief to be able to stop pretending she knew what she was doing in the kitchen and let Ian take over, which she knew he was itching to do. She wasn't much of a cook at the best of times, but cooking in someone else's kitchen, which was precisely how this felt, was torture. If it hadn't been for Sophie showing her, she doubted she'd even have been able to work out how to turn the oven on.

'Cool kitchen,' Lou said. She probably meant the huge oak table. Unless it was the collection of plastic men climbing out of a bowl underneath it.

Ian smiled. 'You like it?'

'It's bigger than our flat,' Lou said, nodding.

Really, Eve would have liked to invite Lily and Melanie, too. Made a group outing of it. Not Mandy, not yet. She hardly knew her. But she had a feeling Clare would have resented that. *Maybe another time,* she thought, *if we get through this in one piece.*

She gave Clare another hug and whispered in her ear, 'What do you think? So far so good?'

Clare hugged her back. 'He seems great,' she said.

'But what?' Eve pulled back and tried to keep the panic out of her voice. Ian was in the utility room, filling an ice bucket from the freezer; Alfie and Sophie were at the table, introducing Lou to the toys that had made it onto the VITs only guest list.

'The house, Eve,' Clare said, her eyes crinkled in concern. 'It's, well, I've only seen the hall and stairs, but it's a *museum*.'

'Chablis or Merlot?' Ian was back, a bottle in each hand. 'Or rosé, we've got rosé, if you prefer? Er, somewhere.' He smiled.

'White please, if that's all right,' Clare said. 'It's not really rosé weather.'

'White please,' Lou chipped in.

'Lou, you know . . . '

'Just a small one,' Eve interrupted. 'It is a celebration after all. Ian, where's Hannah? I'd like her to meet Lou.'

Ian shrugged. 'Upstairs, probably. I'll get her in a minute.'

And there it was, the other reason Eve had wanted to do this. She wanted Hannah to meet Lou. To prove to Hannah and Ian, and perhaps herself, that not all teenage girls hated her. There was at least one teenager on the planet who thought Eve was as cool as it was possible for anyone over thirty to be. She had even dared to hope that maybe, if Hannah hit it off with Lou, that she would begin to get on with Eve by association.

They were all seated around the table, Sophie regaling Clare with her ballet lesson, Lou lovingly nursing her forbidden glass of wine and playing with Alfie, when Ian returned with Hannah.

The minute they walked into the kitchen Eve wondered what on earth she'd been thinking.

198

Seeing the two girls eye each other, it was clear they couldn't have had less in common. Only a year apart, their age was about all they shared. It was not just their looks; Lou's Angelina Jolie in her phial of blood phase, complete with black jeans and band T-shirt, to Hannah's *Gossip Girl* blonde with denim shorts and Topshop's finest.

It was *everything*.

'Hannah,' Eve forced a smile into her voice. Maybe if she convinced herself this could work, she could convince the others. 'This is my friend, Clare, and her daughter — my goddaughter — Lou.'

'She's not exactly — ' Clare started.

'I should have been,' Lou interrupted. 'And I would be if you'd known Eve when I was christened.'

Clare nodded. That was true enough. And Eve had been a better godmother to Lou than either of her real ones. The fact that Eve claimed not to believe in God hadn't seemed to matter at all.

'Lou's fourteen. She's in the year above you at school.'

'How do you do,' Hannah said, her tone making it clear that having braces fitted would be more enjoyable than what she was expected to endure here. Still, it was the most she'd said all week.

It was obvious from Lou's expression — part hurt, part contempt — that she got the message. 'Pleased to meet you.'

'Yeah,' Hannah said, squishing onto a pew

next to Sophie, rather than go around the table to the place that had too-obviously been left next to Lou. 'That too.'

Don't panic, Eve thought.

'Would you like some wine?' she asked, knowing that, like Lou, Hannah was always hankering to be allowed a glass. 'As it's a special occasion.'

'No,' Hannah said. 'Thanks,' she added as an afterthought for her father's benefit. And Eve caught Ian looking from her to his daughter, something like panic creeping into his eyes.

'Diet Coke then?' Eve kept her voice bright.

Hannah shook her head.

'Juice?' Eve persisted. 'Mineral water?' She could hear the desperation in her own voice. The neediness. Where had that come from? She hated needy; regarded needy women as agents of their own downfall.

'Tap water,' Hannah said.

Getting up, Eve took a tumbler from the drainer, filled it and came back. If not for the whirr of the fan oven and some generic dinner-party soundtrack from Ian's iPod in the corner, the room would have been silent.

'And what's your doll called?' Clare asked Sophie too brightly.

★　★　★

It was the same with pizza, pasta and garlic bread. Hannah was not hungry, not interested, and hated garlic, which was an entirely new one on Eve.

200

Everyone else ate. Everyone else had firsts, seconds and forced down thirds, even Lou, who could be as difficult about food as Hannah if the mood took her. Eve felt so pathetically grateful she wanted to hug her.

Pushing a scrap of lasagne around her plate, Eve tried to regroup. She'd had stupidly high hopes, based entirely on fantasy and wishful thinking, and ended up with this. Clare was obviously mortified. Eve could tell from her bright, snappy conversation: the teacher-tone had slid in. Lou was playing with Alfie and eating for England, but that didn't hide the fact that every few minutes her eyes slid to the kitchen clock, and disappointment tightened her face when she realized only five minutes had passed.

Let it go, Ian's glance said, when her eyes sought his across the table.

'More white, anyone?' he asked, waving a newly opened bottle in the general direction of the table.

'Me please.' Lou held out her glass.

Not even Clare tried to stop her.

'And me,' said Eve, seeing a flicker of doubt cross Ian's face.

He was right on two counts: 1) she'd probably drunk enough already, and 2) she should simply ignore Hannah. Let Ian deal with it when Clare and her daughter had gone home. But somehow, Eve couldn't. Clare and Lou were her *friends*; closer even than her family. It wasn't much to ask her to be polite for a couple of hours, surely? She was the one who was meant to be well brought-up. The one from a good family, who went to an expensive school. The one with all the privileges. Where the hell were her manners?

'Ice cream?' Eve suggested, fixing a smile onto her face as she pushed the tub towards Hannah. 'Low fat,' she pre-empted. 'Frozen yoghurt really.'

'No thank you,' Hannah said quietly. 'I don't eat ice cream.'

Eve should have taken a deep breath, held it and counted to ten . . . But she didn't.

'What *would* you like?' Eve asked, exasperation, desperation and a touch too much Chablis meeting in four seemingly innocuous words.

It didn't come out how she meant it.

What Eve meant was, 'What do you want if you don't want pizza or pasta or garlic bread or salad or wine or Coke or juice or ice cream, or anything else I offer you? Tell me, and I'll get it for you.'

But that wasn't how the words came out. They came out more loaded. Translation: *There's no pleasing you.*

'I would like,' Hannah said, her voice cold but glinting with triumph, 'to leave the table.'

There were so many worse things she could have said that Eve's body almost sagged with relief.

'Go on then,' Ian said, breaking the silence that had fallen when Eve had spoken.

'Right,' he added, his voice so brittle that Eve couldn't bring herself to look at him. 'What would everyone else like for pudding?'

★   ★   ★

202

'I can't believe Eve thought I'd like her,' Lou said, banging her Doctor Marten's against the seat opposite. The rhythmic thud was working Clare's nerves. 'She's a spoilt princess. I wouldn't be friends with her even if there was no one else in school.'

'I think Auntie Eve just *hoped*,' Clare said. 'And Hannah's not a spoilt princess. She's had a hard time. Her mum died of cancer when she was ten. You have to cut her some slack.'

'Hmph,' Lou grunted.

Thud, thud, thud.

'Yeah,' Lou added. 'When-she-was-ten. That's three years ago. She's still ligging on it. Anyone can see that. Anyway, I don't have a dad and I don't see you cutting me any slack for that.'

Fair point, Clare thought. Although she didn't say it. She didn't have the energy to go there. And even if she did, Will was not someone she wanted to think about right now, let alone discuss with her daughter.

Thud, thud, thud.

'Lou, for God's sake stop that, will you. It's giving me a headache.'

'No it's not,' Lou said. But she let her feet swing slowly to a halt. 'Lunch gave you a headache.'

Annoyingly, that was true too. Lunch and too much wine. Clare rarely drank at lunchtime, even on the weekend, and not just because she couldn't afford to. Wine went straight to her head, in more ways than one. The lights playing at the edge of her vision were a reminder of that.

Even without the ice cream incident and its aftermath — Hannah flouncing from the kitchen, Eve trying to look as if she didn't want to cry, Ian glowering over cheesecake and chocolate mousse and cheese and biscuits that no one but Alfie had the stomach for — lunch would have given her a headache.

Everything about it felt wrong. From the photos on the stairs (*Museum?* Lou said. *Mausoleum more like)*, to Ian's rigid body language and Eve radiating tension the moment they stepped through the door. Normally the least likely person to go off bang, Clare had watched helplessly as Eve let that spoilt brat wind her up and ruin her day. Clare, who, given her experiences with her own stepmonster, had automatically expected to sympathize with Hannah, was surprised to find herself one hundred per cent on Eve's side. And Lou was right. She was a little princess. Not that Clare could admit that. Eve had been so desperate for the people she loved to like each other, she hadn't stood a chance.

'Just f.y.i.,' Lou added, as the Northern Line train pulled into their station. 'I love Auntie Eve — and she did give me twenty quid before we left — but I'm not going there again. I've got better things to do with my Saturdays.'

Clare hadn't spotted the cash handover. If she had she would have tried to prevent it, but she let that go unmentioned. 'I wouldn't worry about it,' she said.

Her migraine was encroaching rapidly now. She made a mental note to buy some Nurofen at the Tesco Express on the way home. It was a bit stable door shut/horse bolted, but it was better than nothing.

'Why not?' Lou asked.

'I very much doubt we'll be invited.'

16

Silence. Finally.

Eve had been longing for the day to end, but now it had, the darkness didn't bring the relief she'd hoped for. It was suffocating.

It shouldn't have been; the heating had long since gone off and the bedroom window was slightly open. Outside, the air had the chill of autumn, but still the room was stuffy, stale with tension and unspoken resentments.

Eve wanted to kick off the duvet, as she would have done at home, because her flat still felt like home, and right now she'd give anything to be there. She'd been tempted to leave when Clare and Louisa did . . . Go back to Kentish town and her flat, and be her old self, just for a few hours. To regroup and remind herself what life was like Before Stepchildren. Or, more precisely, Before Hannah.

But Eve didn't move, not even an inch. Just lay there, straight as a board, her body parallel to Ian's, their hands nowhere even near touching.

She didn't want to wake Ian. Not that he was really asleep, from the pitch of his breathing.

Eve didn't want to break the pretence of his sleep or hers. Instead they both lay in silence so each could pretend to believe the other was sleeping. If she kicked back the cover, the lie would be revealed, and they'd have to talk. Eve had a good idea she knew what Ian was thinking.

Right now she didn't feel up to hearing it.

It's just a row, she thought. *A row without the words. People do that all the time. Couples, friends, lovers, husbands, wives. It doesn't mean anything. It's not the end of the world. People argue and then make up. Hell, some people argue just for the sake of making up. Any half decent relationship can survive a fight.*

So why did this feel so much more than that?

Why was she so reluctant — afraid, even — to say and hear what had to be said? She knew she was in the wrong, that she shouldn't have taken the bait, that she was the grown-up . . . But why? Why did his having children mean she had to leave her rights at the front door?

In the garden, next door's cat was torturing some small creature; the friendly neighbourhood fox was screeching in frustration as a dustbin rocked on its wheels but refused to fall. And in the far, far distance, lorries rumbled down the A4, giving the night a low-level hum she'd never noticed before. But not the cat, the fox or the lorries hid the creak of a bedroom door, the pad of sock-clad feet on the stairs, and the click of the kitchen door being opened and shut.

Be reasonable, Eve told herself, *the kid's gotta be hungry. She hasn't eaten all day.*

But the knot in Eve's stomach grew tighter.

Whose fault was it if Hannah was hungry?

All the loathsome parental clichés she'd promised never to think let alone say, tumbled inside her head: eat what you're given, children are starving in Africa, you're not getting down until you've cleared your plate . . . If she was honest, Eve wanted to follow Hannah downstairs and slap her.

More than that, she wanted Ian to. More than anything, Eve wanted Ian to stand up for her, to show whose side he was on. His silence and the gradual levelling of his breathing told her that right now it wasn't hers.

If anything, the tension had ratcheted up a notch with Clare and Lou's departure, releasing those who had bothered to be on it from their best behaviour, Eve and Ian included. Alfie had grizzled, Sophie had whined and Hannah had shut herself in her bedroom. Then, even more alarmingly, Sophie had joined her. Even Ian could not pretend that was a good sign.

Eve had slammed plates into the dishwasher and knocked back another glass of wine. Ian had coaxed the children through the rest of that afternoon, but on the rare occasions she'd been left alone with him, an uncomfortable silence had settled, and one of them had found a pressing need to be in another room. For Eve, this usually consisted of finding something else that needed washing up.

It was ironic really. Ever since Eve moved in, Alfie had clung to her like a limpet. This evening she was the one who went in search of him.

Bedtime, when it finally came, had been a living hell. It was gone ten before Sophie and Alfie went down. Alfie, normally so sunny, so unaffected by anything other than his tummy, had been cranky and grizzly, demanding story after story; until Eve had been exhausted from 'doing the voices' while Caroline's photo gazed unflinchingly at her from Alfie's bedside table. That cool stare was the last thing she needed. It had taken what little reserves Eve had left not to turn the picture face down.

And now — *now* — Hannah was hungry. Eve wanted to wring her neck.

'Go to sleep.' The sound of Ian's voice coming out of the darkness made her jump. It wasn't friendly or conciliatory. Just sick, and tired.

'I was.'

'No, you weren't. I could hear you thinking.'

'You could hear me thinking?'

'Uh-huh.'

'Well, forgive me if I think too loud.' She hated herself even as she said it. This wasn't her. She sounded as if she were twelve. She sounded like the kind of woman she hated.

A sigh.

'Just go to sleep. We'll talk about it in the morning.'

Great, she thought. *That's something to look forward to*. But what she said was, 'Night.'

'Night.'

She hoped they wouldn't *talk about it in the morning*. How could they? If they couldn't talk about it in private, the two of them cocooned in darkness, unable to see what the other was really thinking, they were hardly going to do it in broad daylight with three children for an audience.

★   ★   ★

An hour later Hannah was back upstairs and Eve was still wide awake. She needed to talk to

209

someone. She was tempted to call Clare, but it was a long time since her friend had welcomed two a.m. distress calls.

She knew that Clare had intended that to be the purpose of the Stepmothers' Support Group. That she had Clare and Lily and Melanie and, now, sort of, Mandy, to get it all off her chest. But how many of Eve's problems could they really put up with, given they had problems of their own? It was a support group — friendship and coffee and a bit of light relief — not the Priory. For a second Eve found herself wishing she still kept a diary, something she hadn't done since that second year at university. But what would she write if she did?

Dear Diary, my thirteen-year-old stepdaughter was nasty to me today . . . It sounded pathetic even to her.

When she was sure Ian was asleep, Eve slid out of bed, slipped into her dressing gown and crept out of the room. A plate in the sink told Eve that Hannah had eaten several slices of cold pizza that had been left in the fridge intended for tomorrow's lunch. The microwave was switched on at the wall, so she'd obviously heated them up first. Eve fought back tears of frustration. Would it have killed Hannah to eat one slice at lunchtime? What was she trying to do? Eve was sure she already knew the answer to that. Hannah was trying to break her and Ian up. And Eve had just ensured phase one of her campaign had succeeded.

While Eve waited for the kettle to boil, she slid her laptop from her work bag, turned it on and idly chewed a pizza crust she didn't really want as her machine connected to the internet.

Pot of coffee, packet of Alfie's favourite chocolate Hobnobs, laptop ... Eve tried to make herself comfortable at the oak table that only hours earlier had been the scene of her humiliation. Kitchens at night had always been a sanctuary to Eve. It was one of the things she shared in common with Clare. Maybe it had even started when they had shared a house together as students.

As recently as a month ago, she'd huddled over her tiny table in the kitchen of her flat, catching up on copy, reading, just mulling over her day. In the past she'd switched off the light as she listened to the radio, and looked out across the sleeping gardens at the windows of the flats that backed onto hers, blank and dark as if the houses were asleep too.

She could learn to love this kitchen too. She just had to set her mind against the fact that the kitchen, like every other room in Ian's house, was haunted by Caroline.

Looking around, she hunted for some small way to make her mark, but one that wouldn't look like petulance. So that ruled out black-bagging the wellies. Eve smiled in spite of herself. It would almost be worth it. Although, of course, it wouldn't.

Instead, she went to the utility room and opened the cupboard where Ian had stashed her boxes. She didn't know what she was looking for until she found it: a large white bowl with a blue fish swimming across the base. She'd bought it in Chinatown several years ago, one lazy Sunday afternoon of wandering and window-shopping. It was close enough in style to Ian's own things not to look like point scoring, but knowing it was there, in the cupboard, would at least make her feel she was putting down markers.

Eve settled herself back at the table, but still the sense of being an interloper remained. It didn't help that Eve could remember sitting at her own table, with a pile of unread newspapers, reading columns written by Ian's late wife as her illness progressed. Written, Eve imagined, precisely where she sat now.

As her children and husband — now Eve's partner and sort-of stepchildren, Eve realized with a jolt — slept upstairs, Caro prepared herself for the death it was obvious from her later columns she knew was fast approaching. Back then, Eve's heart had gone out to her. She had admired the woman's strength and honesty, the dignity with which she had faced the certain knowledge of death.

That was one reason she'd been so excited when *Beau* secured its exclusive interview with Ian to publicize the book of her columns.

But that was then. That was before she found herself tucking Caroline's son into bed, cooking her youngest two beans on toast, and reading them bedtime stories. Before she'd realized the only unbeatable rival was a dead one. Although the dead one's elder daughter was running a close second.

Eve half expected to glance up and see Caroline leaning against the worktop in her

212

waffle dressing gown, coffee in hand, watching her. On her face that cool, knowing smile she wore in all her pictures.

As a distraction, Eve typed the word 'stepmother' into Google. She wasn't sure what she was looking for, but she knew the second she pressed *Enter* that millions of other women were looking for it too. A manual that didn't appear to exist. *Maybe there's a planet full of us, she thought, sitting alone at our kitchen tables in the late and early hours, wondering how the hell we're going to cope and scouring the web for an answer.*

In the early hours in London; bracing herself for the school run in Sydney; grabbing a few minutes' peace after bedtime in Chicago. A cup of tea/mug of coffee/glass of wine in one hand, and maybe the answer to someone else's problem in the other. Two and a half million hits and counting. Link after link scrolled before her eyes.

My Stepmother is an Alien
The Evil Stepmother
The Ambitious Stepmother
I hate my stepmother with a passion.

The URLs that sprang up told her instantly what she suspected. Stepmothers were A. Bad. Thing. Vilified, loathed, hated. Site after site compared horror stories, swapped jokes, or offered anaemic analysis of this most wicked of fairy tale baddies. Eve was shocked by how many of those there were. She clicked on a site that claimed to offer practical help and was assaulted with a litany of teen complaints.

She tries to keep my dad away from us. She wants

213

to start a new family without us. *She bosses my dad around. She thinks she's our mum.*

Not guilty, Eve thought. *Not guilty. Not guilty. Not guilty . . .* Only the last gave her pause. *I don't want to be anyone's mum, I never have*, she thought. *But what choice do I have?*

Back at the search results page Eve scanned the links for some respite. There had to be another side to it. There was. Amongst the litany she could see the women on the receiving end were trying to look out for each other:

The British second wives' club
Blending a family.com
The second wives' café
Stepmothers' milk

Sipping her coffee, which had turned tepid in the time she'd been surfing, Eve read stories of success and failure, hope and despair, from stepmothers around the world. One site had a Stepmother of the Month. How did they do it, these women who were, more often than not, getting it so right that their own stepchildren put them on a pedestal?

Eve found the link to respond to one of the comments and clicked, but as a box opened to register for the site: her name, her e-address, the name she wanted to appear on her posts, she stopped, feeling exposed. How safe was this really? Could she say what she thought? Potentially to hundreds of thousands of others.

Then a thought occurred to her. She loved all the fashion blogs she kept an eye on for work; the blogs slagging off boyfriends and partners; blogs about weight loss, mothers, first loves, and the futility of diets; blogs about working in restaurants and offices; blogs about how crap people's jobs were and how much they hated their bosses.

She could keep the diary she'd been missing on-line. Writing anonymously would give her the chance to get everything off her chest, thinking it through as she wrote. Like most journalists, Eve found it easier to work things out on paper. And the chances of more than a couple of dozen fellow sufferers bothering to read her ramblings when the internet had so many millions of pages of trivia to choose from were minimal.

Opening an account on blogspot, she pulled up a page and started to type. *My name is . . . Well, it doesn't matter what my name is. All you need to know is I'm thirty-two and I'm an Evil Stepmother.*

But she wasn't, not really. She deleted the last few words.

She was an inexperienced stepmother. An accidental stepmother. A reluctant stepmother, that was for sure. But evil? Accidental seemed apt, but somehow she liked the feel of reluctant. It summed up precisely how she felt. Somehow crap stepmother didn't have the same ring. Although she knew that as far as Hannah was concerned she was that too.

I'm a reluctant stepmother. And the truth is, I'm scared. Scared of a thirteen-year-old girl. How pathetic is that? As scared of her now as I would have been when I was thirteen myself. That's just occurred to me, actually. My eldest stepdaughter (I have two, and a stepson) is all

215

long, blonde hair and labels; whatever passes for a cheerleader in this privileged part of West London. She's a bit spoilt if I'm honest, but there's a reason for that. I'll go into it another time. The fact is, X is precisely the kind of girl who'd have looked down on me at school. She's a cool girl, part of the in-crowd, whereas I was a swot, a geek, and definitely not someone to be seen with. Oh, the shame for X of having someone like me — an ex-geek — as a stepmother. She would have looked down on me then and she's doing a damn good job of it now, to be honest. I'm not saying I'm perfect. God no, I've screwed up left, right and centre. I've only been her stepmum for a month, less even, and I've made more mistakes than I can count. Take today . . .

Getting the facts down then reading them back on screen made Eve cringe. Hannah had set her up, and she'd fallen for it. It was so obvious. Anyone reading this would be able to see in an instant that she shouldn't have risen to the bait. But it was too late now. She had. The fault was hers, Eve could see that now. But what could she do about it? Maybe someone would read her blog, know the answer, and post it.

She decided to write that too.

I know what I should have done. Well, I do now. But I couldn't see it at the time. How can I learn to spot the obstacles before I trip over them and they send me flying arse over tit? How can I win her over? Should I even try? That's the question that bugs me more than anything. I understand that X misses her mum and doesn't

216

want me to replace her. I understand I can never truly understand how that must feel. But why does she seem to HATE me so much?

It was flowing now.

And then there's the house. My partner — future husband, God that sounds weird — is a widower. His first wife died in a car crash . . . Eve had been going to write from cancer but she didn't want the blog's author to be that easily identifiable . . . and the house is the one he lived in with his wife. It wasn't a clean death and obviously the children, especially the elder two, were affected by it. Hence all the spoiling I mentioned earlier. He doesn't want to disrupt the children by moving and I get that. I do. They've been through enough (that's his mantra, by the way).

I know it sounds ridiculous, but the place feels almost haunted. It's her presence, even though he says he has started to change things, she's everywhere. Pictures on the walls, bowls in the cupboard, her face on their children . . . I don't even know how much of the decor she chose but I'm willing to bet it was most of it. But it's more than that, she IS the house. It sounds stupid but I feel like I'm in Rebecca or something. Like their mother is Rebecca and X is a sort of mean-girl version of Mrs Danvers.

Eve read it back. It sounded mad, especially that last paragraph. Could she really post it? Why not? Nobody would know it had anything to do with her. The internet was a big place after all, chances were no one else would even read it.

What the hell, Eve thought, and clicked Post.

217

17

'Only one chocolate coin.'

'Two!'

'Rosie, you can have one. Look how big they are,' Lily cajoled. 'They're almost big enough to eat you!'

'Want two!'

'Rosie, you can't have two.'

The negotiations had been in progress for several minutes now and Lily was pretty sure she wasn't winning. Crouching down to bring her eyes level with the three-year-old, Lily tried to keep her voice even so she sounded more in control than she felt, and counted to ten.

The little girl met her gaze, then tipped her head to one side, her topknot swinging as she did so. The look on her face reminded Lily of Liam . . . Liam when he was trying to get around her. 'Can I have juice?'

'You already have a juice, Rosie.'

'Want chocolate coin.'

'We've got a chocolate coin, sweetheart.'

Sweetheart, my foot, Lily thought. The child was being a brat. She blamed its parents. Talking of which, where the hell was this weekend's parent?

'Three chocolate coins,' Rosie was trying a new tack. 'One for Rosie, one for Daddy, one for Lily.'

'That's a nice idea, Rosie, but Lily doesn't

want one.' Lily could feel disapproving eyes burning into her back in the Caffè Nero queue, and tried not to turn into one of those shrieking *Women who can't control their children* Clare always rolled her eyes at in Tesco.

'One for Rosie. One for Daddy,' Rosie said reasonably.

Lily weighed her choices. She didn't want to cave in to this knee-high Kissinger and buy two, having said no countless times already. But one for Rosie, one for Daddy was such a reasonable request she didn't see how she could refuse.

'OK,' she relented. 'One for Rosie, one for Daddy!'

Rosie beamed. 'Thank you Lily,' she said.

Man, the kid was cute. Cute but lethal.

Having paid for the coffees, and tray laden with cups and chocolate coins, Lily threaded her way through a tight network of tables towards a corner at the back, trying to keep one eye on the small girl who was working the room like a pro.

Just as Lily reached the table, Liam rushed up behind her.

'Sorry, sorry, sorry,' he muttered, pecking Lily on the cheek and swinging Rosie up and under his arm and starting to tickle her. The child squealed with pleasure. Bright orange juice squirted onto her pink T-shirt and Lily wondered which was the lesser of two evils: washing it herself when they got back to the flat or risking the wrath of Siobhan by sending the child's dirty T-shirt back with her.

'Am I late?' Liam asked. Knowing the answer perfectly well, he made his 'please don't be mad at me, I'm having a bad day' face.

Lily sighed. 'Bloody late,' she hissed, knowing swearing was well out of bounds where three-year-old ears were concerned. 'Three and a half hours bloody late to be precise.'

'Come off it Lil,' Liam said. 'You know I had to be at work when Siobhan dropped Rosie off. You said you'd cover. *That* was three and a half hours ago. I'm only half an hour late to meet you here.'

Lily rolled her eyes indulgently, but something nagged at the back of her mind. Her friends . . . they would die laughing if they could see her now. Not that most of her college friends' opinion of Liam bore a second hearing anyway: divorced, three-year-old kid, over ten years her senior . . . They just hadn't got it. She had thought they'd be happy for her; they had thought she was mad. In the end, their constant attempts to fix her up with 'one of the crowd' whenever they met for a drink had worn thin. She hadn't seen much of them since she'd moved in with Liam.

'What have you got there Rosie-posie?' Liam was saying, tucking Rosie onto his knee.

'Two chocolate coins? Goodness! How did you manage that?'

'They're not — ' Lily started to say.

'Easy Daddy,' Rosie announced. 'I asked for three!'

Liam roared with laughter. 'That's my girl!'

Lily stared, dumbstruck. She'd been had. By a three-year-old. But, she was starting to realize, not just any three-year-old. One whose dad was a man who hadn't just kissed the Blarney Stone, he'd swallowed the damn thing whole. And if the toddler could pull that off, what was her father capable of?

She didn't know who to be more furious with. Rosie for being deceitful or Liam for thinking it was the best joke he'd heard all day. Come to that, she didn't know whether to be furious with herself for being so gullible.

★ ★ ★

Later that night, with Liam putting Rosie to bed and the child's giggles echoing from the other end of the flat, the incident still rankled. It wasn't so much that Lily minded a three-year-old stitching her up. Clearly it wasn't Lily's finest hour, but she could work it into a routine, not that she'd done much stand-up lately. It was Liam's pride in his daughter's skills that bothered her.

What hope did the kid have if her father thought it was the funniest thing in the world that she'd conned Lily into buying her two chocolate coins?

Not conned, *negotiated*. Lily forced herself to be charitable. After all, Liam's own negotiating skills were legendary. He'd scored exclusives that other sports reporters only dreamt of, simply by talking his way in.

Although she was reluctant to admit it, Lily was beginning to see where Liam's ex was coming from, and she wasn't sure she liked being put in that position one little bit.

'So, what would you do?' she asked Eve, looking up from her latte.

'What would I do?' Eve pulled a face. 'Since when did I become the font of all stepmother knowledge? Seriously, don't ask me. I'm one big screw-up on the stepmother front. Would you take skincare advice from one of those scary sales women in department stores who assault you with fragrance and look like they've been Tangoed?'

Lily shook her head.

'Then don't take childcare advice from me!' She smiled to soften her words but she knew she sounded fed up.

'I know it's none of my business . . . ' Mandy had been so quiet the others had almost forgotten she was there. In fact, Eve had been surprised she'd turned up at all, and suspected that Lily had dragged her. Melanie had already pulled out of that evening's meeting, her e-mail citing some unspecified crisis at work.

'I think you're being too hard on yourself. Both of you. But especially you.' Mandy looked straight at Eve, her grey eyes surprisingly steely.

Eve looked away. Mandy had had her highlights redone since the last SSG meeting and she was wearing jeans. They suited her. She seemed more confident, somehow. Eve was beginning to see how Mandy controlled five teenagers on the weekends when John's children came to stay.

'Go on,' she said.

'If you don't mind me saying,' Mandy said, 'coping with children is a learning curve, and a steep one, even when they're your own. When they're not you don't have the benefit of automatically loving them, no matter what.'

'On a good day,' Clare put in.

'On any day. Even when you're furious. They're yours, your flesh and blood, for what that's worth, and I don't care what anyone says, it *is* worth something. When you inherit someone else's children, like Eve has, full-time, it's straight in at the deep end. No let up.'

'You're not trying to say I didn't screw up with Hannah?'

'Of course not. I mean, I wasn't there, so I only have your account to go on. But from what you and Clare say, you did. Royally.'

'Cheers.' Eve was taken aback.

'But you weren't evil or wicked or any of those stupid labels. You made a mistake. That's all. Real parents make mistakes all the time. And you want it to work out so badly you're trying too hard.'

'You're saying Hannah can smell it?' Eve asked. She was intrigued. 'The way cats always head for the person in the room who's allergic to them?'

'Yes, but I'm not really talking about Hannah, I'm talking about you. I think you expect too much of yourself. You can't be a brilliant mum straight off. You can't even be a brilliant stepmum.'

'Ahh,' Clare smiled wryly. 'That's where your argument falls down. Eve's been straight-As her

223

entire life. No fuck-ups, no flaws. Perfect degree. Perfect job. Now perfect man. She's not about to tolerate B minus at this point.'

'I'm here, you know.' Eve tried forcing a smile, but none came. 'You're talking about me like I've gone to the loo.'

'Am I wrong about straight As?'

'Very.'

'OK. What have you ever fucked up?'

'Plenty of things.' Eve wasn't planning to expand.

'The point is,' Mandy interrupted, 'you're not used to being around children all that much, let alone full-time. I'm impressed you're doing so well with Alfie.'

'Alfie's easy,' Eve said. 'It's not that I'm good with him. He's good with me.'

'See, there you go again,' Lily said, leaning forward. 'Mandy's right. Give yourself some credit. You've been brilliant with Alfie from the start. He loves you. Clare told me.'

Eve glanced at Clare, who nodded.

'So,' Mandy said. 'You're great with Alfie. What about the younger girl?'

'Sophie? So-so. I thought I was doing well, until that Saturday happened. Then she went and hid with Hannah for hours and we haven't been right since.' Eve took a deep breath. 'To be honest, I'm scared I've blown it with her too.'

'I doubt it,' Mandy said. 'She's, what, eight? Nine?'

'Nine.'

'Well, then, she's bound to be influenced by her big sister. You can get around that. It's

Hannah you need to reach some sort of compromise with.'

'Easier said than done,' Eve muttered into her coffee. She'd thought she needed some advice. Now she was getting it, she wasn't so sure.

'Teenagers are a different kettle of fish,' Mandy explained. 'They're going through all sorts of stuff, even without what Hannah has already experienced. She's lost her mum, remember. She watched her deteriorate. That's not easy for anyone, let alone a ten-year-old. And girls are more of a challenge than boys for a new woman coming into the picture. In my experience anyway.'

Eve caught Lily's eye and knew they were both thinking the same thing: Clare had definitely been a challenge for the Stepmonster.

'What experience do you have with teenagers?' Mandy asked.

'I've been one!' Eve said flippantly.

'Seriously.'

'Seriously? None. I don't know where to start.'

'Yes, you do!' Clare said. 'What about Lou? She thinks you walk on water. It's Auntie Eve this, Auntie Eve that. Gets on my nerves to tell the truth.'

'Lou's different, Lou's my goddaughter, give or take the God bit. I've known her since she was a baby. Plus . . . ' her voice trailed off.

'Plus what?' Mandy asked.

Eve wondered if she dare say it. It was one thing to think it, even to write it on a blog, but saying the words out loud felt like a betrayal of Hannah, of Ian, of everything.

'Plus what?' Mandy repeated.

'She's not spoilt to death and she doesn't hate me.'

There was a silence.

'I'm willing to bet Hannah *doesn't* hate you,' Mandy said at last.

'She does!' Eve said. 'She wants me out.'

'No, she hates the *idea* of you. She hates the change. She hates there being an important new person in her dad's life, in her house, but she doesn't hate *you*. There's a crucial difference. Think how well you get on with Clare's daughter. And even allowing for all the obvious complications that exist between you and Hannah, there have to be some bits of your relationship with Lou that you can draw on with Hannah.'

Clare glanced at Eve. They were seeing another side to Mandy. This Mandy ran an office, a home and an extended family like a military operation. There was nothing diffident about her words, and her voice had strengthened. It made Eve wonder what she'd be like if she'd got her roses around the door, or gone to university like the rest of them.

'Be her friend,' Mandy said. 'An aunt if you like, or a godmother. The way you are with Lou. That's your mistake Eve, if you don't mind me saying so. You're trying to be a mother-figure. And there *is* no mother in stepmother.'

★ ★ ★

'What about me?' Lily asked. She was fascinated by this new, previously unseen, side to Mandy;

quietly proud that she'd found her and introduced her to the group. 'What am *I* doing wrong?'

'I can answer that,' Clare said.

'You always could,' Lily retorted.

Eve winced.

'I can get your opinion any time I like,' said Lily, softening her words. But she knew her sister well enough to know she was on a hiding to nothing.

'Eve doesn't have a choice,' Clare was saying. 'Ian's children don't have a mother. Rosie has a mother and a father. And if I may say so —'

'No,' Lily interrupted. 'You may not. But I'm sure you're going to anyway.'

'From where I'm sitting, they both look pretty useless. They're using that child as a pawn in their divorce.'

Lily scowled. 'With respect,' she said tartly. 'You hardly know Liam and you *don't* know Siobhan. They're just trying to work it out. They're only human. Well,' she added under her breath, 'Liam is.'

'She's right, Clare,' Eve said. 'You're not being fair.'

'Aren't I? Lily's not Rosie's mother. Unlike Hannah, Rosie has one. So why is Lily being treated like an unpaid childminder? Why's she doing the child's washing? Why isn't Liam doing it? Rosie's not Lily's kid, she shouldn't be Lily's problem.'

'What do *you* think, Mandy?' Eve asked.

'Yes,' Lily said pointedly. 'Let's hear if Mandy thinks I'm a total mug.'

227

'Yes and no,' Mandy said. 'Speaking personally I do think the dad can make or break things. I mean,' she looked at Eve, 'Ian's in a tough spot and it's partly of his own making, but he seems to be trying. Those children are his responsibility and from what you say, he takes that responsibility really seriously. My ex . . . to say he couldn't give a shit is the understatement of the year.'

The others were shocked. They'd never heard Mandy swear before. She didn't seem the type. Mandy shrugged and moved on.

'Whereas John, my new partner, he misses his kids so much he spends most of his time trying to fit in around both them and his ex. And his ex uses his guilt to run rings around him. Meanwhile, my ex does what his new girlfriend wants, like forgetting to pay maintenance, and seeing his sons as little as possible and never overnight. Not sure what that says about me.'

Mandy sat back, examined her cup and found it empty. 'Let me sum up,' she said. 'My new man is running around after his ex, and most of his salary goes on maintenance. My old one is useless and pays as little as possible. Ladies, stop listening to me right now!'

Clare and Eve laughed, but Lily wasn't listening, she was thinking that the only time she and Liam ever went to a restaurant that didn't have pizza in its name was when he'd managed to blag it on someone else's expense account.

'And Liam?' she said. 'Where does Liam fit on the Crap Dad scale?'

Mandy thought for a moment. 'Second

Division. Not due for relegation but absolutely no hope of making the Championship this season.' She smiled reassuringly. 'But you never know, maybe next.'

★ ★ ★

As south London slid past the window of the night bus, Lily couldn't get Mandy's words out of her head. Were she and Clare right? Was Liam a Second Division Dad, who would never improve if she didn't put her foot down and tell him that Rosie was his responsibility? He could do his own fetching and carrying and packing and washing. Was withdrawing cooperation really her only solution?

If Lily were honest, it sounded attractive.

Life would be much easier if she didn't have to run it around Rosie's weekends and Liam's shifts. It wasn't that she and Liam had ever discussed it. Lily worked fewer hours and he earned more, although, one way or another, most of his cash vanished into a Rosie-shaped hole. It was no trouble for Lily to do a quick Tesco-run to get Cheerios because that was all Rosie would eat for breakfast, or bung some clothes in the washing machine. It was where the scales had settled. But where would it leave Rosie if she stopped?

Maybe Rosie wouldn't come so often and Liam and Lily could have their weekends off to themselves. She knew Brendan, the stage manager, was getting cheesed off with her dodging her weekend shifts, plus getting her free time back would mean she could concentrate on writing new material. *Any* material.

As Lily considered the prospect of a reduced-Rosie existence, her spirits soared. And then plummeted. Almost in spite of herself, she liked the little horror.

Lily could understand why someone wouldn't want their partner's kid from a previous relationship around full-time; or even part-time. It wasn't rocket science. Rosie was living proof there had been someone before her. Someone who, thanks to Rosie, Lily could never, ever, erase from history. Remove the living evidence and life would be easier, full stop. But it was hardly Rosie's fault. She hadn't asked to be born, hadn't asked for her mum and dad to split up, and didn't ask to be shipped from A to B to C every third weekend.

How would the child feel in years to come? Would Lily even be in Rosie's life in ten years, if she washed her hands of the cleaning, feeding and playing now?

Wouldn't doing that make her just as bad as the stepmonster?

And if Liam let Lily disengage well, wouldn't he be an even crapper dad than he was now? As crap a dad as her and Clare's own father had been?

18

He hadn't changed.

It had been so long. Fourteen and a half years long. How could Will not have changed?

Despite the rain dripping down the back of her coat, and the moisture-laden wind that plastered her fine hair to her scalp, Clare didn't move. She would have said she couldn't, if she was given to melodrama. But she wasn't.

Put one foot in front of the other and eventually you'll reach the door, she told herself.

But she didn't move.

While she stood outside, getting soaked and staring through the steamy glass door, she felt she had some sort of advantage. Dusk had fallen and it was not yet five; the lights inside were bright over the head of the tall, dark-haired man who stood at the counter waiting for his drink, his broad back exposed to her gaze. She stared and stared, trying to get over the shock of seeing him, before he got a chance to take a look at her.

Not that it was helping.

Now that she'd seen him, Clare felt worse. The fury that had driven her since she had received his first letter, the rage that had propelled her from the school gate forty minutes before to this Bloomsbury side street had gone. There was not one *How dare he?* left.

He was Will, the Will she remembered. The one who'd promised to love her for ever, if only she loved him back.

All Clare felt now was sad. Lonely, sad and middle-aged. All washed up at thirty-three. She wanted to run back to the safety of her flat, close her curtains and lock the door behind her. She knew she couldn't. Now Will knew where she lived it wasn't possible any more. He would come to her, if she didn't come to him.

He would come for Lou, if he had to.

Will was tall and slim and his coat was expensive. His hair was cut shorter, but he still had it all. Of course, he did. Louisa had inherited her father's thick hair. It was not the sort that thinned and fell out in men. It was thick and glossy and there didn't even seem to be any flecks of grey. The looks gods had smiled on Will, just as they had smiled on their daughter.

'In or out, love?' an elderly man held the door open as his wife put up her umbrella, but he was looking at Clare.

'In or out?' he repeated, a little more testily now.

'Oh, thanks,' she said. 'In.'

There it was. Decision made for her. In.

Starbucks was crowded and noisy, steamy in the way wet English afternoons in November sometimes are. Warm with wet bodies and steam from the coffee machines that slowly covered the windows with condensation.

'*Clare!*'

It was him. If she'd had the slightest doubt, she didn't now.

He smiled, a little awkwardly, his eyes crinkling in that familiar way; and she almost smiled back. Her memory responding instantly to that shout, his smile . . . In the park, outside the pub the sixth form used, the one that was happy to turn a blind eye to their underage drinking, running up the High Street towards her. It was as if fifteen years had melted away.

'Will.' Her brain forced the smile away and his smile dropped too.

'Let me get you a coffee.' He pulled out a high chair-backed stool he'd just saved for her at the counter. Clare sat, not bothering to take off her sodden coat.

'No need, thanks, I'm fine.'

His smile was tense now. 'Let me get you a coffee, please.' It wasn't quite an order, and, anyway, she needed something to do with her hands.

'Skinny latte. Grande.'

Why had she asked for skinny? She didn't usually bother, unless Melanie was buying, and then only because Melanie was someone for whom skinny was a default position. Surely she wasn't trying to impress him, after all this time?

Will rejoining the queue gave her another chance to examine him; to calm the feelings that had surged in her when she saw him smile. This was why she hadn't wanted to see him. He was still Will, only better if anything. He had the sort of spare body that wore clothes well, and his clothes were good. Thirtysomething suited him: that loping walk, the gentle lines around his mouth giving his face character, his temples, close up, showing the tiniest flecks of grey . . .

She had to stop this. She had to be angry.

'Still no sugar?' he asked on his return.

She shook her head.

'You look great,' he added, sitting easily on the stool.

'As only a thirty-three-year-old single mother on a schoolteacher's salary can.'

He held up a hand. 'OK, OK . . . I'm sorry. I know it's way too late. I should have said this fourteen years ago. But I am sorry. And I know I shouldn't have done anything to have to apologize for in the first place, but what's done is done. All I can do is hope to make up for it.'

He gazed at her for a second, as if searching for a safe path through the years of resentment.

'I'm sorry, all right? And you do look great. I'm not just saying it. You look like you always did, only better.'

When Clare glared at him, Will looked away. She was trying to call up her fury, only it wouldn't come. Having been her constant companion for weeks — months, even — since his first letter. Now, when she needed it most, the anger deserted her. 'Liar,' she said weakly. 'But, as for looking great, right back at you, as Lou would say.'

'How *is* she?'

'She's good, you know. Although she's fourteen, so good is relative. But, yeah, she's fine.' Clare was about to say, Lou looks like you, but stopped herself. The least she could do was make him work for every bit of information.

'How's school?'

'Good. She's clever, when she can be bothered. Good at maths and science.'

Again, unspoken, like you.

For the first time it dawned on Clare that she'd been living with a female version of Will all this time. Good-looking, stubborn, more intelligent than she had a right to be. Was it any wonder she'd never managed to put him behind her . . .

'Really?' he sounded surprised.

'Yup, hates English lit, French, anything like that. Would rather tidy her room than read Jane Austen, and that's saying something. She doesn't get that from me, obviously enough.'

Will laughed.

'How about you?' she asked, trying to deflect the conversation away from Lou and on to safer territory. 'What's been happening?'

'Me? Oh . . . Went to medical school, um, as you know. Qualified eight years ago. I'm based around the corner at UCH, department of oncology.'

Clare forced herself to ask the question she'd been dreading. Better to get it over with. Better to know. 'Married?'

'Suzanne, she's a doctor too. Obs and Gynae — '

For a second, he stalled, but Clare forced him on. It was like pushing her hand further and further into a flame to see how much pain she could stand. 'Children?'

He nodded again. 'Two. Bobby's three, Katie's eighteen months. Suze is taking time out to look after them.'

'And how does *Suze* feel about suddenly discovering you've got a teenage daughter?' She couldn't keep the bitterness from her voice.

'Nothing sudden about it,' Will said, his voice neutral. 'She's always known. I told her as soon as I realized we were serious. It's a part of who I am. Is that what you think of me? That I would marry someone without telling them something that big?'

Right now Clare didn't know what to think.

'It all went to plan then?' That had been in her head since Will started speaking, but she hadn't meant to say it out loud.

Hurt flashed across Will's face, then he shrugged. 'Guess so. I'm sorry Clare. But it's a long time ago now. Years and years, I thought you'd have . . .' He paused, wary of angering her further. 'What I'm trying to say is, I did try to . . .'

'What? You did try to what?'

'I tried to make it up to you both.'

'The cheque?' Clare spat. 'You tried to buy me off! You thought you could buy me.'

'I didn't. We wanted to help.'

'So Mummy and Daddy wrote you a cheque for me! Life's not like that Will, you can't write a cheque and forget it. Everything's not on offer. It's not Tesco's, you know!' Clare was aware the family seated nearest had stopped talking, but now her fury was back she couldn't, wouldn't, stop.

'Look at you! With your cashmere coat and your successful career and your nice wife and your two point four children, and flash car and foreign holidays and nice house . . . You think you can just walk in here and have Lou back! After fourteen and a half years, no birthdays, no Christmases, no nothing. Well, you can't. She's not your daughter, Will, she's mine, and I won't let you hurt her. She's not for sale.'

Will was gazing at her, his expression sad. But behind the sadness Clare saw a determination in Will's eyes she'd seen once before, long ago, one drizzly afternoon in the park.

'She's our daughter, Clare,' he said slowly. 'Not yours, not mine, *ours.*'

Clare shook her head.

'And, for the record,' he said. 'I've never forgotten her birthday, ever. But you — *you*, not me — tore my peace offering to shreds. Then you put the pieces in an envelope and you sent it back without so much as a note. Are you surprised that I assumed any birthday cards would receive the same treatment?'

She opened her mouth to speak, but Will held up his hand. To her annoyance, Clare shut up.

'I admit I made a mistake. I can see that now. For a long time I put my head in the sand and tried not to think about her. But I never succeeded, not really. And then we had Bobby and Katie, and I realized what it meant to be a father and how much I'd let Louisa down. I'm sorry Clare, I gave up too easily.'

Clare was taken aback, but she wasn't about to show him. 'That wasn't the mistake. Being gutless and running away was the mistake.'

Will flushed. 'I was terrified, if you want to know. We were kids, Clare. And I want to make it up to Lou, get to know her. I don't want to hurt her; I just want to see my daughter. She has a right to see me. You know that. How do you think she'd feel if she found out I wanted to see her and you were stopping me?'

'*Found out!*' Clare shrieked. 'How would she find out? Who would tell her? Not me!' But she knew the answer, and she knew he was winning.

'I would rather do it with your blessing.' Will's voice was calm now. 'I'd rather make this as easy as possible. I'd have thought you would too. But if you don't, then, I'm sorry, but I'm going to see her anyway.'

'Bastard,' someone muttered.

Will glared at the family sitting next to them until they looked away embarrassed. Then he reached out and touched Clare's wrist. It took all her willpower not to flinch. Instead, she counted down from five in her head before gently pulling away.

The last time she'd sat this close to Will she'd sobbed and wept, pleaded and begged, and he had closed his heart to her. But she was wiser now and she would not do so again. Anyway, she knew the outcome would be the same. Even after all these years she could see that Will's mind was made up.

'Go near Lou,' she said, 'and I'll hit you with so many lawyers you'll be living in a shack.'

When Will opened his mouth to reply, it was her turn to hold up a hand and his to shut up.

'And for the record,' she said, 'your name's not even on the birth certificate. Legally Lou has no father. Where our daughter is concerned, your rights are precisely zero.'

*   *   *

It was a while before Eve realized that the grating noise of a bicycle bell was coming from her pocket. Alfie must have changed her ring tone without her noticing. It was bound to be her boss, wanting to make Eve feel bad for working the hours she was paid (for once). So she ignored it.

She'd left *Beau*'s office on the dot of six, having tap-danced her way through an interview at the Dorchester with a B-list Hollywood celeb who seemed to have more advisors than the head of the United Nations. And that wasn't even the worst part of her day. The worst part was that Miriam, her editor, had a *really good idea* for a feature. And Eve could think of a dozen reasons why Miriam was wrong.

Now she was halfway to High Street Ken to pick up the Circle Line, having promised Ian faithfully she'd be home in time for a family supper. She'd even remembered to buy the profiterole gateaux — a pyramid of E-numbers and saturated fat — that Alfie and Sophie loved. And if Hannah wouldn't eat it — wouldn't eat anything — well, fine . . . More for the other two. This would be the first time the entire family had sat down together since Black Saturday. Everyone — well, mainly Eve and Ian — had been on their best behaviour for weeks now; and when Ian suggested he make one of his famous chillies with nachos, tacos and enchiladas, Eve had recognized it for the white flag it was. After weeks of skating on ever-thinner ice, safety was so close she could almost touch it.

Supper, a quick update of her blog, and then bed. Nothing more complicated than that, she hoped.

The bicycle bell resumed within seconds. Huffily, Eve dragged her mobile from her pocket and was surprised to see Clare's number on the screen for the first time in weeks. Eve had been feeling bad about that. Before Ian, she'd spoken to Clare if not every day, then every other. Now they sometimes went whole weeks without speaking. In fact, they hadn't been in touch, give or take the odd text message or cursory e-mail, since the last meeting of the SSG.

And Eve knew she'd been a bad friend to Clare lately. Precisely the kind teenage magazines used to run articles about — probably still did. Every girl knew no boy ever came between *real* friends. But this was different. This was Ian — The One — and unfortunately The One came with baggage. Industrial quantities of the stuff.

'Hello stranger,' Eve said. 'What's up?'

Nothing came down the line but static and traffic. Glancing at the screen, Eve checked Clare's name was still there, lit a sickly shade of green. Perhaps her friend had sat on her phone and it had just dialled the last number in its memory.

'Clare? Are you there?'

'Eve?'

Eve could just make out her friend's voice over the sounds of traffic coming from both ends. Traffic and something else. It was the sound of sobbing, the hysterical gasping for breath of

240

someone who'd been crying so hard they could hardly speak. Panic gripped her.

'Clare? What's happened? Is Lou OK?'

'Yes . . . Lou's . . . fine . . . '

Thank God. 'What is it then, are you OK? Are you ill?'

'It's Will . . . '

'What about him?' Clare hadn't mentioned Will since she'd received that letter at the end of summer, and that was months ago. Eve had been so absorbed in her own dramas, she'd just assumed that no news was good news.

'Will's come back. He wants . . . He wants . . . Lou.'

'What?' Disbelief mingled with outrage. 'He wants to take her away from you? That's ridiculous.'

'No, no . . . ' There was another pause while Eve heard Clare take a deep breath. 'I've just seen him and he means it, Eve. I know he does. He's determined to see her whether I like it or not. I *know* him. He'll just come around to the flat and knock on the door if he has to.'

The knot in Eve's chest loosened itself a little. This was bad, but not as bad as she'd first thought. Then it dawned on her. 'You've *seen* him?' she said. 'I mean, actually seen him? When? Why didn't you tell me?'

'Hold on, hold on.' On the other end of the line, Eve could hear Clare struggling to regain her composure. 'I didn't know what to do. He kept phoning and then he threatened to come around to the flat if I didn't agree to meet him.'

Eve was horrified. 'He threatened you? Why

didn't you say? I could have come with you. We could have told the police. We . . . '

'No, we couldn't. And I didn't mean it like that, not *threatened*. Not violence. Although I just threatened him if he goes anywhere near Lou.'

'*Clare*.'

'His name's not on her birth certificate. He has no rights.'

Eve kept her silence.

'So, no . . . ' Clare was saying, 'he didn't threaten me. This is Will we're talking about, remember? I mean he threatened to talk to Lou without my permission. Anyway, I'm not being funny, but when would I have told you? You've got enough on your plate right now. You don't need my problems too.'

Eve was impressed. Clare had gone from hysterical to back together in a matter of minutes. Nearly fifteen years of coping clearly did that for you.

She glanced at her watch and hated herself for doing it. *Bad friend. Bad, bad friend.*

It was six-fifteen. Barring a Tube disaster, she would still make it back to Ian's in time. But there was Clare, plus Lou. And they were practically, if not literally, family.

Clare needed her. She'd seen Eve through some rough times. Whenever Eve had needed a shoulder Clare had been there. Now, it was payback time. Ian would understand. He'd have to.

'Where are you?' Eve asked. 'I'll come and take you home.'

'Don't be silly, I'm nearly at Euston.'

But Eve could hear the hesitation in Clare's voice. She knew her friend was tempted.

'Honestly, I'll jump in a cab and be with you in no time.' Eve cast around, there was not an orange taxi light in sight. Never was when the heavens opened and you needed one.

'No need, honestly. I'm fine now.' Clare sounded anything but. 'I'm almost at the station anyway and I promised Lou I'd be back by half six. I shouldn't have bothered you.'

'Of course you should.' Eve hoped her relief wasn't obvious. She would have gone to Clare without question. They'd always sworn they wouldn't let a mere man come between them, toasting the promise to make it binding. But Eve was grateful not to have to make that call. Nor the one to Ian telling him his big family night in was cancelled.

'What are you going to do?' Eve asked.

'I don't know. Nothing. For now.'

'Nothing?' Eve sounded as sceptical as she felt. 'Doesn't sound like nothing's an option, to me.'

'Nuh-huh.'

'OK,' said Eve, snapping into work mode. 'How hardball are you prepared to play it?'

'Pardon?'

'How tough do you want to be?'

'I'm not sure now . . .'

'Tough enough to deny that Lou is his? Tell him you need DNA tests before you let him anywhere near her?'

'Eve . . .'

243

'Well, that answered that one.'

'He was my first,' Clare said. 'I thought he was going to be my only . . . ' She was crying again.

'Sorry,' Eve said. 'I just needed to know how dirty you were prepared to play it to keep him away from Lou.'

'Not that dirty,' Clare said, hiccupping. She was back in control.

'How did you leave it?'

'I've got Will's mobile number. He's got mine. He'll call me if I don't call him.

'I know, I know,' she said, anticipating Eve's comment. 'But at least this way I'll know when it's him and I know Lou won't answer it.'

'Will you call him?'

'What do you think?' The sadness in Clare's voice was unbearable. The question was rhetorical, but Eve answered it anyway.

'I think you haven't got any choice, my love,' she said.

19

She was late, but only by fifteen minutes. Not late enough to require UN intervention.

'Tubes, rain, Clare, in no particular order,' Eve muttered, as she hurried into the kitchen, thrust the profiterole pyramid, its box now soggy from the rain, into the fridge in the vain hope it hadn't already collapsed, and hugged Alfie, Sophie and Ian in quick succession.

'Clare . . . ?'

'Tell you later.'

The kitchen was warm and welcoming. Exactly as it would have been in Eve's fantasies, if she'd ever had those kinds of 'comfortable kitchen/bubbling pots on the stove' fantasies. The windows were hidden by steam from an enormous saucepan of chilli; the table laid with glasses, plates and forks, bowls of tortilla chips and a stack of tacos and enchiladas. Alfie was in his pyjamas, Sophie was still in her school uniform. Only Hannah was missing, and Eve tried not to wonder what that meant.

'Upstairs,' Ian said, reading her mind. 'On her mobile . . . Just for a change. Thank God it's pay-as-you-go and when it's gone it's gone until next month.' He grinned to show it was no big deal, everything was going to plan. 'I told her to come down whenever she's ready.'

And what if she's not? Eve wanted to ask. But she knew the answer. *If she's not, we leave her there.* Those were the new rules.

'Inge?' Eve asked, lifting an already open bottle of Rioja off the table and waving it at Ian.

'Please,' he said. 'She's out, with the au pair posse.'

Eve poured a glass of wine and took it to him, sneaking in a hug as she did so. Ian let go of the wooden spoon he'd been using to stir the chilli and wrapped both arms around her. 'Love you,' he whispered into her hair.

'Cuddle! Cuddle!' Alfie shrieked, dropping his plastic men onto the table and throwing himself at their legs.

A stupid grin broke across Eve's face as the small boy locked his arms around them. Sophie slid down from the table and came to lean against them; not hugging, but close enough. Reaching down, Ian tousled his younger daughter's hair. For a moment Eve forgot Hannah and felt at peace. They'd done it. They'd got through their first crisis as a proper couple, and come out the other side in one piece, more or less.

Then she thought of Clare, her carefully constructed existence — a Jenga built from sheer force of will, hard slog and determination — shattered by the whim of a man who'd turned his back on her almost fifteen years ago.

Eve felt both incredibly fortunate and terribly, terribly guilty.

* * *

Three hours later the steam and the rich, dark scent of chilli still lingered in the warm kitchen, where Eve sat typing on her laptop.

'Work,' she'd said, swinging her feet off Ian's lap as he settled in to watch Newsnight. 'Just going to catch up on a few e-mails.'

He'd nodded distractedly and squeezed her hand. 'Put the kettle on while you're in there, will you?'

Eve did check her e-mails first, so it wasn't a lie, exactly. She wasn't sure why she still hadn't told Ian about the blog. Why she hadn't, in fact, told anyone. Apart from the obvious. An anonymous blog was meant to be anonymous. Telling him, telling anyone, would defeat the object.

Just scratch the surface, Eve thought, logging on and waiting for her page to download. The broadband was slow tonight.

Nobody went around announcing that they were a stepmother. As if. *Hi, my name's Eve and I'm a stepmother . . .*

It wasn't as if it was anything to be ashamed of, or even that unusual any more, but still, it didn't seem to be something most stepmothers spoke about in polite company. Yet, the minute you announced you were one, the stories came flooding out.

Now every time Eve logged on there were new comments. Some from the few regulars whose names she'd begun to recognize, but more and more from first-time visitors every day.

And then there were the hits.

She held her breath and looked at the counter. The first time Eve had worked out where it was, there had only been twenty or so hits. Women, she assumed, who'd stumbled across her blog by accident. Then, what literally seemed like overnight, several other blogs and a couple of the 'Blended Family' sites had fixed inbound links to her, and the hits started rising. One thousand six hundred and thirty-seven. Even higher than last time. Half of the returning traffic, Eve suspected, was to read each other's comments, rather than her posts, which she only updated a couple of times a week at the most.

Eve hadn't expected her blog to take off in the way it had. Of course, she'd fantasized about there being thousands of women out there like her; all looking for advice and support, and ways to blow off steam about their partners, their partners' exes, their partners' children. She hadn't realized it was actually the case until the comments started coming thick and fast.

At first it had been exhilarating. Now it was terrifying. Her own personal Frankenstein's monster.

It was cathartic enough, but private was the last word she could use to describe what *thereluctantstepmum* had become. The other day it had even been name-checked in *Sidelines* on the *Guardian*'s women's page, spotted and picked up by a journalist who was also a stepmother.

And the fact she was writing a blog that was read by thousands of people every week was hardly something to drop, cold, into conversation — even if you were getting on well, which they hadn't been. *Oh, by the way Ian. You know that blog in the paper? The reluctant stepmum?*

Well, that's me. No, didn't think to mention it sooner . . . Slipped my mind.

And so, she still hadn't told him.

Or anyone else for that matter. Not even the SSG.

But the mention in *Sidelines* had changed things. Miriam had seen it, and now she was on Eve's case. The editor wanted an article for the next issue of *Beau* on stepmothers, and she wanted it hung around this blog. Eve being one herself, Miriam had announced, made her the perfect person to write it.

Eve's first task was to track down the author.

If only Miriam knew.

Thank God she didn't.

Miriam would have outed Eve in *Beau* before you could say 'exclusive'.

Eve shuddered. It didn't bear thinking about, so she opened a blank frame and began to type. She was looking forward to writing tonight's entry. An upbeat one, for a change. How that would go down she wasn't sure. Eve suspected some of her readers would be less than thrilled. The bad news crew, as she thought of them, only wanted to hear that someone was having a worse time than they were. It made them feel better about their own situation.

They were cut from the same cloth as the readers who only liked gossip mags when they were slagging off celebrities: sweaty armpits and cellulite, broken marriages and rehab. *See*, you could be famous and a wreck. Life could be much worse.

But one regular, a woman calling herself Bella,

would be delighted.

As far as Eve could tell from the little Bella had given away about herself in the comments she'd left, Bella was a bit older than most of the other visitors to the site. Her stepchildren were grown up for a start, and the few experiences Bella described sounded very much in the past. Like Mandy, she'd advised Eve to give both herself and her eldest stepdaughter a break, and leave her to her own devices. For a while, Eve had even wondered if Bella *was* Mandy; but her posts were all about taking on someone else's kids, not blending another family into your own.

With Herculean effort Eve had heeded the advice and she wanted them to know it. Despite the fact Hannah had taken ten minutes to eat precisely two tortilla chips, then pushed a single tablespoon of chilli around, smearing it like a dark red glaze across her white plate, Eve let it sail over her head.

The supper had gone without a hitch.

It had been weeks since she had seen Ian looking so happy. Poor Ian, he must have felt as if he had four children this past month. Eve had been so busy wondering what she'd got herself into, it hadn't occurred to her that Ian must have been feeling the same.

As she'd expected, there was a post from Bella near the top of that day's comments. And it was, like most of Bella's comments, brutal in the honesty Bella applied to herself.

I've been thinking about you, it started. *Thinking that the differences in our situations are so much greater than the similarities, and* wondering how I dared give you advice. For a start, I can see now that regardless of how brattish my stepchildren were — and one of them was quite, quite vile — I have only myself to blame.

Back then, I was selfishness personified. (Still am, but at least these days I tend not to inflict myself on other people!) You moved in with a man and found yourself a full-time stepmother to his three children, knowing right from the start that they were to be your new family. That was non-negotiable, from the sound of things. Take it or leave it, and you took it.

I never factored my ex-husband's children into the equation. I met him, fell in love with him; his children from his first marriage were obstacles to be got around. I understand that now, but I can't tell you how hard it is to put it down in black-and-white. I didn't want his ex's children messing up my nice neat life. I thought we'd have a family of our own, one day, and that would be enough.

Turned out we didn't, but that's another story.

You're already streets ahead of me. You are trying (too hard, dare I say?) to be a good stepmother. I was never even prepared to try.

Eve read the post again, fascinated by this mea culpa. She was desperate to know more. Was Bella's situation irredeemable?

Beneath Bella's post was a shorter comment from Amiamug123.

It may be none of my business, Bella, but where was the steps' father when all this was

251

going on? He didn't have to go along with you. He could have just said, 'They're my kids, take it or leave it'. It's that whole wicked stepmother conspiracy again. Think about it, if Cinderella's father had stood up for her, would Cinderella have ended up in rags, sweeping out ash from the hearth and waiting on her big-footed stepsisters? Forget the stepmother for a moment. What kind of father allows someone to treat his daughter like that? I mean, really!

Bella had already responded, less than half an hour earlier.

You're right, of course. My ex was weak. He should have stood up to me. Who knows what would have happened if he had? Maybe our marriage would have collapsed sooner than it did. Maybe it would have improved. And, today, I'd be the proud stepgranny to a wonderful extended family. Who knows? Better not to linger on what might have been and never was, I find. Either way, the blame is still mine. I tried to mould his children to fit my life, and when they wouldn't be moulded, I told him it was them or me. Knowing full-well he'd choose me. And then our marriage fell apart anyway. I dread to think what they think of me now they're adults, but I doubt it could be broadcast before the nine p.m. watershed.

★ ★ ★

Next door the low murmur from the television died. Eve could hear movement as Ian turned off the lights and headed for bed, just as he had

252

pretty much every night since she'd moved in.

Things had been better this evening. Or so she'd thought. She'd even dared hope . . .

The expected sound of his feet on the stairs didn't come. Instead, the kitchen door opened and Ian stuck his head through the gap.

'Can I come in?'

He looked tired; but his skin, usually pallid from lack of sun and exhaustion, was flushed pink with the last of the Rioja and the warmth of the house. The tension, which had been etched across his face twenty-four hours a day for weeks, had eased. Eve realized she'd almost forgotten what he looked like without the worry lines threading his forehead.

'It's your . . . ' Eve stopped herself.

The reminder that it was his house, his kitchen not hers, was on the tip of her tongue, but to her surprise she realized it wasn't true, not really. Not any more. Since that first time she'd sought sanctuary here, sitting late into the night, drinking coffee and fiddling with her laptop, she'd felt increasingly comfortable. Fleetingly, stupidly, Eve wondered if Caroline had, too.

'Of course,' she said, closing down her laptop. 'I was just finishing.'

'You work too hard.'

'Pot, kettle.'

He shrugged. 'Not really.' He stopped. 'May I?' he inclined his head towards the bench beside her. 'I don't want to interrupt if you're busy.'

Shaking her head, Eve scooted up. Why was he being so formal? It was making her nervous. Did he know about thereluctantstepmum.com after all? No, he couldn't, that was the guilt playing tricks on her.

'Eve . . . I just wanted to say thank you.' Ian squeezed her knee through her jeans.

'What for?' She grinned. It was mainly relief. 'You were the head chef, as usual. All I did was buy the most fattening, unhealthy pudding I could find. According to instructions, I might add. And then only just get it home before it collapsed.'

'Alfie and Sophie didn't seem to mind,' Ian said. 'But that's not what I meant and you know it.'

With his thigh resting against hers, Eve felt a familiar pang of longing. Familiar, but distant. It had been too long . . . Not since they'd had sex, they'd gone through the motions plenty of times since the row. Although neither of their hearts had been in it, and Eve still felt discomfited by Caroline's presence. No, it had been too long since she'd felt that surge of passion for him. Life had been too hard. Her work, his work. Both of them creeping around each other's feelings and expectations; the school runs and bath times, ballet and riding lessons, and dietary requirements; with Eve constantly resisting the urge to hide in Alfie's bedroom playing with him for fear of being charged with the favouritism she knew she felt.

All of that trying not to do or say the wrong thing to Caroline's children under their mother's ever-present, stylized, black-and-white eye had left her too drained to think about herself and Ian as a couple, let alone lovers. She knew the same went for him.

'I mean thanks for this,' said Ian. 'For taking us on. I know it hasn't been easy.'

Eve opened her mouth, but Ian shook his head then touched one finger to his lips. He was looking at her intently, his blue-grey eyes holding hers. For once, being silenced didn't anger Eve. 'Let me finish,' he said. 'I have things I need to say.'

There it was again. The pang of longing, mixed with an undertow, growing stronger now, of fear. *Grow up*, Eve thought, *This isn't some sixth-form romance. It's not like he can just dump you.*

'It's been tough,' Ian interrupted her thoughts. 'It still is. And there's a long way to go, I'm not fooling myself otherwise.' Ian was watching her. 'But Eve, I'm incredibly lucky. We all are . . . the girls, Alfie and I, despite any appearances to the contrary, to have you in our lives.' He stared at her, his eyes earnest. 'Can you forgive me?'

'Forgive *you*?' Eve asked. 'What for?'

'For thinking about myself, not you. For rushing things, for not giving you time, for expecting too much too soon, for asking you to live in this house and not realizing how hard it would be for you. For not . . . ' He paused. 'For not supporting you as much as I should. For allowing there to be sides at all.'

This was not what she'd expected. If she'd allowed herself to think of it at all (and she hadn't), Eve would have decided that tonight was make or break. That Ian was giving her one last chance. If she didn't perform this time it would be her or them. And, unlike Bella, she would have been the one who was out. Because, God knows, the kids had nowhere else to go. Not that she did, right now.

'You're kidding, right?'

'Kidding?' Confusion was written all over his face.

'I'm the one who's lucky,' Eve said. 'I'm not saying it's been easy. It's been beyond hard. Beyond what I could have imagined, if I'd thought about it properly, which I didn't. Thank goodness, because if I had . . . '

'You wouldn't have done it?' Pain flickered in his eyes.

'I don't know . . . No. Yes. I mean . . . We rushed into this headlong . . . ' she stopped. 'Didn't we?'

Silence.

She could tell from Ian's face that it hadn't been like that for him. He *had* thought about it. Eve was coming to realize that he never made a single move, a single call, without thinking about it long and hard first. The lone father of three children, he didn't have the luxury of rushing headlong anywhere. All spontaneity had vanished the moment he became a widower. It had died with Caro.

Eve felt sick at her own stupidity. 'Don't get me wrong, I'm glad we did it,' she said. 'I'm so glad you asked me to marry you, to move in, and I'm even happier I said yes.'

'Really?' The hope in Ian's voice made her want to hold him, or cry, or both.

'Really,' she said, her heart pounding now. 'I

256

fell in love with you, Ian. Pretty much the first moment I met you. I love you. I love Alfie . . . ' she paused, lacing her fingers through his. 'OK, so it's hard, but I don't regret this for a minute. We can make it work. I know we can.'

He slid his free hand up her leg and his eyes did that thing they'd always been able to do. Since the first time he'd pulled out a chair for her, he had only ever had to look at her to make the pit of longing in her stomach slide downwards. To make her want to rip off his clothes where he stood; in the tiny hall of her flat, in its kitchen, in her living room . . . Something they hadn't done once since she'd moved in here. How could they with three children around?

'I love you,' he said. 'I love you so much. I can't believe I nearly fucked it up.'

'You didn't,' she whispered. 'I did.'

And then he was kissing her, his tongue in her mouth, one hand tangled in her curls, holding her face tightly as if he couldn't get close enough, his other inside her shirt, and then fumbling at her zip.

'Bed . . . ' she gasped through their kisses. 'Ian . . . The children . . . we should.'

'Fuck that,' he said.

20

'I know it's none of my business, but . . . '

There she went again.

Melanie looked up from checking the digital images of that day's new stock before it was uploaded to the site and put her face into neutral before answering Grace. 'You're right, it's not.'

'Well actually, I think it is.'

Melanie spun her seat around and faced her office manager. 'How so?'

'Vince's company runs our systems. With you and he not on speaking terms, it's affecting the quality of support we're receiving.'

'Are you suggesting Vince would be so unprofessional as to . . . ?'

'No,' Grace stood firm. 'I'm suggesting that while you and Vince were together he provided our systems' support personally. Now he's trying to avoid you, we don't get special treatment any more. We have to make do with the twenty-four-hour helpline like everyone else. Call me corrupt, but I preferred the old system.'

Melanie felt her shoulders sag. The attrition was wearing her down.

'What makes you think he *wants* to speak to me?' she asked, using the same petulant tone she found herself adopting with her mother on the rare occasions guilt made her call Boston. 'If Vince wanted to talk to me he could pick up the phone.'

'Perhaps Vince feels you should call him.'

'Perhaps Vince feels? You know how he feels, don't you? Grace! You've been talking to him behind my back, haven't you?'

Grace shrugged, as if to say, *So what if I have?* But her fingers went to tuck her short dark hair behind her ears when she'd already done so less than a minute earlier. 'His company provides our systems' support. Of course I've spoken to him. Anyway, what if I have? It's my own business who I'm friends with in my own time.'

Melanie stared at her.

'But since we're on the subject,' Grace said crossly. 'Here's what I think. This has gone on long enough. It was a small — and, dare I say, alcohol-fuelled — row that has got way out of hand. You have to call him either way, before it starts affecting the business. If you want him back, call him. If you don't, call him anyway. Call him and say he's right. You're not over Simeon. You can't give Vince what he wants. It's too much, too soon; It's not him, it's you. Use every cliché in the book if you want, just sort it out.'

Turning on her heel, Grace slammed out of Melanie's office.

Melanie wanted to yell after her. Ball her out for speaking to her like that. After all, Melanie was the boss here. Who did Grace think she was? But Melanie didn't, because the worst of it was, she knew her office manager was right.

'All right, have it your way!' Melanie yelled at the shut door, adding under her breath, 'Who do you think you are, my mother? If I wanted this

259

kind of shit, I could phone home.'

And then she picked up the phone.

★ ★ ★

'So, Melanie's not coming?' Lily asked.

'Looks that way.' Eve sipped her Americano and replayed Melanie's call in her head. There wasn't much to replay, other than the fact she'd called. First off, it was unlike Melanie to phone. Second, she'd sounded odd, like there was someone in the room with her and she couldn't talk.

'How many strikes does she get before she's out?' Clare asked. 'Two, or shall we let her have three?'

'I don't think it's written in stone,' Lily said, but she was smiling. 'Three, I guess?'

Eve nodded. 'Three. But I hope not. I'll miss her if she stops coming.'

'What did she say?' Mandy asked.

'Nothing much. Something had come up and she couldn't get out of it. She'd try to get here, but she'd definitely be late, if she made it at all.'

'How did she sound?'

'Odd. Not her usual self at all.'

'Vince,' the others said in unison.

Eve shrugged. 'Guess so. But that was weeks ago. Surely they've sorted it out by now, if they're going to?'

Mandy gave an involuntary snort.

★ ★ ★

260

'I thought you'd never call.'

Melanie smiled as she sat down, but she didn't answer. What was she supposed to say? *Nor did I?* She could imagine how that would go down.

'Hi, Vince.'

'It's good to see you. You look . . . you look great.' Vince smiled, but he didn't get up. Melanie recognized it for the small gesture of resistance it was. He clearly intended to make her work for this. Even if only a little.

'You too,' she said. Vince didn't. He looked as if he hadn't slept for several weeks. His salt and pepper hair stood in tufts, which wasn't unusual. He needed a shave and his clothes could have done with being reacquainted with an iron. As for the bags under his eyes . . . Steamer trunks more like.

Melanie felt a surge of concern. 'Have you been ill? Is Ellie OK?'

Forcing a grin, Vince shook his head. 'Nothing like that. Just the small matter of being dumped by this great woman I thought I had something good going with. Other than that, everything's hunky-dory.'

'Oh.'

What was she supposed to say?

Playing for time, Melanie scanned the room and waved the waiter over. 'Diet Coke,' she ordered when he appeared. 'Vince, d'you want anything?'

'Same again.' He waved an empty Peroni bottle at the waiter.

'Vince . . . I'm sorry . . . Really sorry, but I didn't dump you,' Melanie stared at the back of the receding waiter. '*You* left *me*. Sitting in a limousine in the middle of Marble Arch roundabout. You walked away and didn't look back.'

'That's not fair.'

'Technically it's true.'

'But it's still not fair.'

He was right. It wasn't fair, but Melanie wasn't going to admit that right now. They could talk about it, analyse the argument to death, play the blame game . . . Who was most at fault. Who'd drunk the most. Who'd behaved worst. Who'd hurt who most. But Melanie didn't want to. That night, all the following nights she'd lain awake thinking about Vince but hadn't called . . . Her rage about Simeon and Poppy, the following day's tabloids, gossip pages emblazoned with her picture. The wronged woman. Melanie's tense smile, defiant, but not reaching her eyes. The happy couple glowing and gorgeous. In love. Fertile.

Melanie didn't want to talk about any of it. She wanted to put it behind her; where it belonged.

But sitting across a table, in a dimly-lit bar, gazing at Vince's scruffy hair and the tiny lines around his eyes, the battered Converse on his feet, jeans so grubby you could mistake him for a mechanic, Melanie was surprised to find she wanted to hold him. This was why she hadn't let herself feel. Because if she did, what she'd feel was that she wanted him back.

God, she'd missed him.

'So, where do we go from here?' he asked,

262

once the waiter had deposited a beer and a glass of Diet Coke with ice and lemon on their table and retreated once more.

'What do you mean?'

'Just that.'

The way he was looking at her, as if he expected her to slap him, made Melanie feel sick. Was she so awful? Had she hurt him that much? He deserved better. 'That depends on you.' She swallowed hard.

His expression was a mixture of hope and confusion. 'In what way?'

'On whether you'll give me another chance.'

★ ★ ★

They were draining their mugs when Melanie whirled through the door, rain blowing in behind her, trench coat so wet it had changed from beige to dark grey. Water poured from her umbrella, her bag and her hair. The taxi she'd hailed had got caught up in traffic and she'd had to jump out and run the rest of the way to stand any chance of catching the SSG before they called it a night.

'Sorry, sorry, sorry,' she said, unintentionally shaking water onto a couple sitting next to them and then turning to shower apologies on them too. 'I thought I'd missed you. I'm not too late, am I? Have you got time for one more?'

'Too late for me,' Mandy said, pulling on her coat. 'I promised I'd be back by nine.'

It took all of Clare's willpower not to add, *Says who?*

'So?' Eve asked, barely waiting for Melanie to ensconce herself in the seat Mandy had just vacated. 'News?'

'Nothing much to report,' Melanie said. Her grin betrayed her, but she couldn't help it. A warm glow of contentment had curled up inside her, like a cat hogging the fire. She was here, with her friends. Women she looked forward to seeing, and saw because she wanted to, not because it was what she should be seen to do. Women who had her best interests at heart. Suddenly, everything felt very right. 'I'm back with Vince.'

Melanie couldn't help noticing Eve throw a triumphant grin in Clare's direction. *See*, it seemed to say, *told you so.*

'That's great news,' Eve said, leaning forward to squeeze Melanie's hand briefly. 'When did it happen?'

Melanie glanced at her watch. 'About forty-five minutes ago.'

Eve choked on her peppermint tea and Clare burst out laughing. 'You win,' she said to Eve. 'Forty-five minutes?' This was directed at Melanie.

'I know, I know. What took us so long? Or what took me so long, more like.' Melanie shrugged. 'The answer is, I don't know. To be honest I don't know what was stopping me. I just couldn't make myself pick up the phone. I could think of a dozen reasons why not; but I couldn't see what was staring me in the face, which was that I just wanted to, and that was reason enough. That's why I didn't come last time. I knew I should . . . See you, talk to Vince, I just couldn't. I wasn't ready.'

'But you have now,' Lily said, 'that's what matters. What happened?'

So Melanie told them. All about the fight with Grace and finally getting it together to call Vince, and him saying if she wanted to meet it was tonight or never. So she'd called Eve to say she might not make it to tonight's meeting — and had been afraid that if she missed two meetings they might kick her out. How she'd hated having to choose between losing Vince and losing them. How that made her realize she couldn't bear to lose either.

'As if!' Lily said, throwing a sideways glance at Clare. 'What kind of people do you think we are?'

'I know,' Melanie said, 'Ridiculous, huh?'

'Yes,' Lily said pointedly. 'Totally ridiculous. So, it's all systems go?'

'More or less. I mean Vince wasn't thrilled when I said I was coming on here. He wants me to go back to his after this, but I think we need to take it slowly, so I'm taking him out for dinner tomorrow night and . . . ' Melanie mimed a drum roll, 'I've agreed to meet Ellie! He's going to run it by her at the weekend, and then bring her around to *personalshopper* one evening next week. That way, it's no big deal. Ellie's just coming to one of the places he works; that just happens to be a warehouse full of accessories and shoes. I'm thinking Ellie and I can have a big, girly dress-up session!'

Melanie's face was alight.

'Blimey,' said Eve. 'If that's you taking it slowly, I'd hate to be there when you're on the fast track!'

'You ain't seen nothing,' Melanie grinned. 'Vince says he'll have me back, but he wants some proof of commitment from me. I don't mean anything heavy,' she added hastily, when she saw the expressions on the others' faces. 'I mean, Vince needs to know I mean it. That I'm not messing him around and won't turn around in a week and say I've made a mistake. I mean, can you blame him? I've just put him through weeks of hell. This matters to him. He won't let me meet Ellie unless we're serious. And he knows I won't agree to meet Ellie unless I am, too.'

'And are you?' Eve asked.

Melanie sipped her latte and looked thoughtful. 'Yes,' she said after several seconds. 'Yes, I am. This has been a wake-up call. Vince is good for me. Vince is what I need.'

The women fell silent while they considered this.

There had to be something going on in the planets, Clare thought. Not that she believed that stuff, but Lily did and, more improbably, so did Lou. Although she pretended a more scientific interest, a magnetic pull if you like, that brought everything into alignment. Eve and Ian were loved up again, and things seemed more settled with Hannah; Melanie was back with Vince; even Lily, Liam and Siobhan seemed to be coexisting, with no blood spilt. Lily had had 'serious words', as she put it, with Liam about doing his own kid's washing, and, for now, at least, he seemed to have listened.

Only Mandy had been quiet this evening. Maybe Clare would phone her later in the week. Did the SSG rules allow for that, Clare wondered, and almost laughed aloud at herself, since she was the one who'd invented most of them. And everyone else seemed oblivious to their existence.

Maybe it was a sign, Clare thought; maybe things would start going right for her too.

'Eve knows some of this,' Clare said, then realized that could translate as *Eve knows, but my sister doesn't . . .*

From the look on Lily's face, that was exactly how she'd taken it.

'Will and I had a meeting, a pretty disastrous meeting,' Clare admitted. 'He wants access to Lou, whether I'm happy about that or not. And I'm not. So I've reached a decision,' she said into their stunned silence. 'I've seen a solicitor — the head of maths recommended him, he looked after her divorce. Anyway, I was right. Will's name isn't on Lou's birth certificate, so he can't just turn up out of the blue and demand to see her. I don't want him to and my solicitor says I don't have to let him.'

A bubble of horror, pregnant with shock, expanded above them and deepened their silence, like one of those glass domes the Victorians used to keep food fresh. The others kept expecting the silence to pop, but it didn't.

Lily stared at Clare. As did Eve.

Melanie simply stared at her mug.

'Whoa,' Eve said, eventually, 'I thought you'd decided to let Will see her. You said you didn't have any choice?'

'Well, I discovered I do.'

'Run that by me again,' Lily said.

Clare gave her younger sister a querulous look but repeated herself anyway. 'I said, I've spoken to a solicitor and Will doesn't have any rights. His name isn't on Lou's birth certificate. He's been AWOL for fifteen years, give or take a few months. He hasn't sent so much as a Christmas card, let alone a penny in maintenance. He can't insist on seeing her now.'

'He sent a cheque,' Lily said quietly. 'That I do remember. You tore it up.'

'That was years ago and it doesn't count. Anyway, who told you about that?' Clare scowled at Eve, who stared back. *Don't look at me*, her stare said.

'Mum,' said Lily. 'Not that that's relevant. The point is I'm sure it would qualify as an attempt to pay maintenance. And I'll put money on Will taking this to court. And if it goes to court Lou will be asked what she wants to happen. What do you think she's going to say?'

'He'll need to get DNA tests first.'

'You think Lou would forgive you for doing that?'

'Lily.' Eve's voice sounded a warning note. None of them took much notice of Melanie, who was obviously wondering whether she was too late to get a cab back to Vince's after all.

'*Well?*' Lily repeated.

'Whose side are you on?' Clare hissed.

'Lou's . . . Since you ask.'

'*Lily,*' Eve said. 'Stop it. Now.'

'Why?' Lily spun to face Eve. 'Someone has to tell her the truth. And don't pretend you don't agree. Lou's the one who's going to suffer if this goes to court.'

But Clare wasn't listening. 'How dare you imply I'm not on Lou's side?'

'She didn't say — '

'I'm Lou's mother. I'm the one who had her.'

'We know that — '

'Clare, she doesn't — '

'I'm the one who sat up all night with her. I'm the one who put my life on hold. I'm the one who sacrificed everything! Not you, not Mum, and not bloody, fucking, perfect Will! How dare you say I'm not on Lou's side!'

Eve was on her feet, a restraining hand on her friend's arm. 'Lily's not saying . . . No one's suggesting . . . It's just . . . '

But Clare was out of her seat, her coat and bag bundled in her arms. 'You're meant to be my friends. *My family!* You're meant to side with me.'

'We do,' Eve started to say.

But it was too late. Clare was gone.

21

The whole room had fallen silent. Even the hiss of the coffee machine seemed subdued.

'Well done Lily,' Eve said wearily. 'Nicely done.'

Lily set her jaw. 'Don't tell me you think I'm wrong, because you don't. You know as well as I do that this is not about Will, it's about Lou. And Lou has a right to see her dad, whether her mum likes it or not.'

'Lily . . . '

'We didn't have a dad,' Lily said defiantly. There were tears in her eyes. 'Birthdays, Christmas, Easter, Bank Holidays. No Dad, only Mum. You'd think she'd remember how that felt.'

'There has to be a better way to convince her.'

'The trouble with my sister,' Lily continued, her voice rising dangerously close to hysteria, 'is she thinks everything is about her, her and Will. It isn't. This is about Lou. This has nothing to do with Clare, nothing to do with her at all. The sooner she gets her head around that, the better.'

'Yeah,' Eve said, rubbing her eyes with her fingers. They came away smudged black with mascara and eyeliner. 'I think we've grasped that.'

She couldn't think straight. Lily was right, obviously enough. But that didn't make the situation any better. Eve had never seen this side of Lily before. After so many years cast in the role of feckless little sister, it was rare for Lily to do more than verbally poke her tongue out at Clare. This tough love act was a whole new persona.

'Erm, I hate to intrude,' Melanie said. 'But don't you think one of us should go after her?'

'Shit, yes.' Eve suddenly woke up from the nightmare turn the evening had taken. 'Of course. I'll go.'

Thanks to the rain, Carnaby Street was more or less empty. Clare would be taking the Northern Line home so Eve took a guess and headed towards Tottenham Court Road. At the far end of Great Marlborough Street a distant, dark figure was hurrying, head down against the storm. It had to be Clare.

Eve started to run. Thank God she wasn't wearing stupid shoes.

'Stop!' Eve shouted as soon as she got within hearing distance. 'Clare! Stop! Wait up!'

She was surprised her friend could move so fast. But then as Clare would have wasted no time telling her, Eve hadn't been running around after a child for the past fourteen and a half years. Eve was gasping, and a stitch pierced her side by the time she got close enough to cause a scene. It was her best chance, Clare hated a scene.

'Clare! Stop! Lily didn't mean it. Please stop, for Christ's sake, before I collapse!'

Eve knew it would work, Clare never could stand being the centre of attention. And the smokers loitering under the awning of a nearby pub were already openly staring. Who knew what they were thinking? Eve didn't much care, but she knew Clare would.

Slowing to a halt, Clare turned and advanced towards Eve. 'Leave. Me. Alone,' she hissed, her voice icy. In the glow of a streetlight, her eyes were wet.

'Not until you listen to me. Lily didn't mean it. She cares about you, she just doesn't want you to be hurt.'

'She doesn't want me to be hurt! What does she think I am now? What does she think I'll be if he takes Louisa away from me?'

'Hurt, of course. But he doesn't want to take her away, he just wants to see her. Your solicitor might be right, Clare. But the reality is Will's not going to let this drop. He'll take the DNA tests if you make him. And he'll pass. He was your first, your only, you said so yourself. Then he'll see you in court. You don't have the money to fight this.'

'I'll get legal aid.'

Clare was listening now, so Eve stepped closer. One more step and she'd be close enough to put her arm around her friend. 'Maybe you will. But what if Will doesn't stop there?'

Her friend waited.

'What if he tells Lou? What if he goes to her school? Think about it. You can't be there all the time. You can't move and change your number. You've got a job, a life. Lou's got a life. You can't just up-sticks and disappear. I love you, Clare. I love Lou. You're my best friend, I promise I'm on your side. I understand you don't want Lou to see him, I really do. But Will's her father. I know he hurt you, but if you stop him seeing Lou and she finds out — and Lou will, eventually — she'll never forgive you.'

Clare sagged forward, tears washing make-up and anguish down her face.

Eve held her.

'How will she find out? How? Who would tell her?'

'Will. He'll tell her himself,' Eve said, her voice low as she stroked her friend's hair. 'I'm sorry Clare, but that's the truth.'

★ ★ ★

Melanie and Lily were huddled in the street under Melanie's umbrella when Eve returned. It was gone ten and the coffee shop had shut for the evening. The rain had let up a little, but they were both still drenched.

'Where is she?' Lily demanded.

'Couldn't you find her?'

'It's fine,' Eve reassured them. 'She's fine.'

'Where is she then?' Lily asked. Her eyes were huge in her thin face. It looked to Eve as if the enormity of what she'd said to her sister had just hit her.

'Don't worry,' Eve promised. 'She's going to be all right.'

Lily didn't look convinced.

'I put her in a cab and gave the driver her address and thirty quid,' Eve said, risking a glance at her watch. She wanted to be home with Ian. She wanted to be sitting on the end of

Alfie's bed, watching his little blond head in the glow of his night-light as he duffed up baddies in his sleep. She did not want to be standing outside Starbucks in the pissing rain, in central London on a Tuesday night.

'She'll be OK,' she repeated. 'She'll get through it.'

Not this week, Eve thought, not next. But at some point. Eventually. She'll get through it.

22

'It's bolognese or nothing,' Mandy kept her back to the table as she spoke.

'But Mu-um, I don't like bolognese.' Jason was whining. Mandy couldn't bear it when her youngest whined. Not least because there was always some other reason for Jason's whining that would need maternal excavation later. Nine times out of ten it was Nathan-related. Tonight, Mandy wasn't convinced she had the energy.

'Yes, you do. You've eaten it a million times. Anyway, that's what's for dinner. Take it or leave it.' Since Jason stayed where he was, Mandy assumed he'd decided to take it.

'Nathan!' she yelled. 'Dinner's on the table.' Mandy didn't approve of yelling, it set a bad example, but needs must.

'Bring it in here Mum,' he yelled back. 'I'm watching the telly.'

'Come and eat at the table like everyone else.'

No answer and no sound of movement.

Well, sod him, Mandy thought. Nathan could come and get it or he could go without. Dumping the last of the plates and a tub of ready-grated dried parmesan on the table, Mandy sat down. Her partner, John, her eldest son, Matt, and John's son Jack were already inhaling great forkfuls of spaghetti, not even waiting for her to pull in her chair. Other than being bad manners, it didn't much matter.

For once, there was no need to rush in the hope of seconds, because there was plenty to go around. Izzy was meant to be here this evening but had cancelled at the last minute. John was sulking because of it. Since Izzy was fifteen, Mandy considered John lucky to see her once a month. She'd rather pull out her own fingernails with pliers than hang around with four sullen teenage boys. Mandy felt sorry for John, she knew he missed Izzy, but frankly Mandy had too much of a headache to care. Right now, she couldn't help wishing at least one of her own boys would spend more time with his other parent, too.

Preferably Nathan.

'What's this?' Jason sniffed the parmesan tub and his face wrinkled in disgust. His bowl remained untouched.

'You know what it is,' she said, taking the tub from him and sprinkling grated cheese liberally across her own bowl of pasta.

'Smells like feet.'

Matt sniggered.

'Mu-um,' Nathan hollered from the living room. 'Where's my dinner?'

Mandy hoped the others didn't notice the shudder that ran through her. Shades of Dave, she thought.

'Come in here if you want to speak to me,' she said, feigning an indifference she didn't feel as she began expertly twirling her spaghetti around her fork.

'*Where's my food?*'

'On the table.'

'Don't answer him,' John said, suddenly banging down his fork. 'It's about time he learnt some manners.'

'*Dad*,' said Jack. Matt and Jason simply rolled their eyes.

'Leave it,' Mandy said. 'Just leave it. He'll come if he's hungry.'

'Fine,' John snapped. 'As long as you don't cook him something else in an hour's time.'

Mandy was taken aback. That didn't sound like John at all, he wasn't Mr Lay Down The Law, that was Dave's domain. Common sense told her John was upset because of Izzy, but common sense was on the backburner. 'It's none of your business,' she snapped back. 'He's my son, not yours. How I deal with him is my concern.'

Matt froze, his fork halfway to his mouth. Her eldest hated confrontation. It was one reason Matt hadn't been as upset as his brothers when their dad moved out. At least the rows had moved out with him. Jack stared at the table, obviously wishing it would open up and swallow them. Or that he could go back to his mum's for the night. Jason looked as if he'd like to go with him.

John stared at her. He looked as if she'd slapped him. 'That's how it is, is it?'

'John, don't be — '

'Is it?'

'Of course not.'

'So this isn't about that group you went out to last night?'

'No, of course it's not. I'm sorry. I'm just

tired, and I've had a bad day. Nathan! Come and eat your tea. Now!'

★ ★ ★

Mandy had a fantasy. Well, she had lots. But her favourite, the one that felt most achievable, involved her, a bowl of pasta, a large glass of a mild red (gluggable, John would call it), the sofa, and the TV — in fact the entire house — to herself.

All night.

She might watch *Corrie* or she might not. Maybe *X Factor*, not that she was into reality TV. It irritated her, although she liked *Strictly*, if she had to pick one. Maybe she'd just watch the news. She was out of touch with what was going on in the world these days. There could be a war going on for all Mandy knew. Usually was. Or she'd put on a bad film and watch that. With no one complaining, no one demanding, no one tramping in front of the television.

Just her, a TV dinner, and a glass of wine. In fact, make that a bottle. It wasn't much to ask, was it? Even Clare had that. And, Clare had drawn the short straw in most every other way. But even Clare got to eat a bowl of pasta and drink a glass of wine in peace occasionally.

Mandy had been surprised to hear Clare's voice when she answered the phone earlier, but pleased. She'd really taken to Clare, despite having only met her a few times. Clare felt like 'one of us'. Plain-speaking, hard-working, a nice woman who was at the back of the queue when

278

life's treats were handed out. *Like me*, Mandy thought. Only she wasn't at the back of the queue. She'd been standing behind the bloody door.

'I hope you don't mind me phoning you?' Clare had sounded uncertain.

'Of course not,' Mandy said. 'Glad to hear from you.'

'I got your number from directory enquiries. I hope that's all right.'

Not Lily? Mandy thought. But what she said was, 'Of course it is. That's what they're there for. I'm not being funny, Clare, but are you OK? It's just . . . you don't sound it.'

'No, I'm not. I need to ask you something . . . something personal.'

'Um, OK. Fire away.' Mandy waited. Clare didn't seem the type to ask personal questions of people she hardly knew. Mandy wasn't the type to answer them.

On the other end of the line, Clare took a deep breath. 'The thing is,' she said. 'I've had everyone else's opinion, whether I like it or not. All of them think I'm wrong. I want to know what you think before I do anything definite.'

And so, Clare told her.

Everything.

About Will, about how he'd left her sobbing and pregnant on a park bench when she was seventeen, taken her heart and her hope with him and never even glanced back.

About the cheque. (*What a mug*, Mandy thought. Although, if she was honest, she suspected she might have done the same, aged

279

eighteen.) Too proud to bank his family's guilt offering, no matter how much she needed it.

Mandy already knew about Will's letter.

But Clare told her more. About his phone calls and the meeting in the coffee shop.

And, finally, about the row at yesterday's SSG, after Mandy had left. The terrible things that Lily had said. How Eve had first sided with Lily, instead of her best friend.

As she listened, Mandy wished with all her heart she'd stayed that extra half an hour. *You couldn't have changed it*, she told herself. *You wouldn't have had the nerve to stand up to Lily.*

But maybe she would. There had been times lately, since her split with Dave, when Mandy had surprised herself. She never knew how much she was capable of, until push came to shove.

'What do you think?' Clare asked. 'What would you do in my shoes?'

'The trouble,' said Mandy, 'is what I think and what I'd do are not necessarily the same.'

'You've lost me.'

'I'd think, *Bastard, where the hell do you get off . . .* '

'I'm with you so far!' Clare managed a laugh that finished as abruptly as it started.

'But what I would *do*,' Mandy said, 'is roll over, probably.'

Clare remained silent.

'So,' Mandy asked when several seconds had slid past without a response. 'What do you think?'

'What do I think . . . ?' Clare paused. 'Bastard. Where the hell do you get off . . . ?'

'And what will you do?'

This time, there was no humour in Clare's laugh. 'Roll over, probably.'

'Is that how you see it? Giving up?'

'To a certain extent, yes.' Clare sighed. 'And a bit of me knows Will isn't a bastard, not really. He was a coward, but he was also young, stupid and terrified. And frankly I was stupid to be in that position at all. All my fantasies of living happy every after, Will running his practice and me writing novels from the kitchen table, with a brood of baby Will-and-Clares playing around my feet. Like we were hobbits or something. It was never going to happen.'

'And?' Mandy prompted.

'You think they're right, don't you? Lily and Eve.'

Mandy did. Although she wasn't about to say so. 'It doesn't matter what I think,' she said. 'What matters is what *you* think.'

Clare swallowed hard. 'I know they're right. I don't have a choice. Much as I want to take it to court . . . Much as I want to throw up at the thought of Lou standing next to Will, looking like his mini-me. I stand more chance of losing Lou if I try to stop it.'

Right answer, Mandy thought.

23

'Anyone would think the queen was coming . . .' Grace was grinning as she put a cup of herbal tea on Melanie's desk.

'Thanks,' Melanie said. She meant for the smart-arsed comment not the tea; but Grace could take it whichever way she liked. Melanie was nervous. She doubted she'd be more nervous if the queen were coming. Everything Eve had said about meeting a knee-high firing squad now made sense. This one small person — or not so small, since Ellie was apparently ten going on fifteen, held Melanie's hopes in her hand. One squeeze and she and Vince were history.

A soft knock on the door took Melanie by surprise. No one ever knocked.

'Hello? Anybody home?' Vince's head appeared around the door. Melanie pasted a smile onto her face. Show time.

'Hi there.' She started to stand up, then sat down again. What was she meant to do? Was she allowed to hug Vince, or did she have to shake hands? Was she supposed to hug Ellie? Where was Ellie? Why hadn't they discussed this in more detail? Why hadn't Vince even realized they would need a plan?

Her eyes met his and she wasn't reassured by what she saw. Naked terror.

'Hi,' she repeated. 'How are you?'

'Good,' he said. 'You?'

'Yes, good, great, thanks.' Melanie wanted to scream.

'Vince!' The voice that came from the corridor belonged to Grace. 'It's so good to see you,' she said, and kissed him warmly on the cheek. He kissed her back and Melanie felt a pang of envy. She'd no idea they were such good friends. But then it occurred to her that she knew little about Grace's private life. She'd never asked.

'It's been too long,' Grace said. 'And who's this? You must be Ellie . . . Hello, it's nice to meet you. I've heard so much about you. To tell the truth, your daddy goes on about you all the time! I'm Grace. I work here with Melanie.'

Melanie tried not to scowl. Her office manager was making it all look so easy. It was all right for Grace, she had nothing to lose.

'Nice to meet you.' The girl who stepped around Vince couldn't have looked less like her father if she tried. She was small and slightly stocky, her body still that of a child. Her thick, wavy, shoulder-length hair was a money-can't-buy-the-dye strawberry blonde, and a smattering of freckles speckled her nose and cheeks. They were the kind of looks women would envy and men would love when she grew up. When being the operative word. Right now they probably earned the poor kid the kind of nicknames that would scar her for life. She was also wearing a rather ugly pair of synthetic navy trousers and V-neck jumper for which there was no conceivable excuse.

For crying out loud Vince, Melanie thought,

you could have at least let her change out of her school uniform first.

'Good to see you Vince,' she said, following Grace's lead and giving him a casual hug.

'Hi Ellie, I'm Melanie, but you can call me Mel if that's too much of a mouthful.'

'Like Eleanor,' Vince put in unhelpfully. And Ellie scowled.

Shut up, said the look both she and Melanie gave Vince. And Melanie grinned, ice broken.

Melanie put out her hand and Ellie shook it. 'Nice to meet you,' she said. Then she stepped back and looked Melanie up and down, almost professionally, as if she'd been doing it her whole life. Which, as a seasoned survivor of the playground, she probably had. Melanie could see her taking in the T-shirt, black jacket, jeans and sequinned trainers. She felt herself hold her breath.

'I like those,' Ellie said finally. 'Amy Bronson at school has Converse, but I'm not allowed them until I've saved my pocket money.'

★ ★ ★

An hour later it was all over, and Melanie felt as if she'd been run down by a pre-teen truck.

Vince had left with a big smile on his face. When Grace had taken Ellie off to find the ladies, he'd hugged Melanie and told her over and over again how happy it made him to see 'his girls' getting on. And Melanie, caught up in his euphoria, had hugged him back with an adolescent fervour she barely remembered

284

feeling in the days when she was one.

Ellie had left with a smile on her face too; carrying the distinctive pink *personalshopper* packaging wrapped around a pair of slightly too big, red, sequinned Converse. She'd found her vocation. When she grew up, Ellie announced as she skipped down the stairs behind her father, swinging her spoils dangerously close to his head, she was going to be Mel's assistant, so she could spend all day in an aircraft hangar-sized wardrobe playing with clothes. If that was work, she couldn't wait to leave school . . .

As the door to the street slammed behind the child, Melanie smiled. There was plenty of time for the truth when Ellie grew up.

The girl was adorable, in a precocious way that seemed to be the new standard, according to the other members of the SSG. In fact, if Eve's experience was anything to go by, Melanie had got away incredibly lightly. If not her father's daughter in looks, Ellie certainly was in temperament. She loved her mum and she loved her dad, and she seemed to have little trouble accepting that while they no longer loved each other, they still loved her. Vince had explained that countless times to Melanie already, she just hadn't believed it.

But when did kids get to be so exhausting?

Melanie was sure she hadn't been so labour intensive at that age. Maybe it was her own strict upbringing, or maybe it had nothing to do with that at all. Maybe, back when she was growing up in the eighties, parents who stayed together — out of love or duty or financial need — didn't

285

feel they had to justify themselves to their children constantly. In fact, if Melanie's experience was anything to go by, they felt you had to justify yourself to them by living your life according to their hopes, dreams and ambitions once you were grown up. Unless that was simply Chinese ones. Absence of guilt certainly equalled absence of presents/treats/outings. Kids today, Melanie thought, realizing too late that she sounded like her mother, had it made.

Or possibly not.

★ ★ ★

Brought up to be seen and not heard, Melanie had spent most of her early life with her nose buried in a book. American classics, usually. *Rebecca of Sunnybrook Farm, Little Women, What Katy Did, The Little House on the Prairie.* School-approved texts her parents encouraged, but which, ironically, created and fed her wilful streak. Well, Melanie had reasoned, much to her mother's disgust; you wouldn't catch Jo/Laura/Rebecca living within the confines of their time, so nor would she. There would be no nice Chinese-American husband for her. It had caused a hundred rows over the years, and more than one protracted period of non-speaking.

But here she was, Melanie Cheung, successful entrepreneur, three thousand miles from home, successfully faking an intimate knowledge of *Gossip Girl, Twilight* and *Bebo* with a ten-year-old whose upbringing was a world away from her own.

Three thousand miles from home.

The thought made Melanie nostalgic. What were her parents doing right now? Her Manhattan girlfriends? Her brother and her niece and nephew? OK, so they'd thought she shouldn't leave — Boston in her parents' case, New York in her friends'. And there'd been many times she'd feared they were right. But now she wanted them to see . . . not that they had been wrong exactly. This was not about one-up(wo)manship, but how happy she was. She wanted to show them that things could go right after all. That Melanie had made her own life and she was finally ready for them to be part of it.

On a whim she picked up the phone.

* * *

'Come to Boston,' she said, when Vince answered his mobile.

'You what?' he sounded dazed.

'Sorry, I wasn't thinking. Is now a good time? Is Ellie still with you?'

'No, no, I just dropped her off with her mum. I've literally just got back in the car. She loved you. Was absolutely full of it.'

'I bet her mum loved that.'

'She's cool,' Vince said. She could hear the shrug in his voice. *Ancient history*, it said. *Water under the bridge*. Was it ever? Melanie certainly hoped so.

'Anyway,' he said. '*What* did you just say?'

'I said . . . ' Melanie took a deep breath. Was she about to do the maddest thing ever? 'Let's go to Boston. It's about time you met my family.'

24

'You're kidding me, right?'

Clare looked into her daughter's dark eyes and wished she hadn't. She didn't think she'd ever seen such hostility. Hostility tinged with disbelief.

'Right?' Louisa repeated, her arms folded tightly across her skinny chest. 'How can I have a dad, just like that?'

Sighing, Clare closed her eyes for the briefest of seconds and braced herself for the inevitable onslaught.

'I've told you before,' she said patiently. And she had, Louisa had known all about her dad as soon as she was old enough to grasp that other children had a mummy and a daddy and she didn't. When she started infants, and juniors, whenever the dad thing reared its head, new questions had come and Clare had done her best to answer honestly.

Admittedly the version Lou knew was censored; young love gone horribly wrong, Will going on with his life, Clare deciding to go it alone.

What Lou didn't know, because Clare hadn't known and couldn't possibly have told her, was that her father might one day return, bringing with him a whole new extended family — grandparents (two of them), a stepbrother and sister . . .

The big family that Lou had always wanted.

'Will, your dad, wrote to me. He wants . . . he wants to see you. To . . . ' the words almost choked Clare. Why should she have to do this for him? Then she chided herself. Will hadn't asked her, didn't yet know that she had decided to. 'He wants to make it up to you.' The words came tumbling out, tripping over each other. 'If you'd like to see him, that is.'

Crossing her fingers under the table, Clare said a silent prayer that Lou would say no. But Louisa just stared at her, dazed. The hostility had faded. In its place was not fury or even euphoria, not even tears.

Just . . . nothing.

'I'm going to my room for a bit,' she said eventually, pushing the chair back with her long Will legs until it butted up against the wall. 'I need to think.'

'Lou . . . ' Clare started to get up.

'Mum,' Lou turned in the doorway. 'S'OK, really. I just need to think.'

Clare swallowed hard and nodded. Her baby sounded so grown-up.

'But do me a favour, just leave me alone for a bit. No toast, no tea, no pizza. I don't want *anything*, OK? And no checking how I'm doing or if I need to talk. I don't. OK?'

Clare waited for her daughter's bedroom door to slam and the music to start, but the gentle click of its catch was barely audible, and the crunch of guitars never came. Staring hard at the scarred kitchen table, Clare willed herself not to cry. Right now, she would give anything

(anything at all, except Lou) to turn back the clock to the moment Lou stomped into the kitchen and Clare suggested she sit because Clare had something to tell her. Let Will do it. Let him live with the memory of that look on her daughter's face. But it was too late now.

What had she done?

★   ★   ★

What had begun as low-level anxiety in the pit of Melanie's stomach when she awoke that morning grew to full-blown nausea when the pilot told the cabin crew to take their seats for landing. Melanie wasn't travel-sick, she was homesick. And not in the usual sense. Not sick for home. Sick at the very thought of it.

She glanced at Vince. She wasn't sure about the pod seats they had in club class on British Airways. When the dividing partition was down, as he'd insisted for the entire flight, eye contact was almost compulsory. It was disconcerting. Vince looked exhausted; his skin waxy from the eight-hour trip, his eyes baggy and bloodshot. Could be the flight, the endlessly recycled air took its toll on even the most scrupulously kept skin. Alternatively it could be Vince's over-enthusiastic champagne consumption when they'd boarded. Either way, they'd both need a good night's sleep before going to see her family.

Catching her eye, Vince grinned, and reached across to squeeze her hand. 'Don't worry,' he said. 'We'll be down soon. Never had you pegged as a nervous flier.'

She wasn't about to disabuse Vince of his notion.

What was the point? How could she even begin to explain? Vince knew Melanie's relationship with her parents was rocky at the best of times. She hadn't been home for three years, not exactly a tell-tale sign of a close family. And she could hardly expect Vince to understand the intricacies of the culture she'd grown up in. Its ancestors and ghosts, and family shrines. The obsession with duty, and its certainty that women took second place. She barely understood it herself.

'They should be proud of you,' had been his only comment when she tried to explain why there was no point telling her parents that *personalshopper* had been shortlisted for an award.

Should be? Maybe.

Would be? Not a chance.

They *would* have been proud of her if she'd married David Deng and given them grandchildren; preferably grandsons, although a granddaughter wouldn't have hurt in the mix. The Ivy League university, the law degree, the promising career as a corporate lawyer. All that was so much and nothing, at least as far as her mother was concerned.

That was just one of the many reasons Melanie loved Vince. His laissez-faire attitude. You live your life and let them live theirs; and somewhere along the line you'll meet in the middle, that was his mantra.

In her dreams.

* ★ ★

Inviting Vince to Boston had been the easy part. Within days of suggesting it, flights had been booked and hotel reservations made. They would fly into Boston Logan and out of New York Kennedy, spending two days in Boston with her parents before getting the Bullet Train to Manhattan, for a weekend of shopping and sightseeing, as Vince put it.

And recovering, Melanie wanted to add.

The only stumbling block arose when Melanie insisted on paying for the flights herself.

'My treat.'

'But I've got a ton of air miles,' Vince protested. 'Let's use those.'

'No way,' Melanie tried to keep her tone light. '*I* really want to do this!' For a minute, the spat teetered precariously on the brink of becoming full-scale row, then Vince pulled back.

'All right,' he said, putting up his hands. 'You feel that strongly, you pay! I've heard about these women who are prepared to fight to the death to pay the bill. Just never met one before. If you're that desperate to be two grand poorer, my love, you be my guest.'

Put like that, he was right. It did sound ridiculous.

What he didn't get was that on the many times Melanie had flown across the Atlantic before — from her first parent-funded trip as a student doing Europe one summer, knees tucked under her chin in the back row of economy, through endless expense-account

292

business trips, to the last flight she'd taken, first class, funded by Simeon — Melanie had never, ever paid for her own ticket. That she put these flights on her credit card had assumed almost mythological significance for her. It was a sign. Of what, she wasn't sure, but it was definitely a sign. Why should she expect Vince to understand that?

The other thing he didn't understand was why she insisted on booking into the Marriot down on the waterfront when her parents had a perfectly good six-bedroom house less than an hour's drive away in Cambridge.

In that, at least, Vince and her parents had been in total agreement.

Even so, inviting him had been the easy part. Calling home was an entirely different ball game. Several times she'd picked up her office phone and started to punch in her parents' number. Once she'd even allowed the line to connect and heard the phone the other end start ringing. But always she hung up before there was any chance of anyone answering.

What was she supposed to say if they did? *Hey Mom, it's me. I've got a new boyfriend and I'd like you to meet him. Yes, I know we've hardly spoken since I phoned to tell you Simeon had dumped me and you said I told you so . . .*

She could always play dumb. *Hey Mom, how's Pete? How're the kids? How's Dad's work? I was thinking, if you're around at the weekend, Vince and I might drop by.*

Or confrontational? *Hey Mom. No, still not pregnant, sorry. But I thought maybe I'd come see you anyway. Maybe you could invite my brother and his brood, just to highlight to my new man what a total let-down I am on the grandchildren front.*

The fact was, when you hadn't seen your parents for three years, had only exchanged holiday and birthday cards since . . . Well, there was no easy way to pick up the phone.

And so she hadn't. Resorting instead to the coward's way out, she e-mailed her father at his office, mentioned that they were going to be on the east coast anyway, and suggested that she and Vince come to visit.

It was so long since she'd lived in the States that it slipped Melanie's mind that they would be there right after Thanksgiving. Thank God they hadn't chosen to go a week earlier. Thanksgiving weekend with her folks would have been way too loaded. Much later and it would have been too close to Christmas for comfort. And anyway, Christmas was out of the question for Vince. His holiday season was fully booked with a complex web of Ellie-related arrangements. Christmas Eve and Boxing Day were his, Christmas Day she would be with her mother. New Year's Eve, Ellie was with Vince again, New Year's Day, back to her mother.

And, as always, Vince would be doing all the delivering and collecting, driving on some of the worst days of the year. Melanie couldn't help feeling he'd been stitched; but she knew she had to keep that thought to herself if she wanted to be part of his complex Christmas equation. And she did.

Melanie had met Ellie twice since her visit to *personalshopper*, and their relationship was growing easier with each meeting. The girl was chatty and friendly and outspoken in the way only children can be. She was certainly easier company than almost everyone else Melanie spent time with. To Ellie, Melanie was Daddy's friend; and now Daddy didn't live with Ellie, Daddy needed a friend because otherwise he would be lonely when Ellie wasn't there.

Having accused Vince of planting this devious, if brilliant thought, Melanie had been forced to accept that Ellie had arrived there on her own. It was that straightforward.

To begin with, Melanie had wondered if Eve was doing something wrong with Ian's daughters. Getting on with Ellie seemed so effortless. How could Hannah be so much more difficult? But Vince had seen it more clearly. Ellie wasn't threatened by Melanie. Melanie was Daddy's friend, so she was Ellie's friend. Ellie was happy to let Melanie keep Vince company when Ellie herself was otherwise occupied. Which was often. After all, Ellie was a busy girl; what with having to look after her mother on top of school and ballet and music lessons and drama.

For Hannah and, to a lesser extent, Sophie, it was different. Their father had them. Why would he possibly need Eve too?

Put like that, Melanie could see Eve's problem.

Melanie's father had responded promptly. Maybe not with as much enthusiasm as she would have liked; but with as much as she could reasonably hope for. His acceptance came with inevitable grumbles. What a shame you couldn't have managed a week earlier and been here for Thanksgiving weekend, after missing all these years. Your mother is surprised you won't be staying at the family home. She says it's no trouble to make up your old room and one of the spare rooms. She has to change your bed anyway, after Peter's eldest will have used it for Thanksgiving.

How one person could pack so much disapproval into a single paragraph never failed to amaze Melanie. All those sly little put-downs. A dozen responses itched to escape her fingers and wreak havoc on the keyboard. A dozen responses to pour oil on fire, as they had a thousand times before when she had bitten her tongue less resolutely.

Instead she decided to ignore it. It was that or get into a family fight before she'd even set foot in America. And Melanie was determined to prove that, this time, she had moved on.

★   ★   ★

Boston's smell always took her by surprise. Briny, pungent, a melting pot of salt and that day's catch stirred by a chill wind off the Atlantic. A constant reminder that the city owed its existence to the sea. Why it came as a shock to her, Melanie didn't know. She had grown up here; since her family had only moved from the Back Bay area to Cambridge when she was well into her teens and her father's business

296

importing electrical goods from Shanghai had hit the big time.

'I had no idea,' Vince said, as he slid into the seat of the car they'd hired, looking better for a night's sleep, in a newly pressed jacket and his smartest jeans. He'd even broken out a pair of real shoes for the occasion. Melanie had only seen him this smart once before . . . It didn't bode well, so she pushed that memory away.

'No idea what?' she asked, unwilling to let black thoughts cloud her day.

'That Boston was a port. I know it probably sounds stupid to you, but I just didn't know. When people say Boston back home you think trees, leaves . . . The whole New England autumn thing, you know.' He shrugged.

Melanie grinned at him. 'Trees I can do. But the beginning of December's a bit late for the leaves. We're all out of them by mid-November, usually. Mind you, the weather's so screwed, there might still be some hanging around for your viewing pleasure.'

He punched her arm gently and settled back in his seat to take in the view. How could one person look so instantly at home? Melanie wondered, pushing the doubts that had plagued her since she embarked on this to the back of her mind and shutting the door on them firmly. Wherever Vince wound up — with the occasional notable exception — he just put his feet on life's desk/sofa/dashboard and let events take their course.

What a skill, Melanie thought as she tried to focus on steering them through the traffic that

297

clogged West End's streets as they made for the Longfellow Bridge.

This was OK, this could work. Vince was a good guy, with a great kid, and she liked being with him. Scratch that, she liked being *here* with him. Now that was something she thought she'd never say. She liked seeing the city she'd known her whole life, and hadn't been able to escape from fast enough, through his eyes. It made her wonder if, just maybe, she could learn to love it again. And, by extension, her family.

Surely they would take to Vince? How could they not? And through him, maybe they would take to her again, too?

25

'What am I supposed to wear?' Lou demanded.

Her mood, which had been ricocheting precariously from exhilaration to thunderous ever since Clare had told her that her dad was back, was now practically murderous.

'I get to meet my dad for the *first* time,' she glared at Clare, making it clear precisely whose fault she considered this, 'and all my clothes are crap.'

Taking a deep breath, Clare tried not to rise to the bait. She had considered taking her daughter shopping to buy a new outfit for the occasion, but there was no way her credit card would stretch to it.

'Wear what you usually do, my love,' she said mildly. 'It's you he wants to see. But get on with it. Will . . . your dad's going to be here in fifteen minutes.'

Dad. The word made her want to gag.

Lou glowered at her as if Clare's comment was beneath contempt, and slammed off up the hall to her bedroom.

Clare thought her heart would break irretrievably the morning she punched Will's number into her mobile and called him to declare surrender. She did not tell him that his victory was down to the unexpected army she had found marshalled against her. The enemies lurking among her closest allies. It was their support for his position — Eve, Lily and even Mandy — that finally defeated her.

Will had the good grace to keep the triumph out of his voice as he suggested he write a letter to Lou, explaining 'everything'. When Clare agreed, but only on the condition he send it via her with a stamped-addressed envelope so she could censor it first and then repost it, he made it clear what he thought of her idea, but went along with it anyway. Why wouldn't he? He'd won. What did it cost him, to give her that particular inch?

As it was, his letter hadn't really explained anything at all. Certainly no more than Louisa already knew.

All it said was that he was Lou's father; he was deeply sorry he had been out of her life for so long; and he hoped to make it up to her now. After reading it what had to be over a hundred times, the first few out loud, the rest huddled behind her closed bedroom door, the fury that Clare had been waiting for had finally come crashing down on Clare's head.

Secretly Clare hoped the fury held firm in the face of Will's charm. She had a horrible feeling it wouldn't.

'What's with the eye-liner?' Clare asked, when Lou emerged fourteen minutes and fifty-nine seconds later.

Her daughter's eyes were rimmed with hard black lines. She looked both much older, and very, very young.

'I'm not taking it off. You can't make me.'

Clare was about to point out that, actually, she

could — if she could be bothered, if she had a death wish — when the doorbell rang. 'That'll be him,' she said unnecessarily.

'You don't say,' Lou shot back as she stomped towards the door.

Keep calm, Clare told herself. *She doesn't mean it. She's just scared.*

'If he hates me it's all your fault!'

Wow, Clare thought as the door slammed with such violence a framed print on the hall wall bounced on its cord. *Where did Lou learn to be so harsh? Surely she doesn't get that from me? Does she?*

★   ★   ★

Clare had promised herself she wouldn't look. That she wouldn't stand at her window, that she wouldn't peer through a crack in the curtain, that she wouldn't make it harder for herself than it already was.

So, of course, she did all three.

He was waiting on the pavement below her window, hovering beside his car, which was something large, midnight blue and new. Something Clare was sure would impress the hell out of Lou. At least he had the grace to look nervous.

His coat was just the right side of too big, his hair the right side of short, his body the right side of skinny and lanky. From this distance he could almost pass for the boy who had stood outside her mother's front door waiting for Clare to hurtle down the stairs into his arms fifteen years ago.

Then the downstairs door slammed and fifteen years vanished and Lou was there. Tall, slender, eyes so dark that, from this distance, they looked like black pools, thick dark floppy hair . . . The mirror image of the man who stood on the pavement with his arms outstretched, the man whose arms she was throwing herself into. The image of her father.

★　★　★

It was an hour before Clare was able to pull herself together. If she thought she'd cried after surrendering to Will, both times, it was nothing to the sobs that had wracked her as she recalled her daughter folded in Will's arms.

The hug had gone on for ever. It had been all Clare could do not to run downstairs and rip them apart, but she had caught herself. Instead she had cried as father and daughter had hugged and hugged, as if hugging could make up for all the years of missed hugs and bath times and birthdays and Christmases. Then he'd opened the passenger door of his big, midnight blue car, and her daughter — *her* daughter — had slid into the seat as if big cars and wealthy fathers were something she'd been born to.

A minute later Clare had watched, tears still washing down her face, feeling her heart twist in her ribs as if Will had grasped it. But Will was already driving Lou away.

She didn't know which hurt her most. That Will had come back into her life and turned it upside down. Or that he had come back, but so obviously not for her. All this time, she saw now, she had been waiting. Waiting for nothing.

★ ★ ★

Clare didn't know what to do with herself.

She couldn't believe how silent the flat was without Lou. It was stupid, because the flat was always silent without Lou, and usually Clare relished the peace and quiet. Not to mention the hot water. But this time it was as if her flat knew the silence was more permanent.

Not permanent, she corrected herself. Three hours was hardly permanent. Lou had been known to spend longer than that in Topshop.

Will had promised he'd have her back by five. And he would. She knew he would. A lot rested on this visit. He wasn't Satan, he hadn't come to steal her baby and feed Lou to the flames. He just wanted to take his daughter somewhere quiet so they could talk. The flat was too small and Clare would have been ashamed to let him see inside anyway. It was pointless to refuse.

She could always pick up the phone and go out, too. Lou wasn't the only one with places to go, people to see. Clare hovered by the handset, running through the names and numbers logged in her head.

Eve, usually her first port in a storm, was tied up with Ian and his kids. To be fair, she'd already offered to bunk off, to distract Clare with a late lunch, alcohol and mindless chat. But Clare had put on a brave voice and refused. Stupidly, she saw now.

Lily? Hardly. She and Lily were only back on speaking terms thanks to Eve's international peacekeeping skills.

Visiting her mum was out, too.

'Finally!' she'd exclaimed, her voice almost exhilarated when Clare called her in search of sympathy and possibly tea and cake, too. 'That girl needs a father, didn't I always say so?'

The answers to that were so many and various that Clare, for once in her life, was speechless. Good job too, since she was running out of family members to fall out with.

There was Mandy of course, but much as Clare liked her, she felt awkward about ringing her again.

Melanie? She would never expose herself to Melanie like that. Ms skinny latte and dressing on the side? No way. The mere thought of the horror written across Melanie's face as the last meeting descended into sibling warfare still made Clare shudder with embarrassment.

There were friends from school, but they were just that, 'teacher friends'. Fine for sharing a coffee in the staffroom and moaning about work, but not people you turned to in a crisis. She could call one if she fancied a shopping trip; but they'd realized years ago that, for Clare, participation in their much-gossiped about monthly shopping hits on Brent Cross was out of the question.

So that was that then.

She was all out of people to phone. Not much to show for thirty-three years of friendships, Clare thought bitterly. A teenage pregnancy did that to your social life. The friends who had deserted you in case your condition was contagious (or if they didn't, their parents did) and the opportunities to make new ones were few and far between.

In the kitchen Clare flicked the switch on the kettle, to make tea, then flicked it off again.

She could cook, she supposed. Maybe bake something for Lou's return? Chocolate fudge cake always went down well. At least when Lou forgot she was on a permanent diet.

Reaching into the overhead cupboard she took down a bag of self-raising flour, cocoa powder and the scales, and then stopped . . .

Lou would have eaten already. And something told her baking wasn't going to cut it today. Her heart wasn't in it. Her heart was speeding along the A10 in a smart blue car.

Replacing the ingredients in the cupboard, Clare opened the fridge. She ate the remaining triangle of Dairylea and peered inside Lou's personal jar of crunchy peanut butter, before pouring herself the dregs of that week's bottle of wine. Barely half a glass. Not enough for her sorrows to even paddle in.

Her purse didn't offer much respite.

It contained a single ten-pound note. If she went out and bought another bottle she wouldn't have enough for delivery pizza tonight. And it was Saturday. Lou always had pizza on Saturday. It was the law.

That said, if Lou ate with Will, she might not want pizza. On the other hand, if she hadn't, spending the money would simply highlight her mother's already glaring financial inadequacies. Unwilling to risk it, Clare slid her purse back into her bag.

At the end of the hall, Lou's bedroom was dark and smelt of teenager. All dodgy perfume and dirty socks. Clare pulled the curtains to let in the weak winter sun, took one look at the mess it revealed, and shut them again. But not quickly enough to avoid her red-eyed, puffy-faced reflection in Lou's mirror.

Her own room wasn't much better. It didn't smell of teenager, obviously, but it smelt of something, and it was rammed with junk. It was where Clare kept the flat's overspill; everything there wasn't room for in the other two and a half rooms lived here, which meant one wall was piled high with cardboard boxes full of the detritus of her and Lou's existence.

She hadn't even known what she was looking for until she'd hefted a box out of its place halfway down the pile and emptied its contents onto her unmade bed. Her teenage diaries. She hadn't looked at them or even thought about them for years. Not since Lou was born. She hadn't had time to keep them up with a baby to look after and a degree to get. And then teacher training, real lessons and marking homework took their places. Or so she'd told herself.

Hadn't had the courage to examine her own fuck-up, more like.

Dumping the rest of the stuff back in its box and shoving the box haphazardly into a corner, she tucked a bundle of old exercise books, each one faded to an age-washed dusty pink, under

306

her arm and headed back to the kitchen.

She took a sip from her half full glass and nearly gagged. The wine was sour, so she tossed it. Tea it was. She put the kettle back on, and settled down to read. Clare wasn't quite sure when she got up to find a notepad and a Biro, or why she decided to copy out the bits that struck her most powerfully.

The pain was as fresh as it had been the day Will turned his back on her by the duck pond and walked away. But there wasn't just pain, there was strength too. Where had she found it? Barely eighteen, no longer a girl and not yet quite grown up. Strength enough to defy everyone and have the baby nobody but her wanted. Not even her, not really, not at the start. Clare was surprised and impressed. Could this fierce and feisty girl really have been her? Where was she now? She couldn't have wandered *that* far, surely.

★　★　★

Five o'clock. Clare looked up, dazed. How could it be that time already?

It couldn't be. But the street door had definitely slammed and now she heard the heavy, unmistakable thud of Lou's Dr Marten's on the stairs. Perhaps things had gone badly and Louisa was home early. Clare's spirits soared, and then she caught herself.

A glance at the clock on the cooker confirmed she wasn't early. It was five o'clock. Five minutes past five.

The hours she'd dreaded from the moment she'd realized she had to let Will into Lou's life, had flown. When she had sat down at the kitchen table and opened the first of the exercise books, the ones BW, Before Will, before love, before her dreams of being a writer had been abandoned on a park bench, the clock had said ten past three. And now, it said five. Almost two hours had vanished. Afternoon dusk turning to darkness outside, as her tea grew cold along with the flat. For some reason the heating hadn't come on. Again.

Fingers cramping, Clare unwrapped them from her Biro and hurriedly scooped up the notebooks and sheets of lined A4 that were now covered with her teacher's scrawl. She was startled to find she was reluctant to stop, but there was no way Lou was getting hold of this until Clare was good and ready for her to see it. If ever. There was nowhere to hide them in the kitchen that would be safe from Lou's scavenging, so Clare ran the short distance to her bedroom and shoved them in her chest of drawers under a pile of jumpers.

The front door was opening as she emerged.

'Hello my love.' She forced herself to sound cheery. As if Lou had simply been out with her friends from school, not her long-lost father. 'How did it go?'

'It's bloody freezing in here.' Lou flicked on the hall light. In her haste to hide her diaries, Clare hadn't noticed how dark the flat had grown outside the sanctuary of the kitchen.

'Don't swear,' she said. It was a reflex action.

308

Lou was clutching a carrier bag to her chest. Not so much a carrier bag as a gift bag, something much flashier and made from expensive white card, with a twisted cord handle and a logo.

The logo was hidden under Lou's arm. Intentionally, to judge by its angle.

'What . . . ' Clare opened her mouth to ask about the bag and then shut it again. On the phone earlier, Will had asked Clare if it was OK for him to give Lou a present. Grudgingly, she had agreed. There was no doubt in Clare's mind that this — whatever this was — was it.

Clare caught a glimpse of Lou's scowl under her curtain of hair and suddenly felt nervous. Her daughter's dark eyes were more impenetrable than ever, her face thunderous.

'What is it?' Clare asked. A wave of nausea surged in her stomach. What had Will done to her baby? 'What's happened?'

'Don't you dare,' Lou said. There was a new kind of anger in her voice. An anger that Clare couldn't remember having heard before. It was more grown-up. Frankly, it scared her.

'Don't speak to me,' Lou said, pushing open her bedroom door. 'Not now . . . ' The door slammed behind her. 'NOT EVER!'

26

'He told her?' Eve was horrified. 'He wouldn't do that. He promised.'

'That's what I thought, but it seems I was wrong. He would and he did. And sadly, he hadn't promised. I think I just hoped . . . I *believed* he wouldn't, if I even thought about it, and I'm not sure I did. More fool me, eh? It just didn't occur to me he would do something so . . . '

'Who? Do what?' Lily asked, flinging herself into a chair beside them. 'Sorry to interrupt,' she added, when Clare glared at her. Jeezus her sister knew how to bear a grudge.

'Will,' Clare whispered, 'told Lou about the cheque. He said he tried to give me money when she was born and I sent it back in pieces.'

The three women sat in silence for a moment, taking in the enormity of it.

'I still can't believe it,' Eve said. 'There has to be some mistake.'

'Believe it,' said Clare. 'And there's no mistaking the fact that, right now, Lou hates me. She won't speak to me, won't look at me, won't even stay in the same room as me for longer than it takes to make a sandwich. I thought nothing could be worse than her glowering moodiness of the last fortnight, but this . . . ' Clare dropped her head so the others couldn't see the tears building.

When she looked up, her eyes were dry.

'Give me the teenage sulks and a bit of harmless door slamming any day of the week.'

'When did she tell you this?' Eve asked. 'If she's not speaking to you?'

Clare's smile was bleak. 'Oh, she found her voice for that long.'

Instead of scowling when Lily put up her hand for permission to speak, Clare simply looked sadder. 'I'm not that bad, am I?'

'I was just thinking,' Lily said. 'This calls for something stronger. Let's reconvene to the pub over the road.'

'Shouldn't we wait for Mandy and Melanie?'

'Melanie's not coming,' Eve said. 'And before you say it, no we're not chucking her out, she's got a brilliant excuse, the best. She's taken Vince to meet her parents . . . I know!' She added, seeing Clare and Lily's shocked expressions. 'But let's save that for later. What about Mandy?'

It was Clare who answered. 'She's on her way. I'll text her and tell her where to find us.'

Eve and Lily exchanged surprised glances.

* * *

'What are you looking so smug about?' Melanie asked Vince as he rolled away from her in response to the beeping of his mobile. 'You're good honey. But you're not *that* good!'

'Not that good?' He grinned. 'Your parents love me. The parents who are impossible to please, I might add. Your brother loves me, you love . . . '

Melanie saw his confidence waver. 'I love you,'

311

she filled in for him.

'And, judging from that, you just had the orgasm of your life. I think a man's entitled to feel a little smug.' Rolling back, he tweaked her nipple.

'Ouch,' Melanie squealed, shifting as far as the king-sized bed would let her, but she was hamming it up. The truth was, one tiny tweak and she'd felt herself grow wet again.

'Text from Ellie,' Vince said, scrolling down. 'She says hi, she hopes Boston is nice, and can she have a purple iPod nano for Christmas.'

'In that order?'

Vince's mouth twisted. 'Not precisely.'

'Oh well, it makes a change from pink, I suppose.' Scooching up behind him, Melanie slid her legs either side of his body, her small breasts squashed against his broad back. Idly, she meshed her fingers in his chest hair.

'Don't,' Vince was texting frantically. 'You're distracting me.'

'You don't say,' Melanie's hands crept downwards. 'Surely a master of the universe — or at least of the Cheungs of Cambridge Massachusetts — isn't *so* easily distracted?'

★ ★ ★

The truth was, Melanie still couldn't believe things had gone so smoothly with her family. So smoothly it was almost unsettling. For the first time since adolescence, there had been no rows, no bickering, and only a few moments of mild friction.

As mellow as ever, Vince had been like a sooth-
ing balm on the prickly heat of years of Cheung
family tension. That her brother Pete and his wife
had brought their kids for the day had helped
dilute the atmosphere as well. Vince and Pete had
hit it off instantly and Melanie had always rated
Lucy, his wife. Although she couldn't for the life
of her see how Lucy put up with her younger
brother. As for her nephew and niece . . .

'How did you get so big?' Melanie shrieked,
trying and failing to scoop up Mikey and Mia, as
they tumbled out of the back of their father's
humvee. Last time she'd seen them they had
fitted one under each arm, no problem.

'We grew, Auntie Melanie,' Mikey said, his
face straight. 'We didn't see you for a long time.'

Stick it to me, kid, why don't you?

'I know,' Melanie said wryly. 'Sorry 'bout that.
I've been really, really busy. But I've missed you
tons and I brought you presents to make up for
all the ones you didn't get.'

'Out of the mouths of babes,' Pete hissed,
rolling his eyes. 'And you shouldn't have. They're
spoilt rotten already. You should see the stuff
Mom and Dad have already got them for
Christmas.'

'It's OK,' Melanie hissed back. 'By the way,
you gotta get rid of that SUV. It's so uncool.'

Sticking out his tongue, Pete herded his
children into the house. 'Whatever! Come see
Granny and Grandpops,' he said.

'But we saw Granny and Grandpops last
week,' Mia wailed.

Out of the mouths of babes indeed.

313

* ★ ★

'Vince seems like a great guy,' Pete said later as 'the children' filled the dishwasher, same as it ever was. 'So laidback. He's got Mom and Pop wrapped around his finger. And you know how easy that is to pull off. Like not at all . . . '

Melanie grinned. She couldn't help it. She felt . . . Melanie didn't know what she felt, happy, she supposed. 'He is a great guy,' she replied. 'You know what bro, I think he really is.'

And Pete grinned back. 'Definitely better than the last one, anyway.'

To say Pete had not taken to Simeon was something of an understatement. Mind you, no one in the family had taken to Simeon. But Melanie's younger brother usually liked everyone. So his loathing for Simeon should have set alarm bells ringing. The fact it hadn't . . .

Well, her college friends didn't call her Bull-Headed Mel for nothing. Still, at least Pete hadn't said he'd told her so. Yet.

'Watch it kiddo,' she said, knuckling his upper arm where she knew it hurt. He was right and she knew it and he knew she knew it. Vince was definitely better than the last one.

Melanie had been worried about leaving Vince with her parents, but as it happened she needn't have. Her father declared him a nice young man (politely ignoring the fact that Vince's hair was decidedly greyer than his own) and gave him a glass of his best scotch. Even her mother smiled approvingly and only mentioned David Deng once. To inform

314

Melanie that David's ultra-fertile wife, Ling, had just produced grandchild number four and grandson and heir number three. Such restraint was something of a record by her mother's standards. Melanie had felt stupidly grateful.

'Who's David Deng?' Vince asked, when Melanie's mother disappeared into the kitchen to embark upon preparations for the third meal of the day. It had been so long since Melanie had spent any time in her parents' house that she'd forgotten about all the food. She wondered if the clothes she'd packed would even fit by the time they got back to the hotel.

'Melanie's intended,' said Pete, ducking from the slap he knew was coming.

'Pete,' Lucy said, rolling her eyes. 'Give poor Melanie a break.'

'Poor Melanie, my foot,' Pete said. 'She's had three years of peace.'

'I've been in exile,' Melanie protested.

'Self-imposed,' Pete shot back. 'I, on the other hand, have done every Thanksgiving, birthday, Christmas, Chinese New Year, you name it. You have some making up to do. And, anyway, it's a statement of fact. That's who David Deng is.'

'He is not!' Melanie protested.

'Was!'

'Only in Mother's dreams.'

Pete shrugged. 'That's enough,' he said.

'The Dengs were family friends when we were growing up,' Melanie explained to Vince. 'David is their eldest son. Good, clean-cut, all Chinese/American guy. Straight As, stratospheric SATs. Went to Harvard. Mother harboured

315

fantasies about us getting married. The union of the eldest daughter and eldest son of two respectable Boston Chinese families to produce a little Deng-Cheung dynasty. In her head it was a done deal.'

'But Melanie wasn't having any,' Pete said. 'All hell broke loose when she announced she was dating some guy who stacked shelves at Home Depot!'

'*Home Depot?*' Vince was unable to hide his disbelief. He'd never figured Melanie as a girl to hang around boys who worked at B&Q, even as a teenager.

'He had a Harley. I was a junior at high. What can I say?' Melanie shrugged. 'He was as close as Boston got to Matt Dillon. It was your basic teen rebellion.'

'A teen rebellion that lasted, ooh, twenty years.' Pete's eyes slid towards Vince, as if to say, 'until now'. Melanie was grateful her brother hadn't spoken the words out loud. She had hoped her family would like Vince, but it had never occurred to her that they would like him *this* much. They seemed to see him as some sort of return to respectability. But then again, she ran through the list, he worked in IT, he owned his own company, he'd admitted his savings had grown large enough to cause him concern. Simeon had been different. He'd been too rich, too flash. Vince was solid. It was an odd realization. She'd never seen Vince as respectable before.

'Anyway,' she said, dragging the conversation back to safer territory (as long as her mother

316

wasn't in the room). 'Who's to say he was ever interested in me.'

'Ah come on, Melanie. You were the local babe, everyone knows that.'

'It wasn't easy being her brother, you know,' he said to Vince.

Melanie struck up the air violin, but both men ignored her.

'All these older guys wanted to be my friend and I never knew whether they liked me or just wanted to date my hot big sister!'

'Including David Deng?' Vince asked.

'He was crazy about her,' Pete said. 'But he didn't have to bother to go through me. His parents approved, our parents approved, he approved. Everybody approved . . . '

'Except me,' Melanie put in. 'He was such a geek.'

'A multi-millionaire geek now, I think you'll find,' Pete said. 'And even if he hadn't been, you wouldn't have dated him just 'cos Mom and Dad wanted you to.'

Melanie shrugged. 'And you would?'

'Date David Deng? No way!'

'You know what I mean! The point is, Vince . . . ' Melanie lowered her voice, not only to prevent her parents overhearing but also to keep out of Mikey and Mia's earshot. 'Mom and Dad never really forgave me. Especially Mom. They held out hope I'd see sense, until about ten years back, when he got engaged to Ling. Since then they've just been straight out furious that I blew my chances. Blew *their* chances of a Cheung-Deng dynasty more like.'

'It got really bad,' Pete said, 'about five years ago, when he opened a legal practice in Boston and bought a mansion on Beacon Hill. I thought Mom was going to combust.'

He glanced at Melanie, who nodded.

'Man, she was furious,' Melanie said. 'Now, not only is David Deng the one that got away, he's a pillar of the local Chinese community *and* he's producing heirs like they're going out of fashion.'

'The inference being,' said Pete. 'That if she'd done what they wanted all along, she, too, would have the enormous brood.'

'Yeah,' Melanie's mouth twisted. 'A whole humvee full of little Cheung-Dengs.'

Her brother graciously ignored the dig.

'They've never let me forget it. Usually when I come home it's David Deng this, David Deng that, isn't it?'

Pete nodded vigorously. 'Yeah,' he said and once again his eyes slid towards Vince. 'Family occasions are pretty intolerable when Melanie's around. And sometimes when she isn't, if we don't manage to keep the conversation away from her. Until now, of course.'

★   ★   ★

'So where were we?' Eve prompted when they were finally ensconced in a corner table in the pub across the street with a bottle of house red. Mandy had joined them ten minutes earlier, and had just got back from fighting her way to the bar. She was drinking a Coke for some reason.

318

'I think my daughter was mid-yell.' Clare downed half the glass Lily had just put in front of her. And Lily raised her eyes when Eve topped it up.

'She came out of her room about an hour later, holding this . . . gadget I'd never seen before. I innocently asked what it was, and Lou told me it was none of my bloody business. I said *don't swear*, and that was it. I walked straight into a knock-down, take-no-prisoners fight. Over fourteen years of being a single mother and I fall for the oldest trick in the book.'

Clare shook her head, as if astonished at her own naiveté.

'Oh my God,' she said, and her eyes widened. 'Lou stuck it to me. Called me a selfish, manipulative bitch. Said her childhood had been crap and it was entirely my fault. That if not for me she'd have had a dad all these years. I'd made us poor, apparently. Because I like being a martyr, when all I'd had to do was let her dad — get that, *her dad*,' Clare's fingers mimed inverted commas in the air, 'pay his way. As if the CSA have been battering down our door for the last fourteen years and I've been sending them away.'

'Ouch,' said Lily.

'But oh no, apparently taking Will's money wouldn't fit with my sackcloth and ashes personality. She said that 'Your sackcloth and ashes personality'.'

'Where did she get that phrase?' Mandy asked. 'It's kind of an odd thing for a kid to say. Is that her father talking?'

'No,' Eve, Clare and Lily all said in unison.

'That's Lou,' Eve finished. 'She comes out with stuff like that sometimes. Stuff that sounds wrong coming out of a teenager's mouth.'

'Probably got it from me,' Clare admitted.

No one bothered to argue with her.

'So what was the gadget she was carrying?' Eve asked.

'Here's where it gets bad,' Clare said. 'Yes,' she added, catching Lily's look. 'It gets worse. He bought her a present.'

Lily shrugged, as if to say And . . . ?

'I mean, I knew he was going to. To be fair, he asked me if he could,' Clare explained. 'But if he'd told me *what* he was planning on getting I would never have said yes.'

'So what was it?' Eve nudged.

Clare took a deep breath and drained her glass. 'He bought her an iPhone.'

Lily whistled.

'An iPhone!?' Mandy exclaimed. 'You're joking? He gave the kid an iPhone? What possible excuse could he have to do that?'

'Oh, you name it . . . early Christmas present in case he doesn't see her again before then; trying to make up for all those birthdays he missed; a camera so she can take pictures of her friends; something for Lou to download music on to. But if that was really the case he could have bought her any old mp3 player and been done with it.'

The others were staring at Clare.

The significance of Will's action was clear to all of them; but no one wanted to be the first

320

to say it. Will had bought Lou a mobile phone. So she could call him. So he could call her. Whenever and wherever they wanted. Without going through Clare.

'How's Lou going to pay the bill?' Lily said, thinking she'd found the flaw in his plan. 'Surely Will doesn't expect you to fund it?'

'He thought of that, obviously. I told you, he's Will. He's got her a prepaid card, and he's going to top it up every time he sees her. You have to hand it to him, he's got a helluva nerve, but he's not daft.'

'Are you going to let her keep it?' Mandy asked. 'I wouldn't. I'd take the damn thing away. At least until Christmas, if only to make a point.'

'I did think about that,' Clare admitted. She eyed her glass and Eve headed to the bar for a fresh bottle, even though the others had barely touched their own glasses. 'But it hardly seems worth the trouble it would cause to make a point for a couple of weeks and then give it back. Anyway, things are so bad I'm scared she'll pack her bags if I push it any further.'

'No she won't,' Lily said. 'She might be fourteen and a half and under extreme stress but she's not stupid. Anyway, where would she go?'

Mandy and Clare turned to stare at her.

'Where d'you think she'd go?' Clare asked. 'Do you really want to open that door marked *Push Me*, just to find out where it leads?'

'No,' Lily shook her head in disbelief. 'There's no way she'd go to Will's . . . ' But even as she spoke, her heart wasn't in it. Louisa had that stubborn Adams' streak in spades. And if her father's behaviour was anything to go by, the Drew family had their share of stubborn genes too. Clare was right. Lou was more than capable of doing that, and worse, if pushed.

'Why would he tell her you wouldn't let him see her?' Lily said, changing the subject. 'That's just plain cruel. And not just to you. It was bound to hurt Lou, too. I thought this was all about making it up to her, not sticking it to you.'

Clare shrugged. 'I don't think Will did say that, actually. When I called him to scream at him, he swore he hadn't. That was her interpretation. That if I hadn't torn up his cheque and mailed the pieces back to him, he wouldn't have gone away.'

'And you believe him?' Eve asked, refilling Clare's glass from the fresh bottle.

'Don't have much choice, do I? But for what it's worth, yes, I do. He sounded shattered, like he'd been in a car crash or something. Said she'd balled him out for deserting her, told him he was a crap dad. But he doesn't blame her, said he deserved worse. Then he told me he couldn't believe Lou was so much like me. Which is ironic, since all I see when I look at her these days is him.'

'He meant her tongue,' said Lily.

Eve kicked her under the table.

'So where do you go from here?' Mandy asked. 'You have to ground Lou at the very least. Stop her seeing her dad for a bit. You can't just let her get away with having a go at you like that.'

'I don't know,' Eve said thoughtfully. 'I think maybe Clare has to cut Lou some slack. If she comes on all heavy, she's just the evil mummy. It's lose-lose. Lou has the upper hand here.'

Mandy shook her head. 'Nobody has the upper hand.'

'Fair point,' Eve agreed. If there was a winner here, and she didn't think there was, then Mandy was right. It was not the teenage girl whose life as she knew it had just come crashing down around her.

'Presumably Lou *wants* to see Will again?' Eve directed this to Clare, who nodded.

'Next Sunday.'

'So soon?'

'Yes. She has *a lot of lost time to make up for.*'

Eve couldn't help grinning. 'She's such a piece of work. Come to us for Sunday lunch, take your mind off it.'

Clare shook her head. 'Thanks, but after last time? You're kidding, right?' She smiled to show she, too, was kidding. Sort of. Eve didn't push it.

Mandy, however, did. 'What about her father?' she asked. She was obviously furious, and didn't bother to hide it. They could see the emotions flickering across her face. *How dare this guy steamroll back in after all these years? Who the hell does he think he is? Men! Where do they get off expecting everyone to run around after them?*

'Did he bother to ask your permission to see her again, or did he just call Lou direct?'

'Both probably,' Clare said weakly. A part of her was grateful for Mandy's fury; the rest just found it exhausting. 'But yes, Will called me to ask if it would be all right if he took her out again so soon. He sounded a bit anxious to be

323

honest. Said she'd have probably found lots of other pieces of her mind she forgot to give him last time.'

'What did you say?' Eve asked, smiling.

'I just said, well, this is what you wanted. Welcome to my world.'

'At least he's got a sense of humour,' Lily said.

In the unlikely event that she ever met Will again, she couldn't help feeling she would like him. He sounded, in spite of everything, like a decent guy. But then would her sister have fallen so deeply in love with a man who wasn't?

27

'Wear something nice.'

Mascara wand halfway to her eye, Melanie stopped and glared at Vince in the bathroom mirror. '*Wear something nice?*' she repeated. 'What are you trying to say? That some of my clothes aren't 'nice'? Coming from you, Mr Trashed Converse and long overdue for the wash jeans!'

Vince grinned and held up both hands in surrender. The towel he'd been holding around his waist dropped to the floor.

'*That's* meant to win me over?' Melanie threw a sarcastic glance towards his groin. 'Well, no dice stud.' But she was grinning.

'What I meant was, I'm taking you out for dinner. My treat to celebrate, you know, our little success, and I booked somewhere smart. I thought we might want to dress up. I brought my suit,' he added by way of enticement.

Melanie's smile lasted as long as it took Vince to leave the bathroom. In the bedroom she heard the creak of springs as he launched himself onto the king-sized bed, and then the sound of voices as he began surfing the news channels.

He'd brought his suit. What did that mean?

That Vince even owned a suit was news to Melanie. He had jackets; he wore them to meetings with the smartest of his large collection of jeans, just as he had to meet her parents. But a whole suit? It was a sign. It meant something. Melanie wasn't sure what, but she wasn't sure it was good.

In the mirror, almond-shaped eyes stared anxiously back at her. One eye framed by long, mascaraed lashes, the other not. She started in on her second eye, matching it to the first as quickly as possible. For some reason she felt uncomfortable watching herself at such close quarters. Ordinarily she wouldn't even have noticed. But tonight . . . There was something off, something wary in her eyes. An unease that had been growing inside her since they'd left Boston.

Get a grip, she told herself. *It's dinner. The guy's allowed to treat you.*

When they had boarded the Bullet Train to New York two days earlier, Melanie had been swept up by Vince's euphoria. He had done it! They had done it! Miracle of miracles, she had finally found a man her family approved of!

And he wasn't Chinese!

Carried along on the wave of Vince's good humour she'd thrown herself onto the tourist trail and hadn't minded a bit. They ate ice cream at Serendipity, oysters in Grand Central and drank New York Sours at the Algonquin. They even went skating in Central Park. Well, Melanie did, Vince just clung to the side. They oohed and aahed over the Christmas tree at the Rockefeller Center, and gazed in the windows of Tiffany *à la* Audrey Hepburn, although Melanie steadfastly refused to go inside. It was too loaded. Instead, they ended up at the Apple Shop on Fifth, where she insisted on buying the purple iPod nano that topped Ellie's Christmas list.

Melanie even allowed herself to be persuaded up the Empire State Building. She'd been unable to refuse when he'd wheedled out of her that, in all her years in Manhattan, she'd never once been to the top. And he'd been right, of course, the view was spectacular. He had crossed a line when he tried to get her to take a pony ride through Central Park, but the good thing about Vince was even he knew when he was beat.

Everything was perfect. It was a magical, pre-Christmas Manhattan break. Good sex, good shopping, good company. So what the hell was the matter with her?

★ ★ ★

'You look great!'

'Nice enough for you?' Melanie said, twirling in the bathroom doorway. She wasn't wearing anything special, just her favourite all-purpose LBD, bought in Bergdorf years earlier. If he'd warned her she'd have brought something special with her. But he hadn't, so she hadn't. And once again, it bothered her that he had.

'You look great too,' she said too late. 'You look good in a suit.' *Odd*, she thought, *but good*. If not much like my Vince.

'Where are we going?' she asked, as the doorman hailed them a cab outside the hotel.

'The Waverly Inn!' Vince grinned triumphantly, naming one of Manhattan's hippest restaurants as he slid into the cab behind her.

327

'The Waverly Inn?' Melanie was surprised, impressed and unnerved all at once. 'How did you manage that? It's the hottest ticket in town.'

Vince's beam was so wide it split his face. 'I have my ways,' he said. However, enigmatic wasn't his natural state and he cracked within seconds. 'Friend of a friend of a friend knows the maître d'.'

His grin turned anxious. 'Did I do good?'

Melanie ruffled his hair and leant in to kiss his cheek. 'Of course you did, Vince, but really, you didn't have to. I'd be just as happy in the hotel restaurant.'

'I know, but I wanted to.'

★　★　★

The restaurant was far too cool to be on the tourist trail, only the great and the good of New York's media and celebrity world were admitted. Melanie recognized most of the bold-faced names from Page Six when she'd lived in New York; it was an exclusive club of which Melanie and Vince were most definitely not members. Once again she wondered how the hell Vince had really got a table. Not the best in the house, obviously, but not social Siberia either. It worried her. Was this how Vince saw her? Was this scene what he thought she wanted?

★　★　★

A draught from the door made Melanie glance up. The conversation had lulled and Vince was

328

making quick work of his macaroni cheese. It had amused her when he ordered it. Fly all the way to Manhattan and eat English comfort food, even if it did come with shaved truffles. Now that was 'her Vince'. He would probably rather have had a pint with it, too. She wished he had, rather than the $55 bottle of red he'd ordered, probably because he thought she'd like it. Not that there was anything wrong with the 2005 Crozes-Hermitage, even if it was one of the cheaper bottles on the list. Far from it. It was just that Melanie knew he'd have preferred a beer.

She was drifting, toying with her half full glass, when she felt a breeze lift her hair. She looked up just as a couple were ushered past. The man glanced down just as she glanced up and their eyes met.

Nothing about Simeon had changed. His hair was the same, his uniform unchanged: white shirt open at the neck, navy blazer, pristine jeans. A Patek Philippe platinum watch around his left wrist, and he was wearing the diamond signet ring his father had given him.

'Hi,' the word was out of her mouth before her brain could stop it.

The maître d' hovered. Wondering whether this interruption was something that might inconvenience his client.

Simeon's gaze was cool, as if he were trying to recall where he knew her from. Was it a business deal gone bad? And then he remembered to smile.

The maître d' relaxed.

'Mel. What a surprise. I thought you were still in . . . '

'I was . . . am . . . We just . . . ' Why was she explaining herself to him?

Vince had looked up from his plate and was staring at Simeon. His expression was as close to the definition of pure hostility as she had ever seen.

'Simeon, this is my boyfriend, Vince Morris.' Melanie forced herself to slide into business-lunch mode.

Simeon held out his hand. It was tanned, his nails pink, the tips so white they could have been manicured. Knowing Simeon, they were. 'Hi,' he said smoothly. 'Vince. Good to meet you.'

'Vince, this is Simeon, my . . . '

'I know,' Vince interrupted. 'Likewise.' He shook, as briefly as he could. 'We've been in Boston visiting Melanie's parents.'

'Really?' Simeon raised his eyebrows. 'Good luck with that.'

'I'm sorry, we haven't met.' Vince was peering pointedly around Simeon to a tall, wafer-thin blonde standing behind him. She was looking anywhere but at them.

'Of course, I'm sorry,' Simeon was unshaken. 'This is my wife, Poppy King-Jones. Mel, I believe you've met.'

'Kind of,' said Poppy. She held out her hand to Melanie, who took small consolation from the weak handshake, the little girl voice. At least Poppy didn't have everything. Fingers crossed she was dumb too.

'And her partner . . . Vince, is it?'

330

'Hi.'

It was agonizing. Frantically trying to find a way to end the encounter, Melanie could have hugged the maître d' when he discreetly cleared his throat.

'Well, we must go, our table is waiting. Good to see you.' Simeon bent down, his lips touching the air a fraction of an inch from Melanie's cheek. 'You too, Vince.' And they were gone.

For a second Vince was silent, then he picked up his wine and drained it. 'Suddenly over-priced macaroni cheese doesn't taste so good any more,' he said, putting down his fork.

'You were enjoying it,' Melanie protested. Her heart wasn't in it.

'Was.' Vince gazed at her. Feeling exposed, it took all Melanie's willpower not to break first. 'Why didn't you warn me?' he asked, after a few long seconds had passed.

'I couldn't,' she said. 'I didn't have time. I just looked up and there he was. Standing right there. How could I warn you?'

Vince looked at her again, long and hard. 'Uh-huh,' he said, it was a verbal shrug. 'I don't much feel like dessert, do you?'

* * *

The cab ride back to the hotel was interminable. The silence only broken by the cab driver gabbling into his mobile in an indeterminate Eastern European language. Vince stared ahead, his eyes fixed unseeing on the driver's head. Melanie glanced at him nervously. It didn't take a genius to see that this was bad. She'd seen that expression on his face once before. It hadn't ended well then, either.

Even now, Melanie wasn't sure exactly what had gone wrong. She knew when it had, and she knew why it had. She certainly knew *who* had. But she didn't have the faintest clue how to get herself out of this mess.

'Nightcap?' she asked, as they passed the hotel bar. 'Or coffee?'

Vince shook his head. 'I'm going to hit the sack.'

He couldn't get back to their room fast enough. For Melanie, it was the reverse. The longer she could stay away from it the better, but Vince didn't give her that option. There was no worse place in the world to have a row than a hotel room, in Melanie's book. Once inside, those four walls became a cell. You were trapped. Just you, him, and a king-sized bed as referee.

Been there, done that, had the irate neighbours banging on the wall to show for it.

No sooner had she shut the door behind her than Vince started in.

'What is *wrong* with you?' he said, rounding on her. Melanie's back was to the door, the tips of her fingers had barely left the handle. The urge to run was overwhelming. But where would she run to? Not the friends she'd never even got around to telling she was in town. Not back to Boston, to the parents who thought Vince walked on water, and would not be remotely surprised to hear it was all too good to be true, and she'd blown it already.

Melanie took a deep breath. 'Nothing is wrong with me.'

'Don't patronize me, Melanie. Something is.'

'Vince,' she tried to keep her voice level. 'I'm not the one kicking off here. I'm not the one who refused to finish my meal. I'm not . . . '

'And I'm not the one playing up to my ex,' Vince spat. 'Did you expect me to sit there like everything was fine after that little performance?'

'Vince!' she said, taking a step forward, holding out a hand. 'Vince! I wasn't. I didn't. I was as shocked to see him — *them*,' she added pointedly. 'As you were.'

'But Simeon gets to you,' he said. '*Still.*'

'He doesn't,' Melanie protested. 'He doesn't get to me. I don't love him, I don't even like him. The guy's a jerk, the biggest mistake of my life. I love you.'

Even as she said it, Melanie realized it wasn't true. She was fond of him. She liked him, really liked him. They were great in bed. But was she in love with him? A heart-pounding, stomach-aching, sick at the thought of life without him kind of love? No.

It wasn't the first time she'd said the words and not meant them, but it was the worst. And she could see from Vince's expression that, whatever her mouth had said, her face told him a different story.

He slumped on the bed and put his head in his hands. 'The difference,' he said, the fury draining out of him as quickly as it blew in, 'is that when I say I love you I really mean it.'

The springs squeaked as she sat down beside

333

him on the king-sized bed that had squeaked so often in the previous forty-eight hours. Somehow it sounded different this time.

'I know,' she said.

It felt like hours before Vince finally looked up, and the pain in his wet eyes was unbearable.

'Look . . . ' Melanie started, but she had no idea where the sentence was going. When he put up a hand to interrupt her, she was almost grateful.

'Don't,' he said. 'There's nothing else to say, is there? You're not over Simeon. I knew it after the fashion awards. I should have listened to my head then. But I'm an idiot. I let myself hope.'

'You're not an idiot,' she said. 'And I am over Simeon, I promise I am.'

'But?' He eyed her warily and Melanie was appalled to see a flicker of hope in his eyes. Even now she could see that it would take only one word from her. With just the slightest encouragement he would be prepared to try again. To give her the benefit of the doubt. To give her a second, third, fourth chance.

It would be so easy, so comfortable, to reach out and take it.

Then there was Ellie. Who, already, only a few meetings in, Melanie was growing fond of. How would he explain that Daddy's new friend had vanished from her life as quickly as she'd entered it?

Ellie almost swayed her.

And she was over Simeon. Well, she believed she was. In a way, however, that made it worse. To be over Simeon and still not want this man who wanted her so badly. This man she really liked and knew to be good for her.

'You're right, Vince,' she said slowly. 'I'm not ready for this. I'm so, so sorry.'

She reached out again to comfort him, but he shook her away. 'It's OK,' he said. 'I knew it was too good to be true. But let me be, all right?'

'I . . .'

Melanie didn't know what to do, what to say. Were they going to sit here like this all night? Would she crack and make up if she did? Cling to him for no other reason than that they were here, in this city, together; and already had some semblance of a shared history?

Maybe she would. For tonight, for the rest of the weekend, maybe even for the rest of the year. Ellie came back into her head. The Christmas they had been planning — skating and shopping, and maybe even baking blondies (Melanie's childhood favourite cookies). She felt her eyes prick, but she knew she couldn't weaken. It wasn't fair on Vince. And, if they stayed together now, only to split next year . . . well, that wasn't fair on Ellie. Because Mel knew in her heart that it would not be enough to keep them together. Not for ever. And only for ever felt good enough now. She had been to the other place too many times already.

It was up to her. Vince would make her do what had to be done. And she didn't blame him. Why should he let her off easy?

'Shall I . . . Shall I go see reception about another room?'

Melanie was pathetically grateful he didn't

look up. At least that way she didn't have to see the hurt in his eyes. The blame.

'Vince?' she asked quietly. 'I think I should . . . Don't you?'

A small, sharp nod was his only reply.

The bed creaked as her weight shifted, a sad, mournful sound, so unlike the joyous cacophony of earlier that day.

In the doorway, something stopped her and she looked back.

Vince was leaning across what had been their bed. Out of the corner of her eye she saw a flash of duck-egg blue as he slid a small square box that had been hidden in his hand into the bedside cabinet, and silently pushed its drawer shut.

28

Well, Clare thought, *at least the worst of it's over.* The lovingly prepared turkey with all the trimmings was cooked and eaten. (Although she couldn't honestly say she'd tasted the devils on horseback she'd painstakingly made from scratch.) The washing-up was done. The row about who got to watch what on TV had been fought and lost.

Eastenders and Granny had won.

And why not, it was her house after all.

All these years of slogging away, and Clare still couldn't afford a flat large enough to fit a table that would seat more than two.

Outside her mum's kitchen window, a damp murky dusk was beginning to fall. Mist clung to the edges of the bedraggled garden. At the bottom, as far away as she could get, Lou was huddled, like a secret smoker hiding their sneaky post-Christmas lunch fag from prying eyes. But it wasn't a cigarette Lou was protecting. It was that damn iPhone. Whether Lou was phoning her father — or waiting to receive his call — she had no idea.

Stop it, Clare told herself. *Don't be so paranoid.*

It was far more likely Lou was just texting a friend to bemoan her boring Christmas; or even, shock horror, listening to the music she'd downloaded on Christmas Eve with the iTunes

337

vouchers Will had given her for Christmas. His 'official' present to her.

Either way, it didn't matter. As far as Clare was concerned, Lou might as well have been shut in her bedroom at the flat, with a neon sign flashing *Keep Out Mum* on the door.

Taking a sip of the dessert wine left over from lunch, Clare winced as the sweet syrupy liquid hit her tongue. Try as she might, she couldn't tear her gaze away from Louisa's back. She hardly recognized her daughter these days. A month, that was all it had taken for Lou to vanish completely and be replaced by a Stepford teenager. Where had she gone? Clare didn't know, but she fervently wished Lou would come back.

It had been just the two of them, Clare and Lou against the world for so long, Clare didn't even know how to begin to function without her. She had a nasty feeling this was how it was going to be from now on.

* * *

Her mother's eyes boring holes in her back seemed to alert Lou to Clare's presence at the window. She looked up from her iPhone long enough to scowl. Then she turned away.

Dismissed, her body language said.

Clare sighed. The dessert wine was disgusting. Mum bought Muscatel every year, and every year it tasted the same. Vile. Like so many of those Christmas things everyone always bought and nobody ever really wanted to eat.

Tipping it stealthily down the sink, Clare took

338

a fresh bottle of white wine out of her mother's fridge, unscrewed the cap and poured herself a glass. What the hell, it was Christmas. And, frankly, after the day she'd had — scrap that, make it the year she'd had — she deserved a bit more than a bottle of wine and thirty quids' worth of M&S vouchers from her mum. Not that Clare didn't appreciate the vouchers. It was just, surely this wasn't it?

'Mum?' she called, sticking her head around the lounge door and waving the bottle at her. 'Want another glass?'

Her mother shook her head. 'No thanks.' she held up a mug of tea. 'You go ahead though.'

Too late, Clare thought.

Christmas day had been as difficult as she had feared. The shaky armistice she and Lou had reached had held, just. But with Lily voting to spend Christmas at Liam's flat, it had been just the three of them for the first time since Lou was born . . .

That tricky first Christmas, when a torrent of tears had fallen long before bedtime, and six-month-old Louisa had screamed all day, as if in protest at the woefully insufficient world she'd been born into. Whenever the baby paused for breath, long enough for Granny to take her, Clare had taken refuge in her bedroom and wept. And when she thought her daughters and granddaughter were asleep, Clare's mother had shut herself in what had once been her marital bedroom, and done the same, unaware that her muffled sobs echoed through the house.

Only Lily had remained dry-eyed. Resilient,

stoic, don't-fuck-with-me, Lily. She'd opened her presents, turned up the television and ignored the lot of them. And now, with Lily at Liam's, Clare was painfully aware she had never truly, appreciated her sister before. Without Lily it had been . . . well, without Lily, dire didn't even begin to cover it.

As she'd sat by the tree handing out presents, Clare had tried not to notice Lou eyeing her scant pile — useful things (for *useful*, read boring) from Clare; Topshop vouchers from Granny, (bought by Clare); and cool things from Lily and Eve — while she listened to Granny's ancient *Now That's What I Call Christmas* CD and made polite 'How's school?' conversation.

It was obvious Lou found them all wanting.

And who, thought Clare, *can blame her?* Clare found herself wanting, too.

As if drawn by a magnet, Clare drifted to the window, unable to look and unable to look away. Lou hadn't moved. Her thin shoulders clad in a new army surplus jacket (courtesy of Lily and Liam) were still hunched over her most treasured possession, but her body language had changed. Suddenly an arm flew up, gesturing wildly.

Clare's heart lurched.

Something was wrong! Then the arm lurched again, this time downwards. And Clare realized that nothing was wrong. Quite the reverse. It was animation, not anguish or fury. Louisa was animated because she was talking to her father.

Planning their Boxing Day celebrations, no doubt.

340

Boxing Day.

First, Christmas Day without Lily. Now, Boxing Day without Lou. Just her and Mum and whatever bloody awful Christmas film the BBC was repeating this year. For the first time in years, Clare squeezed her eyes shut and counted silently down from a hundred in her head until the tears that threatened were beaten back.

Get a life, Clare, she thought. *It's time to get yourself a life.*

★ ★ ★

Liam had been gone for hours. He'd left at ten to collect Rosie from her mother's house, which was fifteen minutes' drive, thirty at most in heavy traffic. Anyway, it was Boxing Day. Traffic wasn't heavy on Boxing Day. Liam should have been there and back in half an hour; three-quarters max. But he wasn't.

Eleven came and went. Eleven-thirty. And then twelve. There was still no sign of them. Where the hell was he?

Surely he wouldn't have picked today of all days to play happy families with his ex-wife? Not after all the effort he knew Lily had put into making their first Christmas, just the three of them, go well. She'd had to sell her soul to Brendan to get the day off, and promise to work the box office on New Year's Eve instead. Even Liam, as distracted as he'd been lately, wouldn't do that. Would he?

No, it had to be Siobhan. She was bound to

have cooked up something to screw up Liam and Lily's day.

Bloody Siobhan, Lily thought, slamming around his flat, redoing chores that had already been done, piling and unpiling Rosie's numerous presents under the tree. *That bloody, bloody woman*.

But there was no getting away from it. That bloody woman was Rosie's mother and, as such, a non-negotiable part of the package.

Christmas day had been idyllic. Like a movie, she thought. A dirty one, admittedly. Not one she'd have wanted to watch with her mother that's for sure. Just Lily, Liam, new sex toys and champagne, interspersed with the occasional parcel. Unwrapping the gifts and each other. The Agent Provocateur underwear had stayed on all of five minutes, before Liam had worked through his entire repertoire of things to do with a mouthful of bubbles.

The day had grown light and then dark again before either of them had realized they were famished. So they'd demolished a loaf of crusty French bread and a packet of smoked salmon and a second — or maybe third — bottle of champagne in bed. It was only then, when Liam came up for air, that it occurred to Lily that, in her twenty-four years, this was the first Christmas she hadn't spent watching the *Eastenders* Christmas special at her mother's. Thinking of Clare, Lou and her mother, Lily experienced a brief pang of guilt.

Caught up in her own private festivities, she hadn't even thought to phone home; but she'd pushed aside her mental image of them sitting on her mum's settee, nursing the last of that awful dessert wine Mum always bought and nobody ever wanted to drink. She'd always been able to do that, push aside things she didn't want to think about. There were too many things it was easier not to think about. Far too many of them. All that Catholic guilt for a start. This was, Lily decided, her best Christmas ever.

Well, it had been.

* * *

The indecently large pile of pastel-wrapped presents under the tree had been rearranged a dozen times when Lily finally heard footsteps on the stairs.

'Merry Christmas sweetie!' she cried, flinging open the front door, just as Liam reached forward to put his key in the lock. Lily wasn't feeling all that merry, but putting a brave face on it was always the best policy where Rosie was concerned.

Except Rosie wasn't there.

'Where is — ' Lily started, but the look on his face as he pushed past, stopped her.

'Liam?' She followed him into the living room where he'd already slumped on his sofa, his eyes red and sore. It could have been the after-effects of yesterday — frankly, they'd drunk enough — but she didn't remember him looking this rough when he'd left three hours earlier. 'Where's Rosie? Has something happened? Is Rosie all right?'

343

'She's fine,' he said finally. 'Rosie's not coming.'

'What d'you mean, she's not coming? Where have you been? What's going on?'

Liam sighed, rubbing his hands over that day's stubble, and then glanced at his watch and shrugged. 'Get me a drink, will you?' It wasn't a question. 'Brandy, if there's any left.'

Lily opened her mouth to object, then thought better of it. Shouting and screaming, her preferred default position, didn't work where Liam was concerned. Like her, he'd long since perfected the art of zoning out. Maybe his reasons were as good as she believed her own to be.

'Here you go,' she said, handing him a tumbler. 'Now, tell me what's going on. Where have you been for the last three hours?'

'Sitting in a lay-by on the South Circular.'

Lily waited for him to elaborate. When he didn't, she tried again. 'Sitting in a lay-by? Liam . . . why were you sitting in a lay-by?'

When Liam looked up his eyes were wet.

Seeing him cry made Lily feel uncomfortable, she couldn't help it, Growing up in an all-female household, she'd never seen a man cry before, except in a play, on screen, or on TV, and those didn't count.

'Liam? Baby? What's wrong?'

'She's going.' He paused, took a large gulp of his brandy and then swiped at his eyes with the back of his hand.

'Rosie? Going where?'

'Siobhan. She's moving. And she's taking Rosie with her.'

344

'Moving?' A thousand possibilities spun through Lily's head. Back to Dublin? To relatives in America? Emigrating? 'Where's she going?'

'Manchester.'

Lily stifled a sigh. It could be worse. Manchester was only three hours in the car, less by train. OK, so it wasn't exactly around the corner, but it was do-able; especially only once every three weeks, which was how often Liam had access to Rosie.

'She's getting married,' he continued, 'to this guy, Robert, you know the one. She's been seeing him for months now. Rosie talks about him all the time.' Liam's words were full of bitterness. 'What she failed to mention is that Robert lives in Manchester. She's moving in with him, and she's taking Rosie.'

'Just like that? Can she do that?'

'She can and she is,' Liam said, downing his brandy. 'I don't have a leg to stand on . . . or so I've just been told. I don't have joint custody, I have access, and I'm so crap I'm lucky to have that apparently . . . '

He paused, staring into the bottom of his glass as if expecting it to refill itself. Taking pity on him, Lily fetched the bottle.

'They're going at the end of January. She just dropped it on me when I went to collect Rosie, but she's been planning it for weeks. I didn't even know our old house was on the market, but there's already an offer on it. Rosie's got a place at nursery, you name it . . . '

'What did you do?'

Liam grinned sheepishly. 'I went fecking mad.

345

What d'you think I did? Like the idiot I am.'

'Don't beat yourself up,' Lily said, ruffling his hair. 'You've got a right to be pissed off with her. Of course you said some rash things. It still doesn't explain where Rosie is now . . . '

'I said bad stuff, Lil. A lot of bad stuff. Siobhan hit me with moving the moment she opened the door. And I wasn't ready. I just lost it, told her she couldn't take Rosie away, I wouldn't let her, I'd get the law on her. Then she said if that was how I felt she didn't feel safe letting me take Rosie away today. She didn't trust me to bring her back, and from now on we'd be talking through solicitors. Then she slammed the door in my face. Left me on my old doorstep yelling through the letterbox. She set me up, Lil. And I fell for it.'

His tears were back now. 'Like I'd hurt my baby girl.'

For once, Lily didn't say what was in her head; that losing his rag like that hadn't exactly helped Rosie. Right now, she didn't need Eve, Clare or anyone else to tell her what was and wasn't helpful.

'So what did you do then?' she asked, picking up his tumbler and taking a slug of the burning liquid.

'Sat in my car and phoned Siobhan, but she just let it ring. After I called a few times she took the phone off the hook.'

'A few?'

'Twenty, maybe thirty.' He looked sheepish. 'I just kept hitting redial.'

'Liam . . . '

'I know, fuck it, I know, all right? I'm an idiot. Eventually I gave up calling and just started driving, but I couldn't see where I was going so I had to pull over.' When he looked up, his eyes were brimming again. 'I've been sitting in some sodding lay-by ever since.'

Lily wrapped her arms around him and he buried his face in her neck.

'She's taking my baby away Lil.' He was sobbing openly now. 'What am I going to do?'

'We'll work something out,' Lily said. 'I promise.'

But she was way out of her depth here, and she knew it. She should have been down the pub with her old college friends as she always had been on Boxing Day, discussing boyfriends or job prospects, not dealing with this grown-up stuff.

You are a grown-up now, she told herself. *You're a grownup, in love with a grown-up man, with grown-up problems. So start dealing with it.*

But the mix of emotions she was feeling shamed her.

Since Clare had started the SSG, Lily had begun thinking about Annabel again, for the first time in years. Only this time, her thoughts didn't involve the woman meeting a nasty end. This time, Lily found herself, if not sympathizing with her father's wife, then at least empathizing. The woman had been young, independent, successful and smart — and suddenly saddled with someone else's children. Was it any surprise that she hadn't fancied it?

After all, in her darker moments, Lily had harboured fantasies of a life where weekends

347

weren't spent running around after Rosie; a life without Siobhan and her last-minute rearrangements.

But now it was happening, it didn't feel as good as she'd expected.

★ ★ ★

In the small Edwardian terrace at the other end of the street, Christmas could not have been more different. Christmas at Mandy's house made the first day of the sales look calm. Her parents, John's parents, her kids, John's kids — only for a few hours and not for the big meal, of course — and then her sister Karen, plus family, for lunch.

Chaos. It always had been and she'd always loved it. A house full of people, a massive piece of chipboard on top of the table to fit everyone around, a turkey big enough to feed all seventeen of them; that was Christmas to Mandy.

That and the mess.

Oh good grief, Mandy thought grimly, *the mess!* Enough discarded wrapping paper to save a rainforest, the presents that would need taking back the second the shops opened the day after Boxing Day, so much washing-up she thought it would never end. And, of course, no one but her sister and her mum to help Mandy clear up. Everyone else already fighting over the telly or sneaking off to the pub or up to their rooms so they wouldn't get handed a pair of rubber gloves or a tea towel.

In a wilder moment, she'd thought adding

John's kids to the mix would be like chucking another handful of dried fruit into the Christmas cake. The more the merrier. Far from it. Maybe because they were teenagers. Maybe because 22 Foxton Road was too small. Maybe because Nathan was having a moment (he was always having a moment these days, but today's was special even by his standards). But the whole charade had set her teeth on edge. Or maybe, Mandy thought, (as she gave up drying the cutlery properly — why bother? No one was watching, let alone helping — and tossed a handful of spoons, some still damp, into the drawer, shoving it shut with her hip), maybe it wasn't them at all.

Maybe it was her.

That thought pulled her up short. In the back garden, leaves still clung tenaciously to the tree in next door's neglected garden that guaranteed Mandy's own perfectly cared-for space year-round shade. The weather was screwed anyway. Snow in October and now the mildest Christmas on record. Mandy wondered if the leaves would drop before the next lot tried to grow. And what would happen if they didn't? Which leaf would win? The leaf that was already in place, or the new one pushing bullishly through?

She had been holding the fort — or a variation on that theme — her entire adult life. Unquestioningly, unstintingly. All around to Mandy and Dave's for Christmas lunch since the first Christmas they were married. Twenty-two years old and cooking turkey, roast potatoes and sprouts for both their families. How grown-up she'd felt.

Looking back, Mandy couldn't imagine how she coped. But she did. A coper, that was her. Always had been. She'd start saving on the second of January and blow it all on Christmas. Only to start saving again when the next January second came around. Even before all the kids arrived, when it was just the two of them — young love, ha! — and two sets of parents, Dave's brother and her sister. And as the kids started coming, and their siblings married and had kids of their own, the numbers grew. Even when Dave left, his parents kept coming. Mandy liked that; she loved Enid, her mother-in-law. A no-bull sort of woman. Mandy couldn't imagine how Enid put up with Dave's dad. Never had been able to. Not one for spotting a red flag, eh Mandy? That red flag had smacked her around the face a good few times before sailing off.

And now, with Dave replaced by John, his family just added to the numbers. This was how Mandy had always believed life should be: one big, happy, extended — what was the word now? *blended* — family. But then she'd always believed marriage was for ever too.

Clearly it wasn't.

For the first time Mandy considered the inconceivable: What if the only person making everyone play happy families was her?

★ ★ ★

Melanie hadn't told Grace she was working over Christmas. Not that she expected any sympathy. Grace was furious with Melanie. Melanie was

350

only grateful the run-up to Christmas had been so psychotically busy for *personalshopper*. In a moment of madness, they'd pledged to fulfil orders right up to noon on Christmas Eve, something that had turned out to be less than straightforward, but they'd managed it all the same. And, with a couple of irate exceptions, deliveries had gone off without a hitch. Otherwise, Melanie was sure, she and Grace would have had a serious fall-out. And Melanie wasn't clear on the etiquette, but she *was* Grace's boss. And much as she couldn't conceive of running the company without her, she didn't know how rude she should let Grace be before sacking her.

Thankfully, when they'd officially shut up shop at Christmas Eve lunchtime, they'd all been too exhausted to mutter anything but 'Happy Christmas' as they bundled into their coats and headed into the drizzle.

Melanie was tempted to lock herself away with a case of Merlot and a bottle of brandy, but she'd been there before, when Simeon had dumped her. It hadn't been pretty.

Work was the only thing capable of occupying her mind over the break. Anyway, there was plenty to do. Melanie reckoned if she worked solid twelve-hour shifts on Christmas Day and Boxing Day, the sale would be fully ready to go at six a.m. on the twenty-seventh of December.

So she filled her head with discounts and stock levels, concentrating on walking the fine line between getting rid of unsold stock to free up warehouse space for the new season, and not selling it off so cheaply they ended up out of pocket. And whenever a forbidden image sneaked into Melanie's head of Ellie unwrapping her purple iPod or wearing red sparkly trainers; of Vince and Ellie wrapped against the cold, wobbling hand-in-hand around the ice rink at Somerset House, two of them where it should have been three; of Ellie licking leftover mixture from the bowl as Mel showed her how to make Blondies; of the look of resignation on her parents' faces when they opened her cowardly 'Happy holidays and by the way Vince and I have split up' card, Melanie pushed it away, hard.

So many things it was better not to think about.

But much as she knew she'd acted selfishly, disappointing everyone she cared about; for the first time in her life there was one person Melanie hadn't let down. Herself.

She took a bite of the mince pie she'd bought in a token holiday gesture. It wasn't the first Christmas she'd spent alone, but this one was strangely liberating.

★   ★   ★

As always, the queue in Starbucks snaked back almost to the door.

'You first.'

A voice dragged Melanie away from her thoughts. What a grim bloody Christmas it had been for all of them.

'No, no,' she said, ruefully eyeing the long line of people in front of her. 'It's OK. You were here first. Thanks, though.'

'One more not going to make a difference, eh?' the guy said.

Melanie shrugged, and avoided eye contact, not wanting to appear unfriendly but trying not to encourage him, either. Why did people always want to talk when you were just trying to mind your own business?

'Honestly, it's not a problem,' he persisted. 'I'm just getting take-out.'

Fixing a polite smile on her face, Melanie forced herself to look at him. He was cute, scruffy — weren't all British men? — a little taller than her, with dark hair cropped close to his head, heavy brows framing dark eyes, evidence of a piercing in his ear and another above his eyebrow. And young. Late twenties at most.

Cradle snatcher, she thought. *You're old enough to be his elder sister, if not quite his mother.*

'No honestly,' she said. 'I've got a whole list.' She jerked her head towards the table where Eve and the others were sitting. 'You go ahead.'

'OK then, I will . . . ' He stopped, looked at her. 'I don't mean to push it, but are you all right?'

'Why shouldn't I be?'

'You look . . . I don't know, sad, I guess.' The man hesitated, as if predicting how his words were going to sound. Said them anyway. 'You're too beautiful to be sad.'

Melanie looked at him and laughed in spite of herself. 'I can't believe you just said that.'

He shook his head ruefully. 'I can't believe I said it either.'

The man was picking up his cardboard tray of cups when Melanie reached the end of the counter to collect the group's order. 'Nice to almost meet you,' he said, as she twisted sideways to let him pass. Then something occurred to him and he turned back. 'You might as well have this.' He handed a loyalty card across. It was ragged, torn at one corner and only half full. 'I don't use this place often, so chances are I won't be needing it.'

Melanie smiled. 'Oh,' she said. 'Well, thanks. Nice to nearly meet you too.'

★ ★ ★

'What about you Eve?' Lily was asking as Mel sat down. 'Don't tell us you had a black Christmas too? Law of averages, one of us must have had a good time?'

Eve grinned. 'Comes to something when I'm the great hope for festive cheer!' But her smile was real and her eyes sparkled. The holiday had been, if not a success, then not an abject failure. And compared to the rest of the Stepmothers' Support Group, it was beginning to feel like the best Christmas ever. Happiness surged inside her. If Christmas was anything to go by, she had high hopes for the new year. Very high hopes.

Even Boxing Day — a day she'd dreaded for months because it was a Newsome family tradition to have cocktails and canapés from eleven until three and, of course, the step-in-laws were invited — had gone off without a hitch. If she removed Hannah from the equation.

That had become Eve's mantra. If she removed Hannah from the equation everything was hunky-dory. Unfortunately, she couldn't, not always. But she'd stepped as far back as she could, concentrating on making sure Alfie and Sophie got what they wanted from Father Christmas, and leaving Ian in charge of Hannah. As a result, even with Hannah in the equation, things had been tolerable.

She had thereluctantstepmum.com to thank for that. Over the last months she'd come to recognize the styles of the women who posted regularly; they had become a font of wisdom, generously sharing their experiences, both good and bad. Eve found herself logging on more and more frequently, feeling a surge of disappointment if there was nothing new, particularly from Bella, who had become her own e-stepmother.

Under Bella's instruction, Eve was slowly learning to let Hannah be. Personally she wasn't convinced that letting Hannah be was best for Hannah in the long run, but it certainly made for a quieter life, and Ian seemed happier so she'd gone with it.

When Hannah had refused turkey, sprouts, pretty much everything Eve offered her, Eve just shrugged and ignored it. Just as she ignored the footsteps on the stairs in the middle of the night, and the total absence of cold roast potatoes in the fridge the following morning.

On Boxing Day, when Hannah had clung to Caroline's parents as if they were the only people in the world who understood her — earning Eve disapproving glares and Ian, *a quiet word in the kitchen* — Eve had smiled through gritted teeth and kept Ian's parents' glasses topped up.

On New Year's Eve, when Hannah had insisted on staying over with a friend instead of having dinner at home, Eve had just shrugged and ignored it. Hannah was a teenager after all. Just.

If Eve was honest, Hannah's total rejection hurt, but Eve had something to take her mind off it. Her period had been due before Christmas. When it hadn't come, she'd thought nothing of it. It wasn't as if she'd ever been that regular, anyway. It would turn up, it always did. But on Christmas Day there was no sign of it. Nor Boxing Day. Even then, she wouldn't have used an imaginary shortage of milk to sneak out the following day if her breasts hadn't started tingling and she hadn't suddenly been assailed by smells wherever she went. Ian's Lexus reeked of petrol. Sophie's Gwen Stefani perfume — something she'd been wearing for months — suddenly made Eve's stomach roil.

And garlic!

When Ian had slathered baguettes with home-made garlic butter and slid them into the oven for Boxing Day supper she'd had to make her excuses and leave the kitchen. It had taken a feat of willpower to stay in the house at all.

That was what had made up her mind. It had happened once before. Years earlier. In entirely different circumstances. Her breasts hurting, a metallic taste in her mouth. The way everything stank. She knew what the test was going to say before she removed it from the packet.

Nobody knew. She hadn't told them yet. Not Clare, not Lily, not even Ian. Her heart pounded in her ribs with joy and fear as she pictured the early amazement and eventual pleasure on his face when she told him. This would make them complete.

She knew when it had happened. That night in the kitchen. The night things started to go right. It was only five weeks, six at most.

It wasn't exactly part of the plan, but Eve was pregnant.

29

There was a pile of newspapers on her desk when Eve arrived at work. So far, so normal. They took turns to read all the day's papers first thing and today was Eve's turn.

It was the usual mix of celebrity trivia, health scare stories (red wine being good for your heart on Tuesday, causing cancer on Wednesday and rendering you infertile on Thursday) and New Year divorce statistics. It had been an even worse Christmas than usual for marriages, it seemed. A fact borne out by Eve's own friends.

She had barely started on the tabloids when she heard her editor calling her. 'Eve? Have you got a sec?'

Eve rolled back her chair and wandered into Miriam's office.

'So, who's playing you?' Miriam asked before Eve had a chance to open her mouth.

'I'm sorry?'

Beau's editor waved that morning's *Times* in Eve's direction. 'I said, who's playing you? Do you get a say? If it were me, I'd want right of veto.' The grin on her face was unnerving. In Eve's experience, Miriam grinning meant only one thing. Trouble.

'I haven't got to that one yet.' Heart pounding, Eve took the newspaper from her boss's hand and began to speed-read. Her stomach plummeted. Nausea had been threatening since she

358

woke, but that had nothing to do with this. She should have known this would happen, when she had stuck her head firmly in the sand in the summer and left it there. In her defence, there had never been a right time to raise the film with Ian. First there'd been the whole upheaval of moving in, then the trouble with Hannah, and then, once things improved, Eve hadn't wanted to rock the boat.

It had been easier to pretend it wasn't happening.

In her three a.m. moments, Ian's mother's comment about *that damn film* — so seemingly innocent, and yet so glaringly ominous — had loomed large, but she'd told herself it would never happen. There had been no updates on Google for months now. She'd checked.

Miramax had bought the rights before the book was even published, long before Eve had met Ian. Before, before, before . . . before you started shooting you needed finance, before you got finance you needed a script, before all that you needed a treatment. Film rights were optioned all the time; it meant nothing. Ninety-nine times out of a hundred the treatment stayed in the drawer until the option lapsed. What were the odds of Caro's being the one in a hundred that got made?

Skimming the feature, Eve saw that Rosamund Pike had been cast as Caroline, and Jude Law had signed up to play Ian.

Ridiculous, she thought. *Ian looks nothing like Jude Law. Ian Glenn, maybe. Or that guy in Spooks with the roman nose. Jude Law is too short. Way too . . . pretty. Still, it could be worse, they might have cast Hugh Grant.*

Filming was scheduled to start at Elstree next month.

Next month? Eve tried to keep her face composed. How could it be so soon?

Of Eve there was no mention. *Small mercy,* she thought, her eyes scanning the lines and trying to keep from straying to the full-colour picture of a statuesque blonde actress on the red carpet, with a drop-in of Caroline's press shot.

'She's too young,' Eve said. The words were out of her mouth before she could stop herself. 'Caroline was *older.*'

Miriam raised an amused eyebrow. 'So,' she said, her voice a study in casual. 'I was thinking . . . '

Eve's heart, which was already in her boots, sank through the floor. She knew what was coming.

'Write something,' Miriam said. 'If we move fast we can get it in the April issue. Then you can write a follow-up when the movie's released. Two thousand words, first person. We'll need collects, family snaps, that kind of thing. Old family, new family. After all, you have a unique perspective. And we have you . . . '

Miriam smiled. '*Exclusively.*'

The last word was an instruction.

'Work from home today if you want.' Miriam's voice followed Eve as she headed back to her desk, happiness crushed. 'Might inspire you writing it there. In the heart of the home, so to speak.'

''S all right,' Eve muttered. 'I'll stay here.' Right now, home was the last place she wanted to be.

★　★　★

'We've got a problem.'

'Really? What kind of problem?' Eve concentrated on hanging her coat on the peg.

'A Hannah-shaped problem,' Ian said.

Glancing up, Eve raised her eyebrows. When were their problems ever any other shape?

'What's up this time?' Eve knew it was mean, but she was going to make Ian say it. All day she'd been wondering how he was going to broach the subject of the film. Whether it was as big a deal for him as it was for her.

'Can I get you a drink?' Ian asked.

Eve shook her head. He must be distracted, have been distracted for days come to think of it, because Eve had cut right back on her drinking and Ian, usually observant, hadn't noticed.

'Where are the kids?' she asked, heading into the kitchen and picking up the kettle.

'Inge's bathing Alfie, and Sophie's in Hannah's room, annoying Hannah by touching her stuff. The usual. They were all fine last time I looked.'

'Tea?' Eve waved the kettle at Ian.

He shook his head. Behind him, Eve could see a half-empty glass of red on the table. She glanced at the clock. Seven p.m. Not early, but he didn't usually start drinking without her. It was a bad sign, but not a surprise.

361

'There's something I never told you,' Ian said, taking a deep breath. 'Well not so much never told you, as forgot to mention.'

'Forgot?' Eve said.

'Ages ago, before we met, I had an offer for the film rights to Caro's book. You know how I felt about the columns, about doing a book at all . . . How we all felt. The last thing any of us wanted was for someone to make a film. But the offer was . . . sizeable.'

'How sizeable?' Eve asked. 'Just out of curiosity,' she added, when she saw Ian's discomfort.

'Too sizeable to turn down without a second thought. I discussed it with Caroline's parents and we decided to accept it. We put the money in trust for the children. I thought it was what Caro would have wanted. Her . . . ' Ian paused, 'legacy, I suppose. I thought . . . well, to be honest, I thought it would never get made.'

Eve looked up, trying to keep her face impassive.

'You know, don't you?' Ian said.

Eve nodded. 'It's all over the papers.'

'Why didn't you say anything? You could have e-mailed or called.'

Eve shrugged. 'I've been absorbing it,' she said. She hardly trusted herself to say more, she'd been a mess of emotions and hormones all day. Ian wasn't to know that wasn't all his fault. Well, it was, but not in that way.

'And?'

She forced a smile. There were so many things she wanted to say. One of them — I'm pregnant — more important than all the rest. But they'd

362

have to remain unsaid, at least for now. Today was not a day for more boat rocking.

'You look nothing like Jude Law,' she said, at last.

His body visibly sagging with relief, Ian grinned. 'You're right,' he said. 'He has more hair.'

'And more money. And more girlfriends. At least I hope so.'

'Unfortunately, Jude Law is the least of our problems. The real problem is, *The Times* want Hannah to go on set so they can hang a story around her and the actress playing her.'

'No!' Eve said, before she could think better of it. 'No way!'

'I know,' Ian said. 'That's exactly what I said. In triplicate and with expletives. No set visit, no interview, no photos, no way. Hannah, of course, sees it differently.'

'How does Hannah even know what they want?'

'She answered the phone when the publicist called. They're desperate for Hannah to do it.'

'Of course they are,' Eve said. 'It's a great story, and brilliant publicity. But she's a minor, she can't do it without your approval. No parental approval, no story. It's that simple.'

'I know. That's what I said. But they've asked me to sleep on it. Offered me copy approval, picture approval, the works. I don't see how I can refuse. They were so good to Caro.'

'You can refuse,' Eve said firmly. 'You're Hannah's father. I'm a journalist and, take it from me, you can't trust journalists. Hannah's thirteen, for Christ's sake. She could say anything! And they'll use it. It's their job to find the best angle and print it. Have they given you headline approval? Coverline approval? In case they flag it up on the front page. Of course not, and I don't blame them, I wouldn't either.'

'Eve . . . '

'What about Alfie and Sophie? How will this affect them? And what about Hannah herself? It might sound glamorous and exciting, but how will she cope with seeing someone playing her when she was little. When she was going through . . . what she was going through. Hannah might think it will make her a celebrity, like *Gossip Girl* or something — maybe it will — but what else will it do?'

Ian sighed and reached for his glass.

'You're probably right. My mother and father aren't keen on it either. I just needed you to confirm it for me. I should stick to my guns, for her sake, for all our sakes. I'll go and tell Hannah now. Give her time to get over it.'

★ ★ ★

Eve heard Hannah before she saw her. A shriek of indignation from upstairs. The quiet mono-tone of Ian's voice rising to a shout. The pounding on the stairs. The kitchen door slamming back against its frame. All in a matter of seconds. And then Hannah was there, standing in the kitchen, her face a mask of fury. Eve couldn't tell whether the tears were despair or anger.

'You're a journalist, you know what they're like . . . '

Hannah screamed. 'Why can't you just keep your big nose out of my life? It's none of your business what I do!'

'Hannah, I . . . ' Eve started, as Ian entered the kitchen behind his daughter. His eyes were wide in warning.

'Who do you think you are telling me what to do? I don't have to do anything you tell me. You're not my mum!'

'Hannah!' Ian said. 'That's enough. This is nothing to do with Eve.'

'You're right, it's not. So why are you taking her side?'

'I'm not taking anyone's side . . . '

'It was all right before *she* got back. You said you'd think about it. You were going to let me, I could tell. And now, I can't, just like that, because *she* says so.'

'It's not because *Eve* says anything.' Ian was forcing his voice to stay calm. 'It's because *I* don't think it's the right thing to do. Nor do Granny and Grandpa Newsome. None of us do.'

'Don't lie!' Hannah rounded on him. 'Don't try to blame Granny and Grandpa. You're doing what she says, just like always.'

Eve was stung. This was not the way she saw it at all. From where she stood, she was the odd one out in this house. Ian put his children before her, and that, she'd decided, was how it should be. Or if not the way it should be, the way it was.

'H-Hannah,' she ventured, 'that's not fair. Your dad — '

'Shut up!' Hannah screeched, cutting her off. 'Just shut up! You've ruined everything. Everything was OK before you moved in. Now it's shit! And it's all your fault. I wish we'd never met you.'

The kitchen was silent. The silence swallowed the whole house.

An image of Alfie and Sophie sitting upstairs in their pyjamas, listening to every word, Inge trying to coax them away from the car crash downstairs, forced its way into Eve's head. She hadn't even seen Alfie and Sophie yet, hadn't said hello, let alone goodnight. The urge to run upstairs and cuddle them, reassure them everything was going to be all right, was overwhelming, but she knew she couldn't.

It would only make things worse.

'That's enough!' Ian said. His voice was so cold with fury Eve shivered. 'I don't want to hear another word. You're not going and that's final. You're grounded. Until Easter. Now go to your room and stay there. I will come and speak to you later.'

'I'm sure you will,' Hannah said, the iciness in her voice matching her father's. 'When you're allowed.' Throwing him a look of contempt, she marched towards the door. When she reached it she turned and stared at Eve through bloodshot eyes. 'I hate you,' she said simply. 'I hope you die.'

The lack of passion in her voice chilled Eve.

Then Hannah walked out and shut the door behind her.

★ ★ ★

I hate her, Eve typed.

There had been many times in the months since she'd moved in that she'd thought things couldn't get any worse, any more difficult, any more painful. But the last three hours had been the most painful in her life. Even her second year at university hadn't compared to this. And she'd thought that was the worst life could throw at her.

Things had been so good. How had it all turned to shit so quickly? If only they hadn't both stuck their heads in the sand. If only they had talked about the film before, they could have planned for this.

If only. If only. If only.

There was no sound from upstairs. Sophie and Alfie had taken hours to coax to sleep, and since then, Ian had been shut in Hannah's room. Inge had long since taken refuge in her attic.

I know I'm not allowed to, Eve typed. *But there, I've said it. I Hate Her. She wishes she'd never met me. Well, we're quits. I wish I'd never met her. I would like to go to sleep and wake up in a parallel universe where she'd never been born.*

Clicking *Send,* she leant back and waited for a response. She hadn't written that on her blog. It was too much, too personal. And, increasingly, she worried, too identifiable. This time, she was writing on a live link to Bella.

A minute later, a reply from Bella popped up. *Of course you do,* it read. *But you don't need me to tell you that you can't have her out of your life if you want her father in it, do you? It's the great unspoken. I hated my stepchildren too. I wanted them out of my life. I achieved that, as you know. At the cost of my relationship with their father. But in my case they hadn't done anything to deserve it, other than exist and give me a bit of a hard time. A dose of playground bullying. Nothing more. And then, only one of them. The other one was too young to do more than play with her food.*

Eve smiled. So Bella's stepchildren had been girls. She sympathized. Maybe it was Alfie's age, maybe it was because he was a boy, but she certainly found him much easier to handle, much easier to love, than Hannah or Sophie.

What would she do without Bella? Thanks to the distance between them, their mutual anonymity meant she could accept unpalatable truths from Bella she wouldn't dream of taking from anyone else. If Clare had said half the things Bella had, Eve would have resented it. Not that that usually stopped Clare trying. Eve was peculiarly grateful Clare hadn't answered when she had called her half an hour earlier. Anyway, Clare had problems of her own. The last she'd heard, Lou had had such a great time at Will's on Boxing Day she was demanding to stay overnight with her new family.

Kids, they sure knew how to hit you where it hurt.

Tell me about them, Eve typed. *What happened? You've referred to it before but never elaborated. It can't be that bad, surely?*

I'm ashamed even to think about it, Bella typed in return. *Self-disgust about sums it up. If*

368

I tell you, you'll lose all respect for me.

Eve paused. *It couldn't be that bad. No I won't. I promise. And I'll delete it as soon as I've read it.*

The laptop hummed for a few seconds, and then a new message popped up.

All right, here goes. But don't think too badly of me for it. I was young and selfish and had no experience of children. My ex's daughter baited me and I forgot I was meant to be the grownup. I lived down to all her expectations. I have no excuses . . .

The kitchen clock ticked and the fan on Eve's laptop hummed. *Go on . . .* she typed eventually when Bella didn't.

It was over a pizza.

Smiling, Eve typed, *What is it about stepchildren and pizza?*

What do you mean?

Nothing, sorry to interrupt. It seems everyone has a pizza story. Go on.

My husband was desperate for me to meet his children. It was an odd set-up, actually. The marriage had been bad for a while before he met me. I was the catalyst, I suppose. And take that look off your face, I know what you're thinking!

There's no look on my face! Eve typed.

There was a big gap between his two girls. The eldest was in her early teens, the youngest just a toddler. My ex said she was an accident on his part. The implication being, not on his ex-wife's part. But he loved them both, and it killed him to leave, or so he said . . .

Silence.

That's not fair. Of course he loved them. But, as I've said before, he was weak. If he wasn't he would have made me behave.

Would you? Eve typed. *Have behaved I mean?*

This was fascinating. How many women's stories were in fact the same story with slightly different players? Stepmothers, some selfish, some not, pizzas, weak fathers, confused children crying out for their parents' affection . . . She would have to tell Clare and Lily at the next meeting.

Maybe. Maybe not. Who can say? Anyway, we took the girls to a trattoria. The eldest made it clear she hated me right from the start. Everything I said, she rejected. She had quite a repertoire in dirty looks that girl. I had some funny ideas then, about how things should be. I wanted us to be a family, but on my terms. And my ex wanted us to be a family so badly, he let me play it any way I wanted. And the way I was brought up was children were seen and not heard. We were big on table manners in my family, and these girls . . . Well, let's just say they hadn't been taught any manners, table or otherwise.

Eve realized she was holding her breath.

What was wrong with their table manners? she typed. *If that's not an odd question.*

They didn't have any. It was that simple. The little one had mauled her garlic bread until it was unrecognizable. The elder one just scowled, ignored her food, and kicked the table leg over and over again. Everything I offered her she refused.

370

Sounds familiar!

Quite. It was like Chinese water torture. I should have ignored it, but I didn't. Lunch rapidly went from bad to worse. I'd made a big effort. Dressed up to the nines. Stupid, of course. Like a couple of kids cared what I wore. But I was wearing a white trouser suit. Foolish, looking back. I'd have been better off in old jeans and a jumper. Of all the things I'd change if I could, that's the main thing. Because when the eldest one tipped her Coke over me — she pretended it was an accident, but it wasn't — if I hadn't been wearing that trouser suit . . . Well, it's easy to be wise after the event.

Eve stared at her screen. Surely not?

Annabel? she typed before she could stop herself.

They had typed at the same time and Bella's message popped up before she received Eve's own. *The drink went all over me. And the triumph on that girl's face. I just lost it. I told my ex it was them or me. The girl was a monster, true enough. But she was thirteen and traumatized by her parents' divorce; it was up to me to win her over . . .*

Then suddenly another one: *Did I tell you my name was Annabel?*

Shit, Eve thought. What should she do now?

Another message popped up. *Do I know you?*

No, Eve typed.

But you know me?

Not exactly.

A pause. *You must do.*

371

Eve waited. Shit shit shit. Why had she done that?

If you don't know me, you must know about me.

Yes, Eve typed. Honesty was the only way to salvage this.

My ex's daughters?

Yes, it sounds like it. My name is Eve and Clare Adams is my best friend, but I didn't know you were connected to her. Not until just now. Eve pressed *Send* and crossed her fingers. There were so many questions Eve wanted answered for Clare she almost had to sit on her hands to keep from typing them. How long ago did you split up with Clare's father? And how come he hasn't bothered to get in touch with them since? Does he even know he has a granddaughter? Eve's mind reeled. If she got even half of the answers, how would she explain them to Clare?

It was nice to meet you, Eve.

Eve eyed the message warily. What the hell did that mean?

Bella? she typed.

Nothing.

Bella, are you still there?

Nothing.

Bella, please don't go. It's not a put-up. I didn't know. I swear.

But there was nothing. Bella had gone. What the hell should she do now?

Then, just as Eve was about to give up, another message popped onto her screen. *Do yourself a favour, Eve. Learn to live with your stepdaughter or learn to live without the man*

372

you love. In my experience, you can't have both.
Good luck.

    Bella, don't go . . .

    Bella, are you there . . . ?

    Bella. I'm sorry. I won't tell Clare.

    Bella?

    But this time, Bella really had gone.

30

It had taken all Clare's willpower not to look out of the window when Will arrived to collect Lou that afternoon; but Lou had made her promise. 'No sneaky peeking,' she'd said. 'It freaks me out and it freaks Dad out.'

Through sheer force of will, Clare held back the retorts that flooded the tip of her tongue. Just as she held back when the doorbell rang and the living room window drew her like a magnet. Instead, she kissed her daughter goodbye, tried not to hug her too hard and turned and walked in the opposite direction. In her bedroom, Clare dragged out her box of old notebooks, just as she had every time since Will's first visit.

Old exercise books, and photographs (those hurt). A photobooth snap of Clare and Will with a dozen drawing-pin holes in one corner and a Blu-Tack map on the back. And notes, pages and pages of notes. And something that might have been a chapter breakdown for a novel, if you stretched your imagination.

Reading through her diaries, it was hard to tell when her life had started to go awry. Was it really all Will's fault, or had things soured before that? When her father left them for the stepmonster? Left them, and then left them again, for good? Or even before that? When Lily was born? The Elastoplast baby that wouldn't stick. If Elastoplast babies even existed then. Of course they did, Elastoplast babies had always existed.

No, Clare decided. If there was one person who could not be blamed for the mess of her life, it was Lily. Annabel was a much more obvious culprit. But it was only thanks to the SSG that Clare was beginning to see her father's culpability in all this. She would no more blame Eve for Ian's decisions than she would Lily for Liam's cock-ups. So why was everything Annabel's fault? Because it was easier to blame a woman she'd only met twice than a man who was meant to love her, unconditionally?

The flat still felt weird without Lou, but Clare was surprised to find she was slowly getting used to it. It was almost as if the flat knew Lou would not be back tonight and had closed in protectively around her mother.

Finding a scrap of paper, Clare noted the thought down.

This was the sixth time Lou had seen her father, but the first overnight visit. Not the first night she'd ever spent away from her mother, but somehow this felt different to her other sleepovers. This time Clare felt truly alone.

As a miniature act of rebellion, the ten pounds usually spent on pizza had gone instead on a bottle of Chablis. A scandalous extravagance, but one Clare felt she'd earned. She'd made a mushroom risotto to go with it — ordinary mushrooms but Arborio rice — and now she was sitting in her usual chair at the kitchen table with the decades' old notebooks in front of her. Beside them sat another notebook. Far newer, blue and spiral bound. The first half now filled with her neat, child-legible teacher's handwriting. It was part fiction, part concealed memoir. Although, inevitably, the parts that were fictionalized were far greater. It was the seventeen-year-old revealed to Clare through the pages of her diary that stirred her interest. The young woman, she was astonished to realize, she'd once been. Strong-willed and passionate, full of hope and dreams. Not the woman she'd turned into, sitting with a pile of old diaries in a walk-up north London flat. A woman whose dreams had been shattered by the decisions that seventeen-year-old had made.

★ ★ ★

Lou didn't know about her mother's novel-writing ambitions. Would probably never know, since, once-written, Clare's novel was likely to languish on a publisher's slush pile. Most did. And then only if Clare summoned the nerve to send it out at all. And that was the way Clare wanted to keep it. The girl would only laugh at her middle-aged mother's delusions. That was how it was. Clare saw it every day at school. Only the young were allowed ambition. As far as her pupils were concerned, once past thirty you might as well be dead.

'You?! A writer?!'

Clare could picture Lou's howl of derision now.

And of all the things Clare had had to bear that she'd believed she couldn't over the last six months, her daughter's scorn was the one she was pretty sure she really couldn't. She couldn't stand that.

★ ★ ★

An attack of cramp spasmed through her right hand, forcing Clare to put down her Biro. She filled the kettle and made herself a coffee and went to stand in the bay window, watching the human traffic of a January Sunday, she plotted the second chapter in her head. The one where a seventeen-year-old girl tells her first love she's pregnant and discovers they don't share the same dreams after all.

The growl of Will's engine had grown familiar over the past few weeks. Its hum interrupted her reverie, and she took a step back just as a dark-blue Audi stopped a few doors up, on the far side of the street.

Don't look, she told herself, *You'll only regret it. Go back to the kitchen and clear away the notebooks.*

It was true, on both counts.

Across the street, the Audi's far-side doors had been flung open and Lou and Will emerged. Clare winced as Lou flung herself at her father and for a moment he lifted her off her feet. Then, too late, she noticed a near-side door had opened too.

Clare froze.

Louisa and Will were not alone.

It was hard to tell at that distance, but it looked as if two small dark heads bobbed in the rear seat. Clare took another step back. From

377

where she stood, she could see but not be seen.

Snooping, Lou would say, *sneaking through my things.*

In this case, Lou's life. But Clare couldn't help it. Transfixed, like sitting up late into the night watching a horror film she knew would guarantee her a sleepless night, but unable to turn it off, she watched as slim denim-clad legs emerged from the car. It was too far for Clare to be able to see the woman's face clearly, but from where Clare stood everything looked as if it was in the right place — dark eyes, broad smile, dark hair tossed effortlessly into a knot at the back of her head.

Effortless was the word, Clare decided. Effortless was something she'd never been able to pull off. You had to have money to do effortless.

'Masochist,' she muttered. 'No one's making you do this.'

But she kept looking anyway. Taking in every inch of the woman Will had married, the woman who had borne the children he *did* want. The woman who, Clare could see now, was not, and probably never would have been, her. Not in this life, at least.

★   ★   ★

When Lou's footsteps echoed up the stairs and the door slammed Clare was back at the kitchen table. Her old school notebooks replaced with a pile of marking.

'Hello my love,' she said as Lou bounded into

378

the kitchen. 'Did you have a good time?'

She needn't have asked. Lou was beaming widely.

The fact Lou had come to the kitchen at all, rather than heading straight for her bedroom, told Clare all she needed to know. For three months their relationship had been all scowls and slammed doors. The trust that was the linchpin of their little family destroyed when Will came back into it. Three months and they still hadn't been able to stick themselves back together. Clare felt such a perverse mixture of emotions she hardly knew where to start. But above all she felt guilty . . . Guilty for wishing her daughter had had a bad time.

'Brilliant,' Lou said, pulling out the other chair. She flung herself onto it and began gabbling. 'Dad's house is so great, Mum. You should see it. It has four bedrooms and two bathrooms and a downstairs loo, and the kitchen and sitting room are open plan, like one enormous room. And there's a *huge* garden. It's messy though, because there are trikes and pedal cars, and a climbing frame for Bobby and the house is full of toys and nappies and kids' stuff.

'Nappies, yeuch!' She made a face, and Clare reached out to flip her fringe out of her eyes. Lou let her. It was the closest she'd come to real affection since Will had walked back into their lives.

'And Bobby and Katie are cute. It's great having a brother and sister . . . Sort of,' she added, throwing a nervous look in Clare's direction.

Clare forced herself to smile reassuringly.

'And Suzanne is *really* cool. We just hung out and talked when Dad had a bit of work to do, and Suzanne said I can decorate the spare room any way I want so it's really mine . . .'

As she took a breath, her gaze fell on the pile of homework on the table.

'Mu-um,' she said, rolling her eyes. 'You haven't been doing that the *whole time* I've been gone, have you?'

'Of course not,' Clare said, torn between relief that the litany of fabulousness had finished and gratitude that her old Lou was back, if for all the wrong reasons. 'I do have a life, you know.'

Lou rolled her eyes again.

They both knew that was not remotely true.

'So,' Clare said carefully. 'Suzanne's all right, then?'

Lou eyed her mother as if trying to gauge whether she really wanted the answer. Then she launched into it anyway. 'Suzanne's great,' Lou said. 'She's young and cool. She has great clothes and says I can borrow them when I'm a bit older. Although I'm already taller than her so they're never gonna fit! She's nowhere near as tall as Dad and me. Suzanne said we could go shopping next time. So I've got stuff there instead of you having to keep packing and unpacking . . .'

As Lou rambled on, listing her replacement's many assets, Clare made herself zone out. Slowly she counted down from ten, and then from fifty, trying to suppress the panic that rose inside her. She'd never felt so threatened in her life.

Not even when that first letter from Will had arrived.

Not even when he had called and called, and had kept calling.

Not even when Lou had banged on about how brilliant Eve was and how fun and how much cooler than Clare she was, had Clare felt like everything she had worked for and loved and nurtured could be taken away so easily.

Lou had found her father, and now she'd found a new mother, too. Two for the price of one. Both, *really great*.

Clare was redundant. There was no other word for it.

This was not how it was meant to be. Clare knew all about stepmothers. After all, she'd had one herself, briefly. They were *A Bad Thing*. Lou wasn't meant to like her stepmonster, and the woman was certainly not meant to like her back. Lou was meant to hate her, resent her and despise her. She was meant to see Suzanne as an obstacle in her relationship with her newly discovered father, not an added bonus.

Clare knew she was a bad person, but she'd thought, hoped even, that Lou would come back bursting with bile and resentment at her father's wife. That her father's wife would want this five-feet-six army-surplus-clad evidence of her husband's past out of her cosy middle-class life as rapidly as she had entered it.

But this . . . this Clare had not anticipated. Lou was even more enthusiastic about Suzanne than she was about Eve, and that was saying something.

381

'So can I, Mum?' Lou demanded.

'Can you what?'

'Were you even listening?' Lou was on her feet now, hands on hips. Like Lily. Like Clare. The flash of an Adams' family mannerism reassured her, and Clare grinned at her bolshie daughter.

'Of course I was listening.'

'Then what was I saying?'

'You were telling me how fabulous your dad's wife is.' Her voice was light, but she wasn't fooling anyone, least of all herself.

'Ha!' said Lou. 'That was at least five minutes ago. I was asking if I could go stay with my new family the weekend after next.'

Clare's smile slipped. Catching it, she super-glued it back on.

'Dad's working Friday,' Lou continued, 'but he said, if it's all right with you, Suzanne could pick me up after school and he'll bring me back on Sunday after lunch.'

The eagerness on Lou's face was agony to Clare. Her daughter was alight with anticipation. There was no way she could bring herself to snuff it out.

'I'll have to talk to your father,' Clare said carefully.

'No need! It's cool with Dad. He suggested it. So can I call him to say it's OK? Can I? Please . . .'

Since when had Lou begun using *please*?

'You've only just got back,' Clare protested. 'Give the poor man some peace.' But her heart wasn't in it. After weeks of hostile truce, her Lou was back, and Clare couldn't bring herself to push her away again.

'If you must . . . '

'Thanks Mum,' Lou said, flinging her arms around Clare's neck and hugging her. It was very Lou. But this Lou hadn't been living with her for months. 'I'll go and call Dad.'

Only when her daughter bounded out of the room and up the hall, did Clare let her smile and her head drop. As her forehead landed on the table, she noticed she'd doodled in the margin of the homework she'd started marking when Lou had come in.

Get a life.

31

January was bleak at the best of times. No one really wanted to be at work. Miriam, *Beau's* editor, was in a foul mood about print slots, budget cuts and wobbling advertisers, and half the junior staff were off with stomach flu. Miriam kept demanding they come in anyway. Eve wished they wouldn't. If they did, she was pretty sure, they'd only infect the rest of the office. And, she still hadn't told Ian.

The last two weeks had felt like the longest of Eve's life. Constantly surrounded by people, the staff at the office, Ian's children at home, she didn't think she'd ever been this lonely. Hannah was still not speaking to her, which meant that Sophie, while friendly when her big sister wasn't around, instantly closed down the second Hannah appeared. Which wasn't often, since Hannah was refusing to be in any room that had Eve in it. She was working an effective line in walking out as soon as Eve walked in, whether she was mid-sentence, mid-forkful, mid-anything. The effect could be dramatic. In a different life, Eve might even have been impressed.

It didn't help that Hannah was making a show of having forgiven her father. And Ian, to Eve's disgust, had let her. Even the grounding had been reduced to a measly fortnight. Apparently, they hadn't had groundings at all before Eve arrived.

To Eve's mind things were right back to where they were in the autumn. Eve against the Newsome world, with the honourable exception of Alfie, who immersed himself in his toys, demanded bedtime stories and generally made her long evenings endurable.

But it wasn't just Hannah. It was Bella.

Bella had vanished. Eve had no idea how dependent she'd become on the woman's nightly posts until they stopped appearing. E-mails, comments, messaging, Eve had tried everything she could think of, eventually resorting to appealing to Bella directly on thereluctantstepmum.com. Plenty of other regular posters responded, but there was no sign of Bella.

Eve had to admit it. Bella was gone.

At least there was still Clare, always had been. But, just as Clare had always been there, so there had always been a small part of herself that Eve kept hidden from her best friend. A few details of her life she'd never shared. And the fact she'd discovered Bella only to lose her again added to their number. Eve felt guilty and confused. Once she had even picked up the phone intending to tell Clare everything. Well, almost everything. (*You see, I was e-mailing Annabel . . . Yes . . . that Annabel . . . And she's not so bad . . . You'd like her . . . You should give her a chance.*)

Yeah, right. Some things were too much. But Clare had been so grateful to hear Eve's voice that she forgot to ask why Eve was calling. Ending up, instead, telling Eve all about Lou's 'new family', her 'so cool and so fun stepmother'.

'She adores the woman,' Clare said wryly. 'She thinks she walks on water.'

Lucky Suzanne, Eve wanted to say, but didn't. Getting warm, loving, smart, feisty Lou as a stepdaughter rather than the spoilt blonde brat with a chip the size of Poland that Eve was lumbered with.

And then there were the pregnancy tests. Boots had experienced an unexpected spike in sales in January; Eve had bought so many of them. Bought them, sneaked them to the loos on the executive floor and then hidden the incriminating evidence in a sanitary disposal bin. In an office full of women, no one would ever trace them back to her.

But, just like the first time she'd been pregnant, no matter how many times she did the test, it always came back the same. Positive.

And, just like the first time, now all she felt was dread.

Gone was the surge of euphoria that had shot through her on Boxing Day when she'd realized her period might be more than just tardy; to be replaced by a hollow emptiness when she wondered how to tell Ian. If only she'd told him sooner. If only she'd told him at New Year, when some remains of festive spirit still mellowed the atmosphere between them. Too late now.

Instead she had another *If only* for her collection.

★ ★ ★

'You sure know how to show a guy a good time,' Ian said, when Eve crossed the road towards him carrying two polystyrene coffee cups and a white paper sandwich bag. 'When you said meet me for lunch I thought you had something more glamorous in mind.'

'What could possibly be more glamorous than a picnic in Hyde Park in January?' Eve said. She smiled and stretched up to peck him on the lips, a small bud of hope flowered inside her when he kissed her back.

'Here.' She handed him a cup. 'I can't vouch for the coffee but at least it will keep your hands warm.'

They strolled in something approaching companionable silence across Park Lane, past Speaker's Corner and into the park, their feet crunching the frost-tipped grass.

Companionable. Well, it was an improvement on uncomfortable, chilly or downright frosty. All more apt descriptions of the atmosphere between them over the past couple of weeks. But still, *companionable* was hardly ideal for a couple expecting their first baby.

'Panini?'

'Eve . . . ?'

They spoke in unison, and both laughed. 'Yes,' they both said.

'I'm sorry, it's a fucking mess,' Ian said. 'It's not your fault. I should have made the decision myself, not asked you to make it for me.' He ran one hand over his cropped hair. 'I was going to let Hannah do it, you know that, don't you?'

No, Eve wasn't sure she did.

'Such a mess,' Ian said.

'It's not. Your fault, I mean. It's all of ours.'

'True. What's in those?'

'Mozzarella and tomato. They're hot.' She glanced in the bag. 'Lukewarm. And a bit soggy.'

'Lukewarm and soggy is good.' Ian smiled and slung his free arm around her shoulder. Eve let her body sag into his. Maybe everything would be all right, after all. She would tell him now. For once she had to seize the moment.

'Let's sit for a second,' she said. 'I have something to say.'

Ian's expression was hard to read, but then it usually was. She'd grown used to that. Ian sat, and waited in silence. He was so different to her, Eve thought. In a way it was curious that they'd ever got together. If the situation were reversed, she'd be pestering him to tell her what he had to say, bouncing up and down with anticipation and nerves. Driving him nuts, probably. Eve had never been one for the waiting game. Ian, on the other hand, reached for a panini and chewed in silence.

After a while, he said, 'Lukewarm was a bit optimistic,' and squeezed her hand. 'Are you all right?' he added. There was concern in his eyes.

Eve felt another surge of hope. He did still love her. It was going to be all right. Now the moment was here she felt sick. If she folded her arm under her swelling breasts she could feel her heart pounding against her ribs as if trying to get out.

'I am,' she said. 'We are.'

He looked at her. 'We? I'm glad.' He hadn't got it. Why would he? There were plenty of 'we's in Ian Newsome's life already, and not one of them was the new life inside her.'

'Not you and me *we* . . . ' Eve watched her breath frost in the air, as if she might speak her words and they'd be frozen there for ever. How different from what she'd planned; from what it would have been if she'd done it at New Year. Then, she was sure, it would have been hugs and champagne and celebration, after the initial shock, of course.

'Me and the baby.'

He stared at her, his face giving nothing away.

'Ian, I'm pregnant.'

There was silence. A helicopter banked overhead. A police siren wailed on Park Lane. A gaggle of European students trudged across the grass towards where the ice rink had been over Christmas and New Year. Eve could have told them they'd be out of luck, it had been taken down weeks ago. But she didn't.

'Ian?' she said. 'Say something. Please.'

'How?'

Eve suppressed a smile. 'Erm, I think you know.'

'Don't mock. You know what I mean. We always use something.'

'That night in the kitchen,' she said. 'When you came in to find me. The timing's right and we didn't use anything then.'

He nodded slowly.

She took a deep breath. 'Aren't you at least a little bit pleased?'

'*Pleased*? No, I wouldn't say that's my dominant emotion right now.'

'What is your 'dominant emotion'?' She

couldn't keep the anger out of her voice. *Dominant emotion?*

'Shock, since you ask. How long?'

'Eight weeks, nine.'

'Why didn't you tell me sooner?'

'I was going to . . . And then I didn't because I wanted to be sure . . . And then, well, there was Hannah and I couldn't find the right time.'

Dumping his soggy panini on the ground at his feet, Ian wiped his fingers on his jeans. 'And now *is* the right time?'

'No,' Eve smiled weakly. 'Clearly not. But I had to tell you sometime. Before . . . ' she shrugged. 'Before I was too far gone.'

'So you realize we can't have it.' It wasn't a question. Just a bald statement of fact.

'Sorry?' Eve couldn't take in what he'd said.

Ian looked at her, his face was serious. 'But you just said, 'Before you were too far gone'.'

Eve's voice was shaky. 'I meant before I began to show. Before you or the children noticed, not before it was too far gone to . . . '

His expression was entirely legible now. Horror, disbelief and shock, all rolled into one. 'You're not thinking of having it? We can't. It's not a good time. In fact, it's a terrible time.'

A terrible time?

★ ★ ★

Eve stared at him. 'I thought you didn't really approve of abortion?'

Ian shut his eyes.

'Well?' Eve demanded.

390

'I don't . . . Not really. But come on. Don't tell me you think this is great timing.'

'Of course I don't think it's great. I didn't plan it. Why do you think I was so nervous about telling you? But . . . ' She faltered, forcing a smile onto her face. 'No time like the present, eh?'

Ian shook his head sadly. 'No. I think the present is the worst possible time. Hannah . . . '

Eve leapt to her feet. 'Enough of Hannah. What about us? What about you and me? What about . . . ?'

'Eve, calm down.' Ian was on his feet too. He grabbed her shoulders, but she shook him off. A passing cyclist veered off the path and onto frosted grass to give them a wide berth.

'I'm not saying not ever,' Ian said, 'I'm just saying *not now*. We haven't even discussed it and we're barely surviving as we are. We have to give Hannah and Sophie and Alfie more time to adjust to us, before giving them another brother or sister to get their heads around.'

His face was ashen. He was holding himself so tightly, Eve thought he looked as if at one touch he might shatter like glass.

'There might not be another time,' she said, leading him back to the bench. 'I'm thirty-two, thirty-three soon . . . '

'Precisely.' He tried to smile. 'There's plenty of time. When things have settled down a bit, when we're married . . . '

'But it might not be so easy next time. What if . . . ' She couldn't bring herself to say the words. 'What if we have this chance . . . And blow it.'

391

'We won't blow it,' Ian said. 'We conceived easily enough this time, didn't we? Think how much fun we'll have trying.' He wasn't a kidder. The attempt at levity didn't suit him.

Eve felt sick. This was worse than her worst nightmare. She'd expected Ian to be shocked, reluctant even. And he was right; they hadn't so much as touched on the subject. But never had she imagined he'd ask her to have an abortion.

'No,' she said, her voice firm. 'I won't do it. I want this baby. *Our baby.*'

Ian looked at her, his light blue eyes unnerving. They were so . . . so cool. 'But I don't,' he said. 'Not yet.'

His words hung in the air around them.

'I'm sorry, Eve. I do want us to have a child. But this . . . it's so out of the blue. You can't just get pregnant and hang the consequences. I love you, but we have responsibilities. We have the kids to think about. We can do this, I swear, in a year or two. Just not yet. Life's not a movie, you know.'

★ ★ ★

No, Eve thought, as she lay in a bath later that night, turning the hot tap on and off with her toes. Her life was not a movie. Or if it was, it was not the kind of movie that starred Reese Witherspoon and ended happily ever after. It was more of a Tilda Swinton affair, where the heroine's adolescent misdemeanours came back to haunt her decades later with bleak results.

392

If she believed in divine retribution, which she didn't.

You make your own destiny. That had always been her belief. Wasn't Eve living proof of that? Through sheer force of will she'd dragged herself from being a bog standard pupil at a bog standard Leicester comprehensive, to the top tier of one of the country's top magazines.

'Where there's a will, there's a way,' her grandfather always said. And Eve had that in spades. It was the Owen genes; even if they'd only begun to show when she left home to go to university. They'd been there before, of course, it was just that no one had paid much attention. Eve was just the swotty, dumpy girl at the front of the class, who boys didn't fancy, and who got picked last for games.

So far, so normal.

But in Manchester she had evicted her outer wallflower and began turning into the person she was now. Quietly confident, determined, ambitious.

Accidentally pregnant. Again.

Her ambition had amused the others in the student house she'd shared in Didsbury, Clare more than most. But then Clare, a year older, always affected a slightly world-weary air. Not that she hadn't earned it.

'You'd think differently if you had one of those to worry about,' Clare said countless times, as Louisa, then just a toddler, had slept on the settee between them. Not expecting Eve to pay attention to her words of wisdom. Little did Clare know that Eve had taken every word she said to heart. *Babies change everything.* She'd never let 'one of those' throw her life off-course the way Clare had.

It was obvious Clare adored the toddler in a way Eve had been unable to imagine until Alfie entered her life. Even if offered the chance, Clare would never turn back the clock to make a different decision, no matter what.

But from the moment Clare and little Louisa and their endless bags of stuff turned up at the front door, Eve could see that life, as Clare knew it, had stopped the day she'd decided to keep her baby. Eve respected Clare, admired her. And she was besotted with Lou, but she wasn't Clare and she didn't want a Louisa of her own. Eve couldn't imagine a circumstance in which she might make the same decision.

Then Eve let Steve get too close, get too drunk, and they both became careless. (Careless, what an innocuous word for such a life-changing mess.) And suddenly she had to imagine those circumstances. When Eve got pregnant at the end of the spring term of her second year her whole life hung in the balance.

That was what she told herself.

She could not, would not, let this happen to her.

It was almost like discovering her real self, Eve thought now, watching the tips of her fingers prune. Not necessarily a nice self, but competent and very, very determined. This other competent Eve took over, bought a pregnancy test, bought another to be sure, and another; and then, without telling her best friend, her parents or the boy who'd got her pregnant, phoned a BPAS clinic in London to fix an appointment the following week, and bought a single from Manchester to Euston, and another from Euston to Leicester, where her family lived. She arrived home three days early, claiming a stomach bug. And no one ever knew she hadn't come straight from uni.

When Eve came to . . . Back in Manchester, after the Easter holiday, the problem was gone, as if it had never been.

And so was her boyfriend; dumped by a phone call that said nothing except it was over and she didn't want to see him again. Steve hadn't understood, of course. How could he when he didn't know why she'd left so abruptly the previous term?

Eve liked Steve, a lot.

But the new Eve was here to stay. And how could she stand to look Steve in the eye every day, knowing what she'd done? What she knew and he didn't? So Eve ended it, and then worked solidly for her finals. Clare and the others grilled her on Steve's vanishing act. But, eventually, faced with Eve's constant stonewalling, they gave up.

If Clare noticed that Eve, who'd always been fond of Lou, lavished unreserved attention on her surrogate goddaughter after that term, she never mentioned it.

Honestly, Eve thought, she had made that decision, back when she was nineteen, and she had never looked back. Never once wondered, *What if?* Well, not consciously, not in the daylight hours. But lying in the bath at Ian's house, imagining her tummy was already beginning to curve, Eve couldn't help thinking that if she'd made a different choice, her daughter — or maybe son, but she'd always believed daughter — would have been twelve, nearly thirteen. Not that it mattered. She'd done what was right for her at the time, and had never regretted it.

But do it again? She couldn't.

Once was enough. Once was an accident. Especially if you were nineteen. But twice, and when you were thirty-two, and with a man you loved, and with whom you had always just assumed, rightly or wrongly, you would have children? That was just plain negligent.

The trouble was, Eve had never told *anyone* about that first abortion.

Not even Clare. All right, Clare was her best friend, but how could she not judge Eve when she'd made the opposite decision herself? Eve had always feared the revelation would destroy their friendship. And so she'd kept it to herself. Even when she fell in love with Ian and agreed to marry him she hadn't said a word. It hadn't been deception; it just hadn't arisen, and she hadn't considered it significant enough to mention.

So why did it suddenly matter so much now?

* * *

The creak of floorboards outside the bedroom door interrupted Eve's doze. The TV in the sitting room was off, the corridor outside in

396

darkness. It was almost one a.m. Finally, Ian was coming to bed. Obviously hoping he'd left it late enough for her to have fallen asleep. And she nearly had, if not for that floorboard she might have missed him.

Eve listened to a rustle as he shucked off his clothes and slid into bed before she spoke.

'Ian?' She felt his body jump beside her.

'Thought you were asleep.'

'Can't sleep.' She rolled over to face him and propped her head on her elbow. 'Washing-machine head.' All those thoughts going around and around.

In the darkness, his silence dragged for several, long seconds.

'Ian, we have to talk.'

He rolled over so his face was just inches from hers. In the faint glow of a streetlight she could just see its outline. Tentatively, she reached out to touch his cheek, feeling soft bristles over the hard line of his cheekbone.

'I'm sorry.' He put his hand up to stop hers. 'There's nothing to talk about.'

'At least sleep on it.' Eve tried to keep the pleading out of her voice. She felt rather than saw Ian shake his head.

'There's no need,' he said. 'I'm not going to change my mind. Not tonight, not tomorrow night, not next week. We can't have it. Not right now. Things are too rocky. I think it would . . .' he stopped. 'In a year's time, I promise you, it will be a different story.'

Freeing her hand from his, she rolled onto her back and stared at the ceiling. In a year's time, she couldn't help feeling, their stories would be very different indeed.

★ ★ ★

The next day limped past, and the next. Tuesday became Wednesday and Wednesday became Thursday. They crossed in the kitchen, passed each other condiments and compared the children's schedules. Unspoken words stagnated in the air and, Eve imagined, piqued Hannah's interest as she felt the tension thickening. If it hadn't been so melodramatic, Eve would have sworn the girl scented blood. Tomorrow was Friday. And then what? The weekend. Forty-eight hours of this? Or worse, would Ian just assume she'd decided to go along with it and want to know if she'd made an appointment?

Eve didn't think she could bear it.

★ ★ ★

Throughout the usual chaos of a Friday morning, Eve tried to pretend everything was the same. Although Ian threw her a quizzical glance when she gave Alfie Cocoa Pops, his weekend-only breakfast, he didn't comment. Hannah didn't appear at all, simply shouted to her father from the hall that she didn't want breakfast, before slamming the front door behind her.

So far, so normal.

Then Inge drove Alfie and Sophie to school and Ian headed to Harlesden for a shoot. By eight-thirty, silence filled the house. Eve stacked

398

the plates into the dishwasher and tried not to think about what she intended to do. Then, instead of picking up her bag and heading to the office, she went upstairs and packed.

What to take and what to leave wasn't the problem. After packing up her flat, leaving here was fairly painless. In a material sense the ties were slight. So much of her stuff was still in boxes, probably no one would even notice her things were gone from around the house.

It wasn't the material things that nearly made her stay.

It was Alfie.

What if she never saw him again?

The thought hurt, physically. Alfie had wriggled and squirmed his way into her heart. Could she really just walk away from him? None of this was his fault. None of it was anyone's fault, not really.

Elaine's words echoed in her head. Cornwall felt like a lifetime ago. Had it really only been August, six short months? Eve pictured the woman's face, her eyes kind but her words harsh. What Ian's mother would think of her, Eve couldn't bring herself to contemplate.

Probably, it would only be when she didn't arrive home at the usual time and hadn't called to say she was going to be late that Ian might begin to worry. Unless he went to their room to change. Then he'd see her note on his bedside table, which was where she planned to leave it.

For a moment her resolve wavered. Maybe she could still talk him around?

Then she remembered his words: *I'm not going to change my mind. Not tonight, not tomorrow night, not next week.*

And she knew in her heart he was beyond persuasion.

Eve returned her attention to the note. She had no idea where to start. But then she'd never imagined having to write a letter like this. Always one for grabbing bulls by their horns, she'd done plenty of dumping before and never had any problems saying it to their face. But then she'd never had to leave anyone she loved before. Sitting on Ian's side of the bed, she found she didn't know how to.

In the end it was easier not to try to say all the things she wanted to say. Surprisingly, Eve wasn't even angry with him for refusing to see it her way.

How could he? When he didn't know what her way was.

Just sad. Sad and lonely, with an ache in her stomach that had nothing to do with morning sickness. But she'd been lonely in this house for weeks. So being lonely out of it wouldn't make much difference.

Ian, she wrote, *I'm sorry too. So sorry. But I can't do it, not even for you. I love you. Give* . . . she paused, about to write Alfie . . . *the children a big hug from me. I'll miss them, so much. I'll leave it to you to decide what to tell them. Eve x*

And then she put her house keys beside the note, picked up her case and went downstairs.

For the first time since she'd arrived, Eve didn't feel the ghost of Caroline's eyes following her out of the door.

32

'Auntie Eve? Is that you? Eve? Are you all right?'

No, Eve thought. I don't think I am.

She'd been perched on her up-ended suitcase beside Clare's front door for so long she'd almost forgotten where she was. Let alone why she was there.

Eve had been wandering aimlessly all day. When she left home — Ian's house, she corrected herself. When she left Ian's house, she'd fully intended to go to work. But the tears had begun before the street ended; and when she'd reached the eastbound platform of the District Line, the nervous glances and stealthy side-steps of the other commuters told her she looked like nothing so much as the local bag lady.

Today was a day for being where other people were not.

Luck was on Eve's side when she called in sick with the stomach flu that had been going around the office. Miriam was not yet in, and her secretary was sympathetic, where Miriam would have been suspicious.

'Sick?' she would have said. 'Do you mean, vomiting sick? Like morning sick?'

Miriam had a radar where sick was concerned. In an office staffed by thirty-something women with a maternity leave attrition level that ran at between ten and twenty per cent, Miriam had to

401

be on high alert, always. But her antennae was something Eve could do without today. Telling her boss she was pregnant and suddenly single in the same breath was something that would have to wait until Eve felt stronger. Whenever that might be.

And so she had wandered from park to coffee shop and back. Unable to bear the metallic taste of her usual Americano, unable to bear the stench of petrol, tarmac and garlic. So far, so pregnant. Waiting for enough time to pass for her to take the Northern Line to Clare's tiny flat. A part of her knew going there was selfish. Her own flat was out, but she could afford to check into a hotel in the short-term. But that was too lonely and she'd had her fill of lonely these last few weeks. She could have called her mother and father — or even her brothers — but they were too far away, in more ways than one. Eve couldn't face the inevitable inquisition.

There was only Clare.

★ ★ ★

The first thing Clare felt when she saw an unfamiliar case in the hall was fear. Was Lou going somewhere? Had she got home earlier than usual and thwarted her daughter's escape plan? Instinctively, Clare glanced at her watch.

No, usual time.

Then she heard voices on the other side of the living room door and froze, until she realized both voices were female and both familiar. When she realized the voice that wasn't Lou's belonged to Eve, she took in the case again and pushed the door open.

'What's wrong?' Clare said.

Not 'hello', not 'what a lovely surprise', not 'good to see you'. It was not that those things weren't true; it was just glaringly obvious from Eve's stricken face that none was appropriate. Her best friend sat huddled on the settee, her body a clenched fist or a balled up soggy tissue, depending on how you looked at it. Clare's lanky daughter, still wearing what passed for school uniform in Lou's mind, was sitting at Eve's feet, her arms wound around her godmother-in-all-but-name's legs. A half-used toilet roll lay on the floor next to her. A confetti of soggy tissue balls surrounded them.

'What's wrong?' Clare repeated pointlessly. Eve's damp bloodshot eyes, mascara-streaked face and red nose told her as much as she needed to know.

Only one thing could be *this* wrong. Ian.

Lou and Eve exchanged a glance.

'Eve's left Ian,' Lou said. She sounded forty not fourteen.

'I can see that,' Clare said gently. 'But why?'

The question was addressed to Eve, but Lou answered. 'Mum, you better sit down,' she said. 'You're going to be a not-quite auntie.'

★ ★ ★

It took Clare two hours, a takeout pizza and a very small glass of wine to persuade Lou to go and do her homework and leave them to talk in

403

peace. Clare knew there had to be more to this than Eve had told Lou. You didn't go from blissfully happy to pregnant to moving out in under a month if there wasn't. Not even if you were Eve. Especially not if you were Eve.

'I'm sorry to dump this on you,' Eve said, when they were both sure Lou's door was safely shut. 'I do realize I can't stay here,' she added, glancing around the small room. 'But I didn't know where else to go.'

'You can stay and you will,' Clare said. 'That's what friends are for. Besides, Lou would kill me if I let you leave.'

'I think that's a bit beyond the call.' Eve smiled. 'Anyway, where would I stay? It's not like you have space coming out of your ears. But if it's OK with you, I'll sleep on the sofa tonight and think of something else in the morning.'

'Not a chance. You're staying here. For as long as you need.'

'Now,' Clare continued, putting up her hand to silence Eve's protests. 'Why do I get the feeling there's something you're not telling me? Well . . . ?'

When Eve said nothing, Clare sighed.

'Because there is?' she suggested.

Eve looked at her, Exhausted, broke, with more than enough problems of her own and, Eve had no doubt, a bag full of marking that would still have to be done when Eve had finished sobbing and pretended to sleep. Could she really tell her best friend that she'd been lying to her for the last thirteen years?

If she didn't, how could she possibly explain

the mess she was in? As it was, Lou and Clare were busy putting two and two together and making fifty-four. Eve was pregnant. Eve had left Ian. Therefore, Ian was a bastard. If Ian had stabbed her, Eve felt she couldn't hurt any more than she did now.

But bastard? No.

He was just doing what he felt he had to do. As was she.

'Clare . . . ' she started and then looked at her empty glass as if willing it to refill itself to give her the strength to go on. Catching her glance, Clare went to the fridge and returned with the remains of a bottle. She divided it between their two glasses and sat back down. If she was tempted to remind Eve that half a bottle of white wine and the early stages of pregnancy weren't the best fit she resisted.

'So,' she said, when Eve had half-emptied the glass. 'Tell me. Everything.'

'I will,' Eve promised. 'I will. But I need to warn you up-front, I don't think you're going to like me when I have. In fact, you might hate me.'

'Of course I won't hate you, you're my friend. My best friend. Nothing you can do would make me hate you.'

'Nothing?'

'You're not a serial killer, are you?'

'Nope.'

'You haven't slept with Will?'

'*Clare!*'

'You haven't done anything to hurt Lou?'

'No, of course not. Never.'

'Then, nothing else would make me hate you. I promise.'

Eve took a deep breath. 'You remember Steve?' she said finally.

'Steve?' Clare looked taken aback.

'I went out with him in the second year at university. Tall, floppy hair, tiny glasses, he was sweet. You all took the piss out of him because he hung around constantly. You said he was like a puppy waiting to be kicked.'

'Blimey, that's a blast from the past,' Clare said. 'I always just assumed you finally kicked him. What's he got to do with anything?' And then she stopped, tipped her head on one side and looked at Eve the way Eve had seen her look at Louisa a hundred times. 'Ah,' Clare said, as if a thousand tiny pieces that had always been slightly out of kilter were slotting into place. 'The one you dumped suddenly. Refused to talk about. I always wondered what happened there.'

'I ended it.'

'You always did,' Clare said. 'Every time anyone got too close. But Steve's departure was a little more unexpected. With the others, they were always on borrowed time from the minute you started seeing them. Steve . . . Well, he was sweet, like you say. And it seemed like you loved him.'

Eve nodded. She probably wouldn't have admitted that at the time, but she had.

'He was there. And then, pouf.' Clare mimed Steve disappearing in a puff of smoke. 'He was gone, like magic,' Clare said. 'You never would say why.'

Clare's head was still on one side, as she waited for her friend to explain.

'Are you going to tell me?' she said finally. 'Or am I meant to guess?'

'Do you think you could guess?' Eve said. Her eyes, which had been brimming for several minutes, overflowed and tears began to trickle down her face.

'Oh shit,' Clare said.

'I'm so sorry I didn't tell you,' Eve said. 'I'm so sorry I've kept it from you all these years. I just . . . I just didn't think you'd approve.'

Clare looked at her. 'You didn't think I'd approve? Are you telling me you had an abortion at nineteen and you didn't tell me — your best friend; your flatmate, I might add — because you didn't think I'd approve?'

Eve nodded, gulping for air.

'I'm so . . . sorry. I just . . . Well, you had Louisa, and she was adorable and you'd never looked back. You were so capable . . . Such a good mother and . . . I did what you would never have done. The thing you refused to do. And I did it without thinking about it, well, not for long, and without discussing it with anyone, not even him. I thought you'd hate me.'

Leaving her chair, Clare sat on the arm of the settee next to Eve and wrapped her arms around her friend. Eve turned her face into Clare's waist and sobbed into her work jumper.

'Am I so judgemental my love?' Clare said, stroking Eve's hair with her spare hand. 'I mean, I know I'm bossy and opinionated. It goes with the job. But am I such a harridan? I'm amazed you *want* to be friends with me.'

'N-no,' Eve sobbed. 'I don't mean that . . . '

'Shhh. It's all right. I think I knew. I mean, I didn't . . . But now I do it's so obvious I could kick myself for not getting it earlier. What isn't obvious is why you haven't told Ian?'

Eve looked up. 'I don't know,' she said, her eyes wide to keep tears from breaking through again. 'In the big scheme of things — and there were *so* many bigger things — it just didn't seem relevant. And now, how do I tell him my primary reason for refusing to get rid of his . . . ' She swallowed hard, hardly able to say the word. 'His baby — a baby that he has lots of very good, eminently-sensible, reasons for not wanting right now — is because I already got rid of someone else's?'

★   ★   ★

It wasn't the absence of a living room while Eve was using that as a bedroom; nor even that the only communal space left in the flat was a kitchen so tiny it could fit four standing or two sitting. No, the real problem was the queue for the bathroom. Years of living alone meant Eve was used to having a bathroom to herself. And when she'd moved into Ian's, there were three. One for Eve and Ian, one in the attic for Inge, and another for the children. No question, she'd been spoilt for too long.

For the last thirteen mornings, she'd lain in her sleeping bag on the sofa and listened to Clare's boiler roaring in the kitchen. When it

408

stopped, so did Clare's six a.m. bath. That meant Eve had a fifteen-minute window before Lou emerged to turn the tiny windowless bathroom into a sauna for the best part of half an hour. In one way it was a problem. In another, it was perversely reassuring, like old times at their student house. Not the six a.m. starts, but the bathroom relay.

Not for the first time, Eve wished she hadn't signed over her flat for a whole year. Then she wouldn't have been almost thirty-three, ten weeks pregnant and homeless. All right, so she could give them notice, repay their deposit, be back in her old home within the month. It was just that right now Eve didn't have the heart.

Clare's flat was not designed for three more or less adult women; especially not when one of them had morning sickness and an increasingly unreliable bladder. But Clare and Lou never complained, and Eve was beyond grateful. Every other day she offered to move out, and every time Clare refused to hear of it. But Eve knew she had to do something. Her parents didn't know, and it would be possible to keep them in the dark only a few weeks longer. Work was a different matter. She still hadn't told Miriam. Not that she was pregnant, nor that she had left Ian. And Eve knew she had to do that and soon. Before she started to show.

Next door, the boiler fell silent and Eve heard the loo flush. This was her cue to grab her work clothes. Instinctively, Eve glanced at her mobile. She knew she hadn't missed any calls in the night, but she checked all the same.

She hadn't brought Ian's letter back to Clare's because she hadn't wanted Clare, or worse, Lou, to find it. Instead, she'd buried it at the back of a desk drawer. Who needed it anyway? She knew what it said. Every word. It hadn't been hard. There weren't many of them.

Had it been as painful for Ian to write as it had been for her to read? Part of Eve damn well hoped so. But another part, the part that couldn't picture Alfie's little blond head without welling up, didn't blame him if he hated her. She had left him. And she had left his family.

Recognizing his handwriting as soon as the envelope landed on her desk in the pile of press releases and book proofs, she almost didn't open it. It had passed unopened through an army of interns and the assistant Eve shared with the Celebrity Director. Its passage guaranteed by the *PERSONAL* written in capital letters and underlined twice. Even now, a part of her wished she'd never opened it. Like a child who believes all she has to do to hide is close her eyes. Maybe, Eve thought sadly, if she hadn't opened the letter, it wouldn't exist. And nor would its contents.

Eve,

I can't begin to tell you how it felt to arrive home and find your note telling me you had gone. Thank goodness I found it and not one of the children. Had you considered that possibility? Obviously not.

The children are sad and confused, Alfie

410

especially. As am I. You know how hard it was for me to let someone new into my life. What a leap of faith it was to let you into my children's lives. I can't believe, knowing that, you gave up on us so easily.

I understand your reasons — no, scratch that, I don't — but I know you have reasons. Should you be interested in trying to make me understand them, you know where to find me.
Ian

Her heart twisted at the thought of those cold hard words, in blue ink on a sheet of 100 gsm paper taken from the colour printer in his office. The tension she knew would have been etched on his face as he wrote them.

No *love you*, no *miss you*, no *it's all been a terrible mistake*. No mention of what he'd told Alfie and the others to explain her absence. Or whether he'd told anyone else — his parents, or worse, Caroline's. No reference to Hannah's reaction, which Eve assumed would be triumph. And no request she go home. Not that she could while he would not have the baby, but it would be nice to be asked. Nice to be wanted.

Gathering her thoughts, Eve grabbed her towel and wash bag and clothes for the day, and opened the living room door within seconds of hearing Clare's bedroom door shut. She was always careful never to overlap with her friend first thing in the morning. Their privacy was limited enough as it was, without having to squeeze past each other in makeshift pyjamas.

411

Not that this would have bothered them when they were twenty. Just one of the many things that had changed irrevocably over the years.

The bathroom was warm and damp. Eve's skin goose-bumped as she stepped out of her old striped pyjama bottoms, running her hand over her stomach as she did. It was still flat-ish. If anything, a little more so than it had been a month ago. *The heartbreak diet*: it never failed. She would have to snap out of it though, Eve thought, pulling her vest over her head and stepping under the shower. She should be eating for two now. And then it hit her: for the first time in her life it was time to start thinking of someone other than herself.

Hot water rained onto her face. Closing her eyes for a moment, she tried to empty her mind of everything but the thud of it, washing away the night's fitful sleep, and holding her certain nausea at bay.

She could happily stay here all day. Losing herself in the hot water that rained down on her, heating her chilled body. Its thundering against the bathtub drowning out the noises of the world waking around her. But she couldn't, and not just because her designated time-slot was fifteen minutes. Fifteen blissful minutes until Lou — who had no scruples about privacy — came hammering on the door.

The day had to be faced. Today was the day, Eve had decided, when the rest of her life had to be confronted head-on. Miriam must be told, her parents must be called, something approaching permanent accommodation had to be found.

412

She'd prevailed on Clare and Lou's hospitality too long.

The storm was coming, whether Eve liked it or not, which probably explained the sudden knot in her stomach and the increased nausea.

Leaning forward she groped around for the soap. Clare always left it to the right of the hot tap, but not this morning. Reluctantly, Eve opened her eyes and peered through the steam. Glancing down, she noticed the water pooling around her feet was faintly pink. It took a second for her brain to compute. And a longer second for Eve to force her gaze up, past her ankles and knees, to her thighs where the pink turned to a steady trickle of red.

★ ★ ★

When Clare finished speaking, Melanie stared at her aghast. 'You're kidding? Oh my God, poor Eve. How could this happen? She was so happy last time we saw her. And that was only a few weeks ago. She was glowing. I can't believe we didn't guess she was pregnant.'

'We were preoccupied with our own problems that night,' Mandy said quietly. 'All of us . . . '

Lily nodded.

Her sister looked thin, Clare thought; and not fashionably so. More the hollowness that comes from sleepless nights and endless rows. Too late, Clare wondered when Liam's ex's wedding was, and if Siobhan was really planning to move Rosie to Manchester. To judge by the shadows circling Lily's eyes, Clare guessed she was. Opening her mouth to ask, Clare stopped. Not tonight. Tonight was not open season on the SSG's problems. Tonight, Eve's problems surmounted theirs. That's what friends were for after all. Being there when you needed them. Telling you harsh truths when you didn't want to hear them. And picking up the pieces afterwards. No wonder Eve had announced she wouldn't be coming, barely a week after miscarrying.

'She's not any more,' Mandy said. 'Pregnant, I mean.'

'True enough.' The sadness Clare felt was unbearable. Which was nothing, she knew, compared to how Eve was feeling. Her friend had lost her home, the man she said was the love of her life (and Eve was not a 'love of her life' kind of girl). And now she'd lost her baby, too. A child she'd never known how much she wanted.

'Beside Eve's problems mine pale into insignificance. In fact, thanks to them. Now I think about it, I don't think I've moaned about Will for weeks.'

'Thank God,' Lily said.

Melanie smiled.

Clare had told the group everything, every last detail. The pregnancy, the leaving, the miscarriage and its hideous aftermath — doctors, hospitals, scans . . . Clare closed her eyes to regroup. She thought the misery on Eve's face when the scan confirmed what she already knew would stay with her for ever . . . But she'd drawn the line at Eve's earlier abortion. She knew that without this key piece of information Ian looked heartless; but Eve's leaving him was less

414

understandable. She also knew it was Eve's secret to tell. And if she chose not to tell it . . .

Well, agree or disagree, it was not Clare's decision.

'So, what d'you think?' she asked, looking at the faces around her, two of whom she hadn't even known a year ago. Clare felt comforted, almost unbearably so. This evening, she hadn't imagined herself judged for having full-fat milk in her latte or carrying a handbag that was not just last season's but last decade's, as she had on earlier occasions. Instead, she'd felt accepted and supported. When push came to shove, this disparate group of women had become a family of sorts.

Not for the first time, Clare wished Eve had felt able to come. She knew she would have been better for having her friends around her. For seeing how much they all cared about her. And none of them would have told her the harsh truths, not really. None of them would have questioned her decision to walk away instead of trying to talk it out.

Not even Clare.

There was a time for tough love. Now was not it.

'So, should I do it?' Clare asked, holding first Lily's gaze, then Mandy's and finally Melanie's. Their faces were serious, but each woman nodded in turn.

'Should I risk Eve's wrath and call Ian?'

33

Whose stupid idea had this phone call been? Clare was fully aware of the answer as she waited for the staff room to empty, willing the final few stragglers to drain their cups and head off after the last lessons of the day. In the far corner a man who Clare thought was the new chemistry locum lingered over a pile of exercise books, a wry smile twisting his mouth.

'Davey Winstone kills me,' he said, waving a book in her direction.

Clare jumped. Was he talking to her?

'Sometimes I wonder if we should try introducing community service, since detention clearly cuts no ice at all.' There was no one else in the room, so she guessed he was.

'If that's homework you're one up on me,' Clare said, politeness winning out. 'I can't remember the last time Davey Winstone even pretended to do any of the work I set him. I've given up trying.'

'Really?' He looked genuinely interested.

'Yes, really. Davey Winstone and English homework parted ways a long time ago.'

'I'm Osman Dattu, by the way,' he said, leaving his seat. 'I don't think we've been introduced. Except my first day, when I had as much chance of putting names to faces as getting that boy through GCSE chemistry. Although if, as you say, Winstone doesn't even

416

bother doing his Eng Lit homework, maybe there's a chink in his ignorance. Mind you, if that chink was chemistry it would be a first!'

He had a surprisingly firm grip.

'Clare Adams,' Clare said, trying not to eye the staffroom clock over his shoulder. If he didn't push off soon she'd have to try calling Ian on the way home and she didn't fancy having that particular conversation over the roar of traffic. 'English Literature.'

'I know.' He let go of her hand.

'You know?'

'Some names I remembered.' Dark eyes crinkled behind small glasses and Clare noticed he had the sort of lashes she'd have committed a serious crime for as a teenager, probably still would.

He wasn't bad-looking now she thought about it. Tall, six or seven inches taller than her, and broad, with thick, swept-back black hair and amused brown eyes. Neat dresser, too . . . He had to be about Clare's age, give or take a year or two in either direction.

Concentrate, you've got a call to make, she told herself. But her eyes still dropped to his left hand. No ring. Still, no ring didn't mean no complications.

Wasn't she living proof of that?

★　★　★

The first challenge met, of finding a place to phone from without risk of Eve or Lou eavesdropping, Clare faced a second, greater challenge — that of finding Ian home at all. So

417

far, her success rate was precisely zero. Four calls had turned up two answer-phone requests to leave a message, one au pair and one Hannah. This time, she decided, she'd leave a message regardless of who answered.

The phone was picked up on the second ring, before Clare even had time to consider her approach.

'Hello?'

Clare's heart lurched as she heard the small boy's voice.

'Hello,' she said.

'Who's speaking please?'

The urge to tell Alfie who she was and how much Eve missed him was so overwhelming she was almost forced to hang up. Instead, she said, 'Could I speak to your daddy please?'

There was silence and then the crash of receiver on table, or possibly floor, reverberated in her ear. 'Daddy!' she heard Alfie yell. 'Daddy! There's a lady on the tephelone!'

Clare could hear the echo of footsteps on polished wood as Ian neared the phone. Yes, the receiver was definitely on the floor.

'Did you ask who it was?'

'I forgotted.'

'Alfie, what did I tell you? Don't answer the telephone if you can't do it properly.' And then. 'Hello?'

Ian's voice almost felled her a second time. For some reason it conjured a picture of Eve's face on that terrible morning, barely a week earlier. A morning it made Clare feel sick just to remember. Unsure what she'd find, she had bribed a worried Lou to go to school without her shower, just to get her out of the flat, so she could coax Eve from the bathroom, missing her own first lesson in the process.

It had taken over an hour to persuade Eve to unlock the door. And Clare didn't think she'd ever forget the pain on Eve's face as she took in the splashes in the bath and the bloodstained towels that formed a nest where she was huddled on the floor.

Clare had no choice. She had decided. The SSG had decided. They were unanimous; she had to do this. Eve, fiercely independent as she was, might not agree, but she needed Clare to do this now. Clare was sure of it.

'Ian,' she said. 'It's Clare. Eve's friend.'

Silence, while Clare imagined him contemplating hanging up.

'Don't hang up, please. Eve doesn't know I called.'

There was one of those silences that last mere seconds but feel like minutes, and then Ian sighed. It could have been relief, it could have been exasperation, she couldn't tell. 'Hello,' he said finally and there was no ice in his voice, only sorrow. 'How is she?'

Clare wasn't aware she had been holding her breath until she let it go. 'Not good,' she said. 'Really, really not good.'

★   ★   ★

Enough was enough, Eve decided. Tomorrow she was going back to work.

419

She had to get a grip, get back to her old routines and get on with her life. Eve had called her boss, told her everything, well almost. And, to her surprise, Miriam had been great, amazing, actually. All right, so Miriam had pointed out that Eve should have called in a week ago, rather than simply vanishing. But she told her to take the time as compassionate leave and reminded her she was covered by the company's health insurance. Should she need it.

It was only after Eve ended the call that she realized Miriam wasn't talking about doctors, who Eve had spent more than enough time with already. She meant if Eve needed to talk to someone. A therapist.

Miriam was big on therapists. But Eve didn't need an expert to tell her this was a fork in her personal road. Time to choose left or right. After all, she couldn't just stay in Clare's bed, where she'd been camped for an entire week, and never get out again. Even forgetting the small matter of it not being her bed, her room, or even her flat.

By way of a dry run, Eve pulled on her dressing gown, trying to ignore the fact it smelt less than savoury, and ventured as far as the kitchen. A skinny black jeans-clad bottom protruded from the fridge.

'Mum, did you cook any . . . ?' Lou looked up and her face broke into a smile. 'Eve!' she cried. 'You're up! Would you like a cup of tea? You look . . . '

'Awful? Minging? Like hell?' Eve supplied.

'What you need is a shower, a shampoo and a blow dry,' Lou said with authority. And for the

420

first time in three weeks Eve burst out laughing. And then she burst into tears.

★ ★ ★

'I was going to Amy's to do homework,' Lou said, watching Eve hug a mug of tea. Their knees bumped and Lou instinctively tucked hers as far under the chair as she could. Her legs seemed to grow longer by the day; she was almost too tall for the tiny kitchen. 'Do you want me to wait with you until Mum gets home?'

Eve shook her head. 'No thanks, sweetheart. You head off. I'm fine now, really.'

Lou looked doubtful.

'I promise,' Eve said. 'I'm fine. See?' Standing, she did a twirl to prove it. Not easy in the space between her pushed-out chair and the cooker. 'And I'm going back to work tomorrow.'

'Work? Are you sure?'

The look on Lou's face reminded Eve of Clare and a small shard of pain twisted inside her. 'Absolutely certain,' she said. 'I need to get back to the office, find somewhere to live, get myself a life . . . '

'Bu — ' Lou started.

Eve held up a hand. 'Can't stay here much longer, can I? Your poor mum's been sleeping on her own sofa for a week and I've turned her bedroom into a festering swamp. You haven't had a living room for three weeks. And your mum's been up all night every night marking homework in the kitchen, just to get some privacy.'

'Oh,' Lou shrugged. 'Don't worry about that.

She always does that. Says she can't concentrate if anyone else is around.'

'Yes, she was like that at uni too. But this is different.' Eve frowned. 'We're talking *all night*.' She hoped Clare wasn't taking in extra marking to make ends meet. Tomorrow she would write her a cheque to cover her share of the bills, plus a bit. Better still, transfer the cash straight to her account so Clare couldn't refuse to take it.

'Don't know what I'd have done without the two of you,' Eve said, squeezing her not-quite-goddaughter's hand. 'You've both been wonderful. But you need your lives back. So let's start with you going to Amy's right now.'

★ ★ ★

The phone began ringing seconds after the street door slammed shut behind Lou. As Eve had been ignoring it for the past week, there was no reason to change now. After five rings, the machine picked up, and Louisa's flippant voice warned callers of the futility of leaving a message.

'Eve?'

She froze halfway between kitchen and hall, and turned to stare at the machine. It was almost as if Eve expected to see Ian standing there. It seemed an age since she'd heard his voice, but nothing had changed. Her stomach plummeted and her heart soared simultaneously.

'Are you there?'

A pause. 'Eve, it's me, erm, Ian. If you're there, could you pick up?'

Eve felt rooted to the spot. This was what she'd been waiting for; so what was stopping her from reaching for the receiver? A part of her wanted to grab it and tell Ian how much she missed him. But another, bigger part, was scared of what she might hear, scared that he'd phoned to make sure she wasn't nursing any false hopes . . . Hopes she hadn't even known she still had until she heard his voice.

Come on, she thought, *what happened to facing the future head-on?*

'OK. You're not there. I'll try again later. Or you could call me, you know the — '

'Hello.'

'You're there!'

'Yes, I'm here.'

'I called your mobile and left a message, but you didn't answer.'

'Did you? When?' Eve realized she hadn't looked at her mobile for days, not since . . . In fact, she wasn't sure she even knew where her phone was.

'Fifteen, twenty minutes ago.'

'Oh, right. The battery's probably run out.'

'Eve . . . I . . . ' He hesitated. 'I don't know what to say. I'm *so, so* sorry.'

She stopped, confused. 'About what, exactly?'

'The miscarriage.'

When Eve remained silent, he added, 'Clare called me. She's worried about you. I'm worried about you. She says all your friends are worried about you too.'

And slowly it trickled into her grief-addled brain. Ian was calling her on Clare's landline, which meant he knew she was staying here. All right, anyone with half a brain could have worked that out, but what else had Clare told him?

'What did Clare say?'

'Eve,' he paused. 'She told me about the miscarriage. I'm sorry, I know how . . . How much you wanted the baby.'

Unspoken words hung in the air. *Enough to leave me.*

Eve twisted to sit on the arm of the sofa and decided against. Standing made you stronger, studies had proved it. You could hear it in a person's voice down a phone line.

'That's why you called?' Eve said, fighting to keep her anger in check. 'Because the baby you didn't want is no longer in the picture?'

The stunned silence that filled the line wasn't just his. Because now she'd said the words she realized how true they were. Oh, he wanted her all right. Just not her baby, and now he had his way, he'd have her back.

'No! Eve, be reasonable. You know that's not true.'

'Do I? How do I know? I don't hear from you for three weeks and then, when you discover I'm not pregnant any more, THEN you call.'

'Eve, calm down. That's not true. I wrote to you straightaway.'

'You wrote to me. You call that horrible . . . Opening that *letter*,' she almost spat the words. 'That was the worst moment of my life.' Eve paused. It was true. Reading it was worse even than realizing she was pregnant the first time;

424

worse than the abortion; Ian's letter had gone straight in at number one. Usurped only by the miscarriage.

'You want to know what my worst moment was?' Ian said, his voice chill. 'Coming home, and finding a note from the woman I love telling me she's leaving — had, in fact, already left — without giving me any say in the matter. Without giving me a chance to change her mind. To change mine. *That* was my worst moment.'

Eve felt sick and angry, bereft and very, very sad. 'You had a say,' she told him. 'You said, no.' And with that she put down the phone.

★ ★ ★

The flat had grown dark since Eve had hung up on Ian, her noisy sobs soon giving way to silence. The past month had left her cried out and wrung out. It hurt so much it was almost beyond hurting. She was numb, but not comfortably so. Numb with rejection and Clare's betrayal. Now the only sound was a whirr from the fridge in the kitchen and the boiler clicking as the timer ticked over. She'd intended to retreat to the bedroom before Clare got home, so she could feign sleep and get a grip on her anger. But the keys in the flat door told her it was too late now.

'Hello?' Clare's voice came from the hall. 'Lou? Eve? Anyone home?' She sounded anxious.

The living room light flicked on and they both jumped. Eve at the sudden light, Clare at the unexpected sight of Eve sitting there, in her dressing gown, staring blankly at the wall.

'Are you all right?' Clare asked, slipping off her coat and hanging it on the door.

'Am I all right?' Eve repeated. 'Interesting question. Why would you ask that?'

Clare frowned. 'Perfectly normal question, I'd have thought, in the circumstances.' She backed towards the kitchen. 'Coffee? Tea?'

'Neither, thanks.' Eve followed her and stopped in the doorway, unintentionally blocking it. 'What circumstances?' she asked.

'Well . . . ' Filling the kettle, Clare rinsed one of the mugs Lou had left in the sink, and found a teabag. She kept her back to Eve. 'This morning, when I left, you were in my bed, showing no sign of moving, which is where you've been for most of the last week. Reasonable circumstances for asking how you are, I'd have thought.'

'Why won't you look at me?'

Clare turned, mug still dripping in her hand, and looked at Eve, but her gaze slid away and she turned back to the kettle.

'Why did you do it?'

'Do what?'

'Don't play dumb. It doesn't suit you.'

Eve's voice was quiet. She didn't think she'd ever been this angry in her life. She was surprised how calm she felt.

'How could you?' Eve said. 'How could you call him? What gives you the right to play God with my life? It's not as if you've made such a big success of your own.'

Her friend spun around, eyes wide with hurt.

426

Eve hesitated, but she didn't stop, couldn't. She knew she was hurting Clare, but that was fine. Eve wanted someone to hurt as much as she did. 'You didn't even discuss it with me.'

'When would I have done that? Like I said, you've hardly got out of bed for the past week. The only bit anyone's seen of you is the top of your head.'

'Do you want me out? Is that it? All you had to do is say the word and I'd have gone. You didn't have to do it this way.'

'Where the hell did that come from?'

'That's why you phoned him, isn't it? That's why you told Ian I'd lost the baby. What else did you tell him? Did you tell him everything?'

'*Eve!*' Clare took a step towards her.

'Well?' Eve demanded.

'Of course not. I told him you were staying here, I told him you'd miscarried. He has a right to know, Eve. And it wasn't just my decision, it was all of us. I discussed it with the others and they agreed . . .'

'The others?'

'The Stepmothers' Support Group. Lily, Melanie, Mandy . . . Your friends, remember?'

'You told them? You discussed it with Lily, Melanie and Mandy, but not me?' The tears were back in Eve's eyes, and then they were rolling down her face.

'You weren't in a fit state,' Clare said. 'Of course I did, they're your friends, they care about you.'

'What did you tell them?' Eve stared at Clare and for the first time her friend met her gaze.

427

Guilt replaced with . . . Eve wasn't sure what. She wished she could lose it again, shout, scream and throw things, but she simply felt hollow.

'I told them you'd been pregnant,' Clare said evenly. 'That you'd left Ian when he wanted you to have an abortion, and then you lost the baby anyway.'

'What else?'

'Isn't that enough?'

Eve didn't reply.

'Nothing else was mine to tell,' Clare said, when the silence between them became too much.

'That much wasn't yours to tell.'

'Yes, it was.' Clare was defiant. 'They care about you. They're your friends. You can't go through this alone.'

'Seems like everyone has a say in my life except me.' Eve began to turn away. Where she was going, she had no idea. Back to her bedroom. Clare's bedroom.

Feeling Clare's hand on her shoulder, she shook her off.

'I'm sorry you're angry,' Clare said. 'Truly the last thing in the world I want to do is hurt you more than you're already hurt. But I don't regret calling Ian and I won't apologize for it. You've been so unhappy you can barely function. I thought Ian should know how unhappy he'd made you. Anyway, he had a right to know about the baby.'

'What about me?' Eve said, fighting back more tears. 'What about my rights? Don't I have a right *not* to tell him? Didn't he lose his right

428

when he asked me to get rid of it? Made me choose between him and our baby?'

Clare opened her mouth. Shut it again. 'You want me to answer that?' she said finally.

Eve didn't, not really. Because she knew the answer. Ian already had one Elastoplast baby. Alfie, adorable though he was. And Ian thought he was looking at another one. He didn't know what had happened when Eve was at uni. He hadn't been acting with the full set of information, because she hadn't given it to him.

34

It wasn't as strange being back at work as Eve expected. All right, Miriam had obviously felt she had to say something to explain her features director's absence. But it turned out that that something centred on the collapse of Eve's relationship, the miscarriage going unmentioned. Eve was grateful for that, at least.

Miriam had told the other department heads in confidence, who promptly told their deputies, who got on the phone and e-mailed their friends. So now the entire industry knew that Eve and Caroline Newsome's widower's relationship was over as quickly as it had started; and she'd only been out of the office a week. Admittedly, a week in which she'd been pregnant and then not been; blown her one chance to get Ian back, and thrown her best friend's good intentions back in her face. All in all, not good going, even by Eve's standards.

Work had always been her lifeline. She should have remembered what a safe haven the office provided and run back to it sooner, instead of wallowing in Clare's single bed, feeling sorry for herself and making sure everyone else did too. If she'd done that, maybe Clare would still be speaking to her, not communicating through terse notes.

Poor Lou appeared not to have a clue what the hell was going on between her mother and Eve.

Other than that she was trapped in a war zone. Although, Eve suspected, she did . . . The girl was fourteen for crying out loud. And like most fourteen-year-olds, was fourteen going on forty, and much smarter than most of the adults around her. Smarter than Eve, certainly. Smart enough to use the cold war as an excuse to stay over with her dad as often as possible.

Rolling back her office chair, Eve picked her way past overflowing Marks & Spencer's bags covering the floor around her desk. Peace offerings. Food and wine for Clare, plus a bottle of champagne so they could toast Eve's imminent departure. Tonight Eve planned to tell Clare she'd found a flat via the office message board. Shooter's Hill wasn't perfect, for a start it was south of the river, but it would do as a stopgap until her own tenants vacated. If the landlord would agree a short-term sublet, Eve was ready to hand over her cheque for the full amount that evening and be out from under Clare's feet in just over a week. If not, she'd find a hotel at the weekend. In her purse nestled a hundred pounds' worth of M&S vouchers, by way of paying her share of the bills and an extra apology. And fifty pounds in Topshop vouchers for Lou, simply for putting up with the grief. Whether it was enough to salvage fourteen years of friendship Eve could only hope.

Relishing the routine, Eve took her newly edited copy from the printer and dumped it in Miriam's empty tray. There were times when the endless hamster wheel of ideas meetings/issue planning/commissioning/editing drove her to distraction. If it wasn't spring/summer fashion, it was high summer bikini diets. If it wasn't the autumn/winter catwalk issue it was Christmas, swiftly followed by a New Year, New You life change special. But now she appreciated it. It reminded Eve she had a purpose; there was something she was good at. She felt, if not whole, then a semblance of her old self again.

As Eve wandered back to her desk, Miriam's secretary waggled her fingers. 'Call for you,' she said. 'Sounds like Ian again.' Eve shook her head and turned away, trying not to listen as Beth announced that Eve was in a meeting.

'No,' she heard Beth say. 'I've no idea when she'll be out. Her diary's packed.'

'Why don't you just talk to him?' Beth asked, when she had replaced the receiver. 'That's his third call since lunch. Poor guy sounds desperate.'

'There's no point,' Eve said flatly. 'We've said all there is to say.'

'Don't say that too loud,' Beth warned her. 'They're already forming a not-so-orderly queue in the art department. I had to stop Caitlin asking you outright if Ian was back on the market.'

Eve forced a grin, but it didn't reach her eyes. It hadn't escaped her notice that Caitlin glanced pointedly at Eve's naked left hand whenever she passed her desk.

The truth was, today's calls had thrown her.

The poor guy sounds desperate? That didn't sound remotely like Ian. Even if he was desperate, which Eve doubted, he was far too

432

English to let a total stranger on the other end of a phone know it. *Let's face it*, Eve thought, *he's hardly the type to let the woman he loves know it.*

Loved. Past tense.

It was over. Well and truly. He'd made that clear. As had she. All that remained was to collect the rest of her things and put it down to experience. She wanted nothing from him, except . . .

There was no way that was going to happen. As Melanie said, stepmothers don't get access. Especially not ones who never even married. If they did, Melanie would still be in touch with Vince's daughter, if not Vince himself. But as a step-parent your rights were precisely zero. And so were your responsibilities, she could almost hear Ian say, or you'd never have just walked out on them like that.

Eve forced that thought from her head, and the tears that had threatened to accompany it from her eyes. The whole moving in, stepfamily thing, it was just an aberration. Eve Owen had never been the marrying kind, or the mothering kind for that matter. She should have remembered that and steered well clear of other people's children. It was time to move on.

Clicking away a screensaver, Eve shut down the interview she'd just finished editing, transferred the copy to the magazine's server, and called up her browser. Thereluctantstepmum.com opened to reveal page after page of unread messages, as the old-timers talked to each other and new visitors chipped in. About a third of the way down, was one asking why there had been no updates from reluctant stepmum herself.

Because I've been busy, Eve thought crossly, scanning on down.

A couple of hundred comments later was one from Bella, which surprised her. And in the in-box, among Eve's usual junk and requests for interviews and life updates from readers of the blog who considered her their friend was one from Bella. It was headed, *You Okay?*

No, Eve typed back. *Not really . . .*

And then she added a line saying she was planning to pull the plug on the site — for reasons that had to remain private — but wondered if Bella would be interested in taking it over? Either run it herself, or with the help of a handful of the regulars . . . thereluctantstepmum.com had taken on a life of its own. Whether or not Eve needed it, there were plenty of other women who still did.

Pressing *Send*, Eve wondered if Bella would reply. And then decided she would. Bella hadn't needed to send that *You OK?* message in the first place.

★ ★ ★

The desk phone was driving Eve mad with its constant ringing. Where was voice-mail when you needed it? In fact, where was Beth when you needed her? Not at her desk that was for sure. Instinct told Eve to let it ring, but unanswered phones were one of Miriam's big bugbears. An

434

unanswered reader is a lost reader, she often said. Eve had to refrain from asking what happened to unanswered PRs.

'Hello, *Beau*.'

'Eve, thank God I've got you.'

The caller ID might not be familiar, but the voice was.

'H-hello Ian,' Eve said. Cursing herself for saying his name out loud, she lowered her head behind her computer screen as ears pricked up around her.

'Look, I'm sorry to bother you, but I need to know if you've seen Hannah?' Beth was right. Ian did sound desperate. Eve should have known she wasn't the cause.

'Why would I have seen Hannah?' The words came out before she could think better of it.

'She's gone, missing. Her school called to say she'd sneaked out at first break and hasn't been seen since. She's been gone five hours. I just thought maybe . . . '

'Ian,' Eve said. 'You know as well as I do that I'm the last person she'd run to. And you'd be the first person I'd phone in the unlikely event she showed up here. Have you tried Caro's parents?'

He sighed. 'Of course I have, that was my first thought.'

Of course it was. Where else?

'My parents, her school friends' parents . . . No one's seen her. And her mobile's switched off.' An edge of hysteria had entered his voice.

'So, I'm your last port of call?'

'Pretty much.'

Eve bit back the retort that sprang to mind.

Her voice softened. 'No, I haven't seen or heard from Hannah. Last time she spoke to me . . . ' she stopped. They both knew how that sentence ended, she didn't need to spell it out.

'You're right,' he said. 'I'm sorry to bother you. I'll let you get back to work now.'

'Ian?'

'What?'

'Let me know if . . . ' Eve caught herself. 'It's going to be fine. But let me know when you find her, all right?'

'Really?' Ian sounded surprised. 'All right, I'll text you.'

* * *

'Where've you been?' Eve asked when Beth got back.

Beth looked at her. 'Fag break, freezing on the steps outside with the other social rejects.'

'Can I bum a cigarette then?'

'You don't smoke.'

'I know. But I need one now. I'm going out to get a coffee, d'you want one?'

'No, thanks. I've had my daily quota.' Pulling a packet of Silk Cut and a lighter from her bag, Beth handed them to Eve. 'Don't smoke them all at once.'

Eve headed for the stairs; you always ran into someone you didn't want to see in the lift. And what she needed right now was a fag, a coffee and some fresh air. Failing that, polluted central London smog. In no particular order.

She could kick herself for answering the

phone: she'd been fine before she talked to Ian, something approaching her old self. But now her carefully built façade was cracking. She needed some time to herself, before it collapsed completely in front of the whole office.

The mid-afternoon air was typical late February. A grey, chill drizzle that turned her newly blow-dried hair to instant frizz. So much for Lou's prescription.

Cigarette first, Eve thought, *then coffee*. She tried to ignore her shaking hand as she raised the Silk Cut to her lips. She wasn't crying, definitely not, but she turned her back to the street to shield the lighter from the wind that bit her face and stung her eyes. It was the damn hormones. She'd never been weepy before.

Hunched in on herself, Eve didn't hear the voice until its owner was standing right behind her.

'Can I have one?' The voice was familiar.

'Please?' It added.

Eve looked around, stared at the slim blonde in confusion, and prayed it wasn't obvious she'd been crying. Could this day get any worse?

'Didn't know you smoked,' the girl added. Her tone made Eve think this one small thing had already made her slightly less dull than Hannah had previously thought.

'Hannah . . . I don't. Smoke, that is. And no,' she said, pulling herself together, 'I can't let you have one.' Eve braced herself for the torrent of loathing that could be the only reason for this unexpected visit. It seemed Ian had been right to call her after all.

'Don't smoke? That looks like a fag to me.'

'It is, I mean . . . Does your dad know you're here?'

'I'm not falling for that. So, can I have one?'

'No, they're not mine. And I'm taking that as a no, your dad doesn't know you're here, right?'

'No, of course he doesn't,' said Hannah impatiently. 'He wouldn't have let me come. He doesn't let me do anything these days.'

Eve hoped her sigh was hidden behind the smoke, as the nicotine hit her lungs and rebounded, filling the air with smoke and steam. She badly needed to cough, but pride wouldn't let her.

'You should call Dad,' Eve said. 'He'll be worried.'

'He thinks I'm at school.' Shifting awkwardly from foot to foot, Hannah shrugged, feigning indifference. She looked both incredibly young, in her grey- and red-trimmed school uniform, and far more adult than Eve remembered. But then, Eve had never seen Hannah like this before. Out of the context of being one of Ian's children. Never seen Hannah as just Hannah. A person in her own right.

'Can we go somewhere? Get a coffee or something?' Hannah asked.

'Only if you call your dad first.' Eve heard the adult in her voice, saw Hannah's lips tense and stopped. 'I don't mean to be bossy,' she said, trying a smile. 'And I know it's none of my business, but he *does* know you're not at school, and he *is* worried.'

A sly look crept onto Hannah's face. 'You call

438

him,' she said. 'You know the number.'

'Uh-huh.' Eve shook her head. Did she look stupid? 'You do it. Anyway, I don't have my mobile. I left it on my desk.'

'Coffee first, then I'll call Dad,' Hannah said, knowing she'd won. 'It's my best offer.'

★ ★ ★

'I want to know what's going on,' Hannah said, when they were tucked at a corner table at the back of a small Italian café on a Mayfair side street, with two cappuccinos, one with extra chocolate, in front of them. The only other customers were Polish builders. Eve wondered if they were as conspicuous as she felt.

What did they look like? Mother and daughter? She was old enough, just, to be Hannah's mother. Auntie and niece? Half-sisters? Friends? Stepmother and stepdaughter? Whatever that looked like.

'What d'you mean?'

'I might be 'only thirteen', but I'm not stupid,' Hannah said, eyeing Eve over the froth of her cappuccino. 'I'm fed up with everyone treating me like a kid. I want to know why you and Dad broke up. One minute you're all loved up, the next you've gone and Dad is in the worst mood ever. Just like that. I want to know why.'

'You'll have to ask him,' Eve said evenly. 'It's not my place to tell you, I'm sorry.'

The girl paused. Eve could see her weighing up her choices. 'If I ask you a question,' Hannah said finally, 'do you promise to answer it?'

Never make a promise you can't keep. Ian's words echoed in Eve's head.

'I can't promise,' she said. 'Because if I can't answer it then I'd have to break my promise, and I can't do that.'

'Then answer it and you won't be breaking it.'

'I'm not promising Hannah,' Eve said. 'But ask me the question, and if I can answer it, I will, *that's* a promise.'

'OK . . . Is it my fault?'

Eve was taken aback. 'Is what your fault?'

'You and dad breaking up. Did you leave because of me?'

'Because I said . . . ' Across the table, the girl's eyes filled with tears. For the first time, Eve could see Alfie's big blue eyes staring back at her from Hannah's face. To her shock, it dawned on her that she'd never really looked before. But now she did, the girl looked thinner than ever, and there were grey shadows that should never be under thirteen-year-old eyes.

'Dad's unhappy, Alfie's unhappy, Sophie's unhappy. Everyone's unhappy. It's like . . . Almost like Mummy died all over again. And it's all my fault.'

'No,' Eve said, her own eyes filling up as she reached across the table to squeeze the girl's hand. 'It's not. It's nothing like that. Your mummy was just that. Your mummy. And you only get one of those.'

Eve closed her eyes briefly, struggling to collect her thoughts. Should she say more? Ian would kill her. But that didn't matter now, did it? Ian was gone, and the girl sitting opposite her, eyes red and nose running, well, didn't she deserve more?

'I was never trying to replace your mummy, Hannah,' she said at last. 'At least I didn't mean to . . . if it seemed that way, I, well, I'm sorry.'

The girl sniffed and Eve ploughed on. 'It wasn't easy though, was it?' she said. 'You and me, I mean. We didn't exactly get on like a house on fire. But no, I promise, I didn't leave because of you, not because of what you said.'

'Then why did you go? We just came home from school and Daddy said you'd moved out. It was the worst weekend ever.'

'It wasn't . . . ' Eve started, and then caught herself. It was, she realized. It was a lot like that.

'I'm sorry, Hannah,' she said. 'But I told you. I can't say. You really will have to ask your dad.'

'And I told you, I already asked him, and he won't tell me.

'I'm sick of this.' Suddenly Hannah slammed down her coffee so hard the saucer shook.

Eve jumped, and the builders on the next table, who glanced over, looked hurriedly away.

'Why does everyone treat me like a child?' Hannah wailed. 'I'm so fed up of it. I'm grown up.'

Eve couldn't suppress a smile. A dozen responses flooded her mind, but she kept them to herself. And anyway she remembered the feeling. That powerlessness, the sense that everyone had a say in your life except you.

'Please tell me.' Hannah was staring at her, huge eyes wet and smudged with mascara where she'd angrily wiped away tears. Her bottom lip

441

jutted, threatening a scene.

Eve looked from the girl's face to her empty cup and back again. What did she have to lose? Nothing. She'd already lost the only thing that really mattered. Maybe Hannah should know. Maybe then Hannah would understand that it wasn't her fault. Admittedly, if not for Hannah, Eve might well not be in this mess, but the girl was thirteen. Thirteen and sad and confused and, so it seemed, sorry. Eve was the grown-up here, and she couldn't bear to see her carrying even more guilt and sorrow.

'OK,' she said, decision made. 'I'll tell you. But if I do, I'm telling you now, that will be it. Your dad will never forgive me.'

'It's OK,' Hannah said brightening instantly. 'I won't tell him. *I promise.*'

'All right, this goes back a bit. When I was about six years older than you I really fucked up at university . . . '

Hannah stared at her.

'Yes,' Eve said. 'I know. Don't swear.'

★ ★ ★

When Eve finished, Hannah's eyes were even wider, but they were at least dry. Surprisingly, so were Eve's. 'So Dad didn't want you to have the baby? That's why you left?'

'In a nutshell, yes,' Eve said. 'But don't blame him. It's not that black-and-white. It was an accident. We were careless. We didn't think, and then . . . '

The look on Hannah's face made her smile.

442

'Yes,' she said. 'Grown-ups have those kind of accidents too, gross I know.'

Hannah grimaced.

'Ian . . . Your dad . . . He wanted to wait, because he didn't think it was the right time. And he was right. The timing was awful. It was far too soon for all of us. I mean, you and I weren't even talking to each other.'

Sticking her finger into her cup, Hannah scraped the last remnants of chocolate from the rim. 'Can I have another one?' she asked.

Eve nodded and signalled to the waitress before continuing.

'Dad didn't think it would be a good idea to create any more problems, any more difficulties, for you and Sophie and Alfie, than me moving in had already created.'

Listening to herself argue Ian's case, Eve wished it hadn't taken his eldest daughter to make her see things his way. If she could have done it sooner, told Ian the truths she was now telling Hannah, maybe they'd still be together. But then, if she had, maybe she and Hannah would still be passing each other on the stairs in silence.

It was a strange thought.

'All right,' Hannah said. 'I think I get it.'

She nodded solemnly. Her blonde hair had fallen out of its clip and flopped forward, narrowly missing the chocolate dusting the fresh cappuccino that had just appeared in front of her.

'You wouldn't agree because you didn't want another abortion after the one you'd had at uni?'

She said it matter-of-factly.

Eve winced. Somehow the words sounded worse coming from a thirteen-year-old's mouth. Why had she done it, told Hannah her big secret when she hadn't even told Ian? If Hannah told Ian now, Eve doubted he'd ever forgive her. Probably never even speak to her again.

'Why didn't you just tell Dad?' Hannah asked, as if reading her mind.

'Good question.'

'Then why?'

'I've been asking myself that ever since. So has Clare, for that matter. She's furious with me too. You remember Clare?'

'The woman who came to lunch?'

Yeah. Another day, another Hannah-related screw-up. Eve wished she hadn't brought it up. 'Uh-huh.' That was as non-committal as she could manage.

'The one with the cool daughter who hates me?'

'Hannah!' Eve was exasperated. 'Her name's Lou, and she doesn't hate you ... OK, she doesn't much *like* you now, but only because you didn't give her a chance to do otherwise. Mind you, she'll probably like you if I tell her you think she's cool.'

Hannah shrugged, staring hard at the table. Eve grasped the opportunity to change the subject. 'Now, you have to call your dad, he'll be frantic.'

'One more thing.'

'A deal's a deal.'

'Yes, but this is why I've really come.'

'You mean you didn't come to ask me all that?' Eve frowned.

'No, well, not really. I mean, yes, I did. I wanted to, but I wasn't sure I'd get to see you. When you came out of the building without me even having to go in; it seemed like too good a chance to miss.' Hannah smiled and slurped her cappuccino before licking off the chocolate moustache. 'But I really came to give you this.'

Rummaging in her blazer pocket, she pulled out a folded square of lined paper torn from a pad, and pushed it across the table, steering it around a puddle of milky coffee that had slopped onto the Formica.

'What is it?' Eve asked.

'A letter, obviously.'

The tone was a sarcastic one Eve recognized, but there was no malice.

'I can see that.'

'It's from Alfie. He kept asking to call you, but Dad said not to bother you. He said we had to leave you alone. So I promised Alfie I'd find you.'

'This is why you bunked off school?' Eve asked, unfolding the paper. Through blurring eyes she read the message scrawled in felt pen.

Dear Evie
On Saturday I am six. We are going to see snakes. Will you come? I miss you a lot.
Lots of love
Alfie

The rest of the sheet was covered in crosses. Kisses, swords, birds nose-diving to the bottom of the page, possibly Power Rangers' weapons, but to Eve they looked like kisses.

When she looked up, Hannah was watching intently.

'I miss him too,' Eve said, giving up, and swiping the back of her hand across her eyes. 'I miss all of you so much.'

The look that crossed Hannah's face was far older than her years. 'Even me?'

Eve paused. There was no point lying, but the girl didn't need to hear the truth either. 'I don't miss the fights. Do you?'

'A little.'

Eve was impressed. At her age she'd have lied to any grown-up who asked that.

'Alfie's sad,' Hannah said finally. 'He keeps asking for Evie. It's doing my head in to be honest.' Tossing her hair out of her face, she looked more like the girl Eve had come to know and, sometimes, fear. 'But it makes Dad cry, and I could so do without that.'

It makes . . .

'Oh, not in front of us,' Hannah added, catching a flash of something that crossed Eve's face. 'He wouldn't do *that*. He thinks if he leaves the room I won't see, but I'm not stupid.'

'No,' Eve said, her heart pounding in her chest. 'I can see that.'

'So, I can tell Alfie you'll come?' Hannah asked, downing the last of her cappuccino and flipping open her mobile phone. 'Please?'

Eve looked at her questioningly. 'I'd love to see

Alfie, but I don't think I can. Your dad wouldn't like it, would he?'

Hannah shrugged as she flicked through the pre-set numbers. 'What's it got to do with him?' she said. 'It's Alfie's birthday. And Dad said Alfie can invite anyone he wants.'

35

Trust Alfie to choose the reptile house for his birthday. He could have had penguins or elephants or monkeys or small furry rodents or even polar bears. But no, Alfie, being six and Alfie, had to have snakes.

It was two o'clock on a chilly almost-spring Saturday, and Eve had a serious case of déjà vu. OK, so bustling tourists crowding the streets of Soho had been replaced by bustling tourists crowding the penguins, but was it so different? She'd still spent two hours getting ready, arrived thirty minutes early, and agonized over what to buy. This time, though, she'd given up on books and gone straight for a Power Rangers vehicle. And there had been no guesswork involved. Having asked Alfie what he wanted, Hannah texted Eve a list. Hannah had sent Eve a text. Several, in fact. *Hannah mobile* popping up on her screen.

Now, that was surreal.

No, this time it wasn't the children she was scared of seeing. It was Ian.

★   ★   ★

The small boy spotted her before she spotted him.

'Evie! Daddy, Daddy it's Eve,' he bellowed, losing all interest in the eating habits of the black mamba, and hurtling towards her. Eve was so

448

preoccupied with catching the knee-high blond hurricane who launched himself through the air, that she almost missed the mix of expressions that crossed his father's face. Surprise, confusion, hurt . . . And, dare she hope, relief?

Well, that answered one question.

Hannah hadn't told him she was coming. She hardly dared think what else Hannah might or might not have told him. But it was too late to worry about that now.

'Happy Birthday Alfie!' she said, swinging him up into a bear hug and instantly regretting it. How could he have grown so much? It was only a month. 'When did you get so big?'

Alfie looked at her as if she were an idiot. 'I'm six now,' he said.

Eve grinned and hugged him tighter. Now she had him, she wanted to turn and run, out of the zoo, away from anyone who might try to take him from her. Where had this come from? This feeling that had ambushed her the first time she met Alfie, and had never left her. And why had it not happened with the others? She was fond of Sophie, hated the idea of never seeing her again, but Alfie was different.

'Hello Eve.' Ian was standing beside them. 'Come on Alfie,' he said, prising Alfie's arms from around Eve's neck. 'Let Eve breathe. You wouldn't want to suffocate her on your birthday now, would you?'

'Come and see the black mambas. They eat rats and everything.'

'In a minute,' Ian said. 'I need a word with Eve first.'

'You weren't expecting me,' Eve said, when Alfie had run back to a gaggle of small boys clustered around one of the glass cages. It wasn't a question. It was obvious from the look on Ian's face.

'Should I have been?'

Casting around for a slim blonde girl, Eve realized Hannah had made herself scarce.

'Erm, yes,' she blustered. 'You see, Alfie invited me and I was, erm, told you knew. Well, not that he'd invited me. But that you'd be told I was coming. And I wasn't going to come, but I wanted . . . ' She stopped. What had she wanted? To see Alfie, yes, but not just that.

'And you believed that?' Ian looked amused.

Eve smiled. 'Sucker, huh?'

'You've been had. We both have.'

'I wanted to see Alfie,' Eve said. It sounded pathetic even to her. True, but not the whole truth. She almost wished she hadn't got her hopes up. Almost.

His eyes searching her face, looking for more, Ian nodded. 'Ah, OK. Well, Alfie certainly wants to see you. Better come and be impressed by lots of limbless serial killers, then.'

★　★　★

If it weren't for the awkwardness between Eve and Ian, and the fact that Hannah was speaking to her, after a fashion — something Ian could hardly fail to notice — it would have been like old times. But the awkwardness was undeniable.

After Hannah had called her father to say she

was safe, Eve had put the girl in a taxi, paid the driver up-front and sent her back to Chiswick with a promise she wouldn't tell her father what Eve had said. Any of it. Whether Hannah had kept that promise, Eve had no way of knowing, other than the fact that Ian was tolerating her presence. She very much doubted he would have done if he knew what she'd told Hannah. What she had told Hannah but not told him.

★ ★ ★

The party was over too soon. Small boys were collected by a succession of parents until only Ian's children remained. As they walked to the car, Alfie swung happily between Ian and Eve like a human lightning rod. His little hot hand in hers sent a surge of emotion through her; the closest she could get to touching his father.

When they reached the Lexus, Ian buckled a protesting Alfie into the back and Hannah and Sophie squabbled for the front seat. As they did so, Eve stood aimlessly on the pavement waiting . . . For what, she wasn't sure. It was getting dark now. She should head back to Clare's. She had no plans, after all, other than getting under Clare and Lou's feet.

'So,' she said, leaning into the car to give Alfie and Sophie a big kiss and waggling her fingers in farewell at Hannah over the back of the seat. 'Thank you very much for having me, Alfie. I had a lovely time. I hope I'll see you again soon.'

'Aren't you coming home?' Alfie said.

Eve swallowed hard but not hard enough to

stop the telltale prickle that threatened tears. 'No, Alfie,' she said softly. 'I'm afraid not. You're going home with Daddy and Hannah and Sophie.'

'Then where are you going?'

'I'm going to see my friend Clare, the teacher.'

'And then you're coming home?' His little eyes welled up and Eve turned away as hers came out in sympathy. She hadn't known Ian was standing so close behind her.

'Give Eve a break, Alfie,' he said, pushing the Power Rangers vehicle Eve had given Alfie into his hand and slamming the door shut.

'Sorry,' Eve said. 'The last thing I intended was to upset him.'

Ian looked at her evenly, his blue eyes sad. 'It was bound to upset him,' he said. 'He misses you.'

Eve stared hard at the pavement. The streetlight next to the car had come on, bathing their feet in an orange glow. 'I'm sorry,' she said. 'I'm not very good at this. I miss him. More than I can tell you.'

'Can we talk?' Ian said suddenly.

'We are, aren't we?' She hadn't meant that to sound so abrupt. 'I mean . . . I didn't mean . . . '

'I know.' Ian smiled sadly. 'I meant properly. Will you meet me tomorrow?'

'What about the kids?'

'I'll bribe Inge. How does eleven-thirty, Carluccio's St Christopher's Place sound?'

Eve dragged her eyes from her feet and felt her stomach plummet as she met his.

'OK,' she said. 'Yes. I'd like that . . . I'll be there.'

452

* * *

Eve looked at her watch: eleven forty-eight.

Where was Ian?

It wouldn't have been so bad if she hadn't lain awake half the night working herself up into a frenzy. What if he said this? What if he said that? In all the what ifs had not been What if he doesn't turn up? On top of which, if she hadn't been half an hour early, she wouldn't have read the *Observer* cover to cover and be on her third americano. With forty-eight minutes' worth of caffeine coursing through her veins she was practically vibrating with anxiety.

Eighteen minutes wasn't even that late.

Not really. Except this was Ian, and Ian was never late. It was another of his kid-related things. If you said you'd be somewhere you had to be there when you said you would. She understood that. On more than one occasion she'd been the last kid in the playground waiting for her mum; and when you were five that kind of shame was close to unbearable. But she wasn't a kid, she was a grown-up, and she could stand him being a little late. But still, this *was* Ian.

Eleven fifty-three. Close to half an hour now. The waiters were giving her looks, she knew. Every time the door opened she looked up, she couldn't help it. Every time it wasn't Ian, she looked down, dejected. What must they think of her?

She wasn't at the wrong branch. She knew that because she'd called the other one.

'No ma'am, there's no one answering that

453

description here,' the waiter had said on the phone. *Face it love, you've been stood up,* she could hear him thinking. And who could blame him?

The waiter or Ian?

But no, Ian would never do anything that petty. That wasn't his style. But then nor was being late.

When the door swung open again, Eve forced herself to keep her gaze firmly on the table. What was it her nan used to say about watched pots?

'Eve! You waited!'

Her body sagged with relief. She counted to three, looked up, smiled. 'Of course I waited. Haven't been here long myself.'

If he spotted the lie he didn't let it show.

'Babysitting crisis.' He pulled out the chair opposite and flung himself into it. 'Inge couldn't do it. Not for any amount of money. And we were talking telephone numbers by the end. She had a 'long-standing engagement', for which, I imagine, read hot date. In the end I called my parents.'

'Your parents?' Eve had hardly contemplated Ian's parents since the morning she left. For the past month she'd been so lost in her own agony she hadn't given them a moment's thought.

'Yes, they're looking after the children. That's why I'm late. There was an accident on the A3 and they got held up on the way.'

'They came from Chichester?'

'Where else?' Ian shrugged. 'They know I wouldn't ask if it wasn't important. I was going to call you, but . . . ' He looked abashed. 'I'm not very good on the phone. And every time it

454

matters we seem to end up having an argument.'

'I bet my name's mud with your mother,' Eve said, after a waitress had taken Ian's order. 'She told me what she'd do if . . . Well, let's just say she made her position very clear in the summer.' Eve swallowed. 'I imagine she feels very let down. I'll prepare for hate mail.'

'Wouldn't bother,' Ian said, his face serious. 'You'll probably get mail, but not the hate variety. It's me she's angry with, not you. She could hardly bring herself to speak to me to begin with. I had to eat serious humble pie to get her to come today at all. In fact, she only agreed to come for you. She said as much.'

'You? Why's she angry with you?'

'I behaved abominably.'

'Don't be ridiculous.'

'I'm not. She's right. I did. We were engaged and I brought you into my children's life. And then you were pregnant,' he leant forward, lowering his voice, 'with my child and I . . . I'm so sorry Eve, I was so blinded by what I thought was right for the children, I didn't once think about what was right for you. My mother thinks I'm a fool and wasted no time in telling me so. My father wasn't wildly impressed either, but you might have noticed he tends to leave the talking to her.'

Eve felt a flicker of comfort at Elaine's support. But Ian looked shattered, his eyes were rimmed insomnia-red, and shadows hollowed his cheeks. She'd been so caught up with navigating the eggshells the day before that she hadn't noticed how wretched he looked.

'It's OK,' she said, reaching across to take his hand. Relief surged through her when he laced his fingers through hers. 'I'm at least as much to blame.' She stared at their two hands intertwined; her pale fingers against his tanned ones. How could this be so painful?

'Can you forgive me?' She glanced up at Ian's words. From the look on his face it was a genuine question. 'Please?'

'Of course,' Eve said. 'The question is can you forgive me?'

'You're crazy. There's nothing to forgive you for. Please say you'll come back. I miss you Eve, the kids miss you. Let's make this work.'

She'd never heard him sound so vulnerable, it had always been locked away inside where the children couldn't see it.

'Ian,' she said, taking a deep breath. 'I'd love to. I mean, I really want to, but there's something I need to tell you. And then . . . Well, then, when you know, then we'll see if you still want me back.'

★ ★ ★

Euston station was heaving. Hardly surprising given it was Sunday lunchtime. Packed with people leaving loved ones, or returning to them.

Lily scanned the arrivals board. The twelve thirty-five from Manchester Piccadilly was thirty-three minutes late. It would arrive, when it eventually did, on platform twelve.

Great, Lily thought, wandering back to the end of the platform and leaning against a wall.

456

What a perfect way to spend your Sunday off.

She didn't mean that for a minute.

Despite the fact she'd worked both shifts the day before, the prospect of Liam coming home from Manchester had got her out of bed early. She had been almost lonely since he left. That had surprised her actually. That she missed him. Because the Liam she loved — funny, clever, spontaneous and, OK, more than a little irresponsible — had been missing for months.

Since Christmas he'd been unbearable; drinking too much, snapping at the slightest thing when they were together, which wasn't often, since he was working every hour's overtime he could wangle. When she tried to get him to tell her what was on his mind, he'd snap or storm out. Lily was close to the end of her tether. If this was the way he reacted to his ex-wife packing up and moving to Cheshire, maybe he still wanted Siobhan after all.

This was Liam's first weekend with Rosie since the move. His first weekend staying over at a hotel in Manchester. Lily had offered to go with him, but her heart wasn't in it. It didn't matter anyway, because Liam refused without even appearing to consider her suggestion.

But today she had woken up feeling positive. The situation would either improve now, Lily thought, or it wouldn't, and by the end of the day she'd be looking for somewhere new to live. But somewhere inside she felt sure it would.

She saw his curly hair before he saw her.

'Hey!' Lily waved. 'Liam! Over . . . ' Then stopped. There was a darkness in his expression, something approaching . . . Was it dread? Lily pulled back and wrapped her arms around her body for self-protection. So, her good vibes had been wrong. This was it then, time to look for a new flat.

'Hi Lily.' Liam stopped in front of her. 'You didn't have to come all this way. I wasn't expecting you to.'

'Clearly.' Lily forced a smile and stood on tiptoe to kiss him. He kissed her back, but it was brief and he didn't knot his fingers in her hair to pull on him as he usually did.

The sick feeling growing inside her, Lily looped an arm through his and made to head off through the crowd. Liam stopped her.

'Let's grab a coffee shall we? Or something stronger?'

Something stronger? She tried to smile. 'I'm not hitting the bottle in Euston Station, Liam! I may not have many scruples, but I'm not that big a wino just yet.'

'Really?' Liam didn't return her smile. 'I am.'

★   ★   ★

'So, how's Rosie?' she asked, when they were sitting in a café overlooking the concourse, Lily nursing stewed coffee that no amount of sugar and UHT cream could save, Liam halfway down a flat-looking pint of lager.

'Good. She seems happy, actually. Loves her new nursery.' He looked animated for the first time, the smile softening the darkness in his unshaven face.

Lily felt sick. 'And Siobhan?' she forced herself to ask.

'She's fine. Happy too.'

'What's he like? Her husband?'

Staring into his pint, Liam shrugged. 'Seems like an all-right bloke,' he said grudgingly. 'Obviously besotted with Siobhan.'

'And Rosie?'

'So I'm told.'

This was like getting blood out of a stone. If it was over, it was over, but Lily couldn't take any more of this. Why didn't he just put her out of her misery? 'Come on, Liam,' Lily snapped. 'Let's get this over with, shall we? What is it? I mean . . . I know what it is. Siobhan's taken Rosie to Manchester, but what else is it?'

Taking a long swig of beer, Liam drained his glass and placed it on the table. Then he looked at her. Dead straight, without guile. Lily didn't think she'd ever seen that look in his face before. It made her nervous.

'Lily,' Liam said. 'I'm sorry. Don't hate me. I have to do this. I have to go. I've got a new job. It's local, not national papers, but they've got an on-line push and . . . ' He shrugged. 'I'm going to Manchester.'

She was speechless. 'You what!? How long have you . . . ?'

'Not long, really.' He looked, briefly, his old shifty self. 'A couple of weeks, but I've been thinking about it since Christmas. I know I should have discussed it with you. But I couldn't lay it on you. Your life is here. And mine. Well, it seems like mine just moved to Manchester without consulting me.'

'But . . . ' Lily gasped. 'You and me, we . . . '

'Lily, my love, this isn't about you and me. It's about Rosie and me. I know I'm a crap dad, Lily, I'm not proud of that . . . '

'Liam . . . ' Lily couldn't take it in.

He shook his head. 'Don't deny it. You know it's true. You've said it yourself often enough. You and Siobhan both actually. Well, I need to sort it out — or lose my baby to her new dad.'

'Are you . . . are you going back to Siobhan?'

'No! You're not listening to me. This has nothing to do with her. I love you. You're amazing. I can't believe you're with me. Me and Siobhan were never like this. We're history and we should never have been anything else. Only we had Rosie, didn't we? And now Siobhan's gone and married someone else and taken her away. I don't want Rosie to have another dad, Lily. She's already got one. Me.'

'I'll have that drink now,' Lily said. She needed time to think, to work out how she was meant to respond to Liam's casually lobbed grenade. Except it wasn't casually lobbed, was it? One look at his face told her he hadn't slept in days. Just as she hadn't.

'I'm sorry to drop it on you like this,' Liam said, when he returned with a fresh pint and a bottle of Becks. 'I've been meaning to talk to you about it but there was never a right time.'

'And this is?' Lily asked.

'No, of course not,' he said. 'But now I'm all out of time. My new job starts next Monday.'

'So where does this leave us?' she asked. 'Are

you ending it with me?'

Liam frowned. He was looking at her as if she was a bit mad. Perhaps she was. 'I didn't think I'd be getting the chance, Lily,' he said. 'I assumed when I told you, you'd be ending it with me.'

★　★　★

His scrambled eggs had congealed as she talked, Ian's fork loaded with smoked salmon had got no further than his plate, and the fourth coffee Eve hadn't wanted anyway had grown cold in its cup.

'Say something then,' Eve said. He hadn't taken his eyes off her since she started talking, and his gaze was making her nervous. It felt like several minutes since she'd finished the whole sad, embarrassing tale and Ian hadn't said a word, just gazed at her. Those cool blue eyes taking in every angle of her face, every freckle.

'Is that it?' he said eventually.

'What d'you mean, is that it? Isn't that enough?'

Leaning across the table in Carluccio's, he pushed a curl out of her face. His hand lingered on her cheek. 'Oh my love, I was expecting something awful . . . But that's just a teenage mistake. I'm not downplaying it,' he added, seeing Eve's stricken expression. 'It's sad and it must have been awful for you, but it's in the past. I'm sorry, and I hate to think of you going through that alone . . . ' he stopped, embarrassed.

461

Eve hadn't thought of it like that. She thought she'd just been competent. Done what had to be done.

'I just wish you'd told me before . . . ' He hesitated. 'Before all this. We could have . . . well, I hope we could have done things differently.'

'It's not the kind of thing you drop into polite conversation, is it? I fucked up at nineteen, had an abortion without telling the father, dumped him and got on with my life.'

'True,' Ian said and he grinned. 'But I don't recall all our conversations being that polite.'

Eve laced her fingers through his and smiled back. 'Also true, but there weren't that many conversations anyway, were there? Not those long, all-night conversations you normally have early on in a relationship. And we spent so little time alone once I met the kids. And then I moved in and there were the children again, and . . . '

'The rows,' Ian finished for her.

Eve nodded. 'There were so many things we never talked about.'

Ian looked sad. 'Like having children,' he said. 'I'm sorry, Eve, I just thought we had plenty of time . . . '

'And then I got pregnant,' Eve said, matter-of-factly. 'And I couldn't tell you then, could I? What was I supposed to say? Ian, I'm pregnant. I'm sorry you're furious, and I know it's the wrong time, but I can't get rid of the baby because I had an abortion when I was nineteen, and, for me, once is enough? Any anyway, if I'd done things differently, if I'd been

462

more like Clare, my child would have been almost Hannah's age, and.' She shook her head sadly. 'How could I say that?'

Ian hung his head, maybe in exhaustion, maybe in shame. Catching sight of the tired-looking salmon on his plate, he pushed it away. 'You're right,' he said. 'I'm sorry. I should never have done it.'

'Done what?'

'Proposed.'

'Thanks!'

They both glanced at her empty left hand and looked away. The ring was in Eve's pocket, ready either to put back on, or hand back and walk away.

'No, I don't mean it like that,' Ian said. 'I just mean I shouldn't have proposed when I did. I should have waited. I just got carried away. I loved you from the moment we met. And,' he smiled embarrassed, 'that's never happened to me before. And when I saw you with the kids, how good you were with Alfie and Sophie. And my mother and father adored you. Everything seemed so right. But it wasn't. I'm sorry . . . ' He hesitated. 'It was really selfish. I should have thought about what you wanted.'

Eve stared at him. 'I'm a grown-up, Ian,' she said. 'And I said yes. I said yes because I wanted — *want* — to be with you. But if . . . if you regret it, we can . . . I mean . . . I can collect the rest of my stuff . . . '

Ian looked up, his eyes wide with shock. 'No!' He caught himself. 'Not unless you want to.'

Eve shook her head vigorously.

463

'I just wish we'd done it differently,' Ian said. 'Given it more time. What I'm trying to say is, you were right. I bulldozed everything.'

'I didn't say that.'

'No, but I did. I wanted our lives — mine and the children's — to be exactly the same, just with you in it.'

Eve looked at the table. 'Right down to the rugs,' she said. It was meant to be a joke, but Ian took it at face value.

'You're even right about that. I asked you to change everything, give up everything for me and my children. And I was so obsessed with keeping everything the same for them that I wouldn't change anything for you, not even a rug.'

'About that rug. Could you get it down for me?'

'Of course, where do you want to put it? We could get your china out too. And all your books.'

Eve laughed. 'Just the rug for now. I want to give it to Clare, after a month in her living room, I can see it's exactly what that room needs.'

★   ★   ★

'Can I ask you something else?' Ian said. Their arms were wrapped around each other as they walked towards Regents Park in the weak spring sunshine.

'Anything,' she replied. Eve felt so happy right now, nothing could spoil it.

'Hannah was with you that day, wasn't she?

464

The day she went missing.'

Eve nodded. 'Not when you phoned me. If I'd known she was waiting outside my office I'd have told you. But afterwards, I went out for a coffee, and there she was. Frozen to the bone. She didn't tell you?'

Ian shook his head. 'No, I tried everything to make her. Threats, grounding, withholding pocket money, the lot. And that was on top of the detention she got from school for playing truant. But all Hannah would say was she'd gone to see a friend and she'd promised she wouldn't say where she'd been.'

'Oh God . . . I'm sorry.'

Ian nodded. 'I was climbing the walls. I knew it had to be an adult. At least, someone who could afford to pay her cab fare. And it wasn't any of the grown-ups I knew. To begin with I was terrified it was someone she'd met over the internet . . . ' He looked sheepish. 'I know. I shouldn't believe everything I read in the papers!'

Eve smiled, hoping it hid the guilt she was feeling.

'And then you turned up at the zoo. And it dawned on me that no one could have invited you except Hannah. So that had to be where she'd been.'

Eve was silent.

There was no need to say anything.

'But what I need to know,' he said, 'is, did you tell Hannah? Did you tell her why we broke up?'

Why does he have to do this now? Eve thought bleakly. *When everything is going so well? Why* did Ian have to ask the one question that could puncture their fragile happiness? And then she caught herself. This had been their problem, all along. If their relationship was to survive, they had to stop treating it as if it could break at any time.

She turned in his arms to face him, wind whipping her hair into their faces.

'Yes,' she said. 'I did. I'm sorry, but we were talking for the first time, ever. Even when I was telling her, I couldn't quite believe I was. So, yes, I told her everything. Because, until then, she thought my leaving was her fault. And even though I may be a crap stepmother, I've learnt enough not to want her to carry that around with her as well.'

'*Everything?*' His arms were tight around her. 'Even what you hadn't told me?'

'Yes.' Taking a deep breath, Eve waited for him to pull away. When he didn't, she exhaled.

'And what does she think of me?' Ian said. 'Now she knows her father would do a thing like that?'

'What does she think of you?' Eve locked her arms behind him and stood on tiptoe to kiss him. 'The same thing she thinks of me.'

'Which is?'

'We're a pair of idiots.'

'I don't know about you,' he said. Eve felt him smile. 'I think she's right.'

36

Starbucks was packed, as usual. And, as usual, Clare had snagged the best table with the comfiest armchairs.

'It's so good to see you,' Eve said, hugging her best friend warmly. She meant it. She hadn't seen Clare since she gave her back her living room — complete with new rug, delivered by Ian when he came to collect Eve. It was touch and go who had been more surprised, Eve or Ian or Clare herself, when Clare had greeted him warmly, invited him in for coffee and not made a single comment about the lack of space not being what he was used to. As for Eve, she had spent the whole hour trying not to cry. What had happened to her self-control since the miscarriage, she didn't know, but she was just so glad to see him and so glad to have her friend back.

'It's good to see you too,' Clare said. 'I've missed you.' She grinned at the look of disbelief on Eve's face. 'In a sick, masochistic sort of way!'

'Shall I get coffees in?' Eve volunteered.

'Melanie's already up there. Apparently, it's her round. Mind you, it always seems to be her round. If you ask me it's her way of making amends for being here on false pretences.'

Eve rolled her eyes. 'Give Melanie a break,' she said. 'Anyway, it takes one to know one.'

'Aha,' Clare said. 'I have special dispensation.'

* * *

'Can I interest you in any cakes or pastries?' the Polish girl behind the counter asked.

Do I look like I eat cakes and pastries? Melanie wanted to say. She knew she didn't. Too much time on the heart-break diet. Not that her heart was really broken.

Vince, he was just her rebound man. Poor sod. What had she been thinking taking a rebound man to meet her parents? A spectacular misjudgement, even by Melanie's standards. It had been four months now, but still she missed having him around. She missed the sex and the company, and his unflappable good humour. But more than that, she missed Ellie and what might have been. Occasionally, when she let her mind wander, she wondered if Ellie ever thought about her. But that was off-limits. She couldn't have it both ways. No Vince meant no Ellie, that was the rule.

Melanie knew Grace still saw Vince occasionally, but they never discussed him. Her office manager still hadn't forgiven Melanie for hurting him, so they'd reached an unspoken agreement to steer well clear of the topic. Not that it was difficult. Since Melanie had refinanced *personalshopper.com* to expand into children's wear, they'd been too busy to talk about anything other than stock levels and order fulfilment.

A brave decision, her accountant said. Melanie had been worried that translated as *Stupid*. Although the gamble seemed to be paying off, recession or not.

'That'll be £10.80 please.'

Ten pounds? Melanie winced. Handing over a note, she rummaged in the bottom of her bag for loose change and pulled out a handful of coins, some fluff, and a business card. She was about to shove the card back when she noticed it was actually a half-full loyalty card, and handed it over to the cashier.

'We don't take these now,' the girl said. 'That was just a trial.'

Melanie was about to tell her to toss the card in the trash, when she saw something scrawled on the back. 'Hold on a sec,' she said. 'Could I get that back?'

Flipping the card over, Melanie saw the word *Loni*, followed by a sequence of numbers, written on the back in handwriting she didn't recognize.

Who the hell was Loni?

As Melanie headed to the end of the counter to pick up her order, she turned sideways to make room for a middle-aged man in a suit to pass. And the answer came to her. A previous SSG meeting, Melanie making room for someone altogether slimmer and younger to pass on precisely this spot. Someone who'd handed her his loyalty card as he left, saying he didn't come here often enough to need it.

The guy who thought she was too beautiful to look sad.

Turning the card over, Melanie read the name and number again. Was that Loni? She was almost tempted to find out.

★ ★ ★

'So how's it going with Hannah?' Mandy was saying when Melanie returned. 'I mean, has anything *really* changed.'

Eve grinned. Mandy reminded her of Clare with her spade-calling.

'Yes, and no,' she said. 'We've reached a truce. I treat Hannah like a grown-up — sort of — and butt out and leave the parental battles to her dad, which suits me fine, actually. And Hannah speaks to me when we pass on the stairs, occasionally deigns to eat something and talks to me when she thinks no one else is around.'

Mandy looked doubtful.

'Took me a while to get it,' Eve said. 'But I either had to learn to live with Hannah or learn to live without Ian. I can't have both, so I had to choose.' She paused, realizing the words weren't her own. They were borrowed from someone who'd won that knowledge the hard way: Bella.

Glancing up, she caught Clare's eye as the other woman reached for her coffee. They both smiled warily, aware their friendship had been through a lot. What would Clare say if she knew Eve had kept another, bigger secret? Eve had no urge to find out. Not yet, anyway.

'Enough about Eve,' Clare said suddenly. 'I have a news bulletin.'

'Oh God!' Lily said. 'What's Will done this time?'

'Nothing actually. He collects Lou every other Friday and brings her back on Sunday. All very civilized. But this isn't about Lou or Will for a change, this is about me. Is everybody sitting down?' She glanced around. 'Good, because I,

Clare Adams, professional single mother and involuntary celibate, have a date!'

Their shrieks could probably be heard on Oxford Street. Who? Where? When? How? They needed to know.

Clare beamed as she told them all about Osman Dattu. 'It's not such a shock, is it?' she asked. 'Surely I'm not such a minger that no one would ask me out?' But she was too happy to be properly offended.

'Don't be daft.' Eve hugged her friend. 'The shock isn't that he asked. It's that you said yes. I imagine the staffroom has been full of men throwing glances your way for years.' She stopped. 'You *have* said yes, haven't you?'

Clare nodded. 'Next Saturday night, I am officially going out. On my own, with a member of the opposite sex; who, as far as I can tell, is funny, intelligent, not married, in gainful employment and has all his own limbs.'

'Let me sort you out an outfit,' Melanie said. 'On the house.'

Eve smiled. 'Lou can come to ours if you want,' she offered. 'Bizarrely, I think she and Hannah would probably get on better this time.'

'Don't jump into anything.' That was Mandy, obviously.

'Jeezus,' Lily said crossly. 'The woman's going out for dinner, not meeting the queen.'

'True,' Melanie said. 'This is far bigger!'

'I have something bigger than that,' Lily said.

'Bigger than me going on a date?' Clare said, her voice light. 'Not possible sis, sorry.'

'What's up?' Melanie asked. 'Is everything OK?'

471

Lily shrugged. 'Yes and no.' But her eyes were welling up.

'Liam's moving,' she said. 'To Manchester. Siobhan's married a guy who lives there and taken Rosie with her. Liam's decided to go too. So he can see more of Rosie.'

'Well that's a turn-up for the books,' Mandy said. 'Maybe he'll make the Championship after all. When did this happen?'

'Couple of weeks ago,' Lily said. 'He told me he'd decided and moved pretty much straight-away. I'm staying at his flat, for now.'

'Nice,' Mandy said, sarcastically.

Clare shot her a warning glance. It wasn't that she didn't agree. She did, wholeheartedly. But she knew Lily didn't and never would, so from now on she had resolved to keep her Liam-related views to herself.

'We're going to try commuting,' Lily said. 'Once a month I'm going to Manchester to see Liam, and the next fortnight he's coming down to see me. And before you say anything,' she added, anticipating their protests. 'He didn't presume anything. It was my idea. He thought I'd dump him, but I'm not going to. I want to see if we can make this work.'

'Manchester's not far,' Melanie said support-ively. 'Hell, I know people who commute to New York from Chicago.'

'Put like that, I can't think what you're moaning about,' Eve said. 'When does it start?'

'Next weekend,' Lily said. 'Wish me luck.' She raised her latte at them. 'I think I'm going to need it.'

'I have a bit of news too,' Mandy said. 'But I'm not sure now's the right time.'

'No time like the present,' Lily said. 'But only if it's good news. I have the monopoly on bad news this meeting. Aren't those the rules, Clare? One downer per meeting?'

Her sister ignored her.

Mandy looked thoughtful. 'Yes,' she said. 'I think it's good news.'

'You *think*?' Eve sounded puzzled.

'No, I know it is. John and I have split up.'

The other women stared at her.

'When did that happen?' Clare asked. 'I didn't even know it was on the cards. Are you OK?'

'I'm better than OK, actually. I'm good. This is my decision.' Mandy looked surprised. 'I broke up with him. Forty-two years old, and ending a relationship for the first time.'

'Why?' Melanie asked.

'I've been thinking about it since Christmas, before that really. But that was when I realized I didn't know why I was with him. Or rather I did, I was with John because I was scared not to be. Because I've always been with someone apart from that brief spell after Dave left. Years ago, Dave told me I wouldn't be able to survive on my own, and I guess I believed him . . .'

She sighed. 'I looked at myself at Christmas and it occurred to me I didn't know who I was any more. Other than Mrs McMasters, Matt and Nathan and Jason's mum. I've been so wrapped up in being their mum, and then John's partner. Maybe, soon, his wife . . .'

Mandy held up her hand before Clare could

473

interrupt. 'No, he hadn't asked, it was just obviously on the cards. He's that kind of bloke. We were that kind of couple.'

'Anyway, at Christmas I looked at myself and my house full of family — my family, his family, Dave's family, all our children, none of them desperate to be there — and my sink full of washing-up, and asked myself *why*. Who I was doing this for? Who was making me?

'There was only one possible answer to both of those questions: me. So, if only I was making it happen, only I could make it stop.'

'How did he take it?' Clare asked.

'Badly. He thinks I must be menopausal!'

'Are you?' Lily asked.

'No!' Mandy yelped, and Clare swatted her sister. 'But that's what John's like. Not as bad as Dave, by a long shot. But whenever we row he thinks I've got my period, rather than I'm just speaking my mind.'

Melanie grinned.

'And that's not all,' Mandy said. 'I'm selling up.'

'You're leaving Clapham?' Lily asked. 'What about the kids?' As soon as the words were out, she looked as if she wished she could take them back.

''Fraid so. Firstly, Clapham's too pricey for me on my own. I'm fed up with being beholden to Dave, so I'm giving him his half of the house and downsizing. I won't be far away. Tooting probably. The boys won't have to change schools.'

She paused. 'Well, Matt and Jason won't.

Nathan's always saying he wants to live with his dad. Now's his chance.'

'You're kidding?' It was Clare.

'Am I laughing?' Mandy wasn't.

'I'm sorry Mandy, but that's hardcore,' Lily said.

'It's not.' Mandy shook her head. 'It's for the best. We've talked it over — Nathan and me. It's what he wants. So, Nathan's off to live with Dave. And we'll see how they both like that. See how Dave's girlfriend likes it, too. Wouldn't mind a ringside seat for that one. Matt and Jason are coming with me. The odd thing is, Jack wants to, too. Part-time, of course. He's asked if he can stay some weekends.' She smiled, glowing with pride that in some strange way she had kept her blended family together. 'He's mates with Jason now, you see.'

'And Izzy?' Eve ventured.

Mandy shook her head. 'Unlikely,' she said. 'She only ever came to see her dad, and then only when she couldn't avoid it.'

'Win some, lose some,' she said brightly, then asked, 'I can still come, can't I? If I'm not a proper stepmum.'

'Why not?' Melanie said. 'I do.'

'Of course you can,' Clare said firmly. 'We're friends now. And anyway, it wouldn't be the SSG without you.'

★ ★ ★

It still felt strange, walking up a leafy street that screamed a certain kind of comfortable; looking

475

at the lights in the double-fronted Victorian houses; pushing open a wrought-iron gate; sliding her key in the lock and hearing its familiar click. She'd lived there for several months the first time around, far longer than she was away. But those four weeks apart had changed everything. What surprised Eve most was the way the house felt to her now. She hesitated to use the word home, but that was how it felt. Like she belonged.

'Evie?' Alfie's voice echoed down the stairs as soon as she opened the front door. 'Is that you?'

'It's me,' she shout-whispered. 'Shouldn't you be asleep?'

'I am asleep,' he protested. 'Come and say night-night.'

'And me.' That was Sophie.

'In a minute. I'm just going to see Daddy, then I'll be up.'

Ian was sitting at the kitchen table in Eve's favourite spot, editing pictures on his laptop. A familiar patterned cup sat at his right hand, garishly at odds with the white china on the dish rack. 'Where did that come from?' Eve asked, bending to kiss him.

'Your boxes,' he said. 'I got them from the utility room and Sophie helped unpack your things. That's all right, isn't it?'

'Of course it is.' She headed into the utility room to hang her coat. 'But you don't have to.'

'I want to.' His voice was so close it made her jump. When she turned, he was in the doorway smiling at her.

She hooked her coat over a peg and turned

back. He was still there. Still smiling. 'What are you grinning at?'

'Nothing,' he said, but his eyes drifted to the back door.

Following his gaze, Eve's eyes found the row of wellies where they'd always been. A row that started with child's red ones at one end for Alfie and ended with Ian's enormous green Hunters at the other, with two pink pairs in rising sizes and two smaller pairs of Hunters between the girls' and Ian's own. One green pair, Caro's, and between those and Ian's, a new pair, midnight blue with a touch of sparkle.

'Ian,' she said, hugging him. 'I . . . Thank you.'

'Don't thank me,' he said. 'Hannah and Sophie chose them.'

'Hannah?'

'Think yourself lucky. If she hadn't intervened . . . Well, let's just say, thanks to her, Sophie's sparkle quota is seriously toned down.'

He hesitated. 'I can get rid of Caro's, if you'd prefer?'

Eve smiled, shook her head. 'No need.'

Caro was not gone, she never would be. She was the children's mother after all. And that was something Eve would never be. But her ghost had moved over, all the same, to make room in the family for Eve.

Epilogue

Eighteen months later

There was nothing to beat late September in London. The sun, which always seemed to lose its way in August, had finally found a path through the clouds and was beating down on the unsuspecting streets. Leaves, already on the cusp of turning, blazed like burnished gold in the rays, and it felt as if the whole city basked in this first and last glimpse of summer.

'Tell me again why they picked here?' Ian said. 'When they had all of London to choose from.' He handed the cab driver a twenty as Eve herded Alfie and Sophie onto the pavement. Hannah had opted out, preferring to spend the day with her friends. She and Eve had long since reached a truce. But this was still Eve's family, not hers.

'Because Marylebone Register Office is quintessentially London,' Eve said, punching him. 'And don't be a killjoy. This is Melanie, remember. You're lucky she hasn't hired an old Routemaster to take us to the reception.'

Guests from an earlier wedding crowded the pavement, waiting to breach a dozen by-laws with their environmentally unsound confetti. They burst into riotous applause as two men appeared at the top of the steps, whistling and hollering as someone started singing 'Here come the brides'.

'Daddy . . . ?' Sophie started.

478

'I'll leave you to answer that one,' Eve said to Ian. 'You're the parent here.' And she ducked as he swiped at her head.

'Come on,' she told Alfie. 'Let's go and find Clare and Lou.'

At the top of a sweeping staircase inside, Lily was lounging against the banister. A picture of insouciance in a black shift dress, tanned bare legs and treacherous heels, with her signature man's suit jacket slung over one arm. The piercings in her left ear had been reduced to three for the occasion.

'Wow, you look gorgeous!' Eve exclaimed, hugging her. 'Did I see you wear a dress before?'

'First and last time,' Lily said, bending to mess Alfie's hair. 'Hello mate,' she said. 'What men did you bring me to play with?'

Eve took in the hallway as Alfie talked Lily through a complex array of plastic figures in his rucksack. Lily was definitely alone.

'Where is everyone?' she hissed.

'If by *everyone* you mean Liam, he's late. Of course.' Lily rolled her eyes. 'I told him to take the train last night to avoid precisely this. But there was some school thing of Rosie's he had to go to.'

Clocking Eve's expression, Lily laughed. 'I know, who knew Liam had an inner good dad in there after all?'

'And you? How are you doing?'

'Good. You know, I think I like this Liam better. Although it's taken some getting used to. Occasionally I want to shake him awake in the middle of the night and ask what he's done with

479

the old one. I guess Siobhan taking Rosie away was the wake-up call he needed. Use it or lose it. I guess that applies to families too.'

'Eve!' Clare was on the stairs below them. 'I thought we were going to be late,' she said.

'The traffic's a killer.' Then she looked at her sister. 'Where's Liam?'

'Keep your hair on. He just got held up.'

'Where?'

'Erm . . . Manchester?'

'Why am I not surprised?' Clare said. 'Come on slow coach.' Turning, she swept up a small girl with olive skin in a floral dress and neat white socks. 'Where's Daddy, Mina?'

As if summoned, Osman appeared, taking the stairs two at a time, a boy of five or six, who was the mirror image of the girl, on his shoulders. Lou, Ian and Sophie were right behind them.

'Osman! You'll drop him!'

A bony elbow dug Eve in the ribs. 'Who'd have thunk it?' Lily said. 'Our Clare, an anxious stepmonster.'

'I heard that,' Clare said. 'And I'm not . . . Yet.'

'Yet?' Lily hissed.

'She's such a tease,' Eve said. 'Is Mandy coming?'

'Don't think so.' Lily frowned. 'I don't see her much since she moved, and I started spending one weekend a month in Manchester. Clare sees more of her than I do. She told Clare her mother was ill and she probably wouldn't make it.'

'That's a shame.'

It wasn't that the SSG weren't together often

enough, but with Lily's trips to Manchester, Melanie's business demands, and Clare's new 'commitments', the meetings had become less regular, the turnout more sporadic.

'Is that Melanie's mum and dad?' Lily asked, as an elderly Chinese couple rounded the corner, followed by a Chinese guy in his thirties.

'Must be. Did she know they were coming?'

'She was hoping.'

★ ★ ★

How did they look to Melanie's parents? Eve wondered as everyone crowded into the register office and took their seats. No, 'Whose side are you on: bride or groom?' Just a mêlée of friends and children, and a handful of family all piling into whichever seats were free.

What did Melanie's parents see when they looked at the life their daughter had made for herself three thousand miles from home?

Eve hoped they saw what she did: a room full of people who loved their daughter.

Uppermost of the people who loved Melanie was Loni. Standing in the front row, obsessively running anxious hands through his recently grown-out hair, he glanced over his shoulder and caught Eve's eye. He grinned nervously and Eve smiled back.

Who among Melanie's friends could have predicted this?

Not Eve, certainly. Not anyone who knew the first thing about Simeon, even if only from seeing his picture in the paper. Twitching from foot to foot beside Ed, his best man and business partner, Loni even managed to make the Lanvin tuxedo Melanie had borrowed for him look like something dragged from a bin bag at the bottom of his wardrobe.

Eve adored him. All Melanie's friends did.

And so did her parents, much to everyone's surprise. None more than Melanie. Far from disapproving, they marvelled that their daughter had gone halfway around the world only to marry a man whose mother was Chinese. A man of whom, on paper at least, they could legitimately approve. Melanie's brother thought it was the best joke he'd heard in decades.

The fact that Loni was five years younger than Melanie (if older than he looked), and dressed like a bum (an elegantly wasted one, but a bum no less) made no difference. It probably didn't hurt that his film editing company was so busy he could hardly spare time for a honeymoon. And here they were, both her mother and father, chaperoned by her brother. It was not much short of a miracle.

'Where the hell is Liam . . . ?'

'Here, babe. Sorry, train got held up.' Liam slid into the row beside Lily and nuzzled her neck just as the music struck up. Eve and Clare rolled their eyes at each other. Not entirely reformed then.

No bridal march for Melanie. Instead The Kooks' 'She Moves In Her Own Way' blared out of the iPod speakers Loni had set up at the front.

Turning, Eve saw a vision in ivory gliding up the short aisle towards her, the elderly Chinese man at Melanie's side. She looked fabulous. It still surprised Eve that her friend had turned down all the offers of designer frocks for her big day. Instead, she'd found a Fifties' dress in a vintage shop and altered it herself.

'Something old,' she'd said, when she told them. And even Clare had to admit there was far more to Melanie than the skinny-latte-size-zero-lady-who-used-to-lunch she'd once mistrusted.

The bouquet was blue, the bridegroom's tux was borrowed. They knew that for sure, but what was new? Everything else, probably.

A hand on Eve's shoulder made her turn. 'Don't you think Melanie looks . . . glowy?' Clare whispered.

'Of course she's glowy. She's the radiant bride, remember?'

'And . . . ' Clare paused. Eve couldn't quite decipher the look on her face. 'Bosomy?'

Eve smothered a laugh.

'What?' Ian hissed.

'Clare says Melanie looks *bosomy*.'

Ian eyed Melanie as she passed. A touch too long for comfort. 'Oi.' Eve nudged him. 'No need to look that closely.'

'Clare's right,' he said, kissing Eve. 'The bride definitely does look . . . bosomy.' And he gave her a meaningful stare.

★ ★ ★

After the ceremony and the photos and the illegal confetti, the wedding party moved to Marine Ices for the reception. A decision that had gone down a storm with the knee-high guests. 'Who needs a wedding breakfast when you can have wedding ice cream?' Loni had said, and the SSG had shared a secret smirk and wondered if he knew he was marrying a woman who hadn't let ice cream pass her lips since she was knee-high herself. That was when they knew how much Melanie loved him, because she went along with it.

After the knickerbocker glories and before the speeches, the members of the Stepmothers' Support Group gathered outside, on the pretext of keeping Lily company while she had a sneaky cigarette.

'Who's next?' Melanie said. 'It's gotta be you?' She turned to Eve.

Eve shook her head. 'Nah, not us. The Newsome-Owen household is just fine as it is, thanks.' Instinctively she crossed her fingers in her pocket and thought how close they had come to falling apart. It was a distant, bad memory, but she kept it safe in the back of her mind, in case she ever forgot how good things were now.

'How about you Lil?' she said. 'Planning on making an honest man of Liam?'

'Fat chance of that,' Lily laughed. 'He's reformed, not transformed. Anyway, I'll be too busy moving to Manchester.'

'Not yet,' she added, throwing up her hands when everyone started talking at once. 'It's just that I spend so much time on trains it might be worth a try. They have theatres in Manchester, don't they? Anyway, if you're looking for a wedding, I think my sister's a better bet.'

'I didn't say . . . ' Clare protested.

'No, you *implied*.'

'I was winding you up. We are thinking about moving in together, though. But you know, I've been in my flat so long. I'm not sure I want to give it up.'

'Your palatial Finchley abode?' Lily grinned. 'I would have thought you'd be glad to see the back of it.'

'In a weird way, the flat represents freedom,' Clare said. 'Lou doesn't agree. She says it resembles a small hamster cage! Of course, she's judging it by Will's house these days. They're off skiing after Christmas. Will, Suzanne, the lot of them.'

'And you're cool with that?'

Clare shrugged. 'I'll live,' she said, then smiled. 'To be honest, Osman and I will be glad of a few days to ourselves . . . Seriously though, I do have something to say. An agent's agreed to take on my novel.'

'*What novel?*' Lily demanded.

Only Eve knew about *Park Bench Blues*, although she hadn't been allowed to read it. The story of a feisty teenager who fell pregnant and decided to go it alone and have the baby. Eve wondered if the fictional father came back for his long-lost love, as well as for his daughter. Until Osman became a fixture she'd have put money on it. But, to judge by the way Clare had smiled at him during the ceremony, now she wasn't so sure.

'The novel I've been writing.'

'About stepmothers?' Lily demanded.

'Not directly.' Clare looked as if she wished she'd never started the conversation. And the glance she cast at Eve was almost pleading.

'We think *you're* the one with the real news,' Eve said, deflecting everyone's attention to Melanie.

'I'm the blushing bride,' Melanie said.

'Positively glowing,' Clare said.

Melanie looked coy. Checking the coast was clear, she beckoned them closer. 'A ten weeks' pregnant blushing bride,' she added. 'Shhh,' she begged, when their shrieks could be heard on Hampstead Heath. 'I don't want to jinx it. And I don't want my parents to know just yet. Let them get used to having a daughter they can approve of, before I break it to them that I'm giving them a grandchild too.'

Behind them a door opened, and the group grinned at each other.

'I'm not sure you lot need a support group any more,' Ian said. He and Liam were carrying four champagne glasses each. Osman followed with a fresh bottle.

'Quite right,' Liam said. 'We're the ones who need support. How about it?' He flung an arm around Lily, and she groaned as champagne sloshed on to her jacket. 'Oops, sorry Lil.'

'Doesn't matter,' she said. 'It's your jacket anyway.'

Clare laughed. Her sister had been wearing Liam's jackets as long as she'd known him. How could he not have noticed?

Loni appeared around the door. 'Come back,' he hissed. His eyes pleading. 'It's speech time and I feel like the warm-up act in an ice factory in there.'

Melanie let herself be pulled towards him and he folded her in his arms. The others traipsed inside, leaving them to kiss in private.

★ ★ ★

'Now, I have a card here from someone called Mandy.' As best man, Loni's business partner was doing the traditional read-through of cards from people who 'Are sorry they cannot be with us today'.

'Read it, read it,' Melanie said.

'OK, give me a chance.' Ed cleared his throat. 'It says, "To my dearest Melanie, and Loni who's lucky to have her."'

'Too right,' Lily yelled.

'Sssh!' Clare hissed.

Ignoring her mother, Lou stuck her fingers in her mouth and whistled.

'"I propose a toast" — that's Mandy, not me,' Ed continued. 'I haven't the faintest clue what she's on about, so I'm just going to read it out.'

'Get on with it, will you?'

Ed's face turned serious as he read the card. '"Please charge your glasses," he said.

Turning to the bride and groom, Ed raised his champagne flute. '"To the Stepmothers' Support Group. Because Loni, if Melanie hadn't been masquerading as a step-mother, you might never have met her!"'

There was a burst of laughter, a flurry of applause and chairs were scraped back around the room.

Clare caught Eve's eye across the table and

they both grinned. Eve didn't think she'd ever seen her friend so happy. Melanie might be glowing, but Clare looked truly radiant.

Lily, Liam and Louisa were on their feet, glasses raised; Alfie had clambered onto his chair, his glass of Coke held aloft.

Clasping Eve's hand, Ian pulled her to her feet.

'To the Stepmothers' Support Group,' Ed announced.

Gently Ian chinked his glass against Eve's as the toast echoed around them. 'To The Stepmothers' Support Group.'

Acknowledgements

Profuse thanks are due, in no particular order to:

All the stepmums and almost-stepmums who generously shared their experiences (good and bad) of living with and loving, in the main, other people's children. Your tips, advice and good humour were invaluable. Thanks also to the many stepdaughters who vigorously put across their side of the story!

In the course of my research for SSG I read several books by journalists whose candid weekly columns of living with cancer couldn't fail to move all who read them. Notably, *Before I Say Goodbye* by Ruth Picardie, *Take Off Your Party Dress* by Dina Rabinovitch, and *C: Because Cowards Get Cancer Too* by John Diamond.

My brilliant (and eternally optimistic) agent, Jonny Geller, I'm glad you're on my team; Lynne Drew, you're an inspiration — yes, I hated you when you sent me those few small points that stretched to twenty pages, but SSG is a far better book for it. Thanks also to Victoria, Kate and all the team at HarperCollins, and Fiona and Annabel at FMcM.

Tammy Perry for motivational pep talks. Nancy, Clare and Catherine, for all the usual reasons

— mainly involving ears and alcohol! Everyone at *Red* for supporting me in both my day and night job, and being, well, the best in the business. Particular thanks to Saska for tipping me off to the unintended potential of Queen's Park farmers market, and to all the *Red* readers whose vocal response whenever we printed the word 'stepmother' tipped me off to its potential.

Karen at Caffè Nero for letting us treat the corner table like an office.

Mum and Dad for embracing the role of step-grandparents so wholeheartedly. (Yes, I know you were much too young to have a six-year-old grandson, but you were really good at it. Still are.)

And last but so not least, Jon and Jamie, for trusting me to write this book and putting up with me while I did so. Without you there would be no SSG.

We do hope that you have enjoyed reading this large print book.

Did you know that all of our titles are available for purchase?

We publish a wide range of high quality large print books including:
Romances, Mysteries, Classics
General Fiction
Non Fiction and Westerns

Special interest titles available in large print are:
The Little Oxford Dictionary
Music Book
Song Book
Hymn Book
Service Book

Also available from us courtesy of Oxford University Press:
Young Readers' Dictionary
(large print edition)
Young Readers' Thesaurus
(large print edition)

For further information or a free brochure, please contact us at:
Ulverscroft Large Print Books Ltd.,
The Green, Bradgate Road, Anstey,
Leicester, LE7 7FU, England.
Tel: (00 44) 0116 236 4325
Fax: (00 44) 0116 234 0205

Other titles published by
The House of Ulverscroft:

THE LAST SONG

Nicholas Sparks

Seventeen-year-old Veronica 'Ronnie' Miller's life was turned upside-down when her parents divorced and her father moved from New York to Wilmington, North Carolina. Since then she has remained angry and alienated from her parents, until her mother decides she should spend the summer with her father. Ronnie's father, a former concert pianist and teacher, is living a quiet life in the beach town. He is immersed in creating a work of art that will become the centrepiece of a local church. What unfolds is an unforgettable story about love — first love and the love between parents and children — that demonstrates the many ways that relationships can break our hearts . . . and heal them.

LAVENDER MORNING

Jude Deveraux

Jocelyn Minton is a woman torn between two worlds. Her mother grew up in a world of private schools and afternoon tea, yet married the local handyman. When she died Joce was five, and her father remarried into his own class, leaving Joce an outsider. Then she met Edilean Harcourt, sixty years her senior, but a kindred soul. When Miss Edi dies, leaving Jocelyn her worldly possessions, they include clues to a mystery dating from 1941 in a small town in Virginia. However, her benefactor's notorious past ensures that the townspeople know who Joce is, and they've plotted out her entire future, including who she is meant to marry. But Jocelyn has her own ideas about men — and secrets that no one wants revealed.

SMOOTH TALKING STRANGER

Lisa Kleypas

Jack Travis is a rich, tough, Houston businessman — always in control. So when a beautiful young woman approaches his office carrying a baby that she claims is his, he's shaken more than he will let on. Stunned, Jack listens to Ella Varner as she explains that her sister recently gave birth and then abandoned her baby boy — and that enquiries have brought Ella to Jack's door. He virtually has a seizure when she asks him to do a paternity test. But ultimately, will a paternity test set things right? If Jack is the father, will he be the one to care for the baby? Would Ella be prepared to let the baby go? And if not, Ella can't bear to think of an answer . . .